PRAISE FOR

ADÉLAÏDE: PAINTER OF THE REVOLUTION

"This stunning and intense debut novel is historical fiction at its best. Readers will be carried away from the first page as they are swept into the smells, the sights, and the discord of turbulent eighteenth-century Paris. You will feel you are witnessing firsthand the life of Adélaïde Labille-Guiard, a bright, smart and fearless female artist who almost single-handedly changed the world of art and the way women were treated during the French Revolution era. Strube's descriptions are rich and sumptuous. Her research is impeccable. Her knowledge of art and artists of 1700s France is fantastic. Her story of Adélaïde will capture your heart far beyond the last page."

—Laura L. Engel, author of *You'll Forget This Ever Happened: Secrets, Shame, and Adoption in the 1960s*

"This enthralling and beautifully written historical novel illuminates the extraordinary life of the artist Adélaïde Labille-Guiard—her genius, her passion, and her valiant battle for the rights of female artists—as she is caught up in the throes of the French Revolution. It is a novel readers will not be able to put down, and Adélaïde is a woman they will never forget."

—Laura C. Rader, award-winning author of *Hatfield 1677*

"In this epic tale, Janell Strube brings to life the story of lesser-known artist Adélaïde Labille-Guiard. Using brushstrokes as vivid as Adélaïde's own, she illuminates the journey of a woman determined to make use of her talents and live on her own terms, a woman who fights to extend the same right to others. Adélaïde's tale is one you won't soon forget!"

—Alyssa Palombo, author of *The Most Beautiful Woman in Florence*

"Janell Strube's brilliant debut novel is a lush, immersive tale brimming with romance, intrigue, and suspense. Set during the tumultuous era of the French Revolution, the story blends fact and fiction with poetic language and exquisite sensory details that create a captivating narrative and bring history vividly to life. Adélaïde's quest for artistic fulfillment is both moving and inspiring. Highly recommended, this is a stunning read I couldn't put down."

—Jill G. Hall, author of *On a Sundown Sea: A Novel of Madame Tingley and the Origins of Lomaland*

ADÉLAÏDE

PAINTER OF THE REVOLUTION

JANELL STRUBE

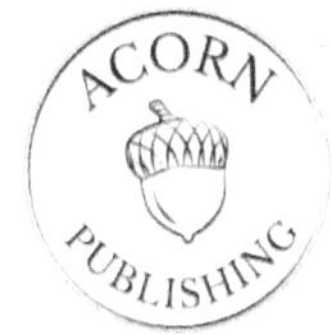

Helping talented writers publish exceptional books

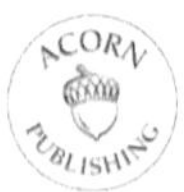

Adélaïde: Painter of the Revolution
Copyright © 2026 Janell Strube

Printed in the United States of America.
For information, address
Acorn Publishing, LLC
3943 Irvine Blvd. Ste. 218, Irvine, CA 92602

www.acornpublishingllc.com

Interior design by Kat Ross
Cover design by Damonza

ISBN-13:   979-8-88528-136-2 (hardcover)
ISBN-13:   979-8-88528-135-5 (paperback)
Library of Congress Control Number: 2025910315

To Dad, to Linda, and to
Adélaïde Labille-Guiard
and the women in her studio

PROLOGUE

PARIS, 1793

A column of fire reached like the Colossus of Rhodes into the night sky.

Shadowed figures waving torches poured into the Place du Carousel.

There, a clamoring mob passed wooden chairs, carriage wheels, and empty wine barrels over their heads toward the center of the square. Anything to feed the growing fire.

The Palais des Tuileries loomed to Adélaïde's left. Its mansard roof jutted into a smoke-filled sky. To her right, the Palais du Louvre's long wings stretched into the dark. The stone walls of the gallery that connected the two palaces flickered yellow and orange.

Adélaïde had never felt as small and alone as in that moment, between the embrace of buildings, in a space designed to dazzle royal spectators with seven hundred horses and jousting riders. Tonight, the square was filled with thousands of milling Parisians. And this time, *she* was the spectacle.

She pulled herself up on the tongue of the wooden cart next to the fire. Squinting against the smoke, she searched for anyone familiar.

Not a soul.

Even the donkeys had balked against their traces and been set free. Their distant braying reached her over the noise of the crowd.

Around her, men lurched about, their faces reddened from the bonfire, their sleeves stained purple from the wine they had scooped into their hands when the king's cellars were raided. The scent of Bourgogne rose into the air. Close by, a woman opened a dusty brown bottle and poured wine into the mouths of her companions.

Then the woman turned to Adélaïde. "Traitor!" she shouted, and drew back her arm, preparing to throw the bottle.

The crowd took up the chant. "Traitor! Traitor!" Others brandished their wine bottles.

Time slowed down. Adélaïde felt each sluggish boom of her heart, the constriction of her lungs, the loss of air she could not drag into her paralyzed chest. Was this the way she was going to die? Sliced to ribbons by a barrage of flying glass?

She raised her hands to protect her head and braced herself, but then a tall man in striped pants and a pointed red hat plucked the bottle out of the woman's hand and emptied the last drops into his mouth. "Any Parisian knows not to let good wine go to waste," he said.

Laughter.

The new citizens of France stomped their feet, shook their fists at Adélaïde, and threw the staves of the wine barrels into the flames. Arms brushed against her skirts. Bodies jostled the cart. She gripped the splintered seat to avoid being knocked into the fire.

The wind changed, and a rush of acrid smoke filled her lungs. She fought the urge to cough. Heat seared through her dress, burned her arms. Her mind screamed at her to run, but she had promised herself not to show fear, not to retreat.

The man in the red cap climbed into the cart. Sweat rolled from his face, and she smelled the sharp scent of his perspiration. Beneath his polished leather boots, the mountain of canvasses shifted. Fragile wood snapped. He stooped and held up a painting, still in its gilt frame. Black paint effaced the portrait sitter.

"Look at this travesty to art," he called to the crowd.

How right you are. She kept her eyes averted from his familiar face.

"Burn it. Burn it all!" the crowd roared.

The man laughed loudly and threw the painting into the fire. She flinched as yellow sparks flew upward. He tossed bundled sketches out to his audience. They cheered, grabbed the drawings, and did their part.

Go ahead, she thought, watching a sketch shrivel into a line of black ashes. *It doesn't matter now. There is nothing left to fight for. It's all gone.*

The man picked up another canvas, paused for a moment, frowned, then held the painting up.

"Brothers," he called. "This sedition especially must be burned."

Adélaïde lifted her head, glimpsed the partially completed canvas.

She had been wrong. Everything did still matter.

"No!" She scrambled onto the cart. "Murderer!" she cried. "This art is innocent."

"Woman," the man said. "There is nothing innocent about your art. And nothing innocent about *you*."

The painting sailed into the fire.

PART I
BEGINNINGS

CHAPTER 1

PARIS, 1764

The day began in its usual way, with her parents arguing over her future.

From her window-seat perch, Adélaïde watched the parish of St. Eustache wake beneath her gaze. She sat with the window ajar—one really did not want *all* the smells of Paris drifting into one's bedroom, but the morning breeze bore the fragrance of baking bread from the *boulangerie* across the street and the voices of her parents from the room below.

"The boys are gone, Claude. Can't you find something better to occupy your time than educating the females of this household?" Her mother's voice, sharp as a crystal bell, clear for Adélaïde to hear on the floor above. "Husband, I tell you, no good will come from this experiment of yours."

"The world is changing, Maman." Her father's baritone, pitched lower, less distinct. "In this age of philosophy, it's the rational thing to do."

"You would do better to invest in Adélaïde's dowry, not waste money on tutors—especially for maids and shop girls."

"We can afford it. Educating the grisettes increases sales because they can better interact with our clientele. But our daughter, Marie-Anne. You should be proud of her. The tutors claim she has surpassed her brothers, God rest their souls."

"Adélaïde will have to marry soon." Her mother's voice rose. "Husband, all this education will be a liability to her."

Maman always addressed Papa as husband when she thought she was right.

"She is too young for marriage yet," her father said, his voice still mild. "Let her pursue her art for a while."

Above them, Adélaïde knelt on the window seat, her hands clasped in prayer.

"She needs to take her place in the shop."

"Marie-Anne, her talents lie elsewhere."

Her mother paused. "I agree, she is a disaster with sales. Even the most laggard grisette does better."

Adélaïde could picture her mother below, tapping her quill on the ledger in dissatisfaction.

"If only she would not be so direct," her mother continued. "She should flirt a little. How will she attract a husband if she does not?"

Adélaïde cringed on the window seat. Her mother knew how to play the coquette, how to coax a reluctant customer to spend a quarter's allowance in their shop, but when she tried, Adélaïde felt like a draft horse pulling a dog cart.

"Perhaps she is selling the wrong thing," her father suggested. "Customers like her little drawings well enough."

"We are not in the business of selling our daughter's scribbles, husband."

The lacings in Adélaïde's dress constricted her chest. The golden weave in the curtain blurred. Was it going to be like her mother's birthday all over again?

"Marie-Anne." Her father's voice was stern.

Her mother did not speak for a moment. "Perhaps she can serve coffee and chocolate to the customers." But she sounded doubtful.

Adélaïde saw herself pouring chocolate and gossiping with the clientele. Dreadful. Maman knew she could never contain her tongue. It was Maman, after all, who had banished Adélaïde from the shop years ago because she was too boisterous. Adélaïde had joined her brothers in the schoolroom while Félicité, her older sister, served their customers. Now that Adélaïde was grown, she understood that working in the shop really meant that Maman could parade her before eligible suiters. With Félicité married, Maman wanted to provide a dowry for Adélaïde, sell the shop, and retire to the country.

"She's no maid, Marie-Anne. She's our daughter. Let her stock the shelves if she must help—or total the ledgers at night. She's good at that."

Maman did not need to know, but Adélaïde would have added the columns in the entire ledger every night to avoid wooing customers and to continue her studies.

There was silence downstairs. Then her mother said, "Perhaps we should get some value from this education. But really, Claude, we have waited long enough to begin our search for a husband. Too long in fact. She is fifteen today."

The window crank dug into Adélaïde's side as she collapsed against the bedroom wall. It was almost worth the pain of Maman's comment about her scribbles.

"Leave her alone today. It's her birthday. And she will love her gifts," her father said, anticipated pleasure in his voice.

Straining to hear, Adélaïde opened the casement window wide. To her right, the door of the wigmaker's shop flew open. Barbers and hairdressers rushed out, covered head to toe in flour, the wig boxes in their hands shedding powder like sugared pastries. At that exact moment, three coffee house waiters scurried past her parents' shop. They collided, the screech of the hairdressers sounding like fishwives in the market.

Doused in flour, shouting curses, the waiters adjusted the straps to the food baskets on their backs and steadied their steaming coffee pots. Dripping hot coffee, the barbers dried off their wig boxes and edged past the waiters on the narrow walkway with the wig boxes now balanced above their heads. Adélaïde laughed at the dance of penguin and powder puff. She grabbed her sketchbook. She had to capture the cloud of white that had flown into the air when the barbers ran into the waiters.

Downstairs, the window slammed shut. Adélaïde sighed. Sometimes Maman was right—a girl could learn a lot if she kept quiet.

Soon after, businessmen, lawyers, and government workers left their elegant townhomes for offices in the stock exchange, the courts, or the treasury. Feathers on cocked hats bobbed in time to the click of walking canes on cobblestones. Jewels pinned to velvet coats caught the sun and threw rainbow-colored light beams across the street. Then grisettes tripped down the alleyways that paralleled their street, their saffron heels and scarlet-and-lemon stockings flashing under demure work dresses.

At precisely nine o'clock, church bells heralded the hour. Up and down the street, sliding bolts shot back, shop bells tinkled, and grisettes came outside to turn signs from *Closed* to *Open*. Curtains swept upward, and window displays filled with cakes, pastries, chocolates, silks, hats, wine, and cheese guided the flow of traffic into their neighborhood like the sides of a riverbank.

The scent of graphite rose into Adélaïde's nose. While the scratch of the pencil across rough paper filled her head like music, she caught the morning neighborhood action in quick slashes of movement and figures. She placed a line of squiggles at the bottom of the grisette's skirts and–voilà–ruffles appeared. She added polka dots to the stockings at the grisettes' ankles. Finished. She put the sketchbook down, then dashed off a note to Félicité, who lived with her new husband on the other side of the Seine.

The words of your birthday poem were as sweet and heady as the scent of perfume gracing your letter. A thousand thank-yous. I have news, dear sister. I have just won the battle against working in the shop.

Adélaïde set the note aside to add shading to a shop window in her sketch, the shadow of someone moving beyond the curtain.

She refused to let her mother's comment sting. With her serious demeanor, long, narrow face, cool gray eyes, and a figure inclined to plumpness, Adélaïde was not their customers' first choice for service, especially after her parents hired Jeanne Beçu. People visited their shop, *À La Toilette*, just to see Jeanne. Her curly blond hair and almond-shaped eyes accompanied a manner that men found compelling. Somehow her gray and white uniform did not hide her figure. Sales had increased since Jeanne was hired. *Thank goodness for Jeanne*, she thought.

Now, if I can just continue my art lessons. Papa is fighting for me. Wish me luck, dear sister . . .

Her whole life would be ruined if that did not happen. Papa had to prevail. She sealed the letter, then tugged the bellpull.

"Deliver this," she instructed when Claudette, the housekeeper's daughter, answered the summons.

Two years older than Adélaïde, Claudette had grown up in the household, studying alongside Adélaïde until she turned twelve. Beneath her maid's cap, Claudette's sharp features and dark eyes bore a long-suffering expression. "A third note already." She took the proffered envelope, muttering, "Because it's your birthday."

A few minutes later, Claudette knocked again. The history tutor had arrived. Adélaïde reached for the books piled beside her, but a movement in the street caught her eye. She leaned out the window. François, their artist neighbor's son, walked up the road. He stooped to pick up a package dropped by the baker's mother. His unruly hair circled his head like a crooked halo. Her insides pirouetted. Now here was a boy she could be bothered to flirt with, if he would notice her, if she knew how to flirt. She opened a fresh page in her sketchbook.

"Mademoiselle . . ." Claudette urged through the door.

Two hours later, Adélaïde was back in her room, a smock over her dress, working on a pastel sketch, her earlier joy erased. Her art tutor had not shown up. Worse, Claudette said he was not coming back.

"You're being cruel," Adélaïde accused.

"You know nothing."

How could her parents take her art lessons away on her birthday? Angry tears fought against the back of her eyes, but she forced herself to focus on the still life before her. It had taken a month of afternoons to blend the right hues of green with purple to create the illusion of half-filled wine bottles. The curves of lemons, brown eggs, and green bottles resting on a white tablecloth against a dark background looked correct, but she had planned to ask her tutor a last question about the shading. She put the work down, wiped her chalk-stained hands on a damp cloth, then went to the window with her sketchbook.

Outside, fiacres and sedan chairs struggled through street vendors and foot traffic. A horse bolted and panic ensued. Her hand flew as she reflected the rider chasing his horse, pedestrians leaping aside, and a flower cart overturning.

A knock at the door. "Your parents want you in the shop," Claudette said.

Drawing the flowers falling from the cart, Adélaïde did not respond.

Claudette opened the door, peered around it. "I knew it. The minute you start drawing, your ears stop hearing, and your brain stops thinking." When that did not work, she said, "I cannot believe you would decline hot chocolate."

Chocolate? Adélaïde's mouth watered. It was her parents' signature luxury, boiled with chili pepper and honey, cooled overnight, boiled again, then served frothy to their most important clientele.

"Never." She might be upset with her parents, but chocolate was different. Her mother always complained about the small fortune they paid to the chocolatier across the street, and the even larger fortune they had paid for the Chinese porcelain they served it in, but her father would remind her of the additional sales they made while the customers sat sipping their chocolate. The family almost never indulged in the treat but today was special.

She put the sketchbook on the window seat and handed her smock to Claudette. "Pastries too?" She had skipped lunch, so she hurried downstairs, taking the completed still life with her.

"Ah, Adélaïde." Her father's face, lined and sagging beneath his powdered wig, lit up when he saw her. Claude Labille sat at the table in the back of the shop, a cup of coffee in his hand. His latest subscription to the *Encyclopédie* lay open atop the day's news journals. Eager to learn how the physical world worked, he read the *philosophes'* work cover to cover when it arrived. "What have you brought to show me today?" He took the pastel drawing from her. One eye squinted, he scrutinized it, then joked, "Not bad, not bad. The fold in the tablecloth through the wine bottles is a nice touch." He propped the drawing on the wainscot where her mother would see it.

Her hands clenched in the folds of her skirt, Adélaïde asked, "What happened to my art lesson today?"

"Sit down, sit down." Claude pointed to the chair beside him, then poured Adélaïde's chocolate into an etched crystal goblet.

"Come, Marie-Anne," he called his wife, who was at the front of the shop.

Her mother tied a package with ribbon, thanked the customer, then left Jeanne Bécu in charge. Maman came toward them, the groove in the middle of her forehead and the ones bracketing her mouth announcing her sorrow to the world. Since the death of Adélaïde's brothers, her mother had changed from a woman who laughed in the center of her sons while tutors traipsed through the house, to this person who argued with her father about continuing to spend money on the education of the one remaining child in the house—Adélaïde. After years of leaving Adélaïde alone, as her birthday approached, her mother had begun to insist that Adélaïde take her place in the shop.

But Adélaïde did not want to quit her studies. She had been happy in the schoolroom. The boys treated their baby sister first as a beloved pet, later as a comrade in their antics. It was the art tutor who had handed her a crayon and a scrap of paper to amuse herself. To everyone's surprise, Adélaïde had drawn Josef's rocking horse beneath the lace-covered window of the nursery, detailing even the faded flowers on its saddle. From that moment on, her hand became an extension of her sight, of everything that her eyes saw and her mind reflected. She was never without a pencil nearby.

Adélaïde drew everyone and everything while she studied alongside her brothers. Away from her mother's disapproving eyes, Adélaïde sometimes did her brothers' lessons so they could play in the park before the sun went down, or, as they grew older, sneak out to visit girls in the neighborhood. In return, her brothers brought her flowers and china bowls with intricate patterns to draw, or posed for her, twisting and climbing on top of one another like the Egyptian acrobats in the *Life of Sethos*.

On days when Claude visited the schoolroom, he would lift Adélaïde in his arms, swing her around, laugh, then chase the boys between the desks. Sometimes he would offer to take them to a science exhibition. Often, her father's good friend down the street, François-Elle Vincent, and Monsieur Vincent's two sons, François and Alexandré, would accompany them. Adélaïde glowed in the love of her father and brothers, undiminished even when her older brothers left for university.

But the day came when Jean-Claude, the eldest, and the next

two after him, Louis, and Josef, were sent home from school. A lung fever had swept the Latin Quarter south of the river. A week later, they realized that Jean-Claude had brought the illness with him, a disease unlike any their parents had experienced. Adélaïde's brothers burned with fever, coughed and wheezed, struggling to breathe. Benjamin, too sickly to attend university, caught their fever and died first. His lips, fingers, even the top of his head, turned blue.

Adélaïde would never forget waking to hear her mother scream, "This cannot be happening," in the hall above her, then beg God for it not to happen. Or her father's tears when he descended to tell Félicité and Adélaïde that Jean-Claude and Josef had not made it.

Once, Adélaïde had been the youngest of eight. Now, only she and Félicité remained, and although her brothers had died four years before, their loss struck the family anew each day. Grief for them was like searing lava in Adélaïde's belly. When she could not bear the pain, she copied her old sketches, worked to improve them. The more time she spent drawing, the more her fingers itched to draw. When she gave in to that tingle, that call from her hands, the ache subsided.

The spirits of the paper brothers came alive as her pencil flew across the page and the edges of her sleeves grew black. James spoke to her through the sparkle in his eyes, Louis smiled his secret smile through the curl of his lip. Charles searched on his knees for Josef's two front teeth while Josef looked brave, the gap in his grin a memory of the day he fell from the top of their human pyramid and struck the edge of a desk. Benjamin studied in a sunbeam, wrapped in a corded quilt. In her art, she returned to the circle of her brothers' love.

On her mother's last birthday, Adélaïde had presented her latest sketches to her mother. Marie-Anne had picked up the sketches, glanced at the faces of her dead sons, then flung the sketches away with a sharp cry. Adélaïde had felt the stab in her gut, a knife thrust so deep she wanted to die right there in the shop. Choking on her sobs, she gathered the scattered papers beneath the gaze of the grisettes. A customer *tsked* in pity.

Clutching the drawings to her chest, Adélaïde ran to her room and fell on the bed. She wanted her brothers. She wanted to be with her brothers. How could she have thought that drawing her brothers would bring her family together again?

Later, she picked up the sketches, seeing them through her mother's eyes. How childish, how pathetic, they were. Her fingers ached to try again, but what was the use? She pushed them off the bed. Tears tore at her sides and splotched onto the sketches on the floor.

At sundown, her father had entered the room. He stooped to pick up the crumpled drawings and sat down beside her, smoothing the papers out.

When Adélaïde heard him catch his breath, she hid her face in the pillow. "Papa, I didn't mean to make Maman cry. I can't remember their faces anymore. I draw to remember them. But I didn't get them right, and Maman hated them."

"Shh." He had gathered her in his arms and stroked her hair. "Maman cries not because they are bad, but because they are good. You've shown your brothers as they were. One day she'll be grateful for what you've done, but she can't bear to look at them just yet."

Now, as Marie-Anne walked toward them, Adélaïde offered her mother a wary smile, wondering what Maman would say about the first artwork Adélaïde had to show her since that disastrous day. But she need not have worried. Ignoring the still life, Marie-Anne sat down.

Letting out her breath, Adélaïde unfisted her hands and sank into her seat. "Papa, what's my surprise?"

"The art tutor says your skills now exceed his abilities. So—" He paused for effect. "We have arranged for you to study miniature painting with that Swiss painter down the street. Oh, what's his name?" He slapped his forehead and snapped his fingers, pretending to forget. "You know him—Monsieur, Monsieur . . ." he teased, his eyes twinkling.

"Monsieur Vincent!" Papa had prevailed. She wanted to fall on her father's neck and kiss him but restrained herself to a wide smile. "I don't know what to say." She could not resist bouncing in her seat.

He laughed. "Starting tomorrow, you'll attend lessons in his studio. And that's not all. A very kind customer has arranged for us to see the art collection at Hôtel Crozat this afternoon."

Claudette appeared, holding a large linen box topped with a pink bow. Her mother took the box, then handed it to Adélaïde.

"For your visit today." A smile warred with her frown lines. "Now that you are fifteen, you must have a dress for special occasions."

Special occasions meant meeting young men, but not wanting to flirt did not mean not wanting to wear beautiful clothes. Cradling the package in her lap, Adélaïde removed the bow. When she opened the box, a nest of pink muslin appeared, from which she drew a pearlescent satin overdress with ruffled sleeves and skirt swags, a Madame de Pompadour pink underdress, and blush leather gloves and matching slippers. She had never worn anything so grand. "Maman, I love it," she exclaimed.

Maman's pinched features eased.

Folding the muslin back over her precious gift, Adélaïde rose with the box. "Come, Claudette. Let's go get ready."

Forgetting her proper place as a ladies' maid, Claudette rushed up the stairs behind her.

"Look what you've done with your talk of equality, Claude," Adélaïde heard from below, then, "Have you no decorum, Adélaïde?"

When Adélaïde looked in the mirror, a radiant princess stood before her, cheeks flushed, eyes sparkling. She lifted her skirts with her gloved hands, trying to look regal as she walked down the stairs. From the bottom step, she saw that her father waited for her, wearing his coral velvet with his dress sword at his side. Behind her father, Claudette waited. When she saw Adélaïde, Claudette sashayed her shoulders and fanned her gray skirt beneath a freshly pressed white apron.

Adélaïde ignored her. "Maman, why aren't you ready?" Her mother, still in her shop dress, had not moved from the table.

"Someone has to mind the shop," Marie-Anne said.

"Can't Jeanne do that, Maman?"

"Yes, Marie-Anne, take the afternoon off." Her father sounded like it was not the first time he had suggested it.

"We are too busy right now," Maman said.

"Too busy to accept an invitation to a palace?" her father pressed.

Marie-Anne glanced toward the shop, then lowered her voice. "If I go, Adélaïde will think that I endorse this dream of hers."

Adélaïde's heart compressed. She knew her mother had waited for her to arrive to say these words. Her joy in the day ebbed.

Claudette dropped her skirts and rolled her eyes. "Hurry up, mademoiselle, or we'll be late."

∼

The Hôtel Crozat sprawled across from the Louvre, as imposing as the royal palace it faced. Adélaïde's father handed her down from the hired carriage. Claudette descended behind them, folding up the blanket she had spread on the carriage seat to protect Adélaïde's dress.

Her father regarded Adélaïde, then broke the silence of their carriage ride. "You are a grown woman, ma petite," he said, his voice gruff. He bowed and offered his arm.

Adélaïde laughed and straightened his wig. Her father always knew how to take away the sting of her mother. She curtseyed, and he kissed her hand.

"Well, now." He cleared his throat. "Shall we go see what's inside this monstrosity?"

In the grand salon, Adélaïde stopped before four large portraits. Spring, Summer, Fall, and Winter, personified as young women, beckoned Adélaïde with dipped heads and direct gazes. The quiver started. She flexed her fingers, but the leather gloves stifled their movement. "Oh, why did Maman make me leave my sketchbook behind? I should be copying these."

Claudette adopted the pose of a marble statue in the room, holding the blanket like a shield, staring at the floor.

"Look, Papa, the artist is a woman. This plaque says she came from Italy."

Papa bent to read the name. "Ah, yes, Rosalba Carriera. She took Paris by storm. Artists have followed her style for decades."

"How did she do it?"

"How did she come to Paris?"

"No. I mean, how did she paint like that? The women look alive. How did she get her colors to glow? How did she make skin look real? How did she make arms round, how did she make their expressions so convincing?" She wanted to know everything—now.

Her father's laugh reverberated through the cavernous room. "Could you paint like this?"

She had only worked in pastels and graphite before but saw herself painting just like this woman. "If someone were to teach me."

"Come now." Her father took her arm again. "Let's explore the rest of Crozat's before Claudette here loses her arm like that wooden Madonna in the corner."

Claudette came alive with an exclamation of relief.

The bells of St. Eustache, the rattles, creaks, and groans of carriages, the cries of street sellers, marked the hours of the day while the sun shone over the close-set houses until it sank in defeat on the western horizon. Shops closed. The Paris of the night awoke, its music and laughter carrying on the wind that blew off the Seine. Adélaïde closed her sketchbook and eased off the window seat. Claudette drew the drapes, then turned to help her don a nightgown.

"Seeing art in person is much better than viewing engraved images in a book, Claudette. It's the difference between listening to a violin play and hearing the whole orchestra."

Claudette rolled her eyes.

"That's twice in one day, young lady." Adélaïde mimicked her mother's voice. The girls laughed. "I thought I had died and ascended to heaven."

"That's understandable—the thousands of putti flying up to clouds painted on the ceiling made me dizzy." Claudette unthreaded the pink ribbons in Adélaïde's braids and then brushed out her hair.

Adélaïde opened the ancient brochure from the Royal Academy's Salon of 1721, a last gift from her father. "Imagine, Claudette. Rosalba came from Italy and became a member of the Royal Academy of Painting and Sculpture. She exhibited her works in the Academy's Salon."

It was Claudette's turn to mimic Adélaïde's mother. "Look what you've done, Claude. Now our daughter will think her works should hang in the Louvre."

Adélaïde giggled. "I hope my talent equals Rosalba's."

Clad in her cap and nightgown, she went downstairs to share a last goodnight with her parents.

Her parents tallied the day's receipts at the back table. Watching them, love filled her heart. She rushed forward and embraced her mother, who sat counting coins. Then she threw her arms around her father. His seat tipped back with the force of her exuberance.

Chuckling, he enfolded her in his arms. "You're too big for this, you know, but you're still my girl."

She wrapped her arms around his neck, kissed his bald head, then sat beside him. "This has been the best birthday. The dress was perfect, Maman. Papa, I can't wait for tomorrow." Taking his hand, she promised to make him proud.

"I know you will. It's time to make your mark on the world. In this great age, you can go anywhere and do anything you want. Even you, Jeanne," he said as Jeanne unfurled the curtains over the bow window.

Jeanne came to the back of the shop, pulled off her apron, and smoothed her hair in the mirror. Green stockings peeped under her dark skirt.

"With the world beating down our door to see you, who knows where you'll go, eh?" her father asked.

"To Versailles, of course." Jeanne batted her blue eyes at him.

Claude laughed. "In a world where women run salons and men study logic, anything is possible."

"Why do you encourage such ideas, Claude?" Maman asked after Jeanne closed the alley door behind her. "I won't have my shop girls chasing our clientele."

He chuckled. "Imagine, Marie-Anne, a grisette of ours becoming a royal mistress and returning to sit in your window." He gave a silent whistle, then said to Adélaïde, "But you, my dear, could become a guild member like your art tutor."

Her mother snapped the cash box shut. "Mistress. Guild member." She turned the words into epithets. "You can best elevate yourself—and our family—by marrying someone above our class."

"I'm not getting married, Maman," Adélaïde said. "I'm going to be a great painter." The words hung in the air above the worktable in the evening darkness. Without realizing it, she had risen to her feet. The candle flame flickered as though even the heat felt the weight of her pledge. The voice that had uttered the words did not sound like her fifteen-year-old self, but in her heart, Adélaïde knew they were true.

Her father looked up and raised his hands to the ceiling.

Across the table, the groove in her mother's forehead formed a downward arrow. "I rest my case, Claude." Her mother shoved the cashbox aside and folded her arms across her chest. The white ruffles at her wrists flashed like gauntlets against her black sateen dress. "We are already too late. Our daughter is no longer a malleable young lady that a husband can mold to suit him."

Her father rubbed a tired hand across his bare head. He gave Adélaïde a look that asked why she had to make his job all the harder. "Now, Marie-Anne," he began. And another fight between her parents commenced.

Adélaïde's head pounded, and her palms moistened. Why, when she was just about to get what she most wanted, did she have to open her mouth and ruin everything? Now, when Maman might understand her a little, when they might be close again. Well, if she was old enough to say what she did not want, she was old enough to say the rest. "I'm not a malleable young lady, Maman."

Her mother threw her hands up in the air, then pointed toward the door. "Go to your room."

"I'm going," she said, but at the stairs, looked back, trying to catch her father's eyes.

Her mother sat with her elbows on the table, hands pressed against her forehead, a tableau of despair. From the stairwell, Adélaïde heard her say, "Claude, if we do not hurry, we will never find anyone to marry her."

Upstairs, her bedroom door and windows shut, Adélaïde was glad she could not overhear the next round of argument. Sketching in the candlelight, Adélaïde thought it would not be so bad if her mother never found someone to marry her, but that it would be tragic if she could not have her art lessons. She would only have herself to blame if her father changed his mind.

CHAPTER 2

MONSIEUR VINCENT'S STUDIO, MARCH 1766

A délaïde squeezed into her seat among the seven other students around the worktable, her sleeve sweeping over a small easel. The boy next to her grabbed his water pot.

"Excuse me," she said, putting down her tiny brushes and gouache colors. A thrill went through her as she observed the small canvasses balanced on easels before the students. She could not wait to get started.

Monsieur Vincent looked up, smiled, and made his way through the crowded room to her. "We have a new student today," he said in his Germanic accented voice. "Mademoiselle Adélaïde. Have you brought some of your work to show us today?"

Adélaïde handed him a pastel sketch of the barbers and waiters colliding.

"Well done, mademoiselle," he said. "You have managed to capture an essence of ghostliness in the barbers. One can feel energy and anger as they wave their curling tongs at the waiters. Still, you must work on the proportion of the arms."

Finally, Adélaïde thought. *Someone who will really teach me.*

The boy next to her glanced at the drawing, then smirked at Monsieur Vincent. "Where is your wig, monsieur?" he asked.

"Is it rational to wear that which one could eat on one's head when many do not have enough to eat?" His voice mild, Monsieur

Vincent took a magnifying glass from his coat pocket and examined the young man's work.

Dressed in black wool, his tall form bony angles of elbows and knees, Adélaïde thought Monsieur Vincent as austere and functional as his studio. With its stuccoed walls, oak table and chairs, the drafting table where his sons studied, the scarred storage cabinet where they ground their colors, and the card table where the Vincents took their meals when it was not serving as a desk, nothing in the studio existed outside its purpose.

Behind his father's back, Alexandré, at the drafting table with his brother François, scribbled a cartoon man wearing a crown of baguettes on a scrap of paper. Like their father, François and Alexandré were tall and thin with aquiline noses, narrow faces, and wavy hair most often neither powdered nor confined to a queue. Alexandré passed the drawing to the students on the other side of the worktable. Everyone snickered.

Monsieur Vincent moved to the drafting table and told Alexandré to rethink the proportions of the building in his sketch. "Redraw it," he ordered.

At noon, when the students placed their metal pails from home on the worktable and pulled out cheese, bread, and pastries, Monsieur Vincent announced a surprise for his sons. Clearing the card table, he placed a protective white cloth over it, then set a package wrapped in brown paper on the cloth. Inside were two leather-bound books.

Alexandré groaned. "We're to eat this?"

François nudged his younger brother.

Monsieur Vincent was determined to educate his sons and spent every available denier on information. A shelf nailed high on the back wall secured his growing collection of books from drifting paint powder and teenaged antics. Today's additions were John Locke's *On Human Understanding,* translated from the English, and its recent rebuttal by Gottfried Leibniz.

"I heard that everyone debates these books in the salons," Monsieur Vincent, who was not invited to salons, said.

"They come to blows," agreed the boy across from Adélaïde, whose father was invited to salons.

"Is man born a blank slate, or with his beliefs already within, waiting to manifest themselves?" Monsieur Vincent asked his sons while the students ate. "Demonstrate your opinion with a sketch."

"If one really wants to understand a human, they could start by understanding hunger," Alexandré grumbled. He thought for a moment, then drew a sleeping baby with empty clouds coming out of his nose.

François sketched a child with devils, angels, and religious symbols struggling to exit the child through his bulging eyes and open mouth.

Adélaïde put down her bread. "Perhaps it is both what goes into the child and what existed within from the beginning," she offered, her heart skipping.

"Defend your viewpoint." Monsieur Vincent stepped aside so she could join them at the card table.

She drew a small child toddling toward a rose. "It is within a child to walk," she said. "But she is affected by the world around her." She added thorns to the stem of the rose, then bows to the child's hair.

"Bravo," Alexandré admired.

"Well done," Monsieur Vincent congratulated her.

"No one can argue with you, Adélaïde." François smiled. He had never spoken so directly to her.

The men's praise thrilled her.

That evening, she entered À La Toilette through the shop door just before closing. Her feet sank into the Turkish carpet. The velvet bergère chairs in the bow window, where customers gossiped and sipped wine or chocolate while grisettes paraded the shop's offerings before them, sat empty. She moved through the shop, her fingertips registering satin and silk, her mind wondering how to paint their difference. Now, she would get to learn. She was thankful her father had not changed his mind, and she promised herself she would do nothing to upset her mother.

She stopped to adjust a swag of fabric, then examined the fruits of her early morning labor. Rising before dawn, she had changed the items on display to match the colors set by the king's designers for the season. A peace offering to her mother.

Her father had been pleased. "How can our customers resist?" he had asked. "As long as one has to change one's attire with the weather and one's looks from breakfast to dinner, and from dinner to breakfast, and on both sides of in-between, we'll always be in business with Adélaïde organizing the shop, Marie-Anne."

"Better she stay home and sell some of this merchandise, husband," her mother had replied.

"No, Marie-Anne, she is going to the Vincents today."

Adélaïde had hurried out of the house before her mother could say anything else.

Tonight, silken scarves from the Orient, lace from Flanders, hats designed in Paris, kidskin gloves, and silk stockings sheer enough to see the color of one's skin rippled across the cabinets in the candle-light. Above them, dyed feathers and entire stuffed birds, jeweled combs, and embroidered purses and slippers shimmered along the walls.

Satisfied with her display, Adélaïde joined her parents at the back of the shop, totaled the day's receipts, then told them how everyone had laughed at Monsieur Vincent's hair, even his own son.

"Their Protestant background makes the family incapable of following the rules of a civilized society," her mother sniffed.

"The man lives according to his beliefs and has paid the price," her father admonished.

Monsieur Vincent had fled Switzerland to avoid religious perse-cution. Once in France, he had moved his family to Paris for artistic opportunities for his oldest son, but many of their neighbors did not accept him for his beliefs. This afternoon, a customer, a neighbor well known to Adélaïde, had walked out when he realized he had stepped into a Protestant establishment, but another neighbor had carried away a gouache portrait created by Monsieur Vincent small enough to fit into a locket an inch high, crowing at the price she paid.

"I don't think he had money for lunch today," Adélaïde said.

When she left for the studio the next morning, Adélaïde carried a small hamper filled with a half-loaf of hardened bread, three apples, a few slices of quiche. "The bread is for your soup." Adélaïde handed Monsieur Vincent the basket. "Our cook still thinks we have lots of young men in the house."

Alexandré reached in and grabbed out a yellow-skinned apple and rubbed it on his jacket. The fruit crunched when he bit into it, and the sharp scent of apple filled the air.

Claiming he was not hungry, Monsieur Vincent watched his son devour the fruit, a slight smile brightening his face.

Months and then seasons sped by as Adélaïde applied herself to her studies.

Each day the neighborhood students took turns sketching and painting miniatures of one another. Adélaïde learned how to add the latest clothing details to her miniatures from the fashion plates in her parents' shop. Lace and highlighted ruffles, created with the thinnest brush, became her expertise. Sometimes she stopped painting and worked on perspective sketches with the Vincent brothers. She told herself that it improved the minuscule backgrounds in her gouache paintings, which it did, but if she were honest, it was to get closer to François. At other times, she rested her cramped fingers and aching eyes by leafing through Monsieur Vincent's books, asking François questions about what she read.

It felt like the entire world was spread before her.

For his part, François would lean over from his seat at the raised drafting table and make a comment on her drawing. Often Adélaïde felt his gaze on her, but when she looked up his hazel eyes darted away. *Still*, she thought, *if François speaks to anyone in class, he speaks to me the most.*

Five years older than her, François had finished his father's training and had applied for a scholarship to study at the prestigious Royal Academy of Painting and Sculpture. While he waited to hear, he sketched, painted, and studied drafting alongside his fifteen-year-old brother. To earn money, he ran errands and ground lead carbonate and lead antimonate into powder and mixed them with oil, selling the resulting paint to local artists.

One afternoon, when Adélaïde had been in Monsieur Vincent's studio for a little more than a year and a half, the man came home with a volume from an edition of Giorgio Vasari's *The Lives of the Most Excellent Artists, Sculptors, and Architects* and gave it to his oldest son. "But in Italian, Father?" François protested.

"To go to Italy one day, you must be fluent, boy. You must know their famous artists."

Adélaïde dropped her brush on the table and stopped to clean up the mess. "Why Italy?" she asked.

"Because all the great artists go to study in Italy," Monsieur Vincent answered.

She wanted to ask why again but thought better of it. After all, Rosalba Carriera had come from Italy.

"Come, François, I want to hear you read aloud," Monsieur Vincent told his son.

"Does he have to drone on and on?" Alexandré asked after a few minutes, and Monsieur Vincent turned to lecture him on the benefits of hard work.

"Look, you have not observed the golden mean. It's the most basic tenet of architecture, Alexandré. How can you be successful if you do not study? Look at your brother's drawing. Follow his example."

Alexandré's face reddened.

Monsieur Vincent turned and grabbed a caricature making its way around the room, an image of himself standing on a box banging a drum that had *Hard Work* written on the drumhead. "Alexandré, you must focus on your studies." He scrunched the drawing in his hand.

François had drawn the cartoon, but the students maintained solemn faces. It seemed to Adélaïde that only Monsieur Vincent did not know that Alexandré struggled to read and hated to study.

When no one said anything, Monsieur Vincent distracted himself by peering over her shoulder. "Adélaïde, you are one of the best artists I've ever trained," he said. "You may begin painting on ivory tomorrow."

"I'm ready?" she asked, feeling pleased. Moving from vellum to ivory meant she was almost ready to sell her own work.

He nodded, and she wondered whether he thought she was better than François but dared not ask.

"Now, check where you have put the shadow against the light. Should it fall on the wall behind the vase or the table before it?"

Later that afternoon, Alexandré took his revenge. When François left to buy paintbrushes, Alexandré made sure his father was busy, then tied a string across the doorway. From the window, the other boys watched for François's return while the girls waited in their seats.

"What's he doing at the flower seller's?" one boy asked.

"What do people do at a flower shop?" another boy asked. "He's buying flowers."

"Here he comes," the first boy said.

When François entered the room, he tripped over the string and executed an awkward tumble, trying to save the flowers, then the brushes. Blushing dark as the dried roses, he chased his brother around the table while the students scrambled out of the way.

Soon, they all were laughing, picking up crushed rose petals and broken paintbrushes while Monsieur Vincent complained about wasted money.

"Who were the flowers for?" Alexandré demanded.

François said nothing but glanced at Adélaïde. The tips of his ears turned crimson. Adélaïde pretended to paint, her insides hot.

Later that afternoon, she and Claudette knelt on the window seat in her bedroom, their shoulders rubbing as they leaned out the window. Down in the street, their neighbors hurried by as the sun fled and twilight approached.

"I think I might get married," Claudette said.

"To whom? Do you have a secret lover you haven't told me about?"

"No, but I accepted a job across the river at a bookseller's shop," Claudette said. "And the owner is a widower."

Adélaïde turned to stare at her friend. Claudette's brown eyes were so close that she could see the starbursts in them. "You don't have to leave us."

"It's dull in the house now. You're always out."

It was true that Adélaïde was going out that very night. Monsieur Vincent had arranged for his students to see a magic lantern show and Adélaïde's father had decided to join them.

"I thought we always said we weren't getting married."

"I have no intention of becoming a kitchen maid," Claudette said.

"Marriage is probably better than that," Adélaïde agreed. Even she had started to believe marriage would not be so bad if she could spend her days with François. But now it seemed that his father planned for him to go to Italy. Perhaps she could study in Italy too.

As though she had conjured him up, François walked past their house.

"Look, there's François!"

Adélaïde told Claudette about the flower episode that day. "I think he likes me, but he's too shy to say anything—while Alexandré never stops talking. I just don't know how to find out."

"Accidentally touch his hand," Claudette advised, then demonstrated, her fingers catching Adélaïde's in the gathering darkness. "See what happens."

Could she be so bold? Adélaïde did not know, but how else could they move beyond furtive looks?

Later that night, Monsieur Vincent walked his students to the theater, telling her father as they walked side by side, "This will be the future of art. Our students must learn about it."

Her father agreed.

At the theater, the lantern girl cranked furiously at her hand organ, the narrator shouted over the music, and the students shivered at the frightening images that flashed on the white-washed wall. In her seat beside François, Adélaïde reached out in the dark, then snatched her hand back.

Was she trying to bring Maman's wrath down on herself?

After almost two years of silence, Adélaïde's mother took up the mantra that her art studies had lasted long enough and that she had to return home. To appease her mother, Adélaïde began to spend more time in the shop, but she begrudged every moment at À La Toilette and longed for the camaraderie and freedom of Monsieur Vincent's studio.

One early winter afternoon, Adélaïde stopped by the Vincents' to find the family celebrating. A half-eaten honey cake covered with purple and yellow marzipan flowers sat on the card table along with a jug of wine.

"Where is everyone?" She placed a basket of food on the empty worktable.

The men rose from their places around the card table. "Did you not receive my note?" Monsieur Vincent asked. "No studying today. But please, join us." He pulled up a chair from the worktable. "Wonderful news, Adélaïde. François made it."

François held out a thick cream-colored piece of paper with

elegant writing on it. Today, even he was ebullient. "I have finally received my letter of support from the Royal Academy. I have earned a scholarship to study with one of its top painters."

"The top painter," his father corrected. "Joseph Vien is the Academy's most renowned instructor. You're on your way to the Academy, son." He clapped François on the back.

She sat down and the men fell into their seats. "What does this mean, François?"

"The government will pay for my art lessons with Monsieur Vien," he said, then told her that he would live in Vien's studio and receive a stipend for food, clothing, even paint supplies.

"If you are training in the Royal Academy, will you eat like a king?" Alexandré rubbed his concave stomach. "If so, I will come to dinner every night."

"You will not." His father cuffed him on the ear.

"If I do well, I can become an *agréé* and then a full member of the Academy. I can display my works in the Salon's biennial exhibition at the Louvre. I will receive royal commissions, and the government will provide me with housing for life."

"It seems your father was right about hard work, François," Adélaïde said.

"I could even paint the king." François jumped up and paced the room while he imagined visiting the palace in Versailles.

This reminded Adélaïde of Rosalba Carriera's portraits hanging in the Hôtel Crozat. "How do I join the Academy?" she asked.

The men burst out laughing.

"Women can't join," François said.

"What?" she asked, heat rushing into her face.

Seeing her expression, Monsieur Vincent said, "Well, that's not entirely true, son. There's talk that they will make Anne-Marie Vallayer, the daughter of the King's goldsmith, a member. Or Marie Thérèse Reboul, the wife of your new instructor, Monsieur Vien."

"But Rosalba Carriera was an Academy member," Adélaïde insisted. "She came from Italy. She did not have royal connections or a husband."

"That was years ago," Monsieur Vincent said. "She was a special case. Now, the Royal Academy has no female members."

How could this be true? For years she had stared at the brochure of Rosalba Carriera and dreamed of the time when she would join the Academy. "Why should a woman be a special case? If she's good and has the proper training?"

"It's just the way it is," François said.

"But how is that logical or reasonable?" It was as illogical and as unreasonable as her mother telling Adélaïde this morning that she needed to start hiding her intelligence and stop debating politics—that it was an unattractive characteristic for a woman of their class, and it had prevented her from finding a husband. For the thousandth time, Adélaïde had retorted that she was not looking for a husband. The one boy Adélaïde wanted to attract never minded—in fact, it was the one certain way to get him to talk to her. But that one particular boy had just mocked her dream. "Why—"

"Oh, here we go." Alexandré lolled back in his seat. "Bring on the debate."

Monsieur Vincent poured oil over her roiling water. "I suppose a truly extraordinary woman could be admitted, but better to gain admittance to the Academy of St. Luke. It's a respected guild throughout Europe and has hundreds of female artists. In fact, if you want to sell your artwork in Paris, you must have a license from the guild."

She could not believe it, did not want to believe it, but what was there to say? She could not tell her teacher that she did not want to be a member of his guild, that she wanted the things his son was about to receive.

"Have some cake." Alexandré put a dessert plate in front of her.

She pushed it away. When she looked up, François stared at her, a stricken look on his face.

"I'm sorry," he said.

"For what exactly?" she asked as though she did not know. A chasm stood between them, but she had not seen the edge until she was upon it.

He shrugged his shoulders. "Everything, I guess," he mumbled. "I know how much your art means to you."

Alexandré shoved the plate back, his fingernail tinging against the china rim. "We were celebrating François's achievement," he reminded, glaring at her.

Shamefaced, Adélaïde picked up her fork. "It's not your fault, François. Maman always says my tongue is a lemon in need of sugar, and she's right."

Honey and butter melted on her tongue, but the cake stuck like chalk in her throat while she mulled over what it took to be an extraordinary woman. She had not anticipated this outcome when she had charted her course. She worked as hard as François, harder than Alexandré, and yet, it seemed, there was nothing she could achieve, no reward for her, no place for her, while every day at home, her mother insisted it was time to stop playing at being an artist and get married. What would her life be if she could not be herself? She wanted to be happy for François, but she was sorry for herself. It wasn't fair. Tonight, even in the Vincent household, the walls closed in on her.

"I must go," she said, her breath catching in her throat. "It's getting dark."

François offered to walk her home.

"Take Alexandré with you," Monsieur Vincent ordered.

They set out for her house, Adélaïde walking between the two young men. Torches above the shop awnings threw flame shadows across their faces. She tried to make up for her earlier behavior. "I'm happy for you, François. This is what you've worked for—to be the best—to study at the Louvre—" They passed the wigmaker's shop. Almost home. Her heart fluttered like a sparrow trapped in her chest. Her steps slowed. "It won't be the same without you." Her voice trembled.

"I'll miss you too." François's fingers brushed her hand in the dark, warm and calloused in the cold air. Suddenly, their fingers locked together.

"It's not as though you're moving to the moon, François," Alexandré said. "You can always walk over from the Louvre."

Snow fell in Paris over Christmas and François's absence loomed over the studio. It was as quiet inside the Vincents' as it was out on the blanketed streets. With no one to provoke, even Alexandré devoted himself to his studies. Adélaïde lived for the times François walked through the darkened streets to dine with his family. On the nights when he came, she lingered to hear about his days in Joseph Vien's studio, then walked home far past the hour her mother deemed appropriate for a young woman from a good family.

"It's a five-house walk, Maman," she would say when her mother complained. Maman did not need to know she was not alone, at least not as far as the corner where François turned for the Louvre.

The first time François came home, he said, "On the first day, Monsieur Vien stood in front of me and managed to look down his nose at me—though I am a foot taller. He looked at my artwork and said it lacked much. I did not know what to think. He explained what he called his revolutionary methods—a live model comes to his studio three days a week. He claimed that he could teach us what beauties to follow and what defects to avoid as we observed the model."

"What does that mean?" Alexandré asked. "Don't draw their fat or their wrinkles?"

François shrugged. "He said he would uplift our souls with electrifying conversations about nature, antiquities, the great masters."

"Electrifying conversation?" Alexandré ruffled his hair, then mimed a spasm.

"I would say the electrocution happens when he critiques our work," François grinned. "He accepts nothing but perfection. Sometimes we have to paint the same object over and over to get it right."

"I wish I could be there with you." Adélaïde said, imagining Vien's studio. "It sounds wonderful."

"There are no girls in Vien's studio, Adélaïde. It is grueling work. Sometimes we must get up before dawn to study the morning light."

"I'm sure it's too difficult for women to rise early enough to watch the sun rise," she said.

That night, she made it home in time for dinner.

From her bedroom window the next morning, she chased pink streaks of cloud with her pastels as the ormolu clock chimed six, still seething at François for being so obtuse.

As winter turned to spring, the snow disappeared, the tulips pushed their way through the earth and the chestnut trees bloomed in the Place Dauphine. During that time, François brought ten canvas squares home, painted studies of the same helmet. In the last study, the metal of the helmet shone like liquid silver and reflected a garden with a Cyprus tree in its midst on the helmet's rounded side.

While his father's students admired his work, François said, "Monsieur Vien says that I have finally produced an acceptable reflection."

Adélaïde wondered what Vien would say about the helmets she had executed in pastel at home.

For once, Monsieur Vincent paid no attention to his son's artwork. "Why are you wearing a bagwig, son?"

François touched the wig on his head. "I must, Father. People have complained that the scholarship should have gone to a real Frenchman, not an immigrant. The Academy officials say I must adopt the standards required of the scholarship."

When Monsieur Vincent began to argue with his son, Adélaïde's father, who had been chatting with the older man while he waited to take her home, stood and extinguished his pipe. "Come, daughter, it's time to take our leave."

They left the studio, arm in arm, her father's pace slow. The night was chilly. Adélaïde tried to hurry her father along, but he appeared not to notice. After he had twice opened his mouth, Adélaïde said, "Papa, you look a bit like a fish out of water. I suppose Maman sent you to scold me?"

His eyes flashed in the dark. "My girl misses nothing."

"Well, please get on with it. It's cold out." She shivered under their shop awning. "What have I done now?"

"You've done nothing, but we are concerned. Before Claudette left, she told your mother that you were carrying on a flirtation with François."

"I—What? I would never do such a thing, Papa. You know that." Why was he bringing Claudette into this? "Claudette's been gone for ages, Papa. Why are you mentioning this now?"

"Because you've been spending so much time at the Vincents' in the evenings when François is there, we are worried. Maman thought it appropriate that I speak to you so that you understand the situation."

"There is no situation, Papa." Even if she wished there were.

"You and François can never be."

"What do you mean?"

He sighed. "It means that we are Catholic, and they are Protestant. You cannot marry him."

"But you don't care about his religion, Papa. Monsieur Vincent is your friend."

"You're right, I don't. But marriage is a different matter."

"Shouldn't you love someone who can be your friend, who wants the same things you want?"

"Marriage between Catholics and Protestants is against the law."

"Why should religion have anything to do with marriage? If two people love each other, why should anything else matter?" What had she ever done to cause the things she wanted most—to be an artist and to be with François—to be denied to her? "That's the most ridiculous law I've ever heard. Besides, it can't be true. Chevalier Roslin is a Protestant and married to a Catholic." Everyone on the street knew of the Roslins' famous romance. The grisettes repeated the story each time Madame Roslin came into À La Toilette to sketch the latest fashions and share a glass of wine with her mother.

"The king knighted Monsieur Roslin. We have no standing to get the king to bend the laws for us, and François has no fortune to make the laws go away."

"Neither money nor position matters to me, Papa."

"But it matters to the Vincents. If not for the charity of the neighborhood, they would starve. Every quarter they barely avoid eviction. For them, everything depends on François doing well. You saw tonight how careful he must be—turning his back on even the appearance of his religion. His father can say nothing."

"I can't believe you would say such terrible things about your friend, Papa."

"He has a fine mind, which I admire very much, but he and I are realists about our children's futures."

A horrible thought struck. "Did Monsieur Vincent ask you to speak to me?"

Her father looked away.

Were her feelings for François obvious to everyone? She left her father standing outside, and ran inside, her cold hands covering her flaming cheeks.

~

François's visits home grew less frequent. His talent had made him one of the top students in Vien's atelier and Vien judged him ready to compete for the prestigious Prix-de-Rome. To make sure no one cheated, the artists had to prepare their competition entries in a special booth. François stayed in his booth for months, painting, sleeping, rising to paint again, leaving only when he remembered to eat.

One evening, François stopped by his father's studio while Adélaïde waited for the rain outside to clear. François sat down next to her at the worktable. "What are you working on?" he asked while his father hurried to get a bowl of soup from the cauldron hanging over the hearth.

She shrugged. "This miniature study of flowers."

"Put all your energy into this competition, François." Monsieur Vincent watched his son wolf the soup down. "Nothing must distract you."

"I am, Father," François said. "See how my clothes hang now?"

"I agree." Alexandré dragged his brother out of the chair and lifted him up. "He's light as a feather."

"Put me down." François punched his brother on the head.

When the two brothers tired of scuffling, François flopped back down next to Adélaïde, his hazel eyes gleaming. "The Prix-de-Rome is the key to everything. If I win, I will receive three years of study at the king's college and four years of study in Rome."

"If you win, you prove that you are the best student in the Royal Academy. You are almost guaranteed an Academy position when you return," his father said. "Your career will be established."

Adélaïde went to the hearth and ladled more soup into François's bowl. His world was expanding with limitless possibilities while her own was contracting to just one, one she did not want. She placed the hot bowl on the table, averting her face to hide her feelings.

If she had not felt so desperate, if, when she had entered the house, soaking wet, her mother had not demanded that her art classes cease at the end of summer—and had her father not agreed—Adélaïde might not have dared to do what she did next.

CHAPTER 3

MAY 1768

I t started with a poster ripped off a wall.

One late spring morning, Monsieur Vincent came into his studio waving a filthy piece of paper, back from a morning spent visiting François at the Louvre. "Here's your opportunity, Alexandré. You have no chance to enter the Academy, but you can try to win some prize money." He handed the poster to his younger son. "You have the skills to do it, you just must apply yourself."

Alexandré pretended to read the poster. Once his father started the afternoon class, he tossed the paper onto the worktable, his face angry. Adélaïde picked it up. It was an advertisement for a student art competition, a Prix-de-Paris to run concurrently with the Prix-de-Rome. While the top Academy students were competing for a place in the Academy's school in Rome, the Academy offered a city-wide competition for art students to compete for a spot in the Academy in Paris. First prize was a scholarship to attend the Royal Academy's art school, second a hundred livres, third, fifty livres. Reading the submission requirements, Adélaïde's heart started to race with excitement. She could win this. She had two months to produce the portfolio pieces required for the competition. She had already done, or could do, each piece requested. But then her eyes reached the bottom of the page, and her hopes plummeted. "Interested young men may submit their portfolio pieces by…"

She arranged her supplies with unnecessary force. When she

splashed water on the gouache paper she had spent hours preparing the day before, she forced herself to calm down. As she wiped up the mess, an idea formed. She pulled the poster toward her, reread the rules, then caught Alexandré's attention.

When she told him what she wanted to do, his eyes lit with glee. "Let's do it," he said. "But first you must help me with these math exercises Father wants."

"Of course," she said.

Alexandré was all her brothers rolled into one.

Adélaïde treated the Prix-de-Paris as her Prix-de-Rome. More than anything, she wanted to show the world her capabilities. Alexandré, who had taken over François's errand running for artists in the neighborhood, smuggled rolls of paper and sepia pencils out of the studio and escorted her home, where she darted up the back stairs with the supplies. The days of summer flew by as she prepared a head study, a hand study, a life study, a study of light and shade, a still life in gray tones, using the memories of her brothers as her models. She sketched Claude lounging in the schoolroom, drew the china bowl Josef had given her filled with fruit on a desk—objects she could almost draw in her sleep, but with the new techniques François had taught her from his time in Vien's studio. Then she prepared a sepia sketch of a master painting.

"What is all this running back and forth?" her mother asked. "And what are you doing hiding up in your room? You should be out walking in the park or working in the shop."

Meeting young men, her mother meant.

"It's a surprise for Papa's birthday," Adélaïde said. To give truth to the lie, she prepared a complicated sketch of her father and Monsieur Vincent demonstrating how an electricity engine worked.

The last day for submissions dawned. At eight in the morning, Adélaïde snuck down the back stairs in stockinged feet, struggling to keep the portfolio from bumping against the stairwell. Alexandré waited in the alley. She went through their plan, making sure they had anticipated everything and forgotten nothing.

"Remember, Alexandré, you are to deliver the art and pose as the artist."

"I know, I know," he said. "I will complete the entry paperwork with your first initial and last name." The entry form was the key to her unsigned submission.

She handed him the portfolio.

He hefted it against his side.

"If you damage my work . . ." She left the threat unsaid.

Ignoring her warning, he loped down the street, her artwork banging against his knee. After he disappeared around the corner, Adélaïde went inside, counting the days until the Academy would announce the winners. She wanted to win so much she could taste it in her mouth, feel it in her bones. Second and third place were nothing. First place was all that mattered. She saw herself standing in the Place Dauphine on the Île de la Cité, stepping forward to claim her reward, her father bursting with pride, her mother at last comprehending her talent and loving her for it.

That is, until she slipped into her seat in Monsieur Vincent's studio that afternoon and saw the strange look on Alexandré's face.

"What happened?" she demanded when they had a moment to speak alone.

"Chevalier Roslin was in the Academy offices when I arrived. He recognized me."

"Oh no." She had not thought of that. Chevalier Roslin knew all the neighborhood children.

"He greeted me by name, just when I had asked for the paperwork to fill out."

Even worse.

"What did you do?"

"I—I had to use my last name."

How could this have happened?

"You need to go back. Withdraw my work from the competition."

"Too late. They took your portfolio into another office before I could figure out how to stop them."

"Oh no." It was all that could come out of her mouth.

"Oh, don't worry, Adélaïde. I'll give you the prize money if I win."

"Who cares about the money? I wanted to win the scholarship."

"You better hope you don't."

"Adélaïde, it's not like you to chatter in class." Monsieur Vincent loomed in front of them. "Alexandré, if you are not planning to study, then you may deliver this portrait."

Alexandré grabbed the hand-sized package and headed for the

door, but not before looking back at her and holding a finger to his lips.

She nodded and picked up her paintbrush. Mixing ochre powder into the water, she imagined Alexandré accepting her prize or, worse yet, winning the scholarship. A sour taste worked its way up from her stomach. Instead of hoping to win—and win big—she had to, at best, hope that she was second best, or not good enough at all.

For the next three weeks, she worked to put the competition she had labored on for months out of her mind, but she could not have imagined how it would end.

"Why did you do it, Adélaïde?" François stormed around his father's studio, looking gaunt and tired. She had never seen him so angry. His hair was wild, his clothing disheveled. He told them he had been up all night, painting in the booth, when a group of officials called him into the Academy office. "They wanted to know why I would enter a competition for a scholarship to the Academy when I already had a scholarship."

"What?" Her mind went blank.

Alexandré stood behind François gesticulating like a mad man.

"When I said I didn't, they showed me where I—*I*—had signed my name to a competition entry. But it was not my signature."

She was confused. "Your name was on the form?"

Alexandré nodded vigorously.

"I asked to see the artwork, and then I knew."

"Alexandré put your name on the form?" was all she could think to say. She turned to Alexandré. "I thought you put your name on the form."

"No, no. Chevalier Roslin said, 'Good morning, young Monsieur Vincent,' so I wrote down François's name."

"You were both in on this?" François sat down at the drafting table. "Don't you understand what you have done?" He raked his hands through his hair.

They shook their heads.

"You won, Adélaïde."

Her muscles went weak, then a slow smile spread across her face. "I won?"

"But it was my name on the form. Now they are investigating me for cheating. They want to make sure my work is my own. I may have to withdraw from the Prix-de-Rome competition. I had just finished my final piece and was going to submit it today. But now, I do not know what will happen. Monsieur Vien was so angry. How could you have done this, Alexandré?" he lashed out at his brother. "What will Father say?" A look of panic came over his face. "Where is Father?"

"He's at the bakery." Alexandré could see Monsieur Vincent's head bobbing in the shop window across the street.

"Adélaïde, how could you do this? My father has spent everything on me. Our family depends on my winning and being able to support us and Father in his old age." His voice was calm, but his eyes were dark with hurt. "What if I am asked to leave the Academy? What will happen when the neighborhood hears of this?"

"We're finished," Alexandré said.

Looking at François slumped at the table, perspiration beaded on Adélaïde's forehead and her stomach grew queasy. What if François lost his scholarship? Would his family ever forgive her? Would their neighbors stop buying Monsieur Vincent's paintings? Would they stop shopping at À La Toilette?

At last, she found her voice. It was small. "What happened next?"

"I said it was not me, that I knew nothing about it. Then Chevalier Roslin came in and agreed that I was not the one he saw that morning, that it was my younger brother, so I said it must have been some prank of my brother's. I begged their forgiveness, but they sent me home while they figure out what to do." He blew out a breath. "Because next week they will they announce the Prix-de-Paris winner, and it cannot be me. The week after that, they will announce the Prix-de-Rome winner—and—and—" He stood and paced the small room. "I have worked so hard for this." His voice broke.

"It's not Alexandré's fault. It was my idea. I–I just wanted to prove that I was good enough to be in the Academy. I–I just wanted to continue to be able to study with you." The agony of her confession came out in a wail. She felt so embarrassed, so dreadful, so stupid, she did not know how she could live with herself. The dream of her studying at the Academy died. "I must go to them and explain." Her stomach lurched.

"Even if you did, they wouldn't let you win, Adélaïde. You weren't eligible to enter in the first place."

Footsteps sounded outside the door.

"Father's coming," Alexandré said.

Monsieur Vincent entered the room, a wheel of cheese in his arms. "What are you doing home, son?" he asked when he saw François. "And why are you crying, mademoiselle?" His gaze settled on his younger son. "What have you done, Alexandré?"

Adélaïde stood up. "I–I'm not feeling well. I have to go home."

She spent the rest of the day in her room, sick for herself that she had won and lost the prize all in the same moment, sick with fear that she had ruined François's chance to be a Prix-de-Rome winner and destroyed his life.

Whatever happened, she had wrecked everything between them.

CHAPTER 4

AUGUST 1768

Two weeks later, Monsieur Vincent walked into À La Toilette at noon, a bottle of wine under his arm. Adélaïde was so nervous she almost missed the outraged look on her mother's face, but the giggling of the grisettes drew her attention to it. She had to admit that the sight of their neighbor, standing among fuchsia and autumn-orange scarves in his puritan black, was comical.

He gave Adélaïde a quizzical look. "Where has my best student been?"

Folding a scarf for a customer, she mumbled something about being ill.

He set the wine bottle on the counter. It was the new sparkling wine from Champagne.

Without looking up, she asked, "Did François win?"

"Yes," Monsieur Vincent exclaimed. "My son has won the Prix-de-Rome."

She sank onto the ottoman her mother had just redone in ruby velvet. Orange cream tassels jiggled beneath her.

"When I heard them call my son's name, when he took his place on the stage with the Academy leaders, I thought I would burst with pride." He wiped his eyes.

Adélaïde also thought her heart would burst, but with relief. François had not been punished for her actions.

"Adélaïde, your customer," her mother said.

Adélaïde jumped up, her face flaming. She refolded the scarf lying on the counter, then wrapped it in tissue paper and tied it with a silk ribbon.

"I came to invite mademoiselle here to a dinner party with my students to celebrate, with your approval of course," Monsieur Vincent told her father.

Her father went to the back of the shop, returning with a bottle of brandy. "Come." He invited his friend to join him in the window. "Congratulations," Papa said as the two men sat in the bergère chairs. "Our young people are going places these days, eh? Even Jeanne Bécu."

Her heart splitting in two, Adélaïde handed the package to her customer with a tight smile. Monsieur Vincent and her father should also have been celebrating her following in François's footsteps into the Academy, not their grisette, who had left to "entertain" customers at the Duc du Barry's casino.

"At least your son earned his place honorably," Maman said. It was rumored that Jeanne Bécu had become a courtesan to the king's ministers, making good on her goal to get to Versailles.

In the folds of her skirt, Adélaïde's fingernails bit into her palms. It seemed to her that a girl had no honorable course of action. She had no desire to become a courtesan—her fingers ached to be back in the studio painting.

Her father turned to look at her. "Daughter, you're quiet today."

"I'm just thinking about tonight," she said.

"Perhaps you should stay home," her mother said. "You don't look well."

"Of course I'm going, Maman. I want to celebrate François's success and wish him well." But would he want her there?

Despite the cramped space, the caterers served a feast for ten jubilant young people and one happy father. To eat like members of the Second Estate was new to the partygoers, who exclaimed over the little forks, big forks, small plates for this course, large plates for that course. They admired the silver serving dishes shaped like the fish, viand, fowl, or vegetables they housed until the beef consommé, veal cutlets, stuffed trout, and breaded partridges had disappeared along with the braised artichokes, green beans, and brandied apricots. The students washed all of it down with copious amounts of cheap wine and Monsieur Vincent's one bottle of Moët champagne.

Adélaïde maintained a veneer of celebration, cheering with everyone else, forcing food into her mouth, waiting for the opportunity to apologize to François. Alexandré and François ate as though they had never eaten before, scraping the serving dishes clean. More than once, she felt François's gaze on her, but, as usual, when she looked up, he was looking away. Dinner ended, the other students said their goodbyes, the caterers packed up and took their table, linens, and dinnerware away. She sat with the Vincents at the card table, drinking the last of the wine.

"You are almost family," Monsieur Vincent said.

If only she could be.

He tilted back in his wooden chair, smoking, reminiscing about the hardships of their moves from Geneva to Turin to Paris. The end of his pipe glowed.

"That was a lot of expense, Father," François said.

"I have saved for this celebration for years, son."

But Adélaïde saw the empty bookshelf and knew better.

François told his father he would have to move into the dormitory of the École des Élèves Protegés by the end of the next week.

The one thing she had refused to think about was before her. François was leaving. How could he be gone for seven years? Though the king's college was in Paris, he would not be free to come home on weekends. When he finished his studies, he would leave for Rome. She tried to imagine how long seven years was and remembered. When she was twelve, she had had six brothers. An eternity.

"I'll be glad enough to leave Vien's, though. There's a new student in the studio. He makes it awkward for everyone."

"Who's that?" Alexandré asked.

"Jacques Louis David. He always thinks he knows what he is doing and does not listen to instruction. Then he gets angry when Vien praises everyone's work but his."

"The one with the scar-face?" Alexandré asked.

"Yes, they call him David of the Tumor."

"I heard about him in the Latin Quarter," Alexandré said. "His duel was the most famous event of the summer." He grabbed the fire poker, danced around François, thrust it at him.

"Put that down," François pushed the poker away. "You've had too much to drink."

Adélaïde jumped up from the table as Alexandré stumbled into her. "Get away, you beast. You'll ruin my dress."

The clock chimed. Midnight.

"I was supposed to be home an hour ago," she said, glancing at François. The night that had dragged on forever had ended without him speaking to her. Was this to be their goodbye, a message of finality said in silence? Even though it was summer, and the windows open to let air in, cold seeped into her chest. Her legs weighed a thousand pounds when she turned to leave.

By the time she made it to the door, François was opening it. "Allow me," he said. "I will walk you home."

From the middle of the room, Alexandré winked at her.

"I will be right back, Father," François said.

Before Monsieur Vincent could order Alexandré to chaperone them, Alexandré moaned and started to retch.

Her body went from cold to hot in the time it took François to take her hand and lead her down the stairs. "François, I never meant to hurt you. I had no intention of involving you—"

"You do not need to worry, Adélaïde. Somehow, Chevalier Roslin made it all go away, because no one at the Academy mentioned it after that day."

A weight lifted inside. She looked up at the sky. Despite the torches burning and the lamps glowing across the intersection, she saw Mars, sailing red among the constellations. She thought of all the days to come, the turning of the earth around the sun, time expanding between them. "François, I can't imagine the next seven years without you."

"Me either." Their steps slowed until they were standing at the edge of the street, in darkness under the wigmaker's awning. "In the last few days, while I was waiting to hear, I would think, what if I do not win? I realized I would not mind, because I would be with you."

The floodgates burst. They talked of their dreams, of how they missed being in the studio together, of how they wanted to be together forever, painting, debating, just being.

"Perhaps I will not go," François said.

"No." Adélaïde shook her head. "You mustn't say that."

In the crisp night air, a window opened in the building next door.

Maman.

"I have to go." At the back door, Adélaïde turned. François gave her a little wave, almost a salute. She could not see his eyes, but she imagined them filled with a happiness that matched hers.

Inside, she tiptoed up the stairs.

Floating in candlelight, her mother's angry countenance materialized at the top of the steps, her arms folded across her chest. Adélaïde groaned and steeled herself.

"Do you know what time it is?" her mother hissed. "I've spoken to your father, and he agrees with me. It's time you left Vincent's studio."

Adélaïde could not believe it. "But Maman—"

"Maybe you have no care for your reputation, but I do. The neighbors are gossiping about it. We have to find you a husband before it's too late."

"I'm only eighteen. I don't want to get married."

"Most girls your age are already married. Even Claudette. Soon, you'll be too old."

"I don't need a husband. I'm going to be an artist."

"You're a fool. Women always need a husband." Then, as though this settled the matter, Maman added, "It's your duty to obey me. It's my duty to find a husband for you."

"Papa has never told me that I have to marry."

"Once I choose a proper husband for you, your father will give his consent. And I don't appreciate your disrespectful tone, young lady. I forbid you from going to the Vincents' again."

"There's no need for you to stop my lessons, Maman. The person you're concerned about won't even be there." Adélaïde closed her bedroom door without slamming it. When the doorknob turned, she pressed her body against the door, saying through her teeth, "Go away."

"If you defy me, I will have your father go to François's school and speak to the authorities."

Adélaïde went cold.

She had conducted the entire argument with her mother in

whispers to avoid waking the household. Now, she buried her head in her pillow to stifle her sobs.

~

It had been the worst week of Adélaïde's life. She missed François, missed her lessons, missed her life. Her mother had gone to her father, who had ended her art lessons. Her fingers ached to feel a pencil flying over paper, her mind cried for the quiet concentration that came when a page transformed into an image with life under her hand, but tonight, she could not even get the sums in the ledger right.

The silence around the table was more than she could bear. Adélaïde stopped pretending to add numbers together and closed the ledger. "Papa, Maman, please, let me go back to Monsieur Vincent's. François won't even be there. He's leaving."

"Your duty is here." Her mother's face was as impervious as stone.

Looking stern, her father warned her to consider the circumstances of others. She knew he was reminding her of her mother's threat.

"But, Maman, you are not considering me."

"Of course I am," Maman said. Her mother looked at her father, then leaned forward. "Adélaïde, we weren't going to tell you yet, but we've found the right man for you. Nicolas Guiard has expressed his interest in you. He's a treasurer in the church." Maman's voice was as breathless and excited as a young girl's, as though Nicolas Guiard had expressed an interest in her.

Adélaïde groaned. She had been right to avoid the large young man with blond hair who had haunted her parents' shop lately, spending too much time buying cravats and sleeve ruffles from her mother. "I'm not interested in him. I just want to go back to my lessons."

"We didn't want to tell you this until you were better acquainted with him, but I see that it's necessary," her father said. "We're working on the details of the dowry. You won't be leaving the house until we've finalized the agreement."

"Papa, all my life, you've told me I could be anything I wanted if I worked hard enough for it. Now you're telling me that all I can do is be a wife to anyone you choose?" She stood up. "What have I been working for then? Was it all a lie?"

Her mother gasped. Thunder gathered on her father's face. The enormity of her disrespect frightened even her. She turned and stormed up the steps, slamming her bedroom door shut. Who cared if she woke the servants or the neighbors in the building next door? How could they do this to her? She flung herself on the bed, not knowing which was more painful, the incomprehensible loss of her father's support, or the blow to her dreams.

Later, she lay in the shadowy candlelight, listening to the steady tick, tick, tick of the mantle clock, considering and discarding various arguments to change her parents' minds before they destroyed her life. She had already tried them all. She had to get away. She would write Félicité in the morning and ask if she could come stay with her. Last week, Félicité had sent a sly announcement saying that the Labilles were expecting their first grandchild. Helping her sister was the perfect escape.

A noise sounded beyond the clock hammer pinging the bell eleven times. Pebbles, hitting the windowpane. She hurried to the window, cranked it open, peered down into the street. François gazed up, his hair a golden nimbus in the moonlight. Her knees went weak. She motioned for François to come around to the alley. Holding her shoes in her hand, she stole down the stairs. She paused at the first floor, listening for her parents. When she heard nothing, she continued down to the ground floor, avoiding the steps that creaked. They must have gone up to bed. She slipped her shoes back on before opening the door and stepping into the alley.

"Are you well?" François asked. "Why have you not come for lessons?"

"I can't," she said, unwilling to say more. How could she say to him, "I already almost ruined everything for you, and I won't do it again?" Their situation was hopeless. She hugged her arms across her chest. They stood in silence for a while. Then she asked, "How did you know which window was mine?"

"I have seen you looking out of it many times." He smiled.

"I didn't think you ever noticed." She tucked a stray tendril of hair behind her ear.

"Oh, I noticed." He took her hand. "I have to accept this prize—my family needs me to. I leave in the morning." His jaw worked and his Adam's apple bobbed. "I will not have a chance to ask you this for a long time, but will you marry me? Not now, but when I return from Rome?"

Her mother had always told her that she must never answer that question without her parents' permission, and she knew their answer without asking. If she said no, and had to tell him why, she would devastate him. She could not do it. "That's a long time from now," she prevaricated.

"I wish I could marry you now, but I do have a bright future. When I get back from Rome, I will have housing and a position as an art instructor. We can spend our lives painting together. Can you see it?"

It was a beautiful picture. It was everything she wanted. But her parents would not allow it. Joy and sorrow were oil and water. She closed her eyes for a moment, struggling to find words that would not hurt. "I would love to wait—"

"I'm so glad." Relief flooded his voice. He swept her into a hug. Before she had time to react, he kissed her.

It was strange, the first time their lips met—soft, cool, sweet, their mouths moving together, releasing, in the darkness. She wanted to do it again but knew they could not. "My parents can't discover us out here." But perhaps her father would listen to her if she got down and begged him on her knees.

"I know." He took her hand again, raised it to his lips. "I wish I had a token of my love to give you."

She made a fist of the hand he had kissed and brought it to her lips. "I will treasure this kiss."

He held her hand in the darkness. They stood there, not knowing what to do, happy in the moment, unsure of what would come next.

Notre Dame's deep bells tolled the midnight hour.

"I know," François said. He held up their twined arms and pointed with their hands still joined. "See that clock?"

She saw the clock tower at the end of their block, lit faintly by lantern light, its filigreed hands clasped together like their uplifted arms.

"Whenever you see a clock with its hands together at midnight, think of me. Remember that my love is as strong and steady as the coming of a new day. Wherever I am, I will stop and remember you."

They waited until the clock hands separated, then said goodbye. Adélaïde watched François walk into the shadows of the alley, her fingers gripped around the memory of his kiss. Then she stared up at the clock, trying to imagine her days without him. The feeling that came when she thought of her brothers washed through her chest. She could not breathe.

This time, both of her parents waited for her at the top of the stairs.

CHAPTER 5

OCTOBER 1768

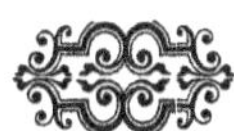

Adélaïde never got to tell her parents about François's proposal. She had not yet drafted her appeal to Félicité the next morning when a letter arrived from across the river, addressed to her father. When he read it, his face turned white. "Come up to the salon," he told Marie-Anne and Adélaïde.

"Did something happen to the baby?" Adélaïde asked when they arrived in the salon.

"No." Her father's voice shook. "Félicité's ill. They think typhus."

Marie-Anne let out a screech. "I told them not to move to that neighborhood. The air is bad." After her sons' deaths from a fever brought across the river, Maman thought any place south of the river dangerous. "I must go to her. Claude, go find a doctor." Marie-Anne ordered a maid to call a fiacre, then packed a nightdress and their supply of medicines into a small trunk. "Adélaïde, you are in charge," she said as she climbed into the hired carriage.

After the carriages left, conveying her father to a doctor, her mother to her sister, the street was quiet, the shop more so. Adélaïde took her place behind the counter, thoughts of art and unwanted marriages cast aside.

Her father returned in the evening. "We can't leave you here alone."

"Will Félicité be all right, Papa?"

"She's a strong girl. Maman will write every day."

But Maman did not write, and Adélaïde sold hats, scarves, and gloves, wondering how her mother had survived each day grieving for her sons while she smiled for the customers. The memory of her brothers' deaths made it impossible for her to think or speak. Inside, she was shaking with fear for her sister.

On the seventh day, Marie-Anne returned, her face stretched somehow, like mottled glass, her mouth an open wound. "Our beautiful, beautiful girl, Claude." She collapsed into her husband's arms. Félicité was dead.

Adélaïde's hand flew to her mouth. *I needed you, Félicité. You were supposed to help me,* Adélaïde thought, then felt selfish. *I didn't even get to tell her I was happy about the baby.*

For the next few days, her father stumbled around their home, speechless. Her mother lay in her bed, shrouded behind the bed curtains. Adélaïde wanted to climb out of her skin, to turn back time, to be anywhere but in this house of sorrow.

On the day of Félicité's funeral mass, her mother did not feel well. "You go on to the church, Claude."

"I should stay with you."

Adélaïde saw the agony in her father's eyes. "Go on, Papa. Come, Maman, let me open the windows so you can see the sun shining. Remember how Félicité loved the sun."

But Maman lay back on the bed, her eyes closed. Adélaïde stood at the window, the light falling on her stinging eyes.

When pustules appeared on Marie-Anne's torso a few days later, everyone knew the worst had happened. The housekeeper placed a black ribbon across the shop door and went to her daughter's. The grisettes rushed out, and the servants fled.

Upstairs, Adélaïde washed her mother with wet cloths to bring down her fever while Claude consulted every doctor in the neighborhood. For two weeks, fevers wracked Marie-Anne's body. She lay, delirious and moaning with pain as the rash spread across her body, but every time the fever subsided and she had a lucid moment, she spoke to Adélaïde of Nicolas Guiard.

"Why is she obsessed with this, Papa?" Adélaïde asked one evening as they stood, exhausted, out in the hallway. "I cannot argue with a sick woman."

"She's had a hard life, Adélaïde. She has nothing left but to see you settled."

"She should try to get better instead."

The fear in her father's eyes told her that he did not know if Maman wanted to get better.

Her mother's weak voice came from the darkened room. "Adélaïde, it's your duty to help elevate our family. You're the only one left."

"Maman, we're fine as we are."

Later, as Adélaïde wiped her mother's forehead, her mother said, "I do not want you to have to work so hard. Nicolas already has a good church pension. We will not have to buy it for him. You will have a life of ease."

"I don't mind working, Maman."

That night, her mother's voice was fretful, querulous, and her body restless under the bedsheet. "Why settle for a bourgeois existence when you can join the nobility?"

"You wouldn't have to pay taxes," Claude tried to lighten the atmosphere. As a member of the *noblesse oblige*, Nicolas Guiard enjoyed rights and privileges bourgeois citizens did not.

Adélaïde gave her father a dark look. "Please, Papa, don't." She looked down at her mother, who resembled a bundle of rags. "Rest, Maman. Concentrate on getting better. Don't worry about me."

Instead, her mother slid closer to death.

Having heard that the old king had survived typhus by drinking antimony wine, her father requested it from the latest doctor. The man refused, saying it was too dangerous and too expensive.

"Never mind the cost," Papa snarled. "I'm losing my whole family."

Adélaïde understood his anger, his desperation, his willingness to pay any price to keep his wife alive. How would he go on without his Marie-Anne? Maman, the warrior queen who had fought and schemed for her family, was not this defeated creature who waited for death to take her from them. Adélaïde wanted to shake her mother, to force her to get well. Then she wanted to climb on the bed, curl up beside her, and take the sickness into herself.

The next night, her father nudged her awake as she slept in the chair outside their room.

"Come," he said. "It won't be long now."

"What do we do?" she asked as she regarded her mother's still form in the candlelight, thinking her father had been through this vigil too many times already.

He sat on the edge of the bed as though he had lost all his strength. "We wait." He rubbed his wife's arm, and she opened her eyes.

"Adélaïde?" Her mother's voice came from a place far away.

Adélaïde picked up her mother's cold hand. "I'm here, Maman."

"Let me go in peace."

Adélaïde could not understand her mother's words and leaned closer.

"Promise me." Her mother's lips moved but there was no sound.

"Anything, Maman," Adélaïde said.

Her mother struggled for breath. "Give me your oath. Promise . . . you will . . . marry him."

All her being screamed, *No.* She did not know to what. No to marrying Nicolas? No to her mother dying? No to Félicité's death? No to everything that had happened to their family? Listening to her mother gasping, choking, gurgling, she wanted her mother's pain to go away. "I promise," she vowed in a strangled voice.

The light left her mother's eyes.

CHAPTER 6

1769

"Papa, you didn't have to close À La Toilette." Adélaïde watched the carters sweat in the noonday sun as they loaded her mother's velvet bergère chairs from the rounded window onto a cart. Her father had laid off the grisettes and liquidated the inventory.

"It was your mother's shop." Sitting at the table in the empty room, Papa added up her mother's final medical bills, his lips forming a silent whistle. He recorded the figure in the ledger book and sighed. "We're not reduced to abject poverty, thank God."

"You could start another business."

"Me? Too old for that." He ran his hand over his smooth head. A great sadness had fallen over him. He refused to don his wig, wear his corset, or maintain the dapper appearance required of a royal *mercier*.

She put her arms around him, rested her head against his. The bristle of his beard poked at her cheeks. "What can I do to help, Papa?"

"Don't worry." He smiled with effort. "We still have enough for a dowry for you, and a cottage for me."

She sighed. Now that Papa had found his cottage, he was determined to see her settled. "Papa, I'm not ready to be married." Seeing the sorrow on his face, she maneuvered the last chair to his side of the table and sat next to him. Her mother's chair. "Let's not argue today. What will you do with yourself in the country?"

"Plant a garden, I think. Contemplate life. Read the journals from the city." He smiled again, this time with more ease. "And wait for grandchildren." Even that made him look sad.

She thought of Félicité, pregnant and dead. "Papa, women die bearing children." Fear fluttered in her stomach.

"Your mother bore eight children. She didn't die in childbirth."

"No, but she died trying to save one of them. What kind of bargain is that?"

"It's the risk we take." A tear made a dark line down his cheek.

"Papa, I don't want to take that risk. I just want to paint."

"I'm carrying out your mother's wishes." He took out a handkerchief and wiped his eyes. "Besides, you can't stay here. I can't leave you alone in the city and nothing awaits you in the countryside."

"I know I said I would marry him, but I can't go through with it. I'm not attracted to him."

"What is so attractive about François?" he asked. "Objectively, he's thin to the point of emaciation. Nicolas, on the other hand, is strong as an ox. The grisettes seemed to like him."

"That's not it, Papa." She tried to find words to make him understand. "François is quiet, but I'm happy when I'm with him. We like to do the same things. He understands how I feel about art. He understands me."

"It's familiarity then. You've spent enough time together to understand each other. So it will be with Nicolas. Love often comes later."

"But I don't want to get to know him." Once she had learned that Nicolas Guiard was interested in her, she had avoided him whenever he came into the shop. "Papa, I just want to paint."

"You're too young to know what you want."

She grunted with frustration, took a deep breath, tried again. "How do I know that marriage won't be the end of all my dreams, all I've worked for?"

"Even if you were to become an artist, someone must still manage your affairs, Adélaïde. You cannot stay in Paris alone. You have to be under the protection of someone."

"But Nicolas Guiard, Papa—" A vision of François rose in her mind. At that moment, her heart was too big for her chest. Her whole body trembled.

"You gave your word. Your word is your honor."

"But you know why I did."

"It doesn't matter. There's very little honor women have to their name, but honor in marriage is the highest honor there is."

"Honoring my husband? Then Jeanne Bécu is better off than I."

"You're not like Jeanne, daughter." Jeanne Bécu, now married to the Duc du Barry, had become the king's mistress. "You're serious, studious, intelligent. Above all, honorable in everything you do. And may I remind you, you've given your word."

It was a circular argument that got them nowhere.

She knew better than to threaten to run away. A girl alone might get lodgings in a *garni* or boarding house but would be under constant attack. Her reputation would suffer. Would any of her family's acquaintances hire her to paint them? She did not have to think too hard on the answer to that. Without her father's approval or blessing, by the time it came to pay the next quarter's rent, she might be out on the streets.

Once, she had set her sights much higher, but now, she would take the one option she did have. "Give me time to be admitted to the Academy of St. Luke. That way, I will have proven my skills and can sell my work. How can I trust a husband to allow me to do this? Once I'm married, he will tell me what to do. I will have to get permission from him on where to go."

He smiled. "I never told your mother what to do, or where to go. That would have been impossible."

"You're different, Papa, and you know it." She grasped his hand. "You were smart. You stayed out of Maman's way and spent your time with the philosophes and your friends. How do I know what Nicolas Guiard will do?"

She saw his resolve weaken.

"Let me become a guild member, Papa. I need to know I've accomplished something. Otherwise, the past five years will have been a waste and Maman was right—I shouldn't have bothered." To realize that hurt her soul. She saw her life as a forest of dead trees, chopped down to the stump, no hope, no possibility of hope. "My life would be a desert." Her voice caught.

"Now, Adélaïde, how you take life is a choice. Bitterness, envy, hatred, those attitudes do not have to be yours."

"But that's just it, Papa," she cried. "You are giving me no choice."

In his eyes, she saw the memories of those arguments between him and her mother. His shoulders lowered. "All right." The ghost of one of his old smiles teased his face. "Your persistence has paid off. We won't set a wedding date until you've been admitted."

Détente reached, Adélaïde focused on her entrance pieces while her father continued to negotiate the terms of her dowry.

The guild admitted her in May. Going to the Academy offices at the back of Saint Symphorien-de-la-Chartre on the Île de la Cité, she paid her membership dues, received her entrance certificate, then walked home. Above her, carmine geraniums opened in the flower baskets lining the walkways. Their sweet scent promised summer, but for her the day was bittersweet. The time had come for her father and Nicolas to set a wedding date.

The next morning Papa handed her a set of documents. "Your marriage settlement," he said.

"Why are you giving me this, Papa?"

"Maman never permitted me to enter into a contract over the shop without understanding its terms. She insisted that a woman must always know what she was agreeing to—even if I was the one doing the agreeing. Good business practice, she would say." His voice was gruff.

Adélaïde unrolled the document, thinking that it was her whole life they had arranged, but she herself had agreed to nothing. "How can you give him your life savings, Papa? Even the dining room table and chairs? And the china? Maman loved that china."

Marie-Anne had bought the new furniture before Félicité's wedding. Her father had protested the expense, but her mother had insisted that the inlaid ivory and marble table and green velvet Louis XIV chairs would be a legacy to generations of Labilles. Félicité's wedding guests had eaten on silver and china that matched a set used by the royal family in Versailles. Her mother had purchased the rented china, saying that she wanted the set for Adélaïde's wedding.

"The furniture and china are part of your inheritance," her father said. "I'm giving *you* our life savings, not him. You will live in comfort and your children will receive the rest upon your death."

"But he controls it."

"That's the law."

She scrutinized the last pages. "But it comes back to me in the event that something happens to our marriage?"

"Well, yes. But that never happens."

On the morning of August 25, 1769, Adélaïde Labille, aged twenty, and Louis-Nicolas Guiard, aged thirty, married in the Church of Saint-Eustache, the church where her parents had baptized a growing family, where Félicité had married, where her brothers, sister, and mother were buried.

The height of the vaulted ceiling made Adélaïde dizzy. It floated a hundred feet above them, resting on soaring buttressed walls whose sides were pierced by religious scenes carved in stained glass. Patterned beams of colored light streamed across the nave.

How small I am, and how short the distance from aisle to altar, she thought, as her father walked her with measured steps toward Nicolas Guiard and the priest. Yet how long a marriage, hidden and mysterious in dark shadows like the gallery rimming the ceiling. She was shaking inside.

It should have been François waiting for her.

When she and her father arrived at the sacraments, the sound of flapping wings startled her. A pigeon trapped in the apse flung itself against the glass barriers that kept it from the light. She imagined it was her frantic soul.

Nicolas Guiard took her hand. Tall, stocky, more bourgeois than aristocratic, he had a round face, a heavy look about the jaw, and a rough complexion that reddened with emotion. With his gray velvet coat and breeches embroidered in floral patterns, his cravat that fell in elaborate folds, the Belgian lace at his sleeves, and the wig with two rows of curls and a sack ponytail covering his blond hair, he was everything her mother would have wanted to see in a bridegroom.

It should have been François next to her, wearing his usual black.

Their distorted images appeared in the chalice raised by the priest, and she observed that he was not handsome, nor she beautiful. But her clothes matched his for elegance. She wore the satin stomacher her mother had embroidered with silver thread for Félic-ité's wedding over a silver satin sack gown with double ruffles, her hair curled, powdered, and piled high over a wig for the occasion. Her mother would have approved of her sartorial choices.

I put more thought into what I would wear today than what my marriage would be like, she thought.

Her whispered words to honor and obey wafted upward into a space that had heard such vows for a thousand years, and beneath the white-washed wooden roof supported by massive, striated stone columns, an ancient ritual transmuted her into a vessel for her husband to have and to hold. When the priest pronounced them man and wife, her father beamed with pride.

In the sacristy, the assistant brushed sand across their names in the register and Claude handed the settlement document to Nicolas, sealed with gold wax and wrapped in a silver ribbon.

The wedding party met at Café Procope. To Adélaïde, the café's marble tables, blazing chandeliers, mirrored walls, and mix of royalty, actors, artists, and bourgeois, represented the essence of Paris. It was also as far as possible from an intimate dinner in their former family home.

The waiters, in fur hats and red caftans, moved among the packed tables, lifting silver coffee pots high to pour coffee into little glasses, Arabic style. Their wedding guests drank the sparkling wine her father had ordered from the country and ate the pâtés and canapés she had chosen by the platterful. Voices rose until people had to shout to hear each other. Her neck ached beneath the heavy wig and her glass remained full.

"Aren't you eating? May I, then? It's delicious." Félicité's former husband took the liver pâté crusting on Adélaïde's plate and popped it into his mouth.

Her brother-in-law had joined the wedding party and sat to her right. She had not seen him since Félicité's death. Drinking glass after glass of champagne, he looked haggard and disheveled, his brown hair escaping under a wig that, as far as she could tell, had not been attended to for some time. "How are your painting lessons?" He set down his fourth glass.

She forced herself to smile. "For now, I've completed them and joined the Academy of St. Luke. I've had one commission so far—very small, enough to pay for my own paintbrushes, but I'm a working professional."

"Such news deserves a toast." He looked around for more wine. "I hope you'll find it a profitable enterprise. I haven't of late."

She could believe it. Her brother-in-law was also a miniature painter, but who would hire an artist who appeared in society in rumpled, stained, and threadbare clothing? Worst of all to Parisians who bathed often, one who smelled.

He accepted a fish pie from a waiter. "Oh, by the way, guess who I saw when I visited the École des Élèves Protégés yesterday?"

Adélaïde froze, fearing what would come next.

"I ran into your old neighbor—François Vincent—the son, not the father. I told him I was coming to your wedding feast. You should have seen the look on his face. He mumbled that you had promised to marry him, then hurried off. Isn't he a Protestant?" He guffawed, then used his fork to skewer the pie.

He had uttered his drunken speech in a sudden lull in conversation. It seemed to Adélaïde that silence reigned in the entire restaurant and a thousand eyes looked at her. Her whole body flushed.

One neighbor muttered that some people should stick to coffee.

"I'm sure it's a misunderstanding," another said. "Here, everyone, a toast to the bride and groom."

It was their neighbor, Chevalier Alexander Roslin, raising his glass. She caught the pitying look in his wife's eyes. Madame Roslin had always been kind to her and, after her mother had died, Adélaïde had visited the Roslin home and looked at Madame Roslin's paintings while the artist shared memories of her mother with her. Could it get any worse?

Then Adélaïde saw the censure in her father's eyes and wanted to run away from them all. She wanted to rush out and find François and tell him that it was not her fault, that she had not meant to hurt him. But it was too late, and she could do none of these things. She prayed that the wedding breakfast would end soon.

To her left, her new husband clenched his fist on the table. The empty plate beneath his hand clattered, and she made a quick movement to steady it before it slipped off the table. Nicolas grabbed her hand in a painful grip.

She pulled away and pressed her bruised fingers in her lap.

Nicolas spent the remainder of their wedding breakfast drinking glass after glass of champagne, growing more morose as the hours wore on.

Adélaïde sat in tense silence, thinking of the minutes draining away until her father would board the evening coach for the country, and she would be left alone with this man.

That night Nicolas was too drunk to consummate their marriage. In the morning, he accused her of not being a virgin and struck her across the face. Before she could attend to her black eye, he forced her to light the fire in the apartment stove using her new paintbrushes as kindling.

So began the marriage she had not wanted in the first place.

CHAPTER 7

SUMMER 1770

Ten months later, Adélaïde would have to say that her wedding day was the high point of her marriage.

Beef stew congealed on a table near the stove while she paced the floor of their lodgings and scanned the darkness outside the window for Nicolas. Past ten, her husband stalked up the street. She snatched a piece of paper off the table and shoved it into the stove, then raked the dying coals. She watched the flame sweep up the letter, thinking, what was the use of writing François anyway?

She slammed the stove door shut and stood as Nicolas came into the apartment, followed by the smell of tobacco smoke and alcohol. They stared at each other, then he went to the table and lifted a cover off a dish, peered at the food inside and set the lid down in disgust. "This soup is cold," he said.

"Super was ready at eight," she said. "It was hot then."

He pounded his fist on the table.

She jumped. The china jumped. Pressing her hands together, she said, "Nicolas, we need to talk." She did not recognize the timid voice that emanated from her throat. A hundred years stood between the girl she had been before their wedding and the wife she was now. "Our marriage was a mistake. Neither of us is happy. I allowed myself to agree to it when my mother was dying, but I was wrong to do so."

"What would you have me do about it, madam?"

"You could let me go out to work."

"No wife of mine will go out to work."

"What am I supposed to do all day? You don't even give me money to go to the market."

"You could occupy yourself being a more pleasing wife." He pushed her into the wall and ground himself against her. His clothes were damp with sweat. A blast of sour wine and cloying perfume assailed her.

Repulsed, she pushed him away and moved toward the door. "I will leave. I can move out tomorrow, but I need you to return my dowry so I can get myself situated."

"You have everything figured out, do you? Go ahead and leave. As a wife, you are useless." In the lamplight, a look of cruel pleasure crossed his face. He lifted another crockery lid and began pouring cold soup onto the table.

"Please, stop." She fought to maintain her composure, returned to the table, and tried to remove her mother's dishes from his reach. Nicolas's steel blue eyes bored into hers. Then he yanked the tablecloth. China hit the floor and shattered. A glass shard drew blood when she picked up the broken bowl. Her mother's tureen. Inside her something snapped. "Is it not enough that you keep me locked up in this place while you waste my parents' savings on wine and women, but must you destroy everything precious to me?"

His eyes were dead. "I've told you before—never take that tone with me."

Her heart began to thud in her ears. She lowered her voice. "Nicolas, please, just give me my dowry and let me go."

"I don't care if I never see you again, but I will not give your dowry back. Consider it compensation for the humiliation of marrying you."

"But it doesn't belong to you."

"Try to get it from me."

"You signed an agreement. You're required to return it if we separate."

"Go anywhere you like, do anything you want, but I will not grant you a legal separation."

"Please, Nicolas, I'm trying to find a rational solution to our problem, but I need money to make it work."

He gave an ugly laugh. "You little fool. You need a lot more than that." Rage flashed in his eyes.

She ran for the door.

Before she could make it, he grabbed her hair and jerked her back. A thousand pain points bit into her scalp. "What you need, madame, is another lesson in obedience."

The force of his backhand caught her cheek and forehead. She fell into a painting on the wall, and the frame hit the floor with a thud. She straightened away from the wall, her cheek stinging, her head spinning.

"You want to leave? Go then. Get out of my sight." She heard his words but the ringing in her ears made them seem far away. He grabbed her arm and dragged her to the door. She tried to keep herself upright as he marched her down the stairs.

His fingers dug into her arm. "Nicolas, let me go," she begged as she tried to get out of his grip.

He dragged her across the courtyard and released her long enough to open the outer door, then pushed her into the street.

She landed on her knees, dazed.

"Use that intelligence of yours to figure this out," Nicolas said and reentered the building. He slammed the heavy door shut. She heard the bar clank into place.

Her cheek throbbed. Her vision swam. One moment she was arguing with Nicolas, the next, she was out on the street. Skirts brushed her face as a group of laughing partygoers stepped around her. She closed her eyes and opened them again, but saw she was still in the street. No one bent to help her up. As Nicolas had said on many occasions, he had the right to discipline his wife, and no one would come to her aid.

Grit dug into her knees, but she rose and saw with dismay that soup from the broken tureen had splashed across her dress. How could she be out in the street like this?

A night watchman passed. Taking her for a prostitute, he told her to clear out. Humiliated, she hurried away. Moving through the crowds hurrying home from cafés and theatres, she was glad no one saw her, grateful this had not happened in her own neighborhood. She did not want people to tell her that it was her own behavior that had provoked her husband, did not want to hear that it was her duty to go back to him.

Not even her father, who was too far away for it to matter, would help her. She could not forget or forgive his last letter.

Imagine my disappointment when I heard from Monsieur Vincent, who no longer counts me among his friends. He wrote of the sorrow of his son, whose hurt at your betrayal was so great your name is never to be mentioned in their house again. How could you have promised to marry him? Daughter, you knew it was impossible. I am grieved by your disobedience.

She thought of her husband, whose veneer of respectability disappeared when he left his Treasury post at night and picked up a bottle of ale. Why had her mother—a person who could recognize a fraud the moment he stepped into À La Toilette—allowed her ambition for their family to blind her? How could her father have given in to the demands of her mother? How could he have gone off and left her with this man?

Righteous anger spurred her forward, and she walked with her chin determined, but after a while, her feet grew tired, and the night's chill seeped through her summer dress. The sun had gone down hours ago. She was out of the house without a coat or a head covering. How could she have been so stupid? She should have foreseen what Nicolas would do if she confronted him.

Raucous feminine laughter startled her. Outlined in torchlight, a trio of scarlet clad women blocked the road, enticing a pair of drunken men. The women's faces were powdered white. Their crimson lips stretched over bared teeth.

"Move along, sister." One of them shoved Adélaïde out of their path. "This is our block."

Shaken, she lifted her skirts and ran until she came to a quiet street and stood in the shadow of a building, gulping air. Somewhere close by, a clock struck midnight. Adélaïde turned and looked up at the black clock hands, frozen together. She thought of François, the time when he had promised to always think of her at the stroke of midnight. Was he thinking of her now? Why had he rushed off to Italy and left her behind? She saw herself, the day her marriage was but a week old, visiting the king's college, desperate to explain herself to him. But she was too late. He had departed for Rome on her wedding night.

Cafés closed, carriages receded, shutters hid lamplight. She walked on, not knowing what else to do, but hesitant now. Homeless mothers, wrapped in clothes the rag pickers would disdain, lay against the stone buildings, clutched prostrate infants. Toddlers, pressed against their mothers' sides, stared at Adélaïde with hollow eyes that glittered in the flames of the torches placed low enough to illuminate misery but high enough to provide no warmth to those sheltering in their flickering glare.

What should she do? Where could she spend the night? She spun around, looking for a church or building to orient herself. She could not bear the thought of sitting down on the cold stones or leaning against a wall, sleeping upright like many whom she had passed, but she was lost. Adélaïde's breath came in harsh rasps.

The torches burned down. The night grew thick with silence.

A pebble cut her foot through a hole in her slipper. She removed it and tossed the small rock into the dark. A rat skittered away. She was too numb to cry out. A low stone wall gleamed in the dark. Despite her volition, she sank onto its mossy marble top and lapsed into a stupor, one of the thousands huddled in the shadows that night, waiting for the sun to rise.

PART II
EARLY SUCCESS, NEW ENEMIES

CHAPTER 8

APRIL 1774

Adélaïde poured a cup of warmed wine and sat by the fire. Her neck ached and her eyes stung from focusing on the miniature self-portrait she had worked on all day. Outside her attic apartment, wind howled over the rooftops and shook the windowpanes while spring lolled in winter's embrace. Though she could not afford it, she lit a third candle, then held her hands over the candelabra until her fingers could no longer bear the heat.

Evenings like this reminded her of the night she had wandered Paris three and a half years before, a night that returned in dreams that woke her, sweating and breathless.

The sound of bells had saved her . . .

Through the stillness, she heard the clock atop La Samaritaine pump station strike four. She woke, her mind clearing. The blackest part of night had loosened its grip on the skyline, and she realized she was on the Île de la Cité. The medieval bulk of a church loomed above her. Somehow, she had brought herself almost to the doorstep of the Academy of St. Luke.

She waited until daybreak, then rose and knocked on the great bronze door until a lock turned. The door inched open. A wizened face regarded her with suspicion.

71

"Please, monsieur, can you help me? I'm a guild member."

The light from the man's candle fell on her. A look of alarm crossed his face, then he opened the door and motioned her in, saying, "There's no one here yet, but you may wait inside." The elderly man relocked the door, then waved an arthritic hard toward a jumble of pews. "Sit where you like." He shuffled up the aisle and disappeared through a side door.

The guild had converted the church into an enormous drawing studio. Moving into the nave, Adélaïde passed easels holding canvases in progress, saw canvasses and sculptures in the chapels beyond. Above her, light rays streamed downward through clear paned windows as the sun cleared the rooftops. A last drop of crimson clung to the bottom of the sphere before it broke free, a ball of burning yellow. She averted her eyes and sat down on one of the scarred pews, sighing with relief. She had survived the night.

Ahead of her, at the transept, a huge portrait hung suspended on wires from the ceiling. St. Luke, patron saint of artists. St. Luke looked down on her, a paintbrush in his hand. His raised arm beckoned her; his open mouth told her what to do. *Keep painting. Your life depends on it now.*

She fell asleep.

Feeling a warm presence, Adélaïde jerked awake.

A familiar face stared into hers. Madame Roslin, her dark eyes emanating warmth, her heart-shaped face radiating kindness. Her mother's friend examined the bruises on Adélaïde's face and sat down on the bench beside her. "Oh, my dear, what happened to you?"

Adélaïde had not seen Madame Roslin or her husband since the debacle of her wedding day. She thought of her parents' neighbors knowing the mess she was in and flushed with embarrassment, then pushed the feeling away. She could not afford to be ashamed.

When she told Madame Roslin everything that had happened since her mother had fallen ill, Madame Roslin shook her head. Putting her arm around Adélaïde, she said, "I was afraid of this." She thought about what to do. "First, let's get you cleaned up and see if we can't find you something to eat. Then we must find you a place to live. It's unfortunate that the Academy of St. Luke has no lodgings. The artists rent out the cloisters or chapels to work in but live elsewhere."

"I have no money. I have nothing."

"Come with me anyway." Madame Roslin rose from the pew and held her hand out. "A solution always presents itself." Threading her arm through Adélaïde's, she guided her out a side door. They climbed a stairway to the cloisters. The smell of linseed oil drifted from an open cell where men and women were already at work.

They came to the rooms Madame Roslin shared with a group of artists.

"You rent space here?" Adélaïde asked. "Don't you have space in the Louvre?" Although Adélaïde had not seen the Roslins for months, she knew that, after a long controversy, Madame Roslin had been admitted to the Royal Academy of Painting and Sculpture along with Joseph Vien's wife.

"Well, my husband has space there," the woman replied, "but I like my studio here, and we like where we live."

Adélaïde sensed the woman left more unsaid but was too tired to ask. Madame Roslin led Adélaïde to an antechamber with a wash-stand holding a pitcher of water and a table mirror. She handed Adélaïde a hand towel, a comb, and a small tin of face powder that she pulled from her pocket. "Make yourself presentable."

Adélaïde washed the blood from a cut on her cheek, dragged the comb through her tangled hair, then covered the bruises on her face with lead powder. Shaking out her underskirts, she straightened the folds of her dress and groaned when she saw the grime ground into the fabric.

"Much better," Madame Roslin smiled her approval when Adélaïde returned. She then introduced Adélaïde to her fellow artists.

Standing there in her ruined dress and shredded slippers, Adélaïde did not understand how the artists did not laugh her out of the room.

"Madame Guiard is looking for work and specializes in minia-tures," Madame Roslin said. "I can vouch for her talent. My husband and I critiqued her entrance pieces for the Academy of St. Luke."

Adélaïde realized she had never thanked the couple for this act. Another wave of shame washed over her.

"Quentin de la Tour was in here last week looking for an apprentice to help him in his studio," one of the women said. "Why don't you speak to him?"

"An apprenticeship for a woman?" Adélaïde asked. An apprenticeship came with lodgings and meals but was something offered to young men and paid for by their parents.

"Yes," Madame Roslin said. "He has a soft spot for women, and he's a great instructor. I, myself, studied under him."

When Adélaïde first met the stooped septuagenarian who refused without excuse to cover his bald head with a wig, his eyes pierced hers with a sharp look and he boomed in his deep voice, "I can penetrate my subjects without their knowledge and capture their spirit. Can you do that?"

Her heart knocking with excitement, she said, "I would like to learn how."

He liked the idea of a woman as an apprentice and cackled that it was the perfect project. "As long as you make me coffee every day, we will get along well enough."

"I don't know how," Adélaïde said. At her parents' home, her father had always ordered his coffee delivered from a coffee house.

Quentin de la Tour looked crestfallen.

"But I can learn," she assured him, and consulted the head beverage steward at Café Procope.

While she found the man to be ignorant when it came to matters of science, as he insisted that the earth revolved around the sun and not the other way around, she considered him a genius when it came to art. His ability to draw out his subjects and infuse their portraits with life, personality, and truth knew no equal. Once he had captured King Louis XV and his mistress, Madame de Pompadour, with his pastels, the wealthiest bourgeois and nobility rushed to pay his exorbitant fees. By the time Adélaïde met him, he was one of the wealthiest artists in Paris.

De la Tour taught her to put together canvases suitable for life-sized portraits, layering sheet after sheet of thick blue paper together to make a large surface. She learned how to make pastel sticks in a hundred different shades and learned to blend and crosshatch her strokes. He then taught her how to observe a subject, speak to them, learn them. The work that emerged from her hands grew vivid and real.

~

For three years, Adélaïde studied and worked under de la Tour. She received a trickle of commissions from the public who visited his studio. She saved enough money to indulge the Labille family passion for fashion and purchased a satin dress she intended to wear for an upcoming exhibition of the Academy of St. Luke. In Paris, it was important to look wealthy, in particular when one was not. Her mother would have admired the line of her new dress, in the latest fashion with bows down the stomacher and lace at the neck and elbows.

Thoughts of Maman had occupied her all day as Adélaïde worked a tiny bust of her mother into the miniature self-portrait she was painting. Under her magnifying glass, under the five individual horse hairs knotted to her brush, Adélaïde painted her mother as she wished her to be, happy, loving, no bitterness or tension between the painted images of the two of them together on the four-inch oval canvas. Sorrow and blame melted away.

Adélaïde wished she could tell her mother about her first public exhibition. Instead, she wrote a long letter to her father, her first in years. She told him how much she had missed him, begged his forgiveness, and told him what she had been doing for the past three years.

Then she wrote about the exhibition to be held at the Hôtel Jabach.

> *I will exhibit a miniature of a magistrate and a self-portrait. You would be proud of my self-portrait, Papa. I am sitting on Maman's red velvet armchair, turned to the viewer, wearing a satin dress that gleams with light, Maman's yellow pearls around my neck. I hold a palette in my left hand and a brush in my right. I'm sitting at Maman's inlaid writing desk which holds the miniature painting I'm working on—a miniature in a miniature. On the desk, a glass vase of freesias and daisies,*

*Maman's favorite. Behind me, a large terra-cotta bust of Maman sits
on a pedestal. We see her in profile, looking off into the distance, into the
past. A suggestion of draperies behind her gives depth to the painting. I
look like plain old me, my hair up in curls, a smile on my face.
Papa, you would be pleased with my progress. You would laugh and say,
"How did you get all that into a painting the size of my big toe?" I
would respond, "With skill, Papa." Or I might say, "You have a very
big toe."*

How she missed her father's rumbling laugh.

*I have pinned my hopes on this exhibition. I must succeed, because
without connections or supporters, I find it difficult to secure steady
work.*

She paused, then crossed out the last two sentences. She would
not tell her father how precarious her situation was. She had made it
this far without his help, and she would not ask for it now, but a few
months ago, Quentin de la Tour had succumbed to a strange mania
and could no longer paint or teach. Adélaïde had had to move out.

With a lot of prompting from the Roslins, and over the objec-
tions of his wife, Monsieur Roche, the king's lock maker, had rented
two attic rooms to her on the basis that he had known her father.
The Roches' mansion was down the street from the site of À La
Toilette. No longer earning wages as an apprentice or having her
lodgings provided, Adélaïde worried daily about paying the rent and
having enough to eat. This exhibition had to be her turning point,
the time when she entered society as a full-fledged working artist.

Adélaïde sealed the envelope, put away her writing desk, and
readied for bed. Life was strange, she thought. For her fifteenth
birthday, her mother had bought her a dress. Now, for her twenty-
fifth birthday, she had bought one for herself. For a long time, she
had been angry, or frightened, or both, but no more. She was ready
for the future she had planned for herself, could not wait for the
exhibition. She returned to the main room to blow out the candles.
In the candlelight, her mother's forehead was marred by a frown.

"Don't worry, Maman," she whispered to the portrait. "I will
elevate myself."

CHAPTER 9

AUGUST 1774

Fading afternoon light turned her apartment into a realm of shadows and possibilities. Adélaïde examined her reflection in the cheval glass. Her narrow face would never resolve itself into the components of classical feminine beauty, but her white court dress and powdered hair made her as elegant as any royal personage who used to shop at À La Toilette. She dabbed a spot of lemon water behind her ears. She might live in a fifth-floor attic apartment, but, as Papa would say, she would do.

Turning sideways, she edged out the door, making sure her paniers did not touch the doorframe. She waited downstairs while the Roches' footman ran to hire a carriage for her. Beyond the courtyard walls, horse hooves clattered to a stop in front of the mansion as a large coach pulled up. Soon, Madame Roche entered the courtyard, her round figure stuffed into a deep purple dress, a tall green hat balanced over her upswept hair.

She looks like an eggplant rolling along the flagstones, Adélaïde thought, then forced herself to maintain a straight face when the woman came through the door, the footman behind her.

When she saw Adélaïde standing in the vestibule, Madame Roche stopped in the act of pulling off her black satin long gloves. Her eyes narrowed, her hands moved to her hips. An aubergine with wings. "Where did you get that dress?"

"I–I bought it," Adélaïde stammered, her levity banished.

77

"You have money for court attire but not for rent?" Madame Roche's eyebrows disappeared into her wig. "Your rent had better be paid in full by the end of the month. If not, you'll have to leave."

The footman smirked as he handed Adélaïde into the waiting vehicle. "So, really, madame, just what *will* you do to pay the rent?"

"Keep your hands and your thoughts to yourself, monsieur." She shoved his hand away and yanked the carriage door shut, mollified when he yelped with pain. The cheap conveyance lurched off, jerking her back into the seat. She fanned her hot face as they moved through the city streets. The show had to be a success. Otherwise, she would be the laughingstock of the building. Worse, a laughing-stock wandering the street in an expensive dress and nothing else.

When she stepped out of the hired carriage half an hour later, worries of Madame Roche's threat fled in the face of wonder. Hôtel Jabach was a palace bathed in yellow radiance. Light from a thousand candles poured through the Palladian windows, spilled over the balustrade, and pooled in the street. On the balcony, an orchestra gilded the night air with Handel's Water Music. In the sky, the evening star trembled over a city spread on a cobalt canvas.

Adélaïde's heart skipped with excitement as she pushed her way through the wine-drinking crowd in the courtyard. Inside the lobby, men dressed as footmen sold entrance tickets and souvenir booklets.

"Get your *livret* here," cried a seller. "Hundreds of paintings and sculptures by the fifty most talented guild members, described inside."

Adélaïde bought a booklet and opened it in the middle of the lobby. When she found her name, joy swept through her.

Hugging the livret, she ascended the marble steps to the exhibition hall, a ballroom designed for five hundred dancing partners. Still early, the room was devoid of people but filled with sculptures, exhibits of painted porcelain, silk fans, and *objets d'art*. The walls lined floor to ceiling with paintings, illustrations, and engravings. Adélaïde wondered how all the people outside would fit through the maze of artwork before her. How would she find her own work?

"Oh, there you are, dear," Madame Roslin exclaimed. She pressed her cheeks to Adélaïde's, left, then right. Her skin felt like ripened peaches and her rosewater perfume reminded Adélaïde of her mother. "You look lovely." Madame Roslin took Adélaïde's arm and hugged it to her side. "I didn't want you to be alone on the first night of your first exhibit."

Unable to squeeze a word past the lump in her throat, Adélaïde nodded. Together they navigated the length of the room, scanning the walls for Adélaïde's submissions. "Here they are." Madame Roslin spied the two miniatures amid a grouping of large portraits and *tête d'expressions*. They heard voices behind them, and Madame Roslin turned to watch two young women walk toward them. "Let me introduce you to your competition."

Élisabeth Vigée, younger than Adélaïde by several years, was tall, slim, with an oval face, rosebud lips, and deep blue eyes. She wore her blond hair piled on top of her head with fat curls that tumbled about her shoulders. Not even her strong jaw detracted from her beauty. "How are you enjoying your first show?" she asked with polite interest.

"I hope it will be a success." Adélaïde pressed her damp palms together.

"It will be." Rosalie Boquet, who had the face of a Greek goddess, linked arms with Élisabeth. "All our friends will be here."

Adélaïde wished she had Rosalie's confidence.

Later that evening, the fourth female artist arrived. Marie-Genevieve Navarre, a pastel and miniature artist in her late thirties who, like Adélaïde, had studied under Quentin de la Tour, rendered her subjects in puritan black and white, a sharp contrast to the other three.

Together, the women stood next to their work as the crowds paraded in front of them. Following the flow of traffic, patrons stopped first at Élisabeth's work. Élisabeth had exhibited two paintings of muses, one playing a lyre, the other standing in a bed of flowers, and several large portraits, including one of the guild's directors. She was often greeted with, "Mademoiselle, your work is exquisite." Adélaïde had to admit it was. And, "When may I schedule a sitting?"

Adélaïde, who was next in line with her two miniatures, would be greeted with a, "Nicely done," comment before the person passed on to Rosalie's portraits and landscapes, and exclaim, "Brilliant work!" Rosalie and Élisabeth would look at each other, smile and clasp each other's hands. Then the art patron would pass on to

Marie Navarre's work, regard the austere colors, nod and say, "Very impressive."

Many people greeted Élisabeth and Rosalie by name and stopped to exchange pleasantries and catch up on gossip. Crowds of young men flocked around the girls, flirting. Footmen flung the balcony doors open. Music filled the room, swirled around them, through them. Waiters poured in, selling wine by the glassful. The atmosphere turned giddy. Every half hour, Madame Roslin squeezed through the throng, dragging someone else she wanted to introduce to Adélaïde behind her.

The orchestra took a break, and, in that moment, she heard the music her ears had awaited all night. "Very nice work." A man bent down to examine Adélaïde's self-portrait in detail.

"Thank you, sir." Adélaïde tossed aside her despair at being placed between Rosalie and Élisabeth. "Did you see how the satin dress changes color in the light?" She moved the oval frame beneath a wall sconce and silver flashed from the miniature painting.

"My wife would like the style, but it's too small," he said. "We want something to hang above our mantel." He glanced back at Élisabeth's paintings. "I just stepped aside, waiting to speak to Mademoiselle Vigée."

Adélaïde heard her mother's voice in her head—*Never let a sale walk away*. Well, here was a sale who did not know he was a sale. She moved to block the man's view of the artist behind her. "I too can paint larger works. I can do any style of fabric, or dress, any seating arrangement you wish." When the man hesitated, trying to peer over her shoulder, she quoted him a fee that was a third of the price Élisabeth and Rosalie had posted next to their portraits. It would barely cover her costs for supplies, but she could not go back to the Roches' tonight without a sale.

At half past ten, Madame Roslin materialized again, this time alone. "Come, my dear. You must be starving. My *chaise à porteur* is waiting outside. I'm taking you out to celebrate."

It was late, but not that late. They managed to make it inside a café near the opera house before the theaters let out. Madame Roslin ordered champagne, then leaned toward Adélaïde and said, "Now tell me everything."

"I wasn't expecting such a crowd," Adélaïde said.

"Summer holidays are over. Everyone's back in town. This event is always the beginning of the fall social season."

"It seemed everyone knew Élisabeth and Rosalie."

Madame Roslin nodded. "Mademoiselle Vigée's father was a beloved member of the Academy of St. Luke. He died when she was quite young. The artists of St. Luke and the Royal Academy practically raised her. Rosalie studied alongside her."

"That explains things."

"You will have your own coterie of followers soon enough, my dear."

"Actually, I sold two commissions tonight." A thrill of pride shivered through her.

The waiter arrived with their champagne. He pulled the cork from the bottle with a soft pop, then a hiss of escaping air sounded as he poured the golden liquid into two crystal glasses.

"This is a celebration indeed." Her friend toasted her.

"It is good and also bad news," Adélaïde said. "I have nowhere to execute these portraits. I cannot afford to rent space at the Academy of St. Luke, but I cannot do them at home as the other girls are doing."

Madame Roslin chuckled. "You would kill off your customers before they made it to the fifth flight of stairs."

"Even if they did not expire on the way up, I would have to have a chaperone, and with an easel for a full-sized canvas and two extra chairs, someone would have to sit out on the landing." Adélaïde set her glass down. "After all this, what if I can't carry out these commissions?"

"I agree, your little garret is out of consideration. You will have to paint them in their own homes, of course. I will come with you if you need a chaperone."

"Thank you," she breathed out. "I don't understand why you've done so much for me."

A tender look crossed the woman's face. "When I look at you, I see myself when I was young. I remember how much I wanted to be an artist, how I would do anything to paint."

Adélaïde blinked and looked away. "I'm trying."

"Besides, I know the lengths you will go to make sure people see your work. It's better that I make sure all goes right from the beginning this time."

"What do you mean?"

Madame Roslin's dark eyes danced. "Several years ago, my husband consulted me about a mysterious affair that the Academy came to call the Prix-de-Paris caper."

"Oh no." Adélaïde said. Somewhere in the restaurant, a clock chimed midnight. A great wind blew through her head. She remembered that terrible time, the poster, the frantic painting in secret, the debacle when she won a prize she could not acknowledge, the separation from François. "You know about that?"

"When I saw the sketches, I recognized the faces of my dear friend's children, and the hand of the artist."

Adélaïde groaned and shrank back in her chair. "How did you have anything to do with me after that?"

The older woman took Adélaïde's hand. "I was lucky that my position allowed me to pursue my dreams—all of them, including my love for Alexander. So, I understand."

Adélaïde struggled to overcome her emotions. "Thank you for all your advice and support, for the people you introduced me to, for everything. And now, for saving me from disaster."

Madame Roslin's heart shaped face broadened into a wide smile. "Enough of this. I'm enjoying shepherding a young artist around. It's a good time to be a female artist. Soon, you'll have people lining up to sit for you." She poured more wine and raised her glass. "To your success, my dear."

The servers changed the candles in the sconces on the mirrored walls and the restaurant brightened. In the shining light, Adélaïde pictured people shoving Rosalie and Élisabeth's admirers aside, insisting that she paint them. It was absurd, but she laughed and raised her coupe glass. Crystal sang, bubbles sailed up through the pale wine, and Adélaïde's belief in her burgeoning career was as heady as the scent of grapes that tickled her nose.

Adélaïde stole up the back stairs, avoiding the footman who had taunted her earlier in the evening. She spent a sleepless night, part of it reliving the wonder of the exhibit opening, the dresses, the champagne, the music, the flirtations, the voices, the clients, and the other part wondering if she had imagined it all. The next morning she rose early, dressed, and rushed down to the kitchens, where the chambermaid pressed the newspaper beneath a layer of toweling.

"May I have a look?" she asked. "I need to know if last night was a dream."

"A dream, you say?" The footman came into the kitchen and swiped a pastry from the cook's table. "Well, here I am. You've got, let's see, thirteen days now."

Adélaïde made a rude noise.

"Ignore him, miss. He's a simple man. He thinks all women are attracted to him." The maid shooed him out. "Go ahead, but don't crease the pages. Monsieur Roche likes his newsprint to be perfect."

What she wanted did not appear in print for three more days.

On the fourth morning, she held up her hand to the footman. "I know. Ten days now." But this time critiques were in. "Here they are!" She scanned them quickly, her heart jumping with excitement. "I was so worried the critics would not find my small pieces among the others, but . . ." Adélaïde turned and ran for the back stairs.

"Wait, madame," the maid called. "What does it say?"

"No time," Adélaïde exclaimed. Sales were bound to be up, and she had to have something new to offer.

CHAPTER 10

AUGUST 1774

Adélaïde arrived an hour before the exhibit opened that afternoon, a freshly completed watercolor on gouache in hand. Overnight, their area of the exhibit seemed to have bloomed into a flower shop. Roses and late summer peonies in vases, gifts from Rosalie and Élisabeth's admirers, lined a counter that Rosalie had borrowed from her parents' shop.

The two artists themselves stood in front of the counter, powdered heads pressed together, giggling over a newspaper article.

"Oh, are you reading the critiques?" Adélaïde asked.

"I read only the society pages," Rosalie said.

"Then you missed the best news of the day. Rosalie, they wrote that your work displayed truthfulness to life." She left out the part *rare to find in a female painter.* "And you, Élisabeth, they called a virtuoso whose portraits and history paintings showed fluent and sure brushwork."

"As if I haven't been painting for years," Élisabeth said. "And you, Madame Guiard, what did they say that has made your face shine with happiness today?"

"One critic said I handled the hair and clothing in my miniature with spirit and grace." Who cared that this critic also said she handled her subject with too much self-love? "Another critic said he expected to see more of my work in the future. A third wrote that while I used lighting to good effect, I had sacrificed shadows."

Adélaïde paused. "How can I use lighting to good effect if shadows cannot be seen?"

"Art critics! Who can make sense of what they say? Best to ignore them," Rosalie said.

"Listen to this," Élisabeth brandished the newspaper. "They've written poetry about us."

Madame Guiard's wisps of art are sure to suffice,
Mademoiselle Vigée's visage, wit, and grace no device
Darling Mademoiselle Boquet's work strong, concise.
These muses, three, with charm, beauty, and talent,
sit on the throne of Saint Luke's. Their artistic skills
the show's success alone.

"Are we really responsible for the exhibit's success?" Adélaïde asked.

"Its wild success, you mean?" Rosalie responded. "Of course we are. How could anyone miss that we, the muses of Paris, are here, our beauty on display?" She picked up a new painting she had brought in that day and strutted in front of the counter, wielding it like a hawker waving a sign along the Seine. "How can they resist our work?"

Laughing, Adélaïde backed up, holding her watercolor out of danger.

Everything seemed to happen at once. The shock of being stopped by a male person against her backside, the watercolor flying out of her hand, her reflexive grab at the counter, hitting a vase that crashed to the floor, the crack of china shattering, water splashing everywhere. With a cry, Adélaïde snatched up her painting. Too late. Wet vellum sagged, hues dripped off the edge, rainbow drops of pink and purple splattered on her white dress.

"Watch where you are going," said a cold voice behind her.

"I beg your pardon, sir. It is you who should watch where you are going." She wiped her face with her sleeve, then turned to confront a middle-aged gentleman in a black velvet jacket and crimson silk pantaloons. "You have ruined my painting. And my dress."

"I did no such thing." Twin flags of ire flanked a hawklike nose under angry gray eyes. "But you have ruined my shoes, madame. I expect you to pay for the damage."

"You must be joking. What is a pair of shoes to a dress or a piece of art?" She could not decide which loss was worse.

"You call this art?" The man swept his arm to encompass their area of the exhibit. "It is a collection of pathetic attempts."

Rosalie and Élisabeth appeared frozen in place.

"Pathetic attempts, sir?" Adélaïde said. "Even the philosophes have remarked on the quality of our work in *The Mercure*."

He laughed. "You actually believe your work warrants critical acclaim, madame?"

"*The Mercure* has been a respected publication for more than a century."

"This time, the philosophes have made a grave error."

"Why do you say that?" She tried to signal to Rosalie and Élisabeth to step in and rescue her from this ridiculous situation. They did not meet her eyes.

"Because they have pandered to the vanity of a bunch of grisettes."

"We are not grisettes, sir."

"You have shop girl written all over you—your dress, your airs, pretending to be something you are not, pretending to be better read than you are."

"Even a grisette is capable of applying herself to learning and improving her situation. Nevertheless, we are working artists, and our toil has produced art, not attempts at it. These philosophes, and the poets who have also written about us, speak a truth you choose not to see."

"You speak of such poetry with pride, madame? May I inform you that art is not a frivolous exercise to be used in the service of young men to woo lovers in such a public fashion."

Were they speaking of the same poetry? Adélaïde looked to Élisabeth for help, but Élisabeth had raised the newspaper to hide her face. "This poetry could hardly be labelled scandalous, sir."

"Nor is it a spotlight to expose yourselves to the world," the man continued. "You should be ashamed of yourselves." Listening to this man made her remember being called a failed specimen of womanhood at her mother's worktable. Well, never again.

"Art is often the subject of poetry, sir. From time immemorial, men have written poetry to their muses. These men are merely following centuries of tradition."

He drew back. "You would lecture me?"

"I would not presume to, sir. We are merely the artists whose character and works you have impugned."

"This proves my point."

"What point, sir? Your argument is without subject or merit."

Behind her, Rosalie coughed.

His face turned the color of his pantaloons. "When a woman in your position presumes to debate with a man in my position, it demonstrates the depths to which our society has fallen." His finger stabbed the air in front of her face. "You grisettes have ruined the kingdom. You rut in palace closets with your skirts flung high for all to see. Then you milk the kingdom dry with your demands for jewels and favors."

Adélaïde's jaw fell open. Élisabeth dropped the newspaper, and Rosalie's eyes widened.

"Monsieur le Comte!" It was Madame Roslin, her voice sharp. She advanced on the group, a pleasant smile on her lips, a steely look in her eyes. "These are young girls, tender of hearing and understanding."

Comte! Oh no. Adélaïde's haze of anger lifted to see the medals gleaming on the man's chest and to take in the deeper meaning of the fleur-de-lis embroidered on his stockings. Someone connected with the royal family. Heat swept through her body.

"Madame Roslin, can you not see how vulgar this is?" The man indicated the entire ballroom. "I had heard rumors about this exhibit—artists placing prices next to their work, bartering like fish-wives in the market. *Impossible*, I said, but came to investigate for myself. And what do I find?"

Madame Roslin did not respond.

"Young ladies prancing in front of the exhibits, claiming to be muses, reveling in the mention of their names in the journals. Surely you, an Academy member, do not condone such behavior."

"You overstate the case, Monsieur le Comte." Madame Roslin measured her words. "You have witnessed the innocent pleasure of three young ladies enjoying the fruit of their artistic endeavors, nothing more."

He snorted. "Given the chance, they would ask for diamonds for the soles of their shoes. I've seen enough to ascertain that this exhibit makes a mockery of art." His cold gaze swept the three artists. "Well, young ladies, be warned. I intend to make sure it never happens again." He marched out of the ballroom, back stiff, shoulders square.

Adélaïde stared after him, her hands covering her cheeks. When they could no longer hear his footsteps, she asked in a small voice, "Who was that?"

"The Comte d'Angiviller," Madame Roslin said. "New Director General of Buildings, Art, Gardens, and Manufactories."

"The Director . . ." She recalled mention of such a title in one of the newspapers. "Don't tell me I've just managed to offend the highest arbiter of art in the entire kingdom?"

"You have indeed," Madame Roslin said.

Adélaïde's stomach churned as she remembered something else. "Doesn't he have some connection to the new king?"

"Yes, he was the governor of the Dauphin's household since the prince was a small child," Madame Roslin said.

Adélaïde groaned. Not only had she offended the head of the art world, but worse, someone who was like a father to the young king.

"And that is why you need to read the society pages," Rosalie said.

"That man is trying to turn everyone upside down." Élisabeth retrieved the flowers scattered on the floor and began to distribute them among the remaining vases. "He has his minions going up and down Rue St. Honoré closing businesses, saying they have not paid their dues to the king. He's the reason I became a member of this guild."

"I don't understand," Adélaïde said.

"He shut my studio down. His men said I was running an unlicensed studio. But how could I do otherwise? I was sixteen, unable to obtain a license."

"Imagine telling an orphan she cannot support her mother and brother, then confiscating her work," Rosalie said.

"My stepfather paid a huge bribe to the Châtelet to get my artwork back." Élisabeth bent to pick up the broken vase.

Adélaïde laid her ruined watercolor on the floor. "Here, let's wrap the pieces in this so you don't cut yourself."

"I hope he doesn't try to close my parents' shop," Rosalie said.

"Could he?" Adélaïde asked.

"He can do anything he wants," Madame Roslin said. "Never forget that."

"He's a hypocrite to lecture us," Rosalie said. "Isn't he the Baroness de Marchais's lover?"

Adélaïde gasped. A name she recognized. "Wasn't the Baron de Marchais the Lord of the Bedchamber for the old king?"

"Yes," Rosalie said. "They say the comte used the baroness to monitor the activities of the old king. So, I ask you ladies—who is the one to use people to get close to the royal family and gain favors?" She raised her eyebrow and crossed her arms. "*He* ought to be ashamed of himself."

"He certainly is a plotting man," Madame Roslin said. "He won his title fighting some war for the old king. Then he became governor of the prince's household, and when the prince ascended the throne, he installed the comte to manage all the kingdom's palaces, palace gardens, and royal factories."

"I heard he could not wait to gain power after the old king died," Élisabeth said. "People say that at the prince's ascension, the comte was actually heard to tell the prince to stand tall and look like a king."

Adélaïde would have sat down, but there was nowhere to sit. "Excuse me," she said. "I have to see to my dress."

"I'm coming with you," Madame Roslin said.

In the empty ladies' retiring room, Adélaïde plopped down on an ottoman and buried her head in her hands. "I failed the least of my mother's instructions."

"What instructions were those?" Madame Roslin asked.

"Never speak disrespectfully to anyone who dresses well. Read the society pages. Memorize the sketches. Never forget a face."

"Your mother did have a way with words."

"I should start chiseling my tombstone now. *Idiot young artiste commits social suicide.*" She spread her skirt out and examined the stains. "This could be my shroud."

"Come, my dear, it's not as bad as that." Madame Roslin pulled a small metal case from her reticule and opened it, revealing needle and thread. She spent the next hour darning seams in Adélaïde's dress to hide the splotches.

"I hope I never see that man again," Adélaïde said. "He's not fit for polite society."

"Unfortunately, the comte is about to *become* polite society. He just announced his engagement to the baroness. The poets, artists, and thinkers in her circle are in mourning. The comte has thrown them out of her salon and replaced them with military men."

"What's wrong with poets and artists?"

"D'Angiviller believes they have destroyed the grandeur of France. That it can only be restored through the demonstration of might. He's ordered the palaces refurbished with new statues and artwork. He even wants to turn the Louvre into a museum to the glory of France. Imagine that pile of stones becoming something useful." She frowned. "You would think that a man"—she lowered her voice to a whisper—"busy propping up a weak king, as some people say, would have no time to attend a guild exhibit. I wonder what he was doing here."

"You mean he didn't come to antagonize us?"

"I doubt it."

"But why does he hate grisettes so much?" Adélaïde asked.

"He hates one grisette in particular. His dislike of Madame du Barry is legendary."

"Madame du Barry?" Adélaïde's head jerked at the name. "Maman's grisette, Jeanne Beçu, the old king's mistress?"

"The very one. He disliked her influence over the king, believed her position weakened the kingdom. He probably got himself installed as the director of buildings just so he could get her out of the king's palace."

A man who would use his own mistress to spy on the sexual acts of the king and his mistress? Who would plot for position of power to remove her? Adélaïde shuddered with disgust. "Whatever he's up to, I had better stay out of his way."

"That's possibly the wisest thing you've said today," Madame Roslin said.

"I'm sure of it."

A frantic knocking registered in her sleep.

Beyond the curtainless attic window, the sky was still black. When the pounding came again, Adélaïde rose and opened her apartment door.

The scullery maid handed her a note and held up her candle so Adélaïde could read it. Her reddened hands smelled of vinegar. "There's a boy downstairs waiting for a response," she said.

"Tell him I'll be there." Adélaïde returned to her room, splashed water on her face, threw on her street clothes, and rushed out. At this time of day, the streets were empty except for the fish carters bringing in the night's catch, the reek of ocean preceding them, and the last of the vegetable sellers returning to their farms in silent wagons. Fog rolled off the river as she crossed the bridge. She wondered what could be so important that St. Luke's rector had sent runners throughout Paris ordering guild members to present them-selves at Saint Symphorien by seven o'clock. This was the last thing she needed today. She finally had a high-profile portrait to execute, and this morning was the first sitting.

Last week, after attending a tragedy at the Comédie-Française, Adélaïde had waited for the lead actor, Henri Louis Cain, to exit the theater, then followed him and his entourage to a restaurant. She ordered a coffee and waited for "LeKain" to finish his dinner. When he had eaten, she approached his table and handed him the sketch she had drawn during his performance that evening.

LeKain, famous for his ferocious expressions and emotive acting, looked from her to the sketch she held out and roared, "What woman brings me this?"

Heads turned.

"It is I, sir, the artist," she said, embarrassed but determined. "I would like to paint you."

He perused the sketch, his shaggy eyebrows waggling with exaggerated surprise above a protuberant nose, caught exactly in the drawing. He passed the paper to a fellow diner. "What think you, my friend?" he asked.

"Impressive," the man said.

"I would like to do a life-sized pastel portrait of you. If you hang it in the lobby of the theater, I'll charge you half my usual fee."

"Shall I?" he asked the men at the table. And they told him, "You shall."

Adélaïde had decided to go hunting for customers, and what better way to advertise one's work than for it to hang before thousands of theatergoers? She would have done his portrait for free to get new customers, but he did not need to know that.

When his laugh boomed through the restaurant, she realized she had voiced the thought aloud.

It was her opportunity, and she could not afford to be late.

At the bottom of Saint Symphorien's crumbling stone steps, familiar figures materialized in the mist: Rosalie Boquet and Marie Navarre, shivering in the cold next to Élisabeth Vigée and her stepfather. Looking around, Adélaïde recognized the artists she had met in the cloister studios after her night of wandering, looking as confused as she felt.

"Do you know what's happened?" she asked the woman who had told her about Quentin de la Tour's apprenticeship. The woman shook her head.

Above them, the cloisters gleamed in the dawn sky, a row of darkened arches against white stone. She remembered walking along that arcade with Madame Roslin on the morning of her rescue. Pain washed over her chest. Madame Roslin, whose radiant visage she most wanted to see emerge from the fog, was one she would never see again.

Just after Christmas, Suzanne Roslin had lost her battle with cancer. It seemed to Adélaïde that everyone she loved was taken from her, but Madame Roslin's death hurt in a special way. She had lost the one person who believed in her without reservation.

At the top of the steps, policemen from the Châtelet blocked the doors of the old church. Alarm swept through her. What had happened to bring the king's officers to their guild?

The sonorous bells of Notre Dame rang. The doors opened and Pierre Dumesnil appeared, his wig and cravat missing, his jacket and pants rumpled, his hose ripped. The crowd on the steps gasped. The rector was already an elderly man, but he looked ten years older than when Adélaïde had met him at the Hôtel Jabach exhibit. Monsieur Dumesnil's watery gaze passed over them.

When the echo of the bells had faded, he addressed them in a wavering voice. "Academy members—friends, brothers, sisters— yesterday the king issued a decree outlawing all guilds. The Academy of St. Luke is now closed. Any further work produced under the auspices of the guild is illegal. The showrooms and exhi- bition halls must be emptied. All artists must remove their posses- sions from this building by sundown tonight or their works will be confiscated by officers of the Châtelet and destroyed." He wiped his eyes with a handkerchief.

For a few moments, shock immobilized the artists. Then, many rushed up the steps, exclaiming in anger or panic.

"What should we do?" Rosalie asked. "We have no artworks here."

"Thank goodness," Élisabeth said. "I wouldn't want to have to pay a second bribe."

"I suggest we leave," her stepfather said. "No sense in getting tangled up with the Châtelet police again."

Thinking of her appointment at the Comédie-Française, Adélaïde turned to accompany them back across the river, but as they descended the steps, she turned back. The sun cast the slate tiles of the church's sloped roof in golden red. She had once waited in this exact spot for the sun to rise, waited for the night to be over. This was the place where she had found hope and haven, these were the people who had saved her, this was her guild. Was there anything she could do? What would Madame Roslin have done?

She headed inside.

She spent the morning helping artists remove their work, thoughts of painting LeKain that day forgotten. Throughout the building, artists asked why the king had done this to them. She too wanted to know and went down to the Academy offices to find out.

Instead, an exhausted Dumesnil asked her to help clean out his office. "We must secure the guild's records," he said. "Some are hundreds of years old. They must be preserved."

Adélaïde cleared cabinets out while Dumesnil and two other guild directors met.

"We need to hire an attorney," Dumesnil said. "Royal agents raided my home at two this morning, as though I were a criminal. They went through the house, saying they were looking for documents. I don't know what they took, but they carried away some of my artwork."

"That happened to me as well," the second director said.

"And me," said the third. "How can they close down a guild that has operated for more than six hundred years?"

"And put more than a thousand members out of work?" the second man asked.

"Jealousy," Dumesnil said. "The Royal Academy does not want any competition with their salon. A few months ago, I received a demand for financial records. Our last exhibit made more than a million livres. I fear Academy officials appealed to the Comte D'Angiviller for his help. He used the finance minister's bid to crush the guilds as a pretext to close ours down."

The second officer agreed. "The timing is right. Think how convenient it is to close us down right before our exhibition this year."

Until that moment, Adélaïde had only thought of the impact on the artists who had to move their work, but now she thought of the loss of income she would experience if this year's exhibition did not happen. Fear shivered through her.

"D'Angiviller did not wait a day after being named to his new position before demanding changes in the Royal Academies," said Dumesnil. "We worried he was going to demand changes of us but grew complacent when nothing happened after the Jabach exhibit."

Adélaïde remembered Madame Roslin's comment about d'Angiviller being a plotting man and understood then that he had maneuvered for months behind the scenes to fulfill his vow to close the exhibit.

At sundown, Adélaïde exited with the last of the artists and officers through the empty church. The portrait of Saint Luke was gone, the wires that had held it aloft snipped and swinging in eddies the artists created as they passed through the nave. As they descended the stone steps, Adélaïde heard the Châtelet officers secure the doors behind them, heard the clank of metal chain against the bronze doors.

She trudged home in the gathering darkness, lugging an ancient ledger filled with guild records.

&

Two weeks later.

Seven hundred Academy members crowded into the ballroom of a wealthy art patron who had lent the Academy of St. Luke its use for the afternoon. Ignoring the women at the back of the room, Adélaïde found a place near the raised platform in the center of the room where Dumesnil and two lawyers waited to speak to the artists.

Dumesnil did not need to shout in a room with curved twenty-foot-high ceilings. "With the closure of the guilds, each individual must apply for a new business license," he told them.

"But, in fact, you cannot do that." One of the attorneys stepped forward. "There is no provision in the law for a business license for artists. For centuries, artists have had two ways to work—either as a member of the Royal Academy of Painting and Sculpture or as a member of the guild of the Academy of St. Luke. At present, the only legal way to exhibit your artwork and sell it is to be a member of the Royal Academy."

"What are we to do?" a guild member asked, his voice trembling. "All patronage, the ability to work, and the right to exhibit are now controlled by the Royal Academy. We don't have the training required, and it takes years to get membership. We can't wait that long. We need to work now."

The crowd started to murmur, and Dumesnil called for order.

The second attorney said, "According to the bylaws of the Royal Academy, as long as you are an agréé, you may work. All you must do is apply for membership and pay the fee to be granted provisional status with immediate effect. This status may exist indefinitely."

"Then I'll just go petition for membership to the Royal Academy," the man next to Adélaïde muttered. Several artists agreed that this solved their problem and left.

Turning, Adélaïde saw that most of those who remained were women. None of them had asked the question they needed answered. She could not wait for bravery. "Can women apply for provisional status?" she asked. "I understand that the Royal Academy has imposed a limit of four females at a time, but the Academy of St. Luke has one hundred thirty-one female members." She had counted their names in the records stored at her apartment. "Will the Academy accept more female members now?"

A woman came to stand with her. "Yes, what will happen to us? This is our livelihood."

The second attorney looked flustered. "You should consult your husband or father, of course," he said.

"Not everyone has a husband or father," a third woman spoke up.

"Some of us have children and sick husbands to support," said another.

A desperation rose in the room, one Adélaïde felt in herself. She approached the platform. "As this woman has said, we also depend on our earnings to eat and pay rent. What are we to do?"

"I have four children to raise." The woman who came to stand next to Adélaïde was gaunt but pregnant.

"Sir, look around you," Adélaïde said. "We need your help."

"I'll look into the rules again," the attorney promised.

The next week.

Hushed female voices echoed in the cavernous ballroom. Adélaïde counted almost one hundred women and a handful of men, mostly husbands. Adélaïde's heart sank when she saw the man who entered the room with Pierre Dumesnil. She would never forget the Comte d'Angiviller's cold gray eyes. She moved back into the crowd. Perhaps he would not recognize her, dressed in sober black, wearing her hair in a plain fashion, looking quite different than the day they had met at the Hôtel Jabach.

"Ladies," Director Dumesnil said, "the Comte d'Angiviller has graciously offered to come and speak to you, to explain the situation."

The comte surveyed the room, speared the few husbands in attendance with a look. "First, I would like to remind all of you that any gathering of former guild members is unlawful."

Dumesnil clenched his fists. When the lace ruffles beneath his jacket sleeve quivered, Adélaïde understood why no other officials had come—they were afraid.

"Our kingdom has embarked on a journey to restore dignity to the arts," d'Angiviller said. "The lightness, frivolity, and weakness expressed through a feminine style of art in recent times has led to the degradation of, and disrespect for, the monarchy. When His Majesty appointed me to the position of Director General, he entrusted me to turn the subjects of this kingdom to patriotism, and pride in the great accomplishments of France. It is imperative that we regain respect for our great country and our king. We will do so through the promotion of noble character, moral themes, and elevation of the ideas we express through art."

"Sir, what does this have to do with us?" a woman near the front interrupted. "We need to know how we may continue our work."

The comte looked down at the woman. "Madame, your efforts are not required."

"But why not, sir?" asked another woman.

"Members of the Royal Academy of Art and Sculpture have been tasked with this great labor."

What would happen if she said anything? Would he dismiss them from the room? Arrest her? Adélaïde stepped forward. "Monsieur le Comte, we too can produce art in the manner you have described. Will you admit us to the Academy so we may also participate in this program?"

The cold gaze passed over her. "Acceptance of women to the Academy is alien to my mission, madame. Admission of women reduces the number of available positions for men. Therefore, only four positions are reserved for female members."

Two years of assiduously avoiding the man, and he had not recognized her.

"Given the closure of the guild, hasn't the Academy reconsidered?" she asked.

"We have not."

"But how will we work, sir?" a woman at the back asked.

"You are welcome to consider employment in one of the king's china or tapestry factories."

Paint china? Embroider? Return to shop keeping?

Never, Adélaïde thought. "Monsieur le Comte, at the present time, the Academy has two female members. How do we apply for the open positions?"

"You may undertake to apply, madame, but we are under no obligation to fill them."

"What are we to do?" Adélaïde asked after d'Angiviller had departed.

"I see no realistic options for you," Dumesnil said. "But perhaps you could apply at the Châtelet for a business license under the new rules."

"Go to the Châtelet where the king's agents demand favors and imprison his enemies?" scoffed an artist's husband.

"Even if that were successful, where would we display our work for sale?" Adélaïde pressed.

"We can't go two years without being able to sell our work," the pregnant woman cried. "Does anyone know a Royal Academy member? They need to know what they've done to us."

Dumesnil nodded. "Several women here have trained under Royal Academy professors. Madame Guiard, Mademoiselle Navarre, perhaps you can reach out to your professors. Perhaps you could apply to become an agréé. Your former professors might be willing to sponsor you."

"Monsieur de La Tour cannot help us." Adélaïde pictured their mutual art teacher as she had last seen him, raving in the hallway, then locked away in his bedchamber.

"Two positions for one hundred thirty women?" Marie Navarre shook her head. "My family would never permit me to pursue such an unseemly competition." Her shoulders bowed. Above her black bodice, her face took on a gray cast, as though the window to her soul had closed, leaving a blank façade behind.

Adélaïde shuddered at the reminder of life before marriage, a world where parents indulged their daughters' desires, but only to a point. At least, she no longer had any family member to hold her back. *Besides*, a voice in her head whispered, *that's one less genuine competitor*. She looked around the room again, assessing the skills of those who remained, her mind calculating the odds. Her prospects for one of those two slots had just improved. "I will apply at the Châtelet," she said. "Then we can see about applying to the Royal Academy."

"The Châtelet is no place for young ladies," the husband who had spoken earlier warned her.

"Living on the street is also no place for young ladies," Adélaïde said. "I have to try."

"That was the most humiliating experience of my life," Adélaïde told Rosalie Boquet, Élisabeth Vigée, and Marie Navarre later that week as they lunched at the Palais Royale. "The official who took my application laughed in my face and threw the paper back at me. He offered a lewd suggestion as to what position I could apply for and where I could perform it. Even the prisoner who looked like he hadn't bathed in weeks laughed." But Adélaïde had seen, and smelled, the festering wound beneath his ankle chains, had seen his fever bright eyes.

"Everyone tried to tell you," Élisabeth said. "When my stepfather went there to retrieve my paintings, he said it was the most wretched place he had ever been."

When Adélaïde hastened past the Châtelet's dark towers that afternoon, she averted her eyes from the sight of its wide, gaping archway. It would take a long time to forget the evil and human suffering emanating from that place.

The one good piece of news from the day was that Monsieur LeKain had understood her situation. He allowed her to reschedule his sitting.

"This could happen to us one day," he said.

It might now be illegal to be paid for work as an artist, but she had not lost her opportunity.

CHAPTER 12

EARLY SUMMER 1777

The women tried everything they could think of to show their works. They organized an exhibit with male artists at the Salon du Colysée on the Champs-Elysée. The Comte d'Angiviller went before the King's Council and accused them of trying to revive the guild. The council issued an injunction. They opened a show at the Musée de la Rue Saint-André. The comte threatened to arrest the museum owners. As a last resort, a wealthy art patron offered his ballroom. When d'Angiviller heard, he paid the man a visit.

An hour later, the man called the women to his house. "I'm sorry," he said. Sweat trickled down his face. "D'Angiviller threatened to imprison me, and I am no Voltaire. I cannot happily exist on the king's meat in the Châtelet's dungeons, and I have no wish to flee the country." His attempted witticism fell flat.

After her experience at the Châtelet, Adélaïde could not blame him. "What do we do?" she asked.

"Find a supporter who outranks the comte," the man said.

"Please, just leave," his wife said, fanning herself.

In silence, the women retrieved their art. This ballroom had been their last hope.

Adélaïde walked home alone. In the past year, her three compatriots from the Hôtel Jabach exhibit had solved their problems the way women most often solved their problems. Rosalie Boquet married an elderly man who managed an estate for the queen and painted when she wanted to paint. Élisabeth Vigée married a prominent art dealer and sold her paintings out of his home with impunity. Marie Navarre withdrew from public life.

Adélaïde climbed the stairs to her apartment, discouragement a giant hand pressed down on her shoulders. Weak from hunger, it was hard to struggle against its grip. She checked the cupboard where she stored food, then pulled her cash box from beneath the bed.

The euphoria of painting LeKain last year and the funds it had brought had dissipated like water into the shoals of the Seine at low tide. Back in the main room, she rechecked the food cupboard, even though she knew what she would find.

Nothing.

Willing panic back, she sat at the table and opened the cash box. A livre and a sou clinked in the bottom.

Without a proper place to paint or sell her art, her commissions had dwindled to nothing. For a time, she had paid Monsieur Roche for the day use of a salon room downstairs and a chambermaid to serve as a chaperone, but fearing he would imperil his position as King's Lock Maker, Monsieur Roche had increased the rent he charged to flout the rules to a price she could no longer pay. Worse, she did not have the money for the next quarter's rent.

She thought of moving to cheaper lodgings but rejected the idea. A woman living alone had to live in a respectable household. Could she go down to one meal a day? Skip a day? Where would it end if she did? Her stomach growled a resolute *no*. Her bony face staring back at her in the mirror also said *no*.

Saving money was no longer an option. She had to have her dowry back, but Nicolas had not responded to any of her letters. She had no choice but to seek him out. She dreaded it, had put it off to the last possible moment, but the moments had run out. *It can't be worse than the Châtelet*, she thought, and set out for the Marais, the site of her husband's most recent lodgings.

It was early evening, not yet dinnertime. The smell of simmering beef and roasting chicken emanated from the alley behind the cafés. She ignored the clench of her stomach and hurried on, at last coming to the small square where Nicolas lived, a set of narrow white stuccoed houses outlined in dark timber, and perforated with mullioned windows.

A soot-rimmed window high in the stairwell emitted a faint light. She climbed the stairs, the creak of rotting treads the only sound. The handrail guided her upward, but splinters tore at her fingers. Smells of onions, garlic, and turnips blended with centuries of wood smoke in the ancient building.

She knocked at Nicolas's door. Moments passed before she heard heavy footsteps. Then Nicolas stood swaying on the threshold, a tankard of ale in his hand, his blond hair disheveled, his face ruddy. His glittery gaze swept her from head to toe. Fear started a drumbeat in her heart.

"What are you doing here?" he asked.

"Please, let me come in," she said. "I need to talk to you." Whatever shame she had to endure from him, she wanted to experience in private.

He moved aside. She stepped into the chamber, heard him shut the door. Her eyes adjusted to the darkened room. A table littered with empty wine bottles and dirty dishes dominated the small room. Beyond it, her parents' wine-splotched couch. Nicolas loomed behind her. She had forgotten how big he was. When he set his tankard on the table, she realized it was her mother's cherished dining table covered in filth. Anger ignited.

He turned to her, arms folded across his chest, a strange light in his eyes.

It had been a mistake to come, but now that she was here, she had no choice but to continue. "I've come again to ask for my dowry," she said.

He shook his head.

"The agreement was that it be returned if we separated. It's been three years, Nicolas."

"I already told you I would not give it back."

She tried to check her temper. Running her hand along the scalloped wooden edge of her mother's table, she said, "Then at least let me have my parents' furniture to sell."

"That desperate, huh?" He laughed, a sound full of anticipated violence. "No." His eyes hardened to pure threat as he moved toward her.

She tensed. "Nicolas, you cannot leave me in this situation. I must have money to pay the rent. This is my property, and you know it."

"Begging, are you?" The sound that came out of his mouth was somewhere between a laugh and a snarl. "I told you to never come back—to never ask me again. The fact that you dare deserves punishment, I think." He now stood next to her. "Don't you?" he asked in a sibilant voice.

Adélaïde shook her head, mute.

He pulled his arm back, knotted his hand into a fist. She took a frantic step back, but the table blocked her way. She raised her arms to protect her face, squeezing her eyes shut against the expected blow. Instead, a punch hit her in the gut. She crumpled to the floor, the wind knocked out of her. Before she could move, he kicked her, his boots slamming into her back, her hips, her shoulders. A crack sounded in the room, followed by instant pain.

My ribs!

She tried to get up, tried to crawl for the door, but the blows kept coming. She felt her head hit the underside of the table, her shoulder crash against a table leg. She tried to scream, tried to beg him to stop, but could not get enough air. She grabbed at his boots, his legs, anything to make the pain stop. Darkness and stars appeared. She stopped struggling.

When she regained consciousness, he stood over her, panting. "Get up," he grunted. "Get out."

Her entire body hurt. She could not move. He grabbed her arm, pulled her up, dragged her to the door. Opening it, he pushed her out into the tiny hall. Her foot gave way, and she pitched forward in the semi-darkness. Air rushed past her. In horror, she realized she was beyond the landing, falling down the stairs. She grabbed for the rail, her arm wrenching when she found it. Agony sliced through her chest. Her dress tore. Clinging to the rail, she maneuvered herself to the next landing. Releasing the handrail, she sank down on the steps and tried not to cry. It hurt too much.

"Get lover boy to help you." Above her, Nicolas's voice sounded loud in the stairwell. "If you come back here again, I will kill you." A moment later, his apartment door slammed.

On the floor above Nicolas, a door opened. Adélaïde felt a presence peer down at her. After a while, the outer door opened downstairs. Soon, wavering candlelight appeared, then an older woman in a frill-edged white cap came up the stairs. She stopped when she saw Adélaïde, averted her gaze, and stepped around her. The scent of rye and yeast clung to the woman's skirts. A door on an upper floor opened, then closed. Silence settled over the building.

Adélaïde wiped her eyes on her sleeve, tested her injured foot, then limped down the stairs, every step fire up her leg, agony in her chest. On the long walk home, it grew dark. Lamplighters climbed ladders at the intersections and lit the lamps hanging over the streets. People pushed past her as though she were invisible. She hurt so much she wished Nicolas had finished her off.

At the foot of the Roches' back stairs, she thought, *I cannot do this*. Then, terrified of what Madame Roche would do if she saw her, Adélaïde knew she had to do it.

Later, she lay in the darkness, half propped against the headboard, breathing in shallow gasps, her teeth chattering. For hours, her mind relived her tumble down the stairs, the feel of Nicolas's boots on her back fresh with every breath. She saw the artifacts of her childhood, the overturned chairs, the broken china, and shattered wine glasses, the ruined vestiges of her hopes. She knew she should be angry, but no feeling came.

For now, Nicolas had won.

CHAPTER 13

SUMMER 1777

Adélaïde had never known such agony. When she could not make it to her apartment door the next morning, the maid returned with Madame Roche, binding strips, and laudanum.

"What happened?" Madame Roche asked. When Adélaïde told her, Madame Roche's usual hard expression softened. "Why did you not tell us of your trouble?"

"I didn't want anyone to know." The shame in her heart was almost worse than the pain in her chest.

Madame Roche ordered the maid to bring Adélaïde food every day and told Adélaïde not to worry about rent until she healed.

In the weeks it took her broken ribs to knit together and for the bruises to fade, Adélaïde lay in bed, the horror of her trip to Nicolas's house coming to her in disjointed dreams, her days filled with nightmarish thoughts of her future. She had done everything she could, but she had failed. The miniature portrait she had done with such high hopes looked down at her from the wall next to the bed, her mother's expression saying, "I told you so." Maman was right.

Adélaïde wrote her father a long letter, asking him to pay her debts and send her coach fare so she could join him in the country. When the maid left with the letter, Adélaïde eased back on to the bed, staring at the space she had made her home for the past three years. Its furnishings were plain: an iron bedstead, a wooden chair, a dresser, a braided rug on the floor, a window bare to the sky. The area beyond the bedroom was equally sparse, but until the last few months, these two rooms had been filled with hope and possibility.

Her gaze fell on a small table wedged in a corner, usually hidden behind the open door to the living area, and the dusty rectangular object on its surface. She got out of bed, went to the table, turned the clock around. Its hands were fused together at twelve, unwound since the day she had banished the clock. Ignoring the pain of her ribs, she dragged the table to her bedside and wound the clock. The device ticked away while she watched the long hand jerk forward with each passing minute.

She had not permitted herself to think of François for so long, but now, memories of their time together rose, and longing for the days in his father's atelier matched the pain from her inhaled breath. Was Nicolas right?

Had François returned from Rome? Had he found success in Italy? Was he happy?

What did it matter? In the morning, she would pack for her move to the country.

August arrived and with it, opening day of the Royal Academy's Salon. From her attic window, Adélaïde watched dawn outline her beloved rooftops and shade them with color and depth. Her hands longed to capture it, but her pastels lay at the bottom of her packed trunk.

When brightness slipped into the room, she picked up her father's letter and reread it.

Daughter, never think that you have disappointed me or that the expense of your training was wasted. Your talent cried for it; it was my great joy to deliver it. While I am sure you know best your circumstances, and I long to see you, I fear that here in the countryside you will be reduced to playing nursemaid to an old man. Much as I know you would take on this role with love and devotion, life here would smother you in quiet obscurity.
And what of your future when I depart this earth?
What can we say of a man who has left his wife to starve? His behavior must not be allowed. While I have enclosed the money you

> *requested, I encourage you to pursue all legal means against Monsieur*
> *Guiard, and I urge you to reconsider whether coming to me is your best*
> *course of action. I have faith that you will succeed despite the obstacles*
> *in your path.*

When she had first read her father's words, his belief in her had lifted her up. But she knew she could not overcome the impediments before her. She placed her father's letter in the trunk and closed the lid. Her coach would leave at first light two days' hence.

She had set herself one last task and needed to complete it before she lost her courage. She powdered her face, donned her finest chintz dress, then walked to the Louvre, a gauze scarf covering the yellowed bruises on her shoulders. Wishing the slow-moving crowds in each room away, she wandered the galleries, her eyes skimming hundreds of paintings hanging floor to ceiling without seeing them, looking for one name, one familiar style.

When she found it, François's name fell from her lips like a whispered prayer. She ached to put out her hand and trace the painted signatures on the two works before her. In *St. Jerome in the Desert Hearing the Trumpet of the Last Judgment*, an angel blared a trumpet in the prophet's face as he sat reading a scripture, wrapped in a claret cloak. The terror on the old man's face, his flying beard, and the bunched muscles exposed by the open cloak conveyed motion and energy. The angel blew his trumpet from a mystic background of black clouds and beckoned with imperial authority, while a lion rested beside St. Jerome, its hairy whorls echoed in the roiling clouds. Adélaïde recognized the religious iconography of the angel and the lion but registered the concrete and scientific rendering of St. Jerome's body and arrested motion.

Next, she regarded *Belisarius*. The general, blinded by the emperor he had loyally served, leaned on a ragged young man who held Belisarius's upturned helmet. A vigorous young soldier dropped coins into the helmet while another soldier and two older men looked on, pity on their faces. The faded red of Belisarius's cloak and the golden cloak of the beggar lad moved in a serpentine swirl across the painting, tied together by the dull gray of a bystander's cloak in the background, the bright red of the soldier's cloak, and the metal shining off the soldier's helmet and armor, all bound in a knot of men's hands at the center of the painting: a circle reflecting the personal price of war. Looking closer, she saw that the sheen in the metal of the soldier's helmet and armor reflected the clouds in the sky. She smiled as she remembered François's frustration with the ten helmet paintings so long ago.

On the way out, she bought the Salon's livret. Standing under a shop awning at the edge of the road, she leafed through the pages until she found François's name, tracing the crisp black letters with her finger. An Academy agréé teaching at the Louvre, he was considered the hope of his school.

In the distance, La Samaritaine's clock chimed. She knew without counting that it was noon. Love and longing for François tore through her so strongly that she staggered against the brick wall of the shop. She had to see him.

But would he want to see her?

By early evening, Adélaïde knew François was not married, knew where he lived. In her heart, she was running through the Louvre, calling out for him. But then she imagined his reaction. Perhaps he had forgotten her, would not know her when she showed up at his door. Perhaps he hated her and would throw her out, like Nicolas had.

The shadows in her apartment lengthened and the scrap of paper with his address on it grew limp in her damp hands.

How could she go to him after what she had done to him?

How could she not?

At midnight, Adélaïde returned to the Louvre, tiptoeing through the Place du Carousel. Sconces placed at intervals along the walls threw flickering light as their candles guttered and burned out. A faint light spilled under the door to number 37. Her heart pounded a riotous drumbeat in her chest, her breath caught in her throat.

She tapped softly, waited, then knocked.

Footsteps approached. The latch turned and the door opened. Then François filled the doorway, his familiar, unruly hair unfamiliar, tamed back into short waves that ended at the nape of his neck.

A day's growth of beard edged his face, and she saw that he had the fuller face and jawline of a man. He was in his shirtsleeves, his cravat hanging like a limp towel around his neck. His eyes gleamed with reflected light from the candelabra he held in his hand, and faint lines radiated from the outer corners of his eyelids.

The frown marring his forehead smoothed into a look of recognition. "Adélaïde."

Their eyes devoured each other in the darkness. Then the candelabra disappeared, and a bright patch showed on the floor beyond the door. François pulled her inside. They came together in a rush, the warmth of his lean body a benediction long delayed.

She began to cry, hoarse, ugly sounds that fought their way past her healing ribs. "I'm sorry. I'm so sorry."

"Do not cry." His thumbs stopped her tears. "Never cry." His voice was as broken as hers.

Hours later, they lay tangled together in François's rough bedsheets, exhausted but not sleeping. He stroked her back while he told her of his experiences in Rome, told her how he had missed her, saying more in one night than he had in the entire time she had known him. She listened, sated by the sound of his voice. Their toes touched, then their ankles, their knees. She moved so that the hard edge of his hip bone rested against hers. He told her of his worry for Alexandré, who had stayed behind in Rome, shirking his studies. She told him of her life living alone in Paris, of how her portraits had become her companions, and how the closing of the Academy of St. Luke had made it impossible to make a living.

When sunlight stole into the room, he saw her bruises. "What is this?" He smoothed the smudges with gentle hands. "Did I hurt you?"

She sat up. "It wasn't you."

When she finished her story, he said, "You are never to see that man again. From now on, I will take care of you."

She was about to say, "I don't need you to take care of me," but stopped herself. The words were automatic, but they were a lie. After all this time, she owed him honesty. "I have always wanted to support myself doing what I love. But right now, I do need help."

"If we were married, you could live here with me."

Her heart dropped. "I'm already married." For a few glorious hours, she had forgotten that.

The reality of their situation sank in.

"Perhaps you could be my housekeeper."

She wanted to cry. To stay in Paris, would she have to reduce herself to a euphemism? "I can't live with you or come and go as your housekeeper. What few friends I do have would close their doors to me. My father would disown me." Wrapping herself in the bedsheet, she thought about it some more. "And I can't get pregnant."

"There are ways to prevent that."

She shook her head. "I need to be able to work, or I must go to my father's."

"Now that I have found you, you are not going anywhere." He pulled her back to him on the bed.

"May I remind you, sir, that I found you."

They laughed, but an edge of sadness crept into their voices.

"We will find a way," François told her. "You are no longer alone."

When the mantle clock chimed eight, he buried his face into her chest. "I have students to teach, but I could stay here forever."

She nodded. She had waited a lifetime to feel the silk of his hair between her fingers.

The sun lathed them in pale lemon light while they tarried in the stillness. When the quarter hour chimed, François groaned, rolled over, and framed her face in his hands. "Be my student. That way we can see each other every day. We'll find a way to pay your rent, but we have to be together."

The next day, she brought a collection of her art to François's atelier. "Your work is as good as anyone trying to join the Royal Academy," he said, "but they will never accept miniatures, and they do not favor pastels."

"But Rosalba Carriera worked in pastel. Quentin de La Tour as well."

"The Academy envied de la Tour's success and despises pastels because of him. For the Academy to accept a woman, her work must be spectacular."

"What do I have to do?"

His voice quickened with excitement. "You must work in oils. You must paint live models, and you must show your ability to teach through your paintings. Expect to work hard."

Her hands tingled. "I'll do everything you ask."

"Your training will be rigorous," he warned.

"You know I relish a challenge."

"Even then, you may not make it."

"I don't want special treatment. I just want to earn my place."

On the way home from François's, she walked along the Seine, watching the flat boats move out on a sluggish tide. A tendril of hair escaped to tickle her cheek. She pushed it back into her bonnet, thinking of the question François had asked before she left. "Who do you love more—me or art?" She had kissed him, saying, one was a person, the other a thing. They did not equate. Once more, she had evaded a question of his. She loved him, but to love art was to love herself. Somehow, her love for him was bound up in her love of art and her girlish dreams of the future. But what of her dreams today, her love today?

Movement on the water caught her eye. A spaniel ran back and forth on one of the barges, leaping around a boy as he reeled in a fish. The dog's tail gleamed in the sun, white against the silver of the fish, whose helpless flopping sprayed the dog with river water. His yaps echoed off the warehouses lining the quays, and Adélaïde laughed, short, joyous sounds that joined the dog's barks.

On such a day, nothing mattered but sun and water, a dog, a boy, a boat. What were dreams, unless you were the fish?

At the Roches', she went upstairs to unpack.

PART III
MASTERY

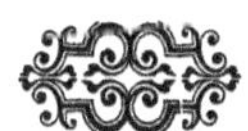

CHAPTER 14

1777–1778

Halcyon weeks passed in a joyous daze. By day, Adélaïde attended classes in François's studio where she learned the latest realistic techniques borrowed from antiquity. By night, she and François dined in cafés along the river. François introduced her to the men with whom he had studied in Vien's studio, agréés like himself.

One of his closest friends was Joseph-Benoit Suvée, a tall, spare Belgian who refused to powder his brown hair or wear it in a queue. He had won the Prix-de-Rome three years after François. Now back from Rome, he and François spent their evenings with Adélaïde, discussing their plans to enter the Royal Academy.

"Strategy is everything," Joseph claimed one night as the three of them dined on roasted quail at a café along Rue de St. Honoré. At thirty-four, Joseph's engrossing concern was how long his entrance would take. "Given the additional years it took to win the Prix-de-Rome, I'm hoping that the quality and maturity of the pieces I sent back from Rome will get the Academy to admit me quickly now."

François worried that his religion would impede his entrance.

"They'll be forced to accept you based on your talent in the end," Joseph said.

"We just have to wait, but it will happen," François said, and Joseph agreed.

For Adélaïde, however, there was no such assurance.

"Your art must be technically perfect," François said.

"And you have to be above reproach," Joseph said.

"Oh, I am," Adélaïde said. For decorum's sake, when the male students painted live nudes in the studio, Adélaïde went out in the corridor, instead sketching the nudes in the paintings hung along the walls.

"It still may not happen," Joseph warned.

"I know," she said, but did not want to believe it.

One night François presented her with a sepia sketch. He had drawn them as teenagers sitting in his father's studio, their chairs side by side as the two of them looked over a sketch François was drawing. In the sketch, their heads were pressed together as though he whispered secrets in her ear, while the paper Adélaïde tucked her arm into the crook of his elbow.

"This never happened," the real Adélaïde said.

"I know." His quirky smile appeared. "But I always wished it had. I was too shy to tell you how I felt about you, and you never paid any attention to me. Look, see how your eyes turn away. You never saw me." The desire François could never express in words was plain on his imaged face. They looked so young in the drawing.

"I noticed you all the time," she said.

It killed her to be married to someone else.

One evening, Adélaïde and François met for coffee. As the theaters had not let out, they were the only patrons in the café. "Everyone says you must teach," François said. "That's how academicians and agréés make their money."

"Not by selling their work?"

"Not really. As members of the Royal Academy, we work for the state, which frowns on commercial activity. We all must make money, and when we can sell our work, we are happy, but income from teaching is steady and reliable."

"I would need capital to open a studio."

"Can your father help?"

"My father gave everything for my dowry." Even saying it upset her.

"You must get it back."

"I've tried." Her heartbeat quickened. "But Nicolas said he would kill me if I came again."

"Then you must file for a legal separation."

"My father advised the same. But I'm not sure I can endure the scandal." She had consulted an attorney about it. "Extreme physical abuse perpetrated by the husband or adultery on the wife's part are the only permissible grounds for separation, and I am not going to engage in a public affair."

"Even though you're engaging in a private one?" He smiled.

"Broken ribs might be easier." She pushed her coffee cup and saucer away.

"I will not let him hurt you again. Do you not have witnesses to the abuse?"

"If they would speak." She buried her head in her arms on the table. "It's not right that I should have to go through this."

"In all the time I have known you, you have never hidden from anything or backed away from a fight. How can you let him get away with this?"

"I know it's not right." Her voice was muffled. "And he has gotten away with it for years." A spark of anger flickered inside.

"The law is bigger than he is, Adélaïde."

"The law, maybe. But society . . ." Her voice trailed off. "People will never accept me."

"I accept you." He took her hand. "All our friends accept you, you know that."

In the kitchen, the cook banged a pot, and the waiter laughed. She tried to picture a studio, but then thought of what she would have to go through. Her ribs hurt with remembered pain, and she could not breathe. She raised her head. "I don't know if I could survive the ordeal."

"Adélaïde, I will stand with you. He cannot hurt you anymore." The intensity of his promise blazed in his dark hazel eyes. He took her other hand. "We all will help you."

She considered. How would it be to have friends helping her? Would it make the difference? Her heartbeat steadied. "He should not get away with this," she said at last. "But I can't confront him on my own."

He squeezed her hands and called the waiter for a round of ale.

Adélaïde bent down and pulled a sketchbook from the bag at her feet. "Let's design my studio then," she said. "I'm going to need something good to hold on to."

CHAPTER 15

SUMMER 1779

I t took two years to get Nicolas into court.

"You are lucky that the archbishop is aged and does not attend to matters the way he used to. In his prime, he would have denied your petition outright." Monsieur Roche, spare as his wife was round, handed Adélaïde into the family coach. "I wish you Godspeed," he said in a tone that implied she would need it.

Her throat constricted, Adélaïde said nothing as she relinquished her landlord's hand.

In the privacy of the coach, sheltered by its closed curtains, her tensed body twanged at every jolt, every cobblestone as the horses set off. She appreciated her landlord's offer to transport her to ecclesiastical court but did not need to hear his doubts. She had enough of her own. Would the men who represented God grant her petition? For the past two years, she had told herself that she had to take that risk or live on the charity of others for the rest of her life. The effort had taken its toll. She was thirty years old, but this morning had found two gray threads snaking their way through her hair.

An hour later, she paced a musty anteroom outside a courtroom in the Ville L'Évèque, steeling herself for the ordeal ahead.

"Madame, please be seated," her attorney, a man with a powdered wig and sober clothing, gestured to the lone chair in the room.

The chair, tatty black velvet, crouched like a spider on spindly legs. She shook her head. If she sat down, she did not think she could stand up again. "Did my witnesses come?" she asked, thinking of the people in Nicolas's apartment building the day he beat her.

"Yes, and your husband as well," the attorney said. "The trial will proceed."

She blew out a breath, not knowing whether to be relieved or terrified. The trial would take the form of an inquisition. A college of at least three judges would question her. Because church law presumed the defendant innocent, a majority of those judges would have to agree that she had overcome that presumption for her to obtain a formal separation. Many women could endure neither the questioning nor the resulting damage to their reputation.

"Try not to look so nervous, madame. Remember, ask no questions, respond only when I instruct you to, volunteer nothing."

She was shaking inside but managed a nod.

When the knock came, her heart floundered like a hare in a trap. She stumbled, righted herself, then entered the courtroom behind her attorney.

For a moment, harsh light from clear paned windows blinded her. The small room was full of men dressed in clerical robes. Three black-robed doctors of canonical law, her judges, sat behind a long table at the front of the room. Distinguished by his mitered cap, the elderly *officialis* occupied the middle seat. To the left, two more church officials stood and talked as they examined papers on a lectern. She surmised that one was the promoter of justice, who would represent the interests of the Church, the other the defender of the bond of marriage. On the right, closest to her, a notary sat at a table covered with ledgers, sheaves of paper, quills, and ink bottles. In the back of the room, two tables waited, large enough to accommodate two chairs apiece, one for her and her representative, the other for her husband and his. Nicolas already stood at his table, a watery look in the bottom of his eyes. He and his advocate also wore ecclesiastical robes. All the men in the room, including her court-provided attorney, were men of the Church.

And ten of them are against me.

Her gaze fell on the void in the middle of the room and her legs lost their strength. In that five-by-five-foot space, she would stand while the judges interrogated her. She could at least be grateful that the benches along the wall for bystanders and supporters were empty.

She forced herself to stay upright.

"What business comes before us?" boomed the officialis. His strong voice belied his wizened appearance.

"A marital case," said the defender of justice, censorious.

The officialis peered at Adélaïde and Nicolas with prurient curiosity. "A case of sexual assault, you said?"

"No, your honor," her attorney said. "A summary case for marital separation."

The officialis looked disappointed. He sat back and waited for the notary to speak.

"Madame Guiard has petitioned for a separation from her spouse, Nicolas Guiard, for the return of her marital property, and any property she has acquired during the marriage through her own efforts," the notary intoned as he recorded the information on a large sheet of paper. "Nicolas Guiard has counter-petitioned, demanding any and all wages Madame Guiard has earned over the past ten years, as is his lawful right."

Adélaïde tried to keep all expression from her face.

"A summary case?" The judge on the right, a jowly man with eyes that protruded beneath heavy lids, leaned forward. "Are the witnesses assembled?"

"Yes, your honor," her attorney replied. Had her witnesses not appeared, her attorney would have had to force them to court, a lengthy and public process that could drag the proceedings on for months. With her witnesses here, a summary trial could be over in a day or two.

"Madame Guiard maintains that the couple has lived apart for years and that she is destitute. She requires the return of her property to support herself."

The defender of the bond spoke. "Madame Guiard would not find herself destitute if she would but return to her husband and allow him to support her as provided for under the law of our Lord."

"Madame Guiard maintains that her husband did not support her when they lived together, nor did he allow her to support herself."

"Madame Guiard should return to her husband and should not

complain about the way her husband chooses to support her as provided for under the law of our Lord."

The legal repartee made her dizzy.

"Madame Guiard maintains that her husband is extremely violent. She is unable to live with him."

Nicolas Guiard shook his head. "She's lying," he ground out.

"Quiet, monsieur. Madame, do you have proof of this?" the judge on the left asked. He was a thin man with a narrow, hard-edged face and stern demeanor.

"Let us first determine the validity of the marriage," interrupted the judge on the right.

The promoter of justice spoke next. "That will not be necessary. The Bishop of St. Eustache has indicated he himself married them."

"The Bishop of St. Eustache?" the thin judge asked. "Why then has she come to our court?"

The promoter of justice spoke in Latin and the three judges sat back in their chairs, disapproval on their faces.

Adélaïde looked at her attorney, who mouthed, *do not speak.*

"We must still examine the validity of the marriage," the judge on the right insisted. "Madame, how long did you live with your husband?" He motioned for her to come to the center of the room. His bulging eyes inspected her from head to toe, then the right side of his mouth made a tiny sneer, as though he had judged and found her wanting.

From the witness stand, she answered the question.

"Madame, did you have conjugal relations with your husband?" he pressed.

Her face burned. She looked at her attorney, who nodded. "Yes, your honor."

"How often?"

"What?" She could not believe what he had just asked. Now they were all staring at her. Prickles broke across her body.

"How many times a week, madame?" The officialis leaned forward in his seat.

She looked at her attorney again, who nodded. "Every time he . . . asked," she whispered.

"Speak up." The officialis cupped his hand around his ear.

The judge on the right turned to her husband. "Do you dispute this?"

"No. However, she was having an affair," Nicolas accused. "How could I engage in marital relations with her? How would I know if any offspring she produced were mine?"

The room darkened around her, and she thought she would faint. Her eyes burned as she stared at her attorney. How could he have let this happen? He had promised not to destroy her reputation.

Again, his look silenced her.

"An affair?" the officialis asked. "With whom?"

"The son of her old art instructor, François-André Vincent," Nicolas burst out.

A roaring sounded in her ears.

"Do you have proof?" the officialis asked.

"No, but I heard rumors."

"Madame, at the time of your marriage, what was your relationship with this Monsieur Vincent?" She saw that the officialis was enjoying his interrogation.

"There–there wasn't any," she stammered. "From the time he went to the College des Élèves Protegés in 1768 until I met him again in 1777, I had no contact with him."

"Were you a virgin when you married?" the officialis asked.

Heat burned through her body, and she felt like a hunted animal with the hounds upon her.

"You must answer the question," the judge on the left said.

"Sir, I am a woman of honor." Her voice shook.

"That's no answer," he told her.

"Yes," she said, agonized.

Appearing disgusted by the proceedings, the judge on the left motioned for her to sit down.

Her attorney stepped forward. "If it please the court, we will call our witnesses now." He first called Chevalier Alexandré Roslin, widower of Madame Roslin, who testified as to how his wife had found her bruised and destitute, and how his wife had helped her find employment and housing.

Her attorney next called Madame Roche, who testified to Adélaïde's four broken ribs from the beating Nicolas had given her two years before. Adélaïde was mortified. She had not authorized her attorney to call these people.

"Your honors, these individuals, though illustrious, are not direct witnesses to abuse," Nicolas's attorney objected.

Her attorney then called one of the occupants of Nicolas Guiard's building in the Marais, who stated that she had come out on the landing when she heard a commotion and heard Monsieur Guiard say that he would kill his wife if she returned.

"How did you know that it was his wife?" asked the officialis.

"I didn't, sir. I had never seen her before."

"Then how do you know that it was this woman?" the judge on the right asked.

"I looked over the railing and saw her." She pointed at Adélaïde.

Nicolas's attorney again objected, saying that it was impossible in the darkness of the building.

"But we do know it was possible," her attorney said, and called another woman to the stand. "Occupation?" he asked.

"Baker, sir," she said.

"How do you know this woman?" her attorney asked.

"One night, I passed her on the stairs, on my way home from work," she said. "She seemed ill. By the light of my candle, I saw that her dress was torn."

Lastly, he called the building's watchman, who confirmed that he had seen Adélaïde enter and leave the premises in short order, appearing injured when she left.

"When I asked people in the building what had happened, they told me Monsieur Guiard had beaten her," he said.

"And you did nothing?" asked the first judge.

"What was there to do?" asked the watchman. "She was his wife, sir."

"If it please the court," her attorney said, "we wish to call our last witness." A man dressed in ermine striped robes and wearing a mortarboard stepped forward. He identified himself as the dean of the College des Élèves Protegés.

"What is your role in this case?" asked the officialis.

"He will respond to the rumor charge, your honor," said her attorney. "Sir," he asked the dean after the notary had sworn him in, "how do you know François-André Vincent?"

"He was a student at the College who conducted himself with

distinction and discretion," the man responded. "He had won the Prix-de-Rome and came to study with us before he went to Italy."

"Can you please provide me with Monsieur Vincent's attendance and dormitory records and the letter of passage for his journey to Rome?" her attorney asked.

The dean presented the records, and her attorney commented that it was most unusual for a student to fully comply with the rules that they not leave the university grounds. The dean agreed, saying that Monsieur Vincent had won an award for his exemplary attendance.

"Your honors, as you can see, this claim of adultery is without merit," her attorney said.

Looking disappointed, the officialis told Nicolas that his allegations contravened the facts and asked if he would swear an oath to them.

Nicolas conferred with his attorney. Shuffling his feet, her husband said, "No, your honor, I will defer to the oath of the petitioner."

Adélaïde understood then that her attorney had known about this issue and devised a way to address it without involving her. A wave of relief swept through her.

"You have requested a formal separation, madame?" the officialis asked.

"Yes, your honor."

"On what grounds?" asked the judge on the right.

"He–he has beaten me many times and threatened to kill me."

"Church law allows for separation only in extreme cases of spousal abuse," the promoter of justice said. "A few broken bones hardly satisfies the requirement."

"Why did you visit him that night?" asked the defender of the bond. "If you were as fearful as you say, why did you not just stay away from him?"

"I had no money, and no food, and my rent was due. I went to ask him to return my dowry."

"You are not asking for a divorce," said the judge on the left. "Why then are you asking for the return of your dowry?"

"In the settlement agreement my father drew up, any separation that lasted more than six months required the return of my property for my support," she said. "It has been almost ten years."

The officialis took her marriage documents from the attorney, then called a recess for the judges to consider the matter.

Back in the anteroom, Adélaïde collapsed onto the chair. She opened her mouth to beg the attorney to stop the proceedings, but he put up his hand.

"Don't say a word," he said. He opened the door and asked someone in the hall to bring her a glass of water.

An hour later, both she and Nicolas returned to the courtroom for the judgment. This time, no amount of fabric could hide her trembling.

"Neither Madame Guiard nor her husband are Protestants, or Jews, and we accept the testimony as to their proper baptism," the officialis read from the ruling with a magnifying glass. "We therefore find the marriage valid. We also find that the marriage was consummated, there being no grounds for annulment. We find no merit to the defendant's claim of adultery on the part of his wife." He set the ruling down on the table. "Turning now to the petitioner's request, the law provides for separation in cases of extreme violence. Gentlemen, I find that the petitioner has cause to fear for her life."

"I too find that the petitioner has just cause," the judge on the left said. For the first time, Adélaïde saw a softening in the man's demeanor.

The face of the judge on the right sagged with disapproval. "I do not believe that the grounds are sufficient for a legal separation. However, I have reviewed the marriage settlement, and I find that both parties agreed that even in the case of a physical rather than a legal separation, settlement property was to be returned."

Adélaïde stifled her exclamation. She had prevailed. All her being wanted to cry out with gratitude, but her attorney had warned her not to display any emotion. A wave of intense relief swept through her, and she felt herself falling. Her attorney grasped her arm and held her up. Her blood pulsed so hard in her ears that she almost missed the officialis order the notary to enter the separation into the record, but she heard him restore her property to her and deny Nicolas's counter petition.

As they prepared to leave the courtroom, the thin judge addressed her husband. "Monsieur Guiard, see that you return Madame Guiard's property without further delay. Had you done your duty, we could have avoided this process. Instead, you have brought scandal on yourself and reproach to the Church. It begs the question of why a man like you is treasurer for St. Eustache."

Bitter hatred flashed in Nicolas's eyes. As she returned to the anteroom, she saw his clenched fists and a familiar fear rose into her throat. She took an involuntary step closer to her attorney.

While they waited for the notary to draft a copy of the ruling, her attorney regarded her with admiration. "You are a strong woman, Madame Guiard."

"No," she said, raising a hand to hide her trembling lips. "Just a desperate one."

CHAPTER 16

FALL 1779

Adélaïde stepped into the early morning quiet of François's studio. She lingered in the shadows by the door, observing the circle of light that fell on François's head, the sure and steady way he moved a brush across canvas, the strength of his forearms beneath his rolled-up shirtsleeves. Beside him, two of his students loaded palettes with paint, speaking in low tones. A faint scent of rain drifted through the double-hung windows at the far side of the room, open at the top to let fresh air in, chase the aromas of turpentine and linseed oil out.

She would miss this spare and humble place, miss watching François work, miss the pleasure of learning from him. Just miss him, she thought, her chest growing tight. Tomorrow she would open her new studio and everything would change.

Sensing her presence, François looked up. "You are here early." He put down his paintbrush and came toward her, his smile widening. "What a pleasant surprise."

Taking a deep breath, she handed him a bank draft, written in her father's hand.

He frowned when he read the scrawled words.

"My tuition, paid in full," she said.

"This is not necessary." He held the cheque out.

"For me, it is," she said, stepping aside.

"No, really, it is not," he insisted.

"Please, let's talk out in the corridor." She glanced toward his students who had stopped talking and turned toward them.

"I never intended to charge you for lessons," he said after he had closed the door behind them.

"I can't accept charity," she said.

He stared at her. "Is that what you thought it was?"

"Without your help, I would have been homeless. I would have starved."

He looked away, his jaw working. "I did this so we could be together. It was never charity."

"Please, François. I must pay you." Her heart sped up.

"Well, I will not accept it. In the first place, this is far more than the tuition I charge, and in the second, I will not take money from your father. That feels like charity, which your family was always extending to us, by the way."

"It includes the rent you've paid on my behalf for the last two years, and it's not my father's money, it's my dowry. I just could not find a bank to cash it for me."

"And that is supposed to make me feel better? I am not going to take money from you."

"Please, François, listen to me," she said, glancing around. She hated standing out in the hallway arguing with him, but she had to make him understand. "For the sake of my honor, you must."

"Enlighten me." He folded his arms and leaned against the door.

She sighed. "Living apart from my husband and trying to accomplish anything has been difficult enough." He looked unmoved, so she tried again. "If people believe that I'm a kept woman, my new studio will fail."

"Being together, however we could, was important to me, not what other people thought."

"Our circle of artist friends may not mind, nor my theater clientele, but parents won't entrust their daughters to my care if any scandal is attached to my name. Now that I have my dowry back, I must pay my debts."

He studied his boots for a moment. "I just do not want you to waste your dowry," he finally said. "You are going to need it."

"You encouraged me to do this, François. It's taken me two years to get this far."

Her landlords, who had become like family to her during that time, had never asked where her rent money came from but thought her new venture mad. This morning, Madame Roche had told Adélaïde that she would always have a home with them.

It was one thing for the Roches to doubt her, but for François to say such a thing hurt in the pit of her stomach. "You think I'll fail?"

He closed his eyes. "Of course, I do not think that. But you should use your money for the expenses of your studio."

"I know how to manage my funds," she ground out.

He saw the look on her face, then threw up his hands in surrender. "I never won a debate with you when we were in my father's studio." He gave her a lopsided grin. "I am not going to try now." He tucked the check in his vest pocket. "I just do not want you to go."

"I know," she said, her voice less defiant. "But I open my studio to students tomorrow."

"So this is your last day?"

She nodded.

"What will this mean for us?"

"We are still us," she said, wishing it true. "I'm not going far, but I have to make my own way."

She moved down the long corridor, trying not to think that this could be the last time she would walk this familiar hallway, trying to forget the image of François standing in his doorway, arms at his sides, looking bereft. He will be fine, she assured herself.

She may have presented a brave face to François, an even braver one to the bankers who sneered at her plans, but if she did not get enough students to pay her expenses, she would be back where she started. Only worse, because she would have thrown away her mother's hard work and ruined her father's hopes. If that happened, she would have to go back to François, not in love but in desperation. If that happened, she would hate herself.

The next morning, Adélaïde stood in her new studio, a half-eaten baguette and a hunk of cheese crusting on the table next to her. Yesterday's rain chased away, yellow light filled the room. Easels bearing blank canvases formed an inviting arc in the middle of the space. Her new license from the Châtelet, permitting her to carry on the business of teaching art, graced a black wooden frame that hung among the oil paintings she had completed in François's studio. On such a bright, happy day, she refused to dwell on the irony that it was acceptable for a woman to teach another woman how to paint, but not for a woman to work as an artist.

Nerves, go away, she admonished herself.

Walking on feet as light as a dancer's, she circled the room, rearranged the empty wine bottles, battered hand baskets, and decorative vases on the high shelf, and aligned sketchpads and pencil jars on the worktables. She opened the back cupboard, a place of wonder, its boxes of pastels and pots of gouache color formed into a rainbow. She went to the stairs, walked up two steps, and turned and surveyed the scene before letting out a sigh of relief. Her studio might be small, the decor not as fancy as À La Toilette, but it was more attractive than any studio in the Louvre.

It had to be. In the time that it had taken her to win her lawsuit and ready her studio, Joseph Suvée had begun to offer classes for women in his studio at the Louvre. "I thought you were my friend," she had confronted him. "It's not as though I can offer classes to boys or men."

"Perhaps I'll find a winning student like you to show off my teaching skills," he had laughed, undeterred. "To gain acclaim as an instructor, your students must be good before they arrive at your doorstep."

"But how can I compete with an Academy member?"

"Oh, don't worry, Adélaïde. There are plenty of parents wanting to spend money on art lessons for their daughters. Besides, the more female students we have at the Louvre, the more Academy members will believe that females belong in the Royal Academy, so think of this as my way to support you."

"I hope you're right," she had said, not mollified.

Down the street, clock bells rang. She tossed back her cold coffee, put her dishes in the pantry closet, then hurried back into the room. When she had first seen the bay window fronting the street, she had known this was the place for her. At the last stroke of nine, she raised the wooden window shades, walked to the door, and turned the sign from *Closed* to *Open*. Then she sat down at the easel in the window and began to paint.

~

It was mid-afternoon before her first potential student walked through the door. Cheekbones protruding from a pale face, her brown hair pulled back beneath a maid's cap, the girl wore an undyed muslin apron over a patched black dress that had faded to gray from many washings. A *mercier's* daughter learned from the womb to assess wealth at first sight. This girl could not afford her fees. Stifling her disappointment, Adélaïde watched the girl wander the room, a rolled sketch in her slim hands.

The girl's expression revealed nothing, but her gaze paused on the pastels from Maison Macle. She came to the window and introduced herself as Marie Capet, telling Adélaïde she was eighteen years old and looking for advanced art lessons.

Recalling Joseph's comment about talented students, Adélaïde asked about her experience.

"I–I believe I have some talent, miss. I took lessons along with the master's children in the house where my mother worked as a housekeeper." Marie unrolled the parchment and revealed a sepia head sketched in profile.

Adélaïde assessed the proportions, the shading, the lifelike representation of a woman who bore a resemblance to the girl in front of her. Hope stirred. She retrieved a sketchbook and a pencil jar from one of the worktables and handed the supplies to Marie. "You have fifteen minutes to draw my face."

Adélaïde sat down in her mother's chair beyond the easel in the window and motioned for Marie to sit in the chair she had vacated.

Before Marie began, she looked at Adélaïde. "My mother saved for my lessons," she said.

Thoughts of her own mother assailed Adélaïde as she caressed the chair's dark green velvet. Without seeing, she stared into the street. Then it was as though she heard her mother's voice urging her to look up. Marie sat in the artist's chair across from her, her face serious, her mouth pursed as she drew. Out in the street, a crowd had formed as people stopped to watch them in the window. "That's the way," she heard her mother's voice say.

"This is excellent," Adélaïde said a quarter hour later. Joy bubbled up. She grinned. "I accept you as my first student."

Marie's face broke into a wide smile. Then she looked around the small studio again. "Will I be able to live in?" she asked. "I saw that you advertised Academy-style teaching, and I know that Academy students live there with their instructors."

Adélaïde had not anticipated this question, having planned for bourgeois students who came to while away the afternoons painting. "I'm sorry, but I don't have the space for that."

The reserve on Marie's face cracked, and Adélaïde saw an emotion beyond disappointment. "I have been staying with my mother, but as I do not have a position in the household, I cannot live there. I have to find an option that allows me to live in."

Adélaïde grew afraid as her first student, a girl with uncommon talent, walked to the door. She had waited for hours for a student—any student—and had nothing to show for her efforts. She might wait a week or a year and never see such talent again. Worse, she might wait another day or week with no student at all. Then where would she be?

As Marie's slim hand turned the bronze doorknob, Adélaïde said, "I have a room upstairs. Perhaps we can find a corner for you up there."

Marie sagged against the door, her hands fisting at her sides. Tears gathered on her eye lashes.

"What's wrong?" Adélaïde guided Marie to the closest chair.

"My mother is dead. I have nowhere to go." Marie wiped her eyes. "My mother was an artist in the Academy of St. Luke. When the guild closed, she took a position as a housekeeper to support the two of us. She earned extra money teaching art lessons to the children of the household. But now," she took a breath, "I have nowhere to go. The funds I have for art lessons are the funds I made selling the last of my mother's paintings." Marie's stomach growled, and she let out a shaky laugh.

Adélaïde went to the pantry and brought back the apple and cheese she had intended for her own lunch. Marie ate without saying a word, but color returned to her face.

After Adélaïde closed her studio that afternoon, she and Marie purchased a used screen from the rag pickers outside the vegetable markets. They hired a street boy to deliver the screen and dragged it upstairs where they cleaned it by candlelight.

A sparkle entered Marie's brown eyes as they scrubbed away layers of dirt and revealed risqué love scenes. "I'll have to paint flowers over that, or at the very least, fig leaves." She laughed. They blocked off a triangle of the bedroom with the screen and set up a pallet behind it.

That night, Adélaïde lay in the darkness listening to the soft breathing of a stranger sleeping close by. What if she had not yielded to the impulse to let Marie stay? Would this girl have said nothing and left, homeless and friendless? Adélaïde shuddered, knowing that if she had been in Marie's place, the answer might have been yes. How many other Maries were out there? Once her former mentor, Quentin de La Tour, had closed his charity school for female artists, none had opened in its place. But what could she do? She was still struggling not to be a charity case herself.

Sleep called. As her thoughts drifted away, she was glad that at least this young woman would not have to spend the night on the street, guarding her small hoard of cash until the morning.

Within two weeks, Adélaïde had acquired a dozen talented students. Marie-Justine de Beaumont, an aristocratic young woman whose beauty, thick dark locks, and deep blue eyes caused men to stop in the street and stare at her through the bay window, wanted to paint in oil. Jeanne Bernard, a bourgeois student, wanted to sketch. Last to come was Isabelle d'Avril, another artist's daughter without a place to live. She offered to serve as Adélaïde's housekeeper in exchange for lodgings.

"I have nowhere to go," she said. "My mother exhibited at Pahin de La Blancherie's salon before she died and taught me everything I know. It was her dream for me to continue painting, but I cannot find work as an artist, so I have been looking for work as a housemaid."

The girl was too young to be a housekeeper, but Adélaïde, who had not realized how much straightening a studio required each day, accepted her offer. "I can't afford to pay you yet, but you can stay and continue your lessons."

"Then I will serve as your painting assistant," Marie Capet said. She had welcomed the students who followed her and organized their workspaces as though she had worked in Adélaïde's studio for years. Marie and Isabelle giggled as they marked off another corner of Adélaïde's bedroom and built a wall out of piled wooden crates.

The studio rang with feminine laughter and the jingle of bells at all hours as visitors came through the studio to observe the women at work. Justine sang as she painted, her contralto voice rich and lusty, her repertoire of folk songs endless. Charcoal drawings of heads and figures joined wet portraits lining the walls. Out in the street, people stopped to watch them work and to listen to Justine through the open windows.

"I could barely get through the crowd," François said one day when he made it into her studio.

"Isn't it fun?" Adélaïde leaned against him, reveling in the warmth that radiated from his body.

"I came to see how your painting is coming along." He looked around. "Where is it?"

"Well, it's hardly one I can display here," she said. "Besides, I'm still planning it."

"You haven't started?"

"Not yet." Demonstrating that she was a master—or mistress—of the nude figure was a challenge she had toiled over for weeks. A female artist actually painting a full nude would have caused a furor, so how to paint one without painting one was a puzzle she had yet to solve.

"You have to do it, Adélaïde. You may have built a successful studio, but without this last painting, the Academy will never accept you."

"It's not as if I'm not trying," she muttered under her breath, stabbing her pencil into the sketchpad propped on the easel in front of her. She could not ask her students to pose for her nude—imagine what their parents would have to say to that? For the same reason, she could not have one of her live models pose nude.

Sitting on a hard wooden chair, drawing nudes in the corridor outside François's studio as young men walked behind her and peered over her shoulder, made her feel naked herself. François had brought some sketches of Monsieur Boucher's for her to copy and tacked them to the wall in front of her.

Why do I have to focus on a woman's hindquarters, or some female posed in an impossible position? she asked herself. *I cannot paint a woman from this mortifying angle and display it for all to see. What would people say?*

A man harrumphed as he passed. She jerked in surprise. The tip of her pencil broke, but not before tearing into the sketch she had spent the last hour creating. Stifling an oath, she pulled a small knife out of her bag and dug the blade into the pencil shaft, wishing it were the flesh of the man who had just disdained her, or better yet, the flesh of the fat buttock of the woman in the painting. No woman she knew looked like that. They were all too thin trying to survive.

Back in her empty studio that night, she examined the drawings she had produced earlier in the day. What had François said when she left his studio?

"Not original enough."

Of course they weren't, they were copies of Boucher's nudes, and no matter what she did to them to make them hers in a painting, everyone would recognize that. She tore the pages out of the sketchbook and shoved them into the stove, listening to the satisfying whoosh of flame as the pages caught fire.

Out in the street, a clock struck one. Releasing a pent-up breath, she put her blank canvas away. She was getting nowhere, and she had classes to teach in the morning. She tiptoed up the stairs, feeling her way in the dark. In the bedroom, between the quiet breathing of Marie and Isabelle, she undressed and slipped into bed. Sleepless, her eyes adjusted, saw the tenebrous form of the screen to her left, the crates to her right. She could not even pose nude for herself before her own bedroom mirror. She rolled over and buried her head in the pillow.

Outside, the city clock struck two. In her mind's eye, the clock hands moved apart, tick by tick, each minute pulling her away from all that she wanted. But then she imagined the pendulum swinging, from what she wanted, to what she wanted.

In the end, she painted herself. Her nude was neither historical nor allegorical, but a *tête d'expression* transformed. It was the head of a young woman, her gaze turned toward a lover outside the painting's view. The woman appeared nude, her upper body wrapped in a sheet, her breasts exposed, her face a flushed reflection of sexual awakening. Rendered in shades of pink, orange, and crimson pastel, *Delightful Surprise* caught the afterglow of a sexual experience.

It was Adélaïde's statement that nudity implied was more daring than nudity exposed, her certification that she could paint a traditional concept in an original manner, her declaration of freedom from the mores and strictures of feminine propriety and modesty in painting.

It was also her gift to François, a testament to their burgeoning love.

CHAPTER 17

AUGUST 1781

The Royal Academy's biennial Salon arrived. To celebrate their fourth anniversary together, Adélaïde and François closed their studios at noon and set off for the Louvre. After the heat of a summer day outside, it was cool and dark in the palace. Adélaïde pulled her scarf over her shoulders.

They craned their necks to view paintings hanging at ceiling level, crouched to peer at ones covering the baseboards, then entered the gallery where François's single submission dominated a wall. *The Battle Between the Romans and the Sabines Interrupted by the Sabine Women* caught the moment when the Sabine women entered the battlefield to save their husbands. At the center of the tableau, a mother with an infant in her arm thrust herself between a Roman soldier and a wounded Sabine. The victor stood with his foot planted on the chest of the fallen man, his club raised to kill him. The baby flailed across the conqueror's knee.

"Oh, François." She squeezed his arm. "I may have watched you work on this for the past two years, but to see it here takes my breath away. The colors, the emotion—I don't understand how anyone could call this painting cold."

"You may be partial," François said. Though he smiled, his eyes were dark with the memory of the leading critic's harsh words. "I suppose we cannot all win favor every time."

"Don't worry." Adélaïde knew he was concerned that the critic's review would further delay his entrance into the Academy. "Everyone says it's political and your time will come. Besides, criticism is a privilege, and usually, when the critics hate your work, the public flocks to see it." She turned away so he would not see the pain on her face. How she wanted the critics to see her own work.

They moved on and came across a gallery that held an entire section of paintings by former members of the Academy of St. Luke.

"At least you don't have to worry about competition from these artists, François. These agréés won't make it into the Academy before you." Despite the lump in her throat, she kept her voice light. "But how does my work compare to theirs?"

"You know your work is of a higher caliber, Adélaïde."

"Thank you." She sucked in a breath and pushed a lock of hair into her cap. "Right now, I need to hear it." Each familiar artist's name on a small white plaque was another stone on Adélaïde's mountain of evidence that her own career had gone nowhere.

In the next gallery, they encountered Marie, Isabelle, and Justine.

"Madame, did you know they have a student exhibition here?" Marie asked.

"No, I didn't."

"We just saw a painting by Laurent Dabos," Isabelle said. Laurent was a teenaged student studying under François.

"Several of my students have paintings on exhibit in the student gallery," François said.

The girls accompanied them as they examined the student paintings, one made by a boy as young as fifteen.

"When can we exhibit our work?" Justine asked.

"Yes, when?" Adélaïde asked François, who pretended to be interested in the folds of a velvet cape in a painting near the floor.

Adélaïde waited until she and François had left her students behind before demanding, "Why, François? I was one of your students too."

"The Academy would not allow it."

She hugged her arms across her chest, holding in the anger. "I've seen enough for today." She headed for the stairs.

On the ground floor, close to the exit, Adélaïde stopped to stare at a truly awful painting. "Is Jacques Louis David trying to copy you?" she asked when François caught up with her.

François glanced at the painting of *Belisarius Begging Alms.* "No, he's trying to outdo me." He grinned. "It was always this way in Vien's atelier. Whatever anyone did, David had to prove he could do it better."

"I do believe he failed. Look at that boy in the arms of Belisarius. He has the stature of a child but the muscled body of a soldier and the face of a young man." She would never forget her first sight of François's painting of the blind general, the way its serpentine lines had drawn her back to François.

"Monsieur David could not bear to paint anything that was not a specimen of perfect manhood," François chuckled. "And, if you are wondering, your work is better than his."

"I don't need anyone to tell me that." She tried to smile.

"I'll see you at the theater tonight," François said as they left the Louvre.

Back in her studio, Adélaïde went upstairs, shut the door, and sank down on the edge of her bed. Going to the theatre was the last thing she wanted. A bar of sunlight fell on the pamphlet on her dresser. She made no move to seek proof that a woman's work had once graced the Louvre. The brochure's binding had disintegrated, its pages too brittle to touch. Like her dreams. For so long, she had imagined her paintings hanging in the Louvre. How much longer would she have to wait? Teaching had been a satisfying and necessary distraction—she had to eat—but no one could assure her that her time would come.

She thought of François's Sabine women. What would she do to save her dying dream, to fight for the future of her work?

That evening, Joseph Suvée inserted himself into their anniversary celebration and joined them at the Comédie Française. After the show, they ordered dinner for four at a restaurant in the Palais Royale, then waited for LeKain to change out of his theatre clothes and join them. Out in the courtyard, beyond the covered gallery, lanterns glittered in the elm trees. Throngs of people passed beneath the sculpted trees, enjoying the palace gardens. Humid air coming through the open windows made her perspire and the tannins in the wine made her mouth pucker, so Joseph and François emptied the wine bottle between them while she sat fanning herself.

"If you're not going to drink the wine, at least enjoy the sunset." Joseph pointed to the rim of gold on the horizon.

"Another day gone." She did not look up. "Here's this young man, he works for a year, and his art is in the Salon. My students deserve this too, but how can I do anything for them when I can do nothing for myself? I've been waiting my turn for longer than he's been alive."

A disturbance at the entrance of the restaurant caught their attention. It was LeKain greeting restaurant patrons who called out to him as he made his way to their table. He sat down in the empty seat, smiled his huge smile, and ordered another bottle of wine. While they waited, the three men struck up a conversation about his play.

"Why the long face, madame?" LeKain leaned toward her. "Was I so terrible tonight you cannot speak to me?"

"You were wonderful, as usual, and you know it. LeKain, here's a question for you—why are women allowed to act in the theater but not to create art?"

"You know it wasn't always this way." He sat back with a grin. "We men grew tired of making love to other men on stage. The moustaches got in our way."

The men laughed.

"I'm being serious."

"We have to get her into the Academy," Joseph said. "She'll give us no peace until we do."

"How do male agréés do it?" she asked. "I'm not talking about the St. Luke ones, who were admitted with the payment of a huge fee and a sample of their work." The Academy had returned her own application with a letter stating they were not accepting women.

"The students take lessons from various professors and exhibit their works in the exhibition hall," François said. "That way everyone is familiar with their work, and they gather the necessary support for entrance."

LeKain, who was watching the door, exclaimed, "This is your lucky night, Madame Guiard. Look who walked in—Jean-François

Ducis. He just happens to live at the home of the Comte d'An-giviller. The comtesse, the former Baroness de Marchais, is his patroness. Now, she was a beauty in her day." He stood and called out in a theatrical voice, "Ducis, come over here. I have someone you will be delighted to meet." He turned and lowered his voice. "Here's your chance. Get him to give you an introduction to the comtesse. She supports women artists."

Ducis, a French dramatist who translated Shakespearean plays into French, approached their table. Adélaïde thought that he had the face of a lion and the body of a hippopotamus, animals she had once seen in the king's menagerie. Everyone stood to greet him. LeKain called for another chair.

"We are plotting to get Madame Guiard into the Royal Academy of Painting and Sculpture," LeKain told him.

Ducis listened with interest as they explained her problem. A gleam entered his eyes. "You need a grand strategy, a master plan of attack, and a patron at the highest level." He tapped out a drumbeat on the table with an unused fork. "You must approach this battle on all fronts, because you have a real general plotting against you, and for him, it is war." A grin appeared in his beard. "You've got to get his wife as your patroness." He laughed and rubbed his hands together. "And now, you have a spy in the enemy's house."

She opened her mouth to protest.

LeKain elbowed her in the ribs. "We accept your kind offer, sir," he told Ducis.

"But I don't know what we're accepting," she said.

The restaurant owner himself presented the covered dishes to his illustrious customers. While they ate, LeKain entertained the group with the story of how Adélaïde had stalked him in this very restaurant.

Joseph snapped his fingers. "I have it. Paint the Academy members for free. That way, they will get to know you and your work."

"Brilliant," LeKain said.

François agreed. "Many Academy members say women can only paint women, or still lifes, but that they cannot paint men. They don't believe they have the capability."

"They know nothing," Adélaïde snorted, then thought about it. "It's such a ridiculous idea, it might work. Who would I paint first?"

"How about our old teacher, Vien?" Joseph suggested. "In his heyday, he identified two great female artists—Madame Roslin and his own wife, both admitted to the Academy."

Madame Roslin's encouraging face came into her thoughts.

"Better to paint Vien after you have the support of the others," François advised.

"They would judge my work the same way as any other agréé?"

Joseph and François nodded.

"Then I'll do it. And prove them wrong."

On the day she painted the great teacher, Joseph Vien, Adélaïde felt like an actress performing in a packed theatre. Despite the fact that it was winter outside, and that she wore the lightest of the new cotton fabrics, sweat trickled beneath the linen scarf wrapped around her hair. Vien sat in her mother's chair in the center of her studio.

François, who had arranged the occasion, peered over her shoulder, his student, Laurent Dabos, beside him, pointing out features in her painting. She worried they would bump her arm and wished them away. Behind Vien, Joseph Pierre, the Academy's director, chatted with Chevalier Roslin. Monsieur Vien's current students, their cropped hair the new rage, wandered the room. They had come to observe the novelty of a woman painter and her female students.

Except for Marie, who sat next to Adélaïde holding her paints and brushes, the girls had forgotten their roles. From somewhere, Justine produced a guitar and strummed as she sang a ballad from *La Caravane du Caire,* as though she were entertaining guests in a Parisian salon. Isabelle floated around the room, flirting while the other girls passed out sweets. The young men did not know where to look first. People passed by in the street, turned, and came inside.

"If one more person comes in the front door, someone's going to fall out the back door," Adélaïde muttered to Marie as she placed a layer of paint on the canvas before her. She took a steadying breath and reminded herself that she had prepared for this performance. She had painted François, then several other Academy artists. Once she had painted a portrait of the famous royal sculptor, Antonin

Pajou, at work fashioning a bust of his teacher, her friends had judged that she was ready to tackle Joseph Vien, instructor to more Prix-de-Rome winners than anyone else in the history of the Academy.

"Your mastery of drapery, color, line, of living flesh and earthen clay has no equal," Antonin Pajou had said in his raspy voice as he admired the portrait she had painted of him. *Stop thinking about past work, or people in the room,* she told herself. *Focus on capturing Vien's soul.*

Vien was not going to make it easy. He sat with his back rigid, a frown on his forehead, lips pressed shut. Even sitting, he looked down his hawkish nose at her and challenged her abilities with a slight sneer. Across the space between them, his eyes seemed to ask, *What do you want from me? What will I have to do with you? Assuming you can produce what you have promised.*

She looked him in the eye. *I'll show you that I can.*

Behind her, François said something to his student. Vien's eyes shifted between her and François, and Adélaïde thought, *How ironic is it that François and I are both fighting for a place in the Academy now.*

CHAPTER 18

JUNE 1782

The Academy relented, and in the appointed time, and the appointed manner, François became a full Academy member. Across the Louvre's Apollo Gallery, morning light silvered the heads of spectators and Royal Academy members alike. In the crowd, Adélaïde sought François's familiar form. She found him at the center of the gallery, a head taller than the other inductees, his wild hair muzzled under wig and powder as he waited to take the oath of allegiance. The room palpitated with excitement. Floating above the light that streamed in from tall windows, the painted ceiling swirled with triumphant battle scenes. For the first time, she heard Director Pierre speak of the importance of art in society, its role to teach, to record, to cause reflection, to inspire. His voice echoed off the gallery arches and into her heart.

When François mounted the stage and raised his right hand, her chest filled with an emotion so big her lungs had no room to breathe. She was too far away to hear the words of the *Proces Verbaux* but mouthed the words in time to the solemn rumble of his voice, knowing he swore to observe the rules of the Academy, uphold its traditions, and honor France through his work for the rest of his life. The crowd clapped as the newest members of the Academy left the platform, but each time her gloved hands met, it was though something she had swallowed had lodged in her throat. What was wrong with her? If she loved him, how could she envy his success? She should only feel joy in his accomplishment. She should have been as relieved as he was when Joseph Vien finally moved to promote him. And she was, she assured herself, but in all the months since she had painted the great teacher, Vien had done nothing to help her. She did not know what to think.

That night, François lay against her breast while she played with his unruly locks, freed from the hated wig that lay like a gutted rodent at the edge of the bed.

"Success has been such a long journey, from Switzerland to France to Italy and back. People said I would not make it because I was not French, I was not Catholic, I was poor. I thought I would not make it."

Her hand grazed moisture on his stubbled cheek.

He gave a great sigh. "I wish my family could have seen it." His father was long gone, his brother still in Rome.

"Well, I saw it," she said, her fingers following the vertebrae ridges down his back. "That was the first time I heard someone talk about the mission of art—to teach, record history, inspire greatness. I never thought of it that way, but I see it now."

He shuddered. "In Vien's studio, that was all we heard. Let us not talk of it now."

She wanted to ask him if that was the power of art, if that was the need that impelled them to produce it. Instead, she let him pull her back into his arms.

A breeze stirred through the room. Then their bodies moved together beneath the open window, beneath the summer sky, and the pale crescent moon.

Afterward, she lay watching as dawn rimmed the darkness, thinking how she would do anything for her turn on that stage.

Which was why she found herself in Pahin de La Blancherie's cabinet of curiosities the next afternoon, perched on a knobby sofa, sipping coffee and nibbling madeleines. Pahin sat across from her drinking brandy and smoking a cigar. A square man with the features of a toad, he bore no family resemblance to any royal person who had visited À La Toilette.

Perhaps Ducis and LeKain were right, Adélaïde thought. LeKain had called him a huckster while Ducis insisted Pahin was a great actor.

"If he's an actor, then what am I?" LeKain had roared. "I challenge you to see if he knows how to play the part of a king."

She had to admit, when Pahin spoke, his gravelly voice sounded unlike any aristocrat she had met. But so far, his claim to descend from royalty had made him impervious to d'Angiviller's machinations, so here she was, negotiating to get her artwork into his exhibition.

"Three years ago, I opened a weekly exhibit of curiosities. It's so popular that I'm moving it to a larger venue this year and expanding the art exhibit. Having a woman artist such as yourself will draw Parisians in droves. You sell your work; I sell my curiosities."

"What else will be exhibited?" She eyed a preserved calf with two heads posed on a lacquered table. Next to it, a large jar held a pair of conjoined twins suspended in gray fluid and beyond that, an orange and white kitten with two pairs of hind legs floated in a blue glass jar. It was hard to imagine her art competing with such oddities.

He grinned. "I assure you, the exhibition is quite serious. Intellectuals will travel from across the world to give lectures and demonstrate the latest inventions."

"Which artists will be there?"

"All the current ones."

She knew this did not mean Royal Academy artists. "Any other female artists?"

"Madame Lebrun."

"But—" She winced. "I heard she was in Flanders."

"Ah, yes." He drew on his cigar. "Her husband's gambling debts. However, I already have her commitment. Don't you see? Having two female artists' works on display will make a splash."

She waved away a cloud of smoke while she considered.

He motioned to a sheaf of papers lying on the sofa table. "I will advertise the exhibit in my journal. People in Europe and the Americas, even the French colonies at the farthest ends of the oceans, will learn of your work."

She picked up his *News of the Republic of Letters* and leafed through it. "My father reads your newsletter."

Half an hour later, she left Pahin's mansion, pleased with herself.

She had agreed to give him thirty percent of her earnings, not the fifty percent he had demanded.

Back in her studio, excitement built as she cataloged her works. This would be her first exhibit in six years. Then, she had shown two paintings to Élisabeth Vigée Lebrun's twenty. If they were always to be pitted against each other, this time she would come prepared.

~

On the morning the exhibit opened, François burst into Adélaïde's drawing class, waving a newspaper. "Look at this. De La Blancherie has advertised that the two goddesses of modern painting will exhibit in his Salon de la Correspondence. You are Diana, the huntress of painting. Madame Lebrun, its Venus. Congratulations, goddess." He grinned.

Adélaïde snatched the paper from him. The girls left their seats to peer over her shoulder. "Under the ministrations of Madame Lebrun's paintbrush, roses bloom in her paintings," she read aloud. "They are sensuous, delightful in color, soft and feminine. Madame Guiard is Diana, goddess of the hunt. Her paintings show that she is strong, virile, ready with the lute, calling for battle and marching to victory." A trill of pleasure rushed through her.

That night, dressed in tight-fitting black taffeta shaped by a constricting corset and heavy panniers, Adélaïde displayed her paintings to thousands of Parisians. Waiters handed out glass after glass of sparkling wine that sloshed on everything and everyone as people moved through the crowded rooms. Stuffed lions and tigers fought for space on the marble floor, the dead twins joined other fetuses in bottles on glass shelves, and her art and Élisabeth Vigée Lebrun's paintings of the queen fought for space on a cloisonné styled wall.

She wondered how Madame Lebrun had come to paint the queen and was surprised to find that this did not upset her as much as it gave her hope. She just had to figure out how she too could paint a member of the royal family.

Pahin, more frog-like than ever in a dark green velvet coat and emerald leggings, pushed his way through the crowd, smiling, bowing, calling out to people he knew. When he saw Adélaïde, he stepped back, looked at the painting behind her, looked at her in full, then winked.

She laughed. Her bosom jiggled above the corset, and heat rushed into her face. When Pahin moved off, she stepped away and went to find the third woman's art on exhibit.

"Why are you exhibiting here?" Adélaïde shouted over the din when she came upon Anne Marie Vallayer-Coster, her plump body squeezed up against the wall next to her own paintings, fanning herself with one hand and clasping an empty coupe glass in the other. "You're a member of the Royal Academy. You don't need to exhibit in this spectacle."

"Good evening to you too," the artist smiled and presented her cheeks for the requisite kisses. "Everyone knows the Academy brings prestige and a stipend, but you have to sell work to make a living. So here I am." She gestured toward her painting of a vase of flowers and plums on a tabletop. White flowers reflected in the curvature of the dark purple fruit.

"The plums look as though you could pluck them up, rub the dust off on your sleeve, and take a bite," Adélaïde complimented.

"Thank you. And may I say, Madame Guiard, your little *tête d'expression*—" She raised her eyebrows. "That certainly is a new way to present one."

Adélaïde smiled, shrugged, and gulped down her champagne. The woman's arch comment served as a warning for the ones that followed. That morning, when Adélaïde had read that Madame Lebrun's work was sensuous and feminine, she had asked François to bring her nude from his apartment. Back at her display, Adélaïde listened to the reactions as *Delightful Surprise,* mounted on the wall behind her, created a scandal.

"Did she give Vincent sex for painting lessons?"

"Someone has touched it up," said another.

His companion laughed and agreed, "It is too good to be a woman's work."

"Nudity is acceptable when used as an ideal way to express historic allegory, but not when used to express sexual desire," bleated another.

"Especially when a woman paints it," his compatriot agreed, then leered at her to see if her chin had the same mole as the woman in the painting.

Adélaïde tried to back away, but her skirt was caught in the snarling fangs of a stuffed jaguar. The dead cat glared at her with onyx glass eyes as she coaxed the silk of her dress from his teeth. She went and found a glass of cool water to press against her burning cheeks.

~

When she read the newspapers the next morning, a well of emotion overflowed. "Madame Guiard's paintings are worthy of the Louvre. She can match any Academy member in technique and ability."

Across the cluttered breakfast table, Marie regarded her reddened eyes. "Was it worth the gossip, madame?"

In her heart, she had known she was as good as any Academy member, but to see it acknowledged in public made her feel relieved and encouraged at the same time. They could not continue to keep her out. They just could not.

"Absolutely."

CHAPTER 19

SEPTEMBER 1782

"At least let me put my back to the door." Ducis frowned as Adélaïde shivered. Her thin shawl was no match for the unseasonable chill in the fall air. Each time the *traiteur* door opened to admit another diner, a blast of cold air hit her. The ladder-backed chair she sat in offered no protection. "What will people say about chivalry in this modern age?"

"That it is dead, as it should be." She picked up her coffee cup and used it to warm her hands. "I don't want that voice of yours ruined by a chill."

"So kind of you to always think of me." He produced one of his famous actor's smiles, more leer than smile.

She inclined her head. "And you are always thinking of me, of course." She and Ducis had become good friends during the time she had spent painting him.

"Oh, I am," he assured her. "I invited you to dinner tonight for that very reason."

"What? Not to tell me about your *Macbeth* project?" The entire time she had spent painting Ducis, his French version of *Macbeth* was almost all he talked about.

"For once, no. I am here to tell you to stop being so proud and get yourself a patron. Er, patroness."

"Why? Can't my work speak for itself?"

He rolled his eyes. "Yes, and no, as you know." He pointed his fork at her. "Or as you refuse to acknowledge." This was the other topic of conversation that occupied their painting sessions—and the source of all their disagreements. He insisted that patronage led to success, while she wanted to succeed through merit.

"My work should be my entrée," she said.

"Pahin de la Blan-cher-ie," he strung the words out, "royalty or not, has made a bitter enemy. The Comte d'Angiviller stormed around his wife's salon last night, ranting that he would close the Salon de la Correspondence. His face was the shade of his raspberry-colored coat. I ran for the hills. That is to say, as far as the other side of the door. That way I could listen in safety. He wants the man arrested."

A different kind of chill ran down Adélaïde's back.

"He can't, can he?" she asked. "The man is of royal blood."

"You know not everyone believes Pahin's claim. Tomorrow is audience day and the comte plans to leave for Versailles at dawn to see if he can have him arrested. Given his connection to the king, the comte may succeed."

Adélaïde saw the serious look in her friend's eyes, and her gut twisted. "How many times does this have to happen? If d'Angiviller shuts me down again, I don't know what I'll do. My life—my future —" She swallowed. "My ability to survive depends on my ability to earn money. But if I can't paint and show my works . . ." Dismay choked her. "What can I do? How do I fight this?"

"It's very simple," he announced in a stage whisper. "Make the acquaintance of the Comtesse d'Angiviller, of course. No fighting needed."

The waiter behind the black-painted bar turned his head toward them.

"What does the comte's wife have to do with anything?"

Ducis lowered his voice to a real whisper. "*He* may know the king, but *she* knows everyone."

While Adélaïde thought about his suggestion, the door opened again. François and Joseph Suvée slid into the two empty chairs at their table.

"Please tell your woman to stop being so stubborn," Ducis said to François after the waiter took their dinner order. "I keep saying that she needs a patron and she's not listening."

"Adélaïde is her own woman." François smiled. "I can tell her nothing. But after tonight, I am beginning to agree." He and Joseph had just attended a quarterly meeting of the Royal Academy.

"Several members broached the subject of admitting women—to no avail," Joseph said.

After their food arrived, Adélaïde told them Ducis's news. "Just when things were falling in place," she said.

"If the comte arrests de la Blancherie, you will have no choice but to get a patron," Joseph told her.

"To me patronage is cheating," she said. Once, cheating had gotten her nowhere and almost cost François everything. She and François exchanged a glance that acknowledged that far-off caper with the Academy.

"More and more voices are calling for women to be admitted, but so far, we are getting nowhere," he said.

"What about Vien?" Adélaïde asked.

"He still has said nothing," François told her.

"Listen to Ducis and go to the comtesse," Joseph advised.

"Bring the little portrait you did of me as a gift to her," Ducis instructed.

When the waiter took away their empty plates, François stood. "I will walk you home."

"Walk her home?" Ducis smirked.

"Not your woman." Joseph grinned.

"If chivalry is dead, madame, I do believe I just saw its resurrection," Ducis said.

Her face burned.

"Don't forget that painting," Ducis called as she and François exited the restaurant.

"Oh, yes, the comte came to see me," Pahin told Adélaïde the next morning. He pulled a calling card out of his pocket and peered at it with a circular glass held to his right eye. "Asked me to close my salon, accused me of demeaning the arts."

"Will you close the salon?"

He pulled a snuffbox from his other pocket and took a pinch. "Of course not. When I told him that, he said he had come to ask me politely. I told him we would have to disagree on the definition of polite." His voice was smug. He pointed the snuffbox at his newsletters stacked on the table beside her. "Imagine the world knowing that France, the center of the highest thinking in science and philosophy, craft and trade, stifles its best artists and thinkers. He did not like that. Threatened me with arrest. I told him he could try and that I did not bow to the likes of him."

Knowing that d'Angiviller was on his way to Versailles to speak to the king, Adélaïde was not reassured. It was like starting out all over again, back out on the street, having no idea what to do next. At thirty-three, married but not married, childless, without extended family, her art was her life. If her paintings could not bring her success, she was . . . She refused to think about what she might be. If the Academy did not relent, a patron was her last hope, and it was not Pahin. She left him to his snuff.

❧

"I hate begging." Adélaïde stood in the middle of her bedroom, arms outstretched while Marie smoothed yards of cotton embroidered with gray lilies over her flimsy new underskirts and adjusted ruffles and bows. "What if this woman throws me out?" She pressed her hand against her chest. Her ribs hurt thinking of it.

"If one believes what one reads, the comtesse is famous for her wit, intelligence, and kindness," Isabelle said. "The society pages used to be filled with news from her salons. Hold still." She placed a black velvet turban over Adélaïde's hair.

"The comtesse still makes the society pages," Marie handed Adélaïde a pair of black ostrich leather gloves. "She and her husband throw parties in their new home all the time."

"You certainly don't look the beggar," Isabelle said.

"One can grovel in any mode of dress," Adélaïde said, "but I cannot look like a shop girl when I visit this man's house."

"It's not begging, madame," Marie said. "It's asking someone to support your cause—and ours. We must sell our works too."

"You're right, but that does not make it easier."

Isabelle handed Adélaïde the portrait of Ducis, wrapped in paper painted with red and gold leaf chrysanthemums. "We are always right, madame. Now hurry. The fiacre is outside."

~

When Adélaïde arrived at the d'Angivillers' grand hôtel, a footman dressed in military-style livery ushered her into a twenty-foot-high entryway. He then led her through a salon where workmen on scaffolds spread plaster on columns supporting the ceiling. Up in the dome, an artist lay on his back on another scaffold, frescoing a battle scene on the underside of the dome. More artisans in the far corner of the room plastered over cherubs cavorting along the coffers at the edge of the ceiling.

The larks of lovers have given way to the hark of battle, she thought. Passing through a gallery, she slowed to stare out a series of *portes-fenêtres* that opened onto a large balcony overlooking a garden along the river. She had never imagined a place with a garden on the river.

"The comtesse will see you now," the footman announced.

As she entered the forty-foot room, she saw a seated woman in her fifties reading a book. Her back was to a large fireplace; before her, a round table with an empty chair beside it. To Adélaïde, the comtesse looked like a lone island in a pale green sea.

The woman put down her book and beckoned her forward.

Adélaïde performed the appropriate curtsey and the comtesse gestured to the chair beside her. Sitting in silence, they assessed each other. Adélaïde saw an aging beauty whose silver hair required no powder and whose graceful movements portrayed her royal training. The woman's warm regard evinced a genuine graciousness that went beyond the superficiality one might expect of a salon leader.

"Aren't you the height of fashion?" the comtesse complimented with a smile. In fact, she wore a dress so similar to Adélaïde's that the only differences lay in the quality of stitching and fabric.

"Thank you, Madame la Comtesse," Adélaïde responded. She recalled the package in her arms and held it out. "A gift for you."

The comtesse removed the paper Adélaïde's students had stayed up half a night to paint and lifted out the portrait of Ducis. The long hand on the mantle clock clicked forward three times before she said, "It's a perfect likeness. One feels the emotion moving beneath his skin."

"Thank you." Adélaïde let out the breath she had been holding.

The comtesse had not thrown her out . . . yet. "Monsieur Ducis does have a face made to paint."

She looked around the room and recognized the work of Anne-Marie Vallayer-Coster in the still lifes that hung on either side of the fireplace behind the comtesse. One was a painting of a basket of plums, a glass vase holding a budding rose, and a cut-open orange resting on a table. Light gleamed across the table and turned the sectioned flesh of the sliced orange into a bursting star. The carved handle of a fruit knife protruded into the space in front of the table as though the viewer could just pick it up and slice another orange.

How had she done that? Adélaïde wondered and felt her fingers tingle.

The comtesse followed Adélaïde's gaze. "They are lovely, aren't they? I have several paintings of hers."

"I have heard that you support women artists." Pride strangled the next words in her throat.

"Did you come to seek my patronage?" the comtesse asked when the silence grew uncomfortable.

Adélaïde turned away. "The Salon de la Correspondence may soon close. It is the one venue I've had to exhibit my work. I–I don't know where to turn. I seek advice."

The comtesse rose. "Come, let's take a turn about the room. I will show you my collection of art and you may decide if you wish to have your art hang on my walls." They toured the room at a sedate pace, the comtesse pointing out paintings done by women. She caressed a writing desk inlaid with pink mother-of-pearl cut in a diamond pattern. "Even this was designed by a woman." She smiled.

They returned to the chairs by the fireplace. The comtesse picked up Adélaïde's portrait of Ducis, then looked at Adélaïde, a curious smile teasing her lips. "Many years ago, the king and his entourage made a trip to Paris. While in the city, I visited a famous shop to buy gloves and a hat. A daughter of the owner sketched the customers while she studied."

Adélaïde's eyes homed in on the deep crease in the comtesse's cheek. She recalled a young woman with thick black ringlets, an oval face, an intriguing dimple. Her parents had plied the woman with expensive wine. At one point, the woman had wandered into the back of the shop where Adélaïde studied and picked up her sketchbook. Adélaïde had sat paralyzed with shame while purple-gloved fingers followed the lines of the geometry theorem she was proving. Beside the math problem was a quick sketch of the woman's face, dimple exaggerated. Embarrassed, her mother had apologized for her daughter's temerity. Laughing, the woman had demanded the sketch.

"I remember that day," Adélaïde said. It was the last time her mother allowed her to study in the shop.

"Monsieur Ducis tells me that you have become a fine portraitist, one of the best in Paris, in fact. I have read of your work on display at the Salon de la Correspondence. Now I see with my own eyes that it is true. I cannot give you advice about the Salon, but I would be proud to support your endeavors."

What kind of universe did she live in where her earliest supporter was married to the man who was trying to destroy her? Where she spent eighteen years struggling and all it took was a childish doodle, a bit of notoriety in the papers, and a gift to succeed? How could it be this easy when it had been so hard? Adélaïde stood and performed a deep curtsey, not trusting herself to say more than, "Thank you, Madame la Comtesse. I appreciate your support and faith in me, more than I can say. I will leave you to your day."

The comtesse pointed to the seat she had just vacated. "Please, sit back down. Ducis also told me about your pride." She rang a bell, and a maid stepped through a hidden door in the wall. The comtesse ordered chocolate. "Now, tell me what you've done with yourself since that day in the shop. And take out your sketchbook. I want a proper portrait of myself this time."

<h1 style="text-align:center">CHAPTER 20</h1>

1783

"Oh, why did I think this was ever going to work?" Adélaïde flung herself back in the wooden chair. "All I've done this past year is eat, sleep, and paint." It was two in the morning. Marie and Isabelle had gone to bed hours ago.

Joseph Suvée jerked awake in her mother's velvet chair. François stopped his ceaseless circling of her studio.

A hundred burning candles made the air hot and sickeningly sweet with the scent of beeswax. The half-finished canvas before her wavered. She wiped her eyes. "I can't even see," she wailed.

"You're supposed to paint the canvas. Not yourself," Joseph laughed.

With an exclamation, she grabbed a wet rag and scraped at her eyebrows.

"On your eyelids." François took the rag from her and wiped the paint away with gentle hands. "You're overwrought," he said quietly.

"I am not." She began to shake.

"You're tired, but you have to push on. We've all done this in our quest to make it to the Academy."

"But you knew you would get there, Joseph."

Spring had arrived, and with it the Academy's annual acceptance of new members. If their ploy for Adélaïde to paint a strategic group of Academy members did not work, she was done.

After six years of rejected applications, she knew it in her heart. Her muscles were so tight she could not lift her paintbrush to the canvas.

The brush fell from her fingers and flipped along the floor.

Joseph got out of her mother's chair and retrieved it. "Keep going," he ordered.

She grasped the brush, looked at his face on the easel before her, its downcast eyes and body turned away from the viewer to accommodate his constant fidgeting, and waited for the familiar tingle. It did not come.

"What if I can't?" Her voice, high and thin, came from a place far away. She bolted for the stairs.

François stopped her flight at the first step. "Come back, Adélaïde. You're almost there."

"How can I be? Seven portraits are not enough." Nausea churned her stomach. "I can't do this, François."

"Why don't you just visit your friend the comtesse and get her to persuade her husband to admit you? That would be far easier," Joseph said.

"She's not my friend, Joseph. And if my work isn't up to the standards of the Academy, I don't belong." She squeezed her eyes shut. "Maybe I don't belong."

"We all feel that way at the end. That is when we must rely on our training." François rubbed at the knots in her shoulders, then picked up her palette. "You've executed your battle plan, mastered your studies, found a patron, exhibited your work, painted in front of the most influential Academy members. Do not give up now, Adélaïde. This is your final assault."

Drawing in a ragged breath, she took the palette.

"The whole world is talking about you," Joseph reminded her.

Pahin had made good on his threat to the Comte d'Angiviller and written a piece about her struggle in his *News from the Republic of Letters,* saying that the arts had languished in France because the government stifled innovation, creativity, and talent, especially if it came from the hands of a woman. Protest letters from as far away as the Caribbean poured in. Pahin had printed those in his newsletter as well.

"At the theatre last night, LeKain spoke about you after his play. The audience stood and cheered. I saw it myself," Joseph said.

"Everyone supports you, but you must believe in yourself," François said.

Joseph took the rag, examined it for a clean spot, then wiped the sweat off his forehead. "Can we get on with it? It's damn hot in here." He dropped the cloth on the table and returned to his seat. "Let it never be said that a woman was not up to this task." He closed his eyes as though he were about to go to sleep again. When she still hesitated, he exclaimed, "Good lord, François. Have we been wasting our time?"

Joseph's sting went deep, but those were the words she needed to hear. She moved a candelabrum closer to the canvas and could see that the jacket lapel was missing a highlight. Without thought, she picked up the palette knife. She mixed yellow and white into a slice of brown, one thought spinning in her head: Would it be enough?

CHAPTER 21

MARCH 1783

A thunderstorm rumbled through Paris. Lightning flashed as Adélaïde hurried to the d'Angivillers' grand mansion.

Come quickly, Ducis's letter had read. *The comte has called a secret meeting of Academy leaders to settle the matter of who will be admitted this year.*

She took the back stairs to Ducis's apartments, which adjoined the comte's study.

"Having a spy in the enemy's house pays off." Ducis motioned her inside. "The comte and his newfangled construction." He laughed. "All these ducts and water pipes. If you have good ears, you can just about hear every word that goes on in there."

She stared at him. "You don't, do you?"

He grinned. "Who, me? I would never. Now, quiet, please." He led her through a hallway to his small salon. "They've been arguing for about an hour. Some members insist these deliberations should be open to the public, but d'Angiviller says he doesn't want any controversy. They decided to admit Jacques Louis David even though half of them think the man is unhinged. They need to keep him away from swords and knives, I say."

He led her to a wall with an elaborate grill placed above the baseboard. "D'Angiviller's study is on the other side." Ducis got down on his knees to listen. Feeling foolish, she crouched down beside him, thinking they must look like two supplicants praying to a piece of metal painted white. Heat radiated from the void beyond the grill.

"Gentlemen, you are aware that the purpose of the Royal Academy of Painting and Sculpture is to embody noble ideals that further the purpose of the State." The clarity of the voice through the wall startled her and she reared back. She recognized the voice of Joseph Pierre, the director of the Academy, from François's induction. "While the Academy has encouraged talent in women by admitting a select few to our body, such admissions are contrary to the purpose of the Academy and must not occur too often."

Her eyes widened. Ducis nodded and spread his hands wide as if to say, "You see?"

Pierre continued, "For the past two decades, it has been my responsibility to ensure that the Academy members meet the criteria of the institution. This is a *royal* academy, gentlemen, not a guild pedaling popular art to the public. Monsieur Vien, I'm surprised to find you here."

Was Vien finally going to speak up for her?

"I am not here to nominate a woman, although I am apprised of the matter," Joseph Vien said in his cool voice.

She could not believe it.

"Well, gentlemen?"

"There's a lot of talk around town about the unfairness of women not having an opportunity to exhibit."

"Who is that?" she mouthed at Ducis.

"A supporter of Madame Lebrun," he whispered.

"We are under no obligation to provide the housewives of France with a place to exhibit their leisure work," Pierre said.

"We are not talking about housewives." She recognized Chevalier Roslin's voice. At least someone in the room was fighting for her. "We are talking about dedicated and talented female artists and their ability to work and promote their art. Without guild membership or a special dispensation from the king, they cannot work."

"We are not responsible for providing a living for the fan painters of Paris," the director said. "You cannot compare the art produced by members of the Academy of St. Luke with the art produced by the Royal Academy."

"Yes, painting stenciled floral arrangements on strips of wood is not art," someone agreed.

"Certain women are very capable painters," Vien said.

After two years, that is all this man can manage on my behalf?

"Women of talent should be recognized for their abilities," someone else said. "Reason demands it."

"Another supporter of Madame Lebrun," Ducis breathed.

"I disagree." A new voice. D'Angiviller's. "I have said before that women have no place in the progression of art."

"It is your closure of the Academy of St. Luke, Monsieur le Comte, that has led to a lot of distress. You, and you alone, have deprived many women of their livelihood." Roslin again.

"Some have faced starvation or worse," Élisabeth's supporter said. "A record is being compiled of the women made homeless by the closure of St. Luke and the desperate acts women have taken as a result."

"Some have made good marriages and gone on to manage the queen's estates," the director protested.

He means Rosalie Boquet, Adélaïde thought.

"That may be true of a few well-connected ones, but not of the vast majority."

"This issue is a topic of discussion in the salons of Paris," Roslin said. "The rest of Europe has begun to take note."

"The *News from the Republic of Letters* has called for people to avoid this year's salon if women aren't admitted to the Academy." When Adélaïde heard the raspy voice of Antonin Pajou, she forgot the ache in her thighs, the strain on her knees. Her pastel portrait of the sculptor had convinced many Academy members that she was their equal in talent. He had been so pleased with that portrait that later he had gifted her a marble bust of her father.

"I will not bow to such pressure," Pierre said.

"Many Academy members will not provide works to exhibit this year if the situation isn't rectified." Chevalier Roslin again.

"If we admit just one woman from the Academy of St. Luke, what is to stop the other female members from demanding membership?" Pierre sounded harassed. "It would turn our Academy into a hen house in no time."

"And yet, all the former male members of St. Luke's have standing in the current Academy structure," the chevalier said. "How is that right?"

"The queen is aware of the plight of female artists," Élisabeth's supporter said.

The room was silent but for the rain that pounded the roof.

"The issue has become an embarrassment to the king," d'Angiviller said. "He has intervened on behalf of Madame Lebrun and asked me to look into the matter."

"We are an independent body," Pierre protested. "The king cannot tell us what to do."

Arguing broke out.

"Gentlemen, this is unnecessary," the comte said. "I have a solution."

Adélaïde listened while d'Angiviller told of the deal he had struck with the king to formalize the practice of admitting only four female members.

Pierre read the king's order aloud and the room was silent again while he weighed his options. "I agree that our rules indicate we will have no more than four women in our ranks, but we are under no obligation to have four women at any one time. Additionally, any woman admitted to the Academy must be admitted by unanimous consent of the Academy members. Well, gentlemen, no woman has my vote."

Beyond the wall, d'Angiviller said, "You have expressed your views, but I advise you not to defy the king in this matter."

The rain once again intruded on the silence. Finally, his voice gruff, Pierre asked for the names of the female artists they intended to nominate.

Roslin said, "I will nominate Adélaïde Labille-Guiard. She meets the requirements. We expect her support to be unanimous."

Adélaïde drooped with relief.

Ducis grinned and whispered, "It's about to happen."

Something was said about Élisabeth Lebrun and arguing broke out again. Chairs scraped across the floor, and men started shouting.

Ducis stood. "The meeting's breaking up. You need to go."

They rushed down the stairs.

"Is that how things are done?" Adélaïde asked as they emerged, breathless onto the street. "Secret deals?"

"Let's not get soaked." Ducis steered her into an arcade at the end of the block. "Look at it this way. Pierre was ambushed. Roslin's a knight and his wife was an Academy member. He's the wealthiest artist in Paris. Even the king of Sweden came to France to be painted by him. Then there's Vien, whose wife is also an Academy member. He's a powerful voice in the Academy."

"That powerful voice sounded mighty puny to me," she said.

"Sometimes that's just how it's done."

"What will happen next?" she asked François and Joseph that night.

"You should receive an invitation to submit an entry piece," François said.

"You do realize that you can say nothing about this," Joseph said. "Considering that secret meetings never happen."

She nodded, then worried as weeks went by without any correspondence from the Academy.

Finally, at the end of April, she went to Chevalier Roslin and asked him if he thought she would be admitted this year.

Later that afternoon, he stopped by her studio and handed her a letter. "This was mislaid in the Academy's office."

I am sure it was, she thought, breaking the wax seal. At first the words did not make sense, and she had to read them again. "Madame Guiard, you are hereby invited to submit a *morçeau d'entrée* for consideration for admittance to the Royal Academy of Art and Sculpture . . ." In that moment she did not care that the letter had sat on someone's desk for weeks. She wanted to leap around her studio, shout for joy, fall on her knees with relief, all at once. Instead, she told the chevalier, "Sir, I can never thank you or your family enough for all you've done for me."

Her students ran across the road to the wine seller's shop and came back with three green bottles. Adélaïde spent the rest of the afternoon in a daze of happiness and relief so intense, she felt like a hummingbird moth flitting through a field of red valerian.

When Joseph and François arrived to take her to dinner that evening, Joseph surveyed the empty champagne bottles, the half-filled glasses on the table, the cake plate adorned only in crumbs. "What's this?" he asked. "Did no one invite me to the celebration?"

Marie presented the men with the Academy's invitation. "Look what has happened," she told them breathlessly.

Joseph frowned. "The Academy always gives us a year to prepare our best work for consideration," he said.

"What?" Adélaïde asked.

"Even if you could come up with a worthy design," François said, "the oil will not be dry. You do not have enough time."

Adélaïde's spirit crashed back into her body, elation replaced by panic. "But the deadline is two weeks away," she cried.

Her final hurdle, and she could not attempt it?

CHAPTER 22

MAY 1783

When the citizens of Paris heard that the Royal Academy would admit two women, they rose early and crowded into the Apollo Gallery. Outside, newsboys stood on their friends' shoulders to peer in through the windows and shouted back to the crowds passing in the streets what they saw.

In the gallery, four hundred Academy members filled the seats in the hall, and beyond them, reporters, pamphlet writers, friends, and family. A thrum of excitement pulsated through the room. From her seat among the inductees, Adélaïde's body was a tuning fork of anticipation.

"Fellow Frenchmen, I am pleased to report on the progress we have made to turn this palace into a repository of great French art," the Comte d'Angiviller said from his place on the stage. Just then, a black pug ran up the aisle with a chicken leg in its mouth. Garlic, onions, roasted meat, Adélaïde's nose informed her. Laughter rippled through the room. Looking severe, the comte called for someone to catch the dog and throw him and his accompanying street urchin out. The newsboys informed the crowd outside.

Élisabeth Lebrun learned over and whispered, "With his medals flashing on his chest, he resembles a peacock." The comte wore last year's green and blue velvet.

Adélaïde stifled a laugh. "He certainly struts about like one, but he's a hawk pretending to be a peacock."

D'Angiviller stepped aside so directors from the various academies could announce their new members. Each time they read a name, polite applause filled the room. When Jean-Baptiste Pierre rose to present the painters and sculptors, exaltation swept through Adélaïde, the same elation she had felt as a child, running through a sunbeam in the shop, waving a sketch and calling for her parents' approval.

Beside her, Élisabeth's eyes were bright with tears. Without volition, the two gripped each other's hands.

"For his painting of *Andromache by the Body of Hector,* Jacques Louis David, History Painter," Pierre called. "For her pastel portrait of Augustin Pajou, Madame Adélaïde Guiard, Portraitist."

François and Joseph had been right; she had no time to complete a new work in oil. Her friends had met, judged her works, and selected her portrait of Pajou, the sculptor.

"This work reflects your mastery of the male form, your ability to manipulate illusions of clay and flesh with a lively fluidity, your control over drapery, texture, expression, your ability to reflect life itself in your art," Chevalier Roslin had said.

In the end, Adélaïde made it into the Academy on the strength of a pastel, executed the year before when she was proving to Academy members that she was a worthy artist.

She stood, her hand still gripped in Élisabeth's, her legs shaking under the heavy skirts of her court dress.

"Madame Élisabeth—"

Beside her, Élisabeth rose to her feet. The room erupted in cheers.

"Madame—" Pierre tried again.

Calls of "Fifteen years" and "About time" came from the crowd.

"Madame Élisabeth Lebrun, member." When clapping began again, Pierre shouted over the audience. "Member admitted by order of the king."

Adélaïde felt Élisabeth's convulsive movement, the loosening of her grip. The crowd began to murmur as they tried to understand the undercurrent roiling through the Academy members.

"Don't give in to them," Adélaïde said beneath the noise. She took Élisabeth's hand again and they turned to face the crowd, raising their clasped hands above their heads.

Élisabeth's husband rose from his seat at the back of the room and began to clap. He bowed to the women and continued clapping. Then the seated Academy members rose to honor them.

"You did it." François's voice came from behind her. She looked back to see the warm light in his eyes.

Somewhere in the crowd, Alexandré emitted a piercing whistle. He had arrived in Paris the night before, joking, "It's finally safe for me to return. From now on, you can no longer blame me for anything that the Academy does to you. And my brother here was getting lonely in his lodgings."

Jacques Louis David, Élisabeth, and Adélaïde remained on their feet while Pierre called the sculptors.

Finally, Secretary Renou stepped forward to administer the Proces Verbaux to all the new members of the Academy. She recognized the voice from behind Ducis's wall, the one who had said she had enough votes.

Jacques Louis David climbed the stage steps to take his oath. Tall, well-built, he kept his dark hair curly and short, but the cut of his clothing was expensive and stylish. When he uttered the words of the oath, the right side of his face bulged outward, and his mouth turned down. From her place near the stage, she should have heard each word, but his vow came in a series of guttural sounds, a remnant, she surmised, of his teenaged sword fight.

Adélaïde was next in alphabetical order, but Renou passed over her name. When he skipped Élisabeth's name, a frisson of worry went down her spine. They waited while the sculptors followed David onto the stage, took their pledge and returned to their seats.

"Ladies, you may be seated." D'Angiviller stepped forward. Raising his voice, he said, "This concludes the entrance ceremony of 1783. We look forward to seeing each of you at the Academy's Salon in August."

Adélaïde's body flushed with embarrassment. She and Élisabeth sank into their seats. Reporters and pamphleteers rushed out and the mass of people moved toward the doors. François and Alexandré joined her while Élisabeth left with her husband, her walk as stately as a queen as she moved down the empty aisle.

"Why didn't they call us, François? They could not have forgotten us."

"Women cannot take the oath."

Her mind whirled. Then, comprehension dawned. The only

oath available to women was the marriage vow. She had worked so hard to rise above being female, had spent so much effort getting to this day, that she had never considered this outcome. She struggled to contain her feelings. "I've waited years to take that vow."

"How could you forget, Adélaïde? If anyone knows about rules and regulations, it's you," Alexandré said.

"You may have gotten older, Alexandré, but you're as annoying as ever."

"It's part of my charm."

"I'm not going to vow another vow until I can take the vow I want."

"An avowal against vows is still a vow."

"Don't be smart, Alexandré," François said to his brother. "It's just a set of words, Adélaïde. No one pays any heed to it."

"Said by someone who took the vow. If it meant nothing, why have it?"

"You do not need to take it. You already are an honor and glory to France." François took her arm. "Come, let's go celebrate."

And celebrate they did.

The Lebruns opened their mansion. The building was so packed that it took half an hour for their party to squeeze through the double doors and make their way up the stairs to the ballroom. By then Adélaïde had started on her second glass of champagne and the edges of the insult had mellowed.

Pahin de La Blancherie pushed through the crowd, Élisabeth at his side. He bowed over Adélaïde's hand. "I knew it," he gloated. "Diana and Venus together."

Laughing, Adélaïde extricated her hand from a tangle of scratchy chartreuse lace. "You opened the door, kind sir."

"Not I," he said. "The stars foretold it."

"There are no stars," Adélaïde said. "Just hard work and people who help pave the way." Careful not to tip her glass, Adélaïde gave Élisabeth a quick embrace, cheek to cheek. "Madame Lebrun, I do believe you've invited the whole Academy and anyone in Paris with the slimmest connection to art." She glanced at Pahin.

"Oh no." Élisabeth's eyes glinted with anger. "Monsieur David is holding *that* party. The important Academy members are at his house."

Adélaïde realized she had not seen d'Angiviller, Pierre, or any other Academy official.

"What do you think of the Academy refusing to accept me as a history painter, or, for that matter, to put me in any category at all?" Élisabeth said.

That I will be forever glad I insisted my work be judged for itself, Adélaïde thought, but said, "No matter what, our paintings will hang in d'Angiviller's museum of the future."

"But the history painting I submitted has been hanging in Versailles for the past three years."

Pahin exhaled a ring of cigar smoke. "The king has better taste than they do."

Élisabeth groaned. "People will always talk about how I got into the Academy by order of the king."

Adélaïde held up her champagne. "We don't need a group of sanctimonious old men to commemorate this auspicious occasion. Congratulations, Madame Lebrun. You made it."

"No." Their glasses clinked. "*We* made it. Despite their best efforts."

"Well said." Pahin turned to the partiers and raised his glass.

The toasting went on until the room spun, and Adélaïde looked for a way to escape.

François appeared with a wine bottle and two empty glasses. "Come with me. It is too crowded in here."

His handsome face wavered. She put her hand in his. "Where are we going?"

"To a party for two." François's grin grew wide.

She glanced around. Élisabeth had turned to speak to another artist, and Pahin's puce green coat had disappeared into the crowd.

"Come on. No one will notice if we slip away."

Adélaïde handed her glass to a passing waiter and followed him out.

PART IV
FRIENDS AND ENEMIES

CHAPTER 23

1784

Justine breezed into the studio, her golden cloak an artistic contrast to the red and white checkered cloth covering the basket on her arm. In the center of the worktable, a delivery of pastels from Maison Macle awaited sorting. She plopped the basket on top of the boxes and whipped off the cover.

"If we must work before class, we should eat first," she said.

"Oh, beignets," Marie said as she smelled the fried dough.

Isabelle stood on a short ladder near the door, posting new prices on the wall. She hurried over to the table and grabbed a pastry. "Madame, how much do you want to charge for posing in the window?" she asked, licking her fingers.

Stacking écus into her cashbox at the end of the table, Adélaïde did not look up. "Thirty livres a sitting."

"A month's rent?" Marie gasped.

In the process of hanging up her cloak, Justine turned and laughed, half in outrage, half in admiration. "When you are poor and unknown, no matter how talented, no one wants you to paint their portrait, but when you are famous, Parisians flock to you, whether you are talented or not." She waved a beignet under Adélaïde's nose. "Soft, warm, delicious."

Adélaïde grunted and waved her away.

Marie rummaged in the bottom of the basket and pulled out a

jar of jam. "But you are talented, Madame." She spread strawberry jam on her pastry. "And you can charge whatever you want."

"Madame, if you aren't eating, do you mind if I take your pastry?" Isabelle asked.

Adélaïde pulled the basket toward her end of the table. "I didn't say I wouldn't have a pastry, just not yet."

"Why so upset, madame?" Justine asked. "Your bourgeois clients love to sit in the bay window, but will they pay that much?"

"These people come to be seen by their neighbors out in the street, not to be painted," Adélaïde said. "And if they're not buying, I don't want them to take the place of a paying customer. Make it thirty-five. They are not the right clientele."

"What's wrong with your bourgeois clients, madame?" Marie asked. "They love your work. You've tripled your prices, and we all get to work on your commissions. We couldn't survive without them."

"There's nothing wrong with them," Adélaïde said around a mouthful of fried dough. "Just never sacrifice your talent. People won't value it if you do." She lost her appetite and went to dump her crumbs in a bucket by the back door. There was everything wrong with her clientele. Actors, businessmen, and their wives might flock to her, but she was still waiting for royalty to step across her threshold. The daughter of royal shopkeepers knew this failure did not bode well for her business.

She returned to the table and watched the girls sort the pastels. "Where's Celestine? She was supposed to help." Celestine, a recent student of great talent but little ambition, often arrived late.

Her students looked at each other. "Didn't she tell you?" Marie asked. "She left to go to Monsieur David at the Louvre."

"Why?"

"He told her there would be better opportunities for her there, and she said there's more room in his studio," Marie said.

"When did he tell her that?"

"One day when you were out, some of his students came and talked to us. Then her parents visited his studio."

"We didn't think you'd notice," Isabelle said. "There are too many students here already. You've turned some away lately."

The issue of turning away students while she waited for her

lodgings in the Louvre had become another worry. Since Marie Capet's arrival, many more destitute artists had knocked at her door. Often, they were not looking for art lessons, but for a place to live and an opportunity to work. These desperate young women reminded Adélaïde of herself. She wished she could offer them more than advanced morning lessons, but it was impossible until she had more space.

"Someone said that he gives his students a discount if they bring in new students," Marie said.

"I've never heard of such trickery." She folded her arms and looked at the girls. "Are any of you planning to leave me for him?"

"No, madame," Marie said.

"I've got to find a way to accept more students," she said.

"I know we're the lucky ones, but you can't save everyone." Isabelle handed the boxes of colored sticks to Marie, who put them in the cupboard. "You have no more corners to give up, and they can't sleep under the table here."

"Well, not without us falling over each other—" Justine said before Isabelle interrupted.

"And getting paint on everything and everyone." Isabelle was constantly washing paint out of their clothes.

"I could design a paint armor suit." Marie giggled.

"We could move into the pantry," Isabelle suggested, referring to the tiny closet that held their food supplies.

Everyone but Adélaïde laughed as she lugged her cashbox up the stairs.

Her cashbox had never been so full. This should have been the best possible news, but suspicion teased at the edge of her enjoyment in her success. She had been an Academy member for a year now, but still had not received her space assignment in the Louvre. It was time to find out why.

She donned a blue redingote, placed a black hat on her fluffed hair—thankful that à la hedgehog meant easy hairdressing these days—and returned to her studio. Twenty students greeted her with cheery hellos.

"You look dashing," Marie said.

"And determined." Isabelle eyed her. "Where are you going?"

"Monsieur David is not going to get away with this."

The shop bell tinkled. Two women entered, dressed as though they had stepped from one of queen's latest fashion books. A flutter of excitement rippled through the studio. Feeling a rush of relief, Adélaïde hurried to greet the duchess and her daughter. When the duchess looked her up and down with a look of offense, Adélaïde remembered to curtsey. Rising, she directed the women to the chairs in the bay window. "May I offer you hot chocolate and bonbons?" she asked.

While they waited for the refreshments, the mother quizzed Adélaïde about her clientele, then asked to see samples of her work.

Isabelle and Justine paraded canvasses before them, and Adélaïde pointed to the transparent scarves and feathered boas in the portraits. "You may pose in your own clothing or use some of the props we have available," she said.

"What does the king think of your work?" the duchess asked.

Adélaïde answered with care. "I have not yet had the pleasure of hearing his views."

Marie arrived with a tray and offered it to the women. The daughter reached for a candy, but the mother refused. "Let's go," she told her daughter. "I'd rather use Madame Lebrun. This woman hasn't painted anyone important. I just wanted to see the studio of a woman of her reputation." They walked out in a cloud of perfume. The daughter turned back to look at the students, her gaze mocking and disrespectful.

After the door closed, Justine used the checkered cloth to fan away the smell of perfume. "Are these really the right clientele?" she asked.

While everyone applied themselves to their artwork, Adélaïde pretended to inspect the cupboard Marie had just stocked, her eyes glazed. This was the root of the problem. No member of royalty would hire her without the blessing of the king, and if she did not have royalty sitting in her window chairs, soon not even bourgeois clients would want to sit there.

Élisabeth Lebrun, who had been ordered into the Academy by the king, had his blessing. But as for her, the Royal Academy's deafening silence was a roaring message that grew louder each day. If the Academy had overlooked her, she would never receive her lodgings or royal commissions until she reminded them. And if the Academy had not made an oversight, she had to know now.

But what had the woman meant, "a woman of her reputation?"

She went to the mirror, made sure the powder on her cheeks was not ruined, straightened her hat, and went to the door. "I'm going to pay Monsieur David a visit, and then I'm going to the Academy to find out what's taking so long to get my lodgings. Until I get back, Marie and Isabelle are in charge."

Marie regarded her, and said, "Be gentle with them, madame."

"May we eat the bonbons?" Isabelle asked.

Adélaïde wove her way among the carters offloading cargo along the river, but when she neared the palace complex, she changed directions and headed for Élisabeth Lebrun's house. She found the younger woman painting in her studio on the third floor of her husband's mansion. Intent on the large wooden panel before her, Élisabeth did not offer Adélaïde a seat, instead saying, "Please wait," so Adélaïde remained standing by the door.

A velvet chair suitable for wealthy guests rested against the left wall. A shelf above the chair held scarves, hats and silk flowers, props Adélaïde recognized from Madame Lebrun's many paintings. On the back wall, above a narrow bed lined with pillows to resemble a couch, hung a large painting of the queen in an elaborate wooden frame. Beneath the portrait, a hand-lettered sign read "Élisabeth Vigée Lebrun, First Painter to the Queen." Squeezed along the right wall, a gray-haired woman who looked like an older version of Élisabeth knitted in a wooden rocking chair while a toddler played on the floor beneath the lone window. The little girl ran behind her grandmother's skirts and peeped out at Adélaïde with curious eyes.

Minutes later, Élisabeth stopped working, wiped her hands on a rag and looked up. Adélaïde had not seen her rival since last year's party. Dark shadows ringed her blue eyes and her clothes hung from her jutting shoulder bones.

"I'm sorry," Élisabeth said with enough frost in her voice to indicate that she was not. "I usually do not permit visitors in my studio unless I've scheduled a sitting."

"I apologize for interrupting your work, but I wanted to know if you had heard from the Academy regarding your lodgings in the Louvre?"

"Lodgings?" Élisabeth looked surprised. "No."

"Have you asked about them?"

Élisabeth made a circling motion with her hand that encompassed the entire building. "I don't need lodgings at the Louvre."

Adélaïde looked around the small room. The place was the size of her old apartment at the Roches'. "Regardless, you're entitled to them. What about space for students?"

"Heaven protect me from students." Élisabeth shuddered. "My husband tells me all the time that I must have students, but I prefer to paint."

"What about attracting clientele?"

"Our concerts and weekly salons attract all the customers I can handle. This year, I've had to work day and night to finish the work I have."

Given her haggard appearance, Adélaïde believed her. "But what about royal customers?" she persisted. "Don't you need a studio for them?"

"Many of them like to come here. They find my studio quaint."

Adélaïde sighed. Painting in a woman's boudoir might work in a gentleman's house, but never in her own circumstances.

"Most of the time, though, I go to them." Élisabeth motioned to the easel, then stepped back and regarded the painting with narrowed eyes. Picking up a small brush, she dipped it in white paint.

Adélaïde came to look at the painting. The half-realized face of the queen stared back at her. "Oh," she breathed. "Does the Academy arrange your royal commissions?"

Élisabeth laughed, an abrupt high sound. "No."

"What about the Comte d'Angiviller?"

"The comte?" Élisabeth looked amused.

"Yes, his project to reflect the glory of France has kept several Academy members I know very busy."

"That man would not ask me to draw so much as a flower on a piece of stationery." Élisabeth laughed again, then returned to her painting as though she had forgotten Adélaïde was standing beside her.

The toddler yawned, climbed onto the bed and lay back against a pillow, staring at Adélaïde while she sucked on her figures.

Adélaïde looked around the room a last time. A feeling of despair rocked her.

The knitting needles paused long enough for Élisabeth's mother to say, "The queen has supported my daughter more than the Academy ever will. If you wish to succeed, you must find your own royal support."

Taking her leave, Adélaïde retraced her steps to the Louvre, her stomach in knots.

A guard directed her to Monsieur David's studio next to the Academy offices. She headed there, but found her way blocked by a group of young men setting finished canvases on easels in the corridor. While she waited for the path to clear, she admired one of the works and asked the artist, who was the same age as most of her students, what was going on.

"The Academy is holding one of its quarterly student exhibitions. The professors will critique our work," he told her.

This is new, she thought. She examined the painting in greater detail. "Your shading is excellent. It follows the proper cast of the light, but here"—she pointed to the painting "you have put the vanishing point in the wrong place, throwing off your perspective."

The young man stared at her. "Who are you?"

Amused, she was about to give her name, when another student with red hair said, "Oh, we know who you are, Madame Guiard."

Mystified, she asked, "And who might you be?"

The young men told her that they were students of Jacques Louis David.

The corridor had cleared, and she saw the sign above the door behind the students. It read, "Atelier: Jacques Louis David."

She walked through the open door of David's studio and entered a long room filled with young men talking and laughing as they sketched statues placed around the room and fabrics hung along the walls to simulate drapery.

The sole female in the room, a girl of about twenty, stood behind a large counter covered with drawings and pamphlets near the door. "May I help you?" she asked when Adélaïde approached. Harsh sunlight exposed the ravages of spots hidden under a heavy layer of white powder on the girl's face, but no amount of elegant attire could disguise her advanced pregnancy.

"I've come to speak with Monsieur David." Adélaïde looked past the woman, gauging the size of the room by counting the number of windows along the east and south walls.

"My husband is not here."

"When will he be back?"

The student with red hair came in behind her and said to the girl, "Madame David, may I introduce Madame *Guiard*?" Adélaïde heard the emphasis he put on her name.

The girl flushed, then fidgeted with the materials on the counter. She pulled a large drawing over a stack of pamphlets, but not before Adélaïde saw the elaborate calligraphy of twining snakes and thorny vines lining the bottom of the pamphlets. She wondered what reading material David was supplying to his students.

"I'm sorry, but my husband will have no time to meet with you. One of his students has won the Prix-de-Rome, and he is off finalizing preparations for their trip."

"Monsieur David is traveling to Italy?" She had never heard of a teacher accompanying a pupil on his Prix-de-Rome trip.

"The Comte d'Angiviller has given my husband a project that can only be executed in Italy to be authentic."

Adélaïde sensed pride and disdain in the young woman's voice.

"What will he do with the rest of his students?" Adélaïde asked.

"He's leaving them in my charge." Madame David stood tall, as though daring Adélaïde to question her ability to do so. The effect was spoiled when a movement tightened her belly, and she absently rubbed it.

"But who will teach them?"

"He'll leave assignments for them, and the advanced students will assist them."

Monsieur David would steal her students, then leave for Rome? Adélaïde could not believe it. She left without saying goodbye.

A familiar figure, tall, broad-shouldered, his brown hair in a queue, hovered outside the doorway.

"I heard that some woman was walking through the halls, criticizing the students' work." Joseph Suvée greeted her with a smile.

"News travels fast here, I see."

He grinned. "Come to offer my students advice?"

"Should I?"

"Absolutely. We hold this exhibition to prepare our students for the Prix-de-Rome. By afternoon, this place will be packed with artwork. I come early to have less to review."

Adélaïde laughed. "My friend Joseph, always looking for the easy way."

Joseph bowed with an elegant flourish. "By that measure, you should return at five o'clock this evening, when all the works will be lined up for your inspection."

"I'm no military officer, monsieur."

"Yet you *are* wearing epaulets." Joseph pointed to her jacket.

"Perhaps because I knew I was going into battle," she said, then entered the Academy's office and asked to speak to an official. She watched as painters stenciled a military scene on a newly painted panel. Apparently, D'Angiviller had ordered changes here as well. A half hour ticked by while she choked on plaster dust, and her patience disappeared. Since everyone knew she was here, why make her wait?

Finally, she was shown down a short hallway to the secretary's office. Antoine Renou rose from his desk. Adjusting his dark gray jacket, he greeted her without any expression and waited for her to speak, so she came straight to the point. "I'm here to inquire about my space in the Louvre."

"I don't have any orders for space for you," he said.

"May I speak to Director Pierre then?"

"He's not here." She saw the slight curl of his lip.

"Who has the ultimate authority to approve space here?"

"The Comte d'Angiviller."

She should have known. "May I speak to him then?"

"He's also not here." This time the curl of his lip was more pronounced.

Did he think she was an idiot?

"When will he be back?"

"I cannot say." His pale blue gaze was wide, innocent. But she knew better.

"Then may I make an appointment to discuss my lodgings?"

"That's not possible." He looked down and picked lint off his jacket.

"Why not?" She waited while he pondered his response.

"It would require a meeting of the leaders of the Academy."

She folded her arms and regarded him with narrowed eyes. "Even though the Comte d'Angiviller has the final authority?"

He nodded.

"When is the next meeting?"

"Not until next month," he said.

"But—"

"I'm sorry, madame. I have urgent business and have no time for further questions." He sat down and turned back to his work.

She regarded him with disbelief. She wanted to stamp her foot and throw the marble bust of the king sitting on his desk at his impassive face. Instead, she dug her fingernails into her palms.

To be in good society, and to be good society, one never showed anger, one always remained composed. Her mother's voice.

Adélaïde took a deep breath and said, "Good day to you, sir." She managed to close the door quietly on her way out.

The bells of St. Germain L'Auxerrois chimed one and Adélaïde's stomach growled. Pushing aside her hunger, she stormed into François's studio.

François worked at his father's drafting table, drawing in the quiet. The comforting smell of turpentine and linseed oil greeted her, and a rush of nostalgia washed over her as she looked around the empty room. Once François had become a full Academy member, he had received a larger set of apartments that allowed him to have a bigger studio and a dormitory to house his students, yet he had organized the new studio in the same manner as the old, and his father's before that. For a moment, she wished herself back to that simpler time.

"Where is everyone?"

"At the exhibition," he said.

"Why aren't you there?"

"I'm working on my latest commission. The Comte d'Angiviller has asked several of us to produce paintings that depict republican glory and resolve—the act of dying for one's country, for example. The government will no longer purchase paintings that focus on such frivolous topics as men and women dallying in the forest. Instead, we are to instruct the children of France on the nature of true nobility."

"Many Parisians would argue that the sole purpose of royalty is to please themselves and cavort. In fact, I would far prefer to see people romping across my ceiling than killing each other."

He laughed.

"Which artists have received this commission?" she asked.

"Those with the designation of history painter."

She sighed. At least she would not have to worry about which ancient story she would choose. "What is your topic?"

"Heroism and sacrifice."

She came and looked over his shoulder, frowning at the couple in the sketch. The man, dressed in a toga, reclined on a stone seat against a chiseled rock wall, while he watched a woman pull a knife out of her side. "A woman killing herself is heroic?"

"I have drawn Arria, encouraging her husband Paetus to fall on his sword."

"A woman sacrificing herself to encourage her husband to sacrifice himself is the true nature of nobility?"

"The Emperor Claudius orders Paetus to commit suicide for his part in a rebellion, but Paetus does not have the courage to do it, so Arria stabs herself to show him it does not hurt."

She looked at the woman's face and the sepia splatters of blood François had shown spilling from the knife wound. "It looks like it hurts to me. I still fail to see how it is heroic for a wife to kill herself for her husband's crime."

"Arria sacrifices herself because she also believes in her husband's rebellion and refuses to live in a world where they cannot enjoy what they both fought for."

"She was willing to die for her convictions then."

He nodded. "More willing than her husband, it would seem."

"But the act of Paetus watching Arria makes him look weak," she said.

They stared at the sketch while François tapped out a dissatisfied drum beat with his pencil on the edge of the drawing board. "That is my difficulty," he admitted.

She considered the sketch. Her hand tingled. "What if you show her snatching the knife?"

He thought about it. "Before she stabs herself? Then it is her act alone."

"If the essential story is how she insisted on dying for their cause—"

"No, they died together."

"Then they were both involved, but when she takes the knife, she shows initiative and free will and accepts the consequence of her rebellion." She plucked the pencil from his hand and executed a quick sketch on the edge of the paper. "Make them in the middle of an argument, then he is not passive, she is not tragic. They are two people caught in a situation from which they cannot escape."

He regarded their two sketches for a minute, then took the pencil back. "You may be right." His eyes probed hers for a moment, then he eased off his stool and stretched. A new light entered his eyes. "I imagine you did not come here to give me artistic advice." He smiled.

"Of course not." For a moment, though, working with him had been a glimpse of heaven again. "I came to ask a question."

"That's all?" He looked disappointed.

She rolled her eyes. "It's the middle of the day."

"But you were the one who mentioned cavorting. And here we are, alone."

"I came for a serious matter."

He sighed and slouched back into his seat. "What is your question?"

"When you became an agréé, how did you get your studio and lodging here at the Louvre?"

He thought for a moment. "I do not recall doing anything. I received a letter from the Academy telling me to present myself at the Louvre to view the lodgings assigned to me."

"But how long did it take? Months? A year?"

"Not long." He shifted in his seat. "Then, of course, once I became a full-fledged member, I received larger quarters."

She looked around the room. "And did you have to do anything to receive them?"

"No, I just received a new assignment of rooms the next month. Of course, it took some time for the renovations."

"That's what I thought." Whatever good feeling she had experienced walking into François's studio evaporated. "I see that Monsieur David has received his lodgings."

He nodded. "He and his wife moved in right after he made it into the Academy."

"That was almost a year ago."

"His father-in-law oversees the construction that takes place here."

"How convenient for him. Is that why his lodgings are right next to the Academy's offices?"

"Perhaps, but I think it is more so that Academy officials can keep an eye on him. Sword fights and all."

She did not appreciate his levity. "What can be taking mine so long?"

"Perhaps they have no available space."

"In a palace with nine hundred rooms?" A headache formed.

He gave her one of his half grins and shrugged his shoulders. "Perhaps it is a question of construction schedules. Do you want me to ask for you?"

"I'll handle it myself."

Outside, the noon sun hung overhead. The summer day sweltered. By the time Adélaïde crossed the courtyard between the Carousel and the Louvre, she was hot, sweaty, and in no mood to be toyed with. She asked again for Secretary Renou and told the young clerk not to keep her waiting this time. When Renou appeared five minutes later, she demanded to see the Academy bylaws. It was another half hour before he handed her a heavy leather-bound book, warning her to take care of the ancient tome.

For the next two hours, she sat at a side table in the hallway outside the man's office, turning the crumbling pages, trying not to sneeze while she memorized a century of Academy rules and meeting minutes. Then she went to the secretary's office and asked for writing materials. She returned to the hallway and spent another hour penning her request.

"According to the regulations," she said as she reentered the secretary's office, "all Academy members are entitled to lodgings and may obtain them upon request. Please accept my formal request." She thrust the petition at him.

Renou took the document and told her that he would get back to her as soon as possible.

"I'll be waiting," she said.

～

The student exhibit was in full swing when she left the secretary's office. She wandered through the young men's paintings, critiquing and encouraging.

By the time she walked back along Rue de Rivoli and reentered the Place du Carousel, the sun had moved low into the western sky.

"Have you been at this all day?" François asked when she entered his studio and sank down into a chair.

She nodded.

"Have you eaten?"

She considered and then shook her head. Justine's half-eaten beignet was a far-off memory.

They ate at an upstairs restaurant on the south side of the river. The Seine turned pink, then purple as the sun set behind a tower of cumulus clouds.

She told François of her day. "While the Academy admitted Madame Lebrun and me, the officials have no intention of providing us with its benefits. They hope that by ignoring us, we'll go away." The breath caught in her throat. "It hurts to say this, but I can't think of any other explanation."

A wind tore across the water, rocking the flat boats against their moorings. Beneath the table, François took her hand in his.

She sniffed and tried to think of something else. "How is your concept drawing going?"

"Much better," he said. "I worked on your idea all afternoon."

She nodded, pleased. "Today I kept thinking what I would have done if I were Arria. How far would I go to change the world, to make it the one I want to live in?"

"That is the question, is it not?"

The waiter approached and poured them another glass of wine.

"François, something odd happened today. When I went into Monsieur David's studio, his wife hid some pamphlets. Then, when

I went to the student exhibition this afternoon, I heard students laughing and whispering behind me. Do you know why?"

He tensed.

"What is it?" she asked.

There was a long pause before he said, "I have no idea." He released her hand and pulled a small pad of paper from his vest pocket. Returning to the subject of Arria and Paetus, he sketched his new idea in miniature.

Her heart fell out of rhythm, as she regarded his bent head, thinking, *This is the first time he has ever lied to me.*

After dinner, they crossed the river. She shivered. Beside her, François walked at a correct distance, making no move to touch her, to brush against her body, to catch her hand in his. Lovers' voices bumped against them in the dark, like the water that lapped against the bridge pilings beneath them. At the end of the bridge, she went on alone, the night obliterated by torches flaming high on the building walls and glowing lamps strung across the intersections. Her own street was dark and quiet, her studio too. She had forgotten that the girls planned to visit the theater that evening. She let herself in and stood at the bay window, looking outside.

She pondered what she had observed that day, thought about what she was missing by not being in the Louvre. Perhaps Madame Lebrun, caught up in tending to a family, did not need or want these things, but she longed for the collegial collaboration of working in a group, and her students wanted the exhibitions and the advice of other teachers that the students at the Louvre had come to expect. She missed working with François but puzzled over his odd behavior this evening.

The silence out on the street intruded and blended with the silence inside. No one walked past the windows, looking in the shops. When she thought about it, she realized that she had passed no one in the street once she had turned on to her road and yet, it was not even nine o'clock. A shiver passed through her. Once her studio's location had thrilled her, but now she saw it for what it was: a cramped space on a thoroughfare losing its cachet. Now, all day long dray horses pulled cargo up from the river and passed her studio while printers and furniture makers moved into the shops beside her, and dressmakers and merchants serving royalty moved out to the Palais Royale. What was she to do?

Arria came into her mind and the tingle in her hands began. Perhaps painting would make her lose her worries and see what was possible. She would do a study of the woman. She lit a candle, then looked in surprise at the unfamiliar arrangement of her studio space. The girls had moved the worktable to make room for more easels, but every easel had a work in progress drying on it, even the one in the window. Tonight, it appeared, she would have to confine herself to a sketch.

The worktable had been pushed to the back of the room. A tubular roll in brown paper rested on it, a package from her father, sent by express post. Inside the roll was a note and another package.

Daughter, I write this not to upset you, but that you may be aware of the dangers you face and take immediate action.

She tore open the inner package. It was a pamphlet made from folded foolscap with familiar serpentine and swirling ivy calligraphy on the bottom. The title, *Twenty-One Men. By Anonymous* blazed out at her. The inside cover read, *Twenty-One Lovers. Twenty-One Positions.* The tube made a hollow sound as it hit the floor. The pamphlet was filled with colored drawings of her engaged in sexual acts with the men who had supported her quest to enter the Academy. Acts she did not understand, did not even know were possible. The faces, drawn in caricature, exaggerated the features of the men in her life: François's wild hair, Joseph Suvée's long nose, Joseph Vien's supercilious mien, Chevalier Roslin's retroussé nose and drooping eyelids. In the last drawing, the cartoonist had depicted Adélaïde as a snake wrapped around a group of struggling men. Above their flailing hands, her face split into a maw with dripping fangs and a forked tongue.

She squeezed her eyes shut but could not blot out the words written beside the drawings. Fear streaked through her.

Her father did not want to upset her? This is what the boys had laughed about as she had walked through the Louvre today? This was what the duchess had meant by a woman of your reputation? Not only had she seen a stack of them in David's studio, but her father had received one out in the country. A vice of pain circled her head. This pamphlet could destroy her.

She felt the thrum of her life's blood rushing through her neck.

Outside, bells chimed the hour. The theatres were about to let out. The girls could not see this . . . this vile thing. She ran up the stairs and shoved the booklet into the bottom drawer of her bureau, then collapsed onto the floor, panting for breath. She was humiliated, horrified, and terrified, all at once. Who would do this to her? And why hadn't François warned her?

CHAPTER 24

MAY 1784

Adélaïde stood in the Comtesse d'Angiviller's enormous drawing room, swallowing equal measures of pride and indignation. On the wall beside the fireplace, her portrait of Ducis winked down at her. She took comfort that the miniature gift to the comtesse held a place of honor on the wall.

The comtesse regarded Adélaïde with concern. "Are you ill, Madame Guiard?" she asked.

Adélaïde gripped her elbows across her aching stomach. She knew her face was gray from lack of sleep.

"Madame la Comtesse." She sounded far more tentative than the last time she had stood in this room. "It is against my nature to ask for favors, but I have nowhere else to turn. I do not object—and never will—to criticism of my work, but this I cannot manage." Her hand shook as she held out the sordid booklet.

When the comtesse saw the obscene cartoons, she flung the booklet away.

Averting her eyes, Adélaïde picked the pamphlet up and placed it face down on the comtesse's reading table. "I have no idea what I have done to deserve this, or who is behind it, but even my father who lives a day's journey from Paris has seen it." Her voice broke. "If I have no honor, I have nothing. This week, several customers cancelled their orders and two of my students left."

The comtesse rang a small, bright bell, and then a larger one.

When a maid appeared from behind a panel in the wall, she ordered a glass of water for Adélaïde. The footman stepped through the double doors, and she directed him to locate her husband.

While they waited for the water, the comtesse said, "Although you have not asked for it, I will offer you some advice. Without a husband or father here to protect you, you must obtain a royal sponsor."

Adélaïde nodded. "But you . . . I had hoped you—"

She shook her head. "My husband will handle this . . . piece of nonsense."

The footman returned and informed them that the comte would see his wife in his study. "Come," the comtesse directed, and they left the room. The scent of the woman's freesia perfume was strong as Adélaïde followed her.

"This is the trouble that comes when a woman attempts to do a man's work," d'Angiviller addressed his wife without looking at Adélaïde. He had not risen from his inlaid marble desk to greet them, but even seated, she could see he was dressed more elaborately than most royals who had attended À La Toilette. He wore a red velvet vest and a silken shirt with many gathers and gold fleur-de-lis embroidered on lace falls. In their muslin gowns, she and the comtesse looked like urchins pleading before him.

"No, this is what happens when men are threatened by a woman's success," his wife retorted. "But you are in a position to stop them, my dear."

The comte stared at his wife. "That woman is a fool," he said as though Adélaïde were not in the room.

"I thought better of you, darling," the comtesse said. "I'm asking you to help her."

D'Angiviller turned his gaze on Adélaïde. She realized that his eyes were not gray as she had supposed but rather the coldest shade of blue she had ever seen. "What did you expect, Madame Guiard?"

Adélaïde bit the inside of her lip and said nothing.

"I don't know what she expected, dearest," the comtesse intervened. "Perhaps to be left alone to pursue her talent?"

D'Angiviller flicked through the pamphlet his wife had placed on his desk and pushed it away with a disdainful finger. "What do you want me to do about this?"

"You must protect her. Her reputation is at stake."

He harrumphed. "As is the Academy's. We can't let the public think that we are a hotbed of impropriety and fornication. I will not have a brewing scandal, not when I have just begun to return the arts to their moral imperative." He picked up his pen. "A police investigation and a threat of an extended stay in the Bastille ought to do it." He wrote out an arrest warrant for persons unknown and rose. "I'll drop this off at the Châtelet on my way to the Louvre."

The comtesse took his arm as he walked out of his study. Just outside the door, the comte raised his voice. "I hope this is the last I hear of this. I have more important things to do than coddle that woman."

The comtesse dropped her arm to her side. "I am sure Madame Guiard does not expect any coddling," she said.

Adélaïde walked back to her studio, her steps precise on the uneven cobblestones, her posture rigid. Passing the fashionable shops along Rue St. Honoré, she felt the stares of shoppers boring into her back, thought she heard the whispers of gossips flying behind her. Her breathing sped up.

The Academy had to grant her lodgings in the Louvre soon. Without a place in the king's palace, everyone who was anyone knew she did not have the protection or approval of the king, and everyone else knew they could say whatever they wanted about her with impunity. D'Angiviller had to suppress the pamphlet. If the booksellers got ahold of it and sold it out on the streets, she would not be imagining stares, she would be fending off shouts and hurtled stones. If the situation did not change, she would be ruined.

CHAPTER 25

DECEMBER 1784

"Would you repeat that?" Adélaïde asked. "I don't believe I understood you."

The Comte d'Angiviller leaned back in his wooden chair in the pantry at the back of her studio. From the sideways movement of his nostrils, she knew he was toying with her.

A rolled piece of paper lay between them like a Roman candle on the checkered surface of the table.

She wished she could have backed away from the scent of rose water and bergamot splashed on his close-shaven cheeks, but her own chair was pressed against the wall. She was so close to the comte that she could see his beard pores from the light falling through the porthole window above his head. Beside her, Marie shifted in her seat, uneasy in her role as chaperone.

"I said, you may have one thousand livres a year, as long as you do not take lodgings at the Louvre and teach your students elsewhere." He repeated the words as though speaking to a dull-witted child.

Under the table, lace-covered buttons dug into her hands as she gripped her wrists and counted the ticks of the clock. She reminded herself that the man had made the pamphlet scandal go away. "For months I've waited for a response to my petition and a bribe is my answer?" She pushed the bank draft back across the table. "What's a thousand livres? This might get me three furnished rooms on a fourth floor in this district, with nothing left for food."

"You could always move into one of the surrounding faubourgs. There, you could rent three times the space for that. It appears you could use it." When the comte had walked into her studio and demanded to speak to her in private, she had had no choice but to usher him into the converted pantry closet the girls called her office.

"Agreed, but I can't leave the city center. My clients and students live here. I don't want money. I want the space I'm entitled to."

"Madame, that is simply not going to happen."

"Because I'm a woman?" When he did not respond, she began to list the female artists who lived at the Louvre. "Madame Vallayer-Coster, Madame Reboul, Joseph Vien's wife——"

"Their situation has nothing to do with yours."

She sat back and folded her arms. "Explain yourself, sir."

"You are not the widow of a former artist. You are not the wife of a current one." Sweat trickled down his face.

"The rules don't specify the type of member who may live there, or under what circumstances. You cannot get around the rules by asking me to leave the city."

Marie's chair squeaked as she moved again.

Adélaïde continued, "My students deserve to have the same opportunities as other Academy students. To get them, they need to study at the Louvre."

D'Angiviller leaned forward and rested his forearm on the table. "Now that is where you are wrong, Madame Guiard. Not one of your students will become an Academy member. Unless, of course, you wish to relinquish your place."

Pain stabbed at her temples. "Don't patronize me, sir. My students are as talented as any Academy student. They have a right to study there."

"The Academy does not teach female students," he said.

"Then you are misinformed. Several Academy members teach female students. Madame Lebrun and I studied there."

His face darkened. "The Louvre is little more than a barrack. It is not an appropriate place for women."

"And yet, hundreds of women live and study there. Why not I? Why not my students?"

"Enough." He shot out of his chair and slammed the table with his fists. The table jumped, and Marie made a sound of distress.

Adélaïde stared up at him, her head pressed against the wall. The scent of animal musk filled her nose as he loomed over her.

"I am the Comte d'Angiviller, madame, the Director of Building Projects. And you, madame, are not a protégée of the queen."

Heat rushed through her body, then cold.

He jabbed the bank draft. "Either take this money and find your own space or discover how unpleasant life can become for someone in your position."

She pushed her way out of her chair, but before she could respond, Marie rose and spoke, her voice high and shaky. "Perhaps Madame Guiard can have some time to think about this. It's possible that we could find a use for this money, Monsieur le Comte."

"I'm glad to see that someone here is willing to listen to reason." The comte stepped back.

"All I'm asking for is what I'm entitled to, nothing more, nothing less, Monsieur le Comte. That is a perfectly reasonable request." Adélaïde forced her tone to be neutral. What would happen if this were the only assistance the Academy gave her?

D'Angiviller picked up the bank draft. "If I leave here with this draft, my offer is revoked."

"But how am I supposed to cash it? I don't have a bank account."

"That is not my concern, madame. You are lucky the Academy has tried to work with you."

"If this is help, as you call it, I can't imagine what hinder looks like," she said.

The flesh around the comte's nose whitened.

Marie moaned and gave her an imploring look.

Adélaïde held her hand out for the check. "Money to help defray the costs of a large studio is better than nothing at all," she ground out.

He held the paper out of reach. "Write me a receipt. I do not want you changing your mind."

A few days later, Joseph Suvée stepped into her studio, looking angry. "Adélaïde, what have you done?"

She stopped her drawing lesson and went to the door. "What do you mean?"

He handed her a letter. She had never seen the signature of the king before but every part of her sank when she read the words.

By order of the King, no woman shall be allowed to attend any art class offered by the Academy or taught by any professor of the Academy at the Louvre.

"Apparently, d'Angiviller wrote the king, calling it a moral outrage that the corridors of the Louvre allow for the unsupervised mixing of young persons of the opposite sex. The king responded by issuing this decree."

"I can't believe d'Angiviller would go that far." She stared out the bay window, seeing nothing. "How do I fight a battle with a man who seems out to get me at every turn? Especially one who has the ear of the king?"

"I have no idea, Adélaïde. I just know that every woman at the Louvre hates the sound of your name, and I have lost half my income." He turned to leave. "We helped to get you into the Academy, and this is how you reward us?"

CHAPTER 26

PARIS, SUMMER 1785

"Let d'Angiviller try to stop us here," Adélaïde told her students as they lugged wooden crates filled with artwork into the Place Dauphine. It had taken her months to figure out how to exhibit her students' works, but this ancient square at the tip of the Île de la Cité, in the heart of old Paris, was the perfect site.

Sunlight splashed the stuccoed walls of the shop fronts lining the space. Overhead, unseen birds chirped in the elm trees, almost as happy on this summer day as her chattering students who pulled their canvasses from the crates and placed them on easels in the center of the triangular square. Yellow and white roses drooping in the heat blessed the air with their heady scent.

"The exhibit's sure to be a success, madame." Marie-Marguerite Carraux de Rosemond sat on a bench, ran a hand through her curly hair, then surreptitiously rubbed her aching feet. She, Marie, and Isabelle had walked the city for hours putting up posters to advertise the show.

At twenty, she was the latest to join Adélaïde's household. She had made her way from Switzerland to Paris to study art in the Louvre, but lost the right to study, and a place to live, when d'Angiviller ordered female students out of the Louvre.

"With the help of the Academy, how can it fail?" Adélaïde said. She had certainly put the comte's money to good use paying to rent space in this square. "If we can just keep the comte away for the next fourteen days, everything will be perfect."

On the second day of the exhibit, the square filled with art lovers, gawkers, and street vendors. At noon, meat pies and sizzling crepes called to Adélaïde, but then she spied the comte shouldering his way through the milling throng. He held a set of pamphlets in his hand. The sight of pamphlets made her nauseated and she braced herself, knowing she was about to get a bellyful of complaints.

"Where are your protectors, madame?" the comte asked.

She pursed her lips, then said quietly, "I have no protectors, as you well know." *Nor even friends who can be seen with me in public.* She and François had agreed they would stop seeing each other until the furor had died down. Joseph Suvée was still angry with her, and many of the remaining twenty-one men in the pamphlet avoided her. It had been a long year.

The comte looked around the square. "This is simply not done," he said.

"But what else am I to do?" she asked, folding her arms. "The Academy has left me no choice."

D'Angiviller wiped his brow with a handkerchief and said under his breath, "Wherever you go, madame, you bring controversy."

Even though the bright summer sun stabbed her eyes, she regarded him with a raised eyebrow. "Let the students you barred from the Louvre back in and grant me my space in the Louvre. Controversy solved, sir." She made sure that the people around them could hear her voice.

His eyes widened. People stopped looking at the paintings and started watching them instead. "I wish to know who gave you permission for this show."

"Do not begin to suggest, Monsieur le Comte, that you've come to close my exhibit down."

"Well, I—"

She stepped up to him, glad for heavy skirts that hid shaky knees. "Well, you cannot. As a member of the Academy, I have the right to organize a public exhibit."

"As a matter of fact—"

A well-known art critic stepped forward and interrupted the comte. "The Young Women's Student Art Show has exhibited here for decades. Do you mean to stop that too?"

Someone across the square started shouting that the comte was closing the exhibit. A crowd gathered around them.

The comte stepped back. "You have proven yourself a worthy opponent, Madame Guiard, but can we not discuss this elsewhere?"

"We can discuss anything you like right here in front of our guests, Monsieur le Comte." When he said nothing, she held out her hand. "I invite you to view our exhibit with me." With the crowd watching, he could do nothing but offer his arm. They walked through the exhibit. His jaw clenched and Adélaïde repressed a feeling of repulsion for having to touch this man who wished her no good.

They stopped at an easel in the middle of the square. "Look at this self-portrait, Monsieur le Comte."

In the painting, Marie Capet had adopted the traditional pose of an artist, paintbrush in hand. Gone was the gawky and emaciated young girl who had walked into Adélaïde's studio. In her place, a young woman in blue silk and lace, tumbling hair wrapped in a coil of blue ribbon, graced the canvas. "Look how this artist has demonstrated her ability to paint fabrics, textures, and accuracy of form. The figure moves through space in an utterly realistic way. I defy you, Monsieur le Comte, to tell me that the work of this artist does not equal the work of any agréé in the Academy today."

D'Angiviller regarded Marie's exposed shoulders painted beneath a transparent shawl edged in gold. "This offends the public's sensibilities," he gritted.

"Which public?" She gestured at the art patrons in the square. "These people don't seem offended."

D'Angiviller shook the pamphlets at her. "This public," he said.

She glanced up at the elm trees, the blue sky beyond, then looked at him. "What is offensive to me, sir, is that my students' works must be shown on a public street and not in the Louvre where they belong. What should be an affront to all is that a woman displaying her professional talents and abilities is called wanton."

He turned to a sketch of a male figure on an easel beside Marie Capet's portrait and opened another pamphlet. "The rules of propriety cannot be respected by a woman whose unashamed eyes are accustomed to seeing a naked man every day," he quoted.

"How is this different from any young man painting a female nude?" she asked.

He ignored her question and continued, "'Flatterers should not encourage a taste in idleness and frivolity for those who are destined to fulfill the important role of motherhood, nor should they foster activities that discourage the highest qualities of womanhood: fidelity and conjugal love.'"

She sighed and pulled a pamphlet from a voluminous pocket hidden in the folds of her skirt. "For every pamphleteer who writes such distressing comments, sir, there are two more that encourage our work. This one says that the glory of the sun cannot diminish the glory of these girls' works and argues that as treasures of France, they belong in the Louvre to reflect the glory of France. I recommend that you consider improving your reading material, sir." She held the booklet out to him.

Several onlookers laughed. Mopping his brow again, D'Angiviller said, "Madame, I cannot support this action of yours."

She bared her teeth in a triumphant smile. "Nor, sir, can you stop it. I have the legal right to hold this show." From her other pocket she withdrew a license from the Châtelet permitting her to hold the exhibition and showed it to him. "Now, sir, perhaps you would be so kind as to leave. You are drawing unwanted attention."

The onlookers laughed. Someone clapped.

"Madame, my troops would never have dared to speak to me the way you have."

"But I am not one of your soldiers, *General.*"

They faced each other in the center of the square while the raucous crowd swirled around them. Nearby, a clock struck a single note. A group of drunken university students entered from the bridge and shouted vulgarities at her students.

D'Angiviller's mouth fell open. "Your students should not be displaying their wares out on a city street."

Adélaïde folded her arms and nodded. "I couldn't agree with you more."

∿

"I thought d'Angiviller would arrest you this afternoon," Marie said from where she sat on Adélaïde's bed. She and Isabelle tallied the exhibition's earnings while Adélaïde paced between Marie's lurid screen and Isabelle's stack of crates.

Marguerite's "corner" was defined by a long cheval glass. She emerged from behind it and sat on the bed. "I cannot believe you spoke to him that way," she said.

"I'm still shaking." Adélaïde held out her trembling hands. "I thought he would drag me to the Châtelet himself."

"Still, a comte, madame," Isabelle agreed with Marguerite.

"When I thought about another exhibit of mine being closed down, I didn't stop to think."

Marie finished counting and ran a loving eye over the stacks of coins. "One thousand, five hundred twenty-two livres. We should go to Café Procope and celebrate."

"No, we must save the money," Isabelle cautioned. "We never know when we'll hold another exhibit."

"Since we promised to include Monsieur Suvée's students in the next one, it will have to be soon," Marie said.

"I hear that Monsieur Suvée and Monsieur David intend to defy the king's order," Isabelle said.

Adélaïde stopped mid-stride and perched on the edge of the bed. Her gaze fell on Marguerite's bowed head. "I feel terrible that my struggles with the Academy caused you girls to be put out." While Joseph had sent Marguerite to her for help, he had not spoken to Adélaïde since he had slammed out of her studio last December. "The Châtelet may not grant me another license, especially if d'Angiviller finds out that I used the bank draft with his signature on it to get it."

Isabelle chuckled, but it was not a happy sound.

Adélaïde reviewed Marie's column of numbers. "An exhibit is not enough. The answer to everything is that we must all be at the Louvre—you, me, the students d'Angiviller expelled." She resumed her pacing. "We are artists. It should not matter whether we are men or women. I wish I could make them understand."

"Imagine an art school for women at the Louvre." Marie looked off into space.

"I would offer studies in perspective, anatomy, history—everything that male students have at their disposal, you would have," Adélaïde said.

A dreamy look crossed Isabelle's face. "I can just picture that school."

"I don't know if it will ever happen," Adélaïde said.

Isabelle locked the cash box and put it under the bed. "Director Pierre is always saying art instructs. You should make a painting that proves that women belong in the Louvre."

"Like a geometric theorem?" Adélaïde asked, doubtful.

"Yes."

Adélaïde sat back down on the bed. "Science and reason have taken our knowledge to a better place, but fear and tradition blind people and hold them back." She rubbed at the tight muscles in her neck. "This battle with the Academy is wearing me down."

"If science can transport man above the trees of Faubourg Saint-Antoine, you would think science and reason could propel women into the Louvre." Isabelle had watched a hot air balloon experiment earlier that week.

"I don't see how," Adélaïde said.

"You have to outwit the Academy," Marie told her. "Otherwise, they will never give in."

They tried to think up ways to do that while they prepared for bed. Just as Adélaïde blew out the lantern, Marie sat up. "I have it!"

When Marie told them, Adélaïde burst out laughing. The idea was so simple, it was perfect.

~

Two months later.

"Hurry, madame," Isabelle urged. "Both Monsieur Vincents are waiting downstairs for you."

"Let them wait." Rouging her face at the mirror above her bureau, Adélaïde allowed herself a triumphant smile. Marie's idea of "transporting" them to the Louvre had been brilliant. Adélaïde had constructed a tableau of herself in court dress, engaged in painting an unseen painting, the turned easel and canvas jutting into the foreground while Marie and Marguerite looked over her shoulder, Marie's attentive gaze focused on the unseen painting, and Marguerite's gaze directed at the viewer. In the background, the bust of Adélaïde's father looked down on the trio of women, a reference to classical tradition and the blessing of a father overlooking his daughter's work.

France's major art critic had called her painting exquisite, and Parisians flocked to the Louvre to see this famous painting of women made by a woman. For the first time in the history of the Salon, the female members of the royal family refused a private showing of Salon paintings in Versailles. Instead, Queen Marie Antoinette, her seven-year-old daughter, and the king's aunts came with such a large female entourage that their coaches blocked the roadways. Academy officials were forced to move Adélaïde's painting into the Louvre's grand ballroom. After the royal women's visit, Adélaïde's painting was the central attraction of the Salon. The irony of Adélaïde's message missed no one: while she and her students were barred from the Louvre, a painting of them—her painting of them—was permitted. Tonight, the Academy would present Adélaïde with a prize for Most Accomplished Painting.

She put down the red tinged rabbit foot and moved to stand in front of the cheval glass. Wearing the blue silk dress from her self-portrait, she looked regal, assured, confident. Downstairs, she greeted Joseph and François, who waited for her dressed in black finery with white lace pinching their throats.

Alexandré looked around the room. "Who is this splendid person? Where is our Addy?"

Adélaïde wrinkled her nose at the old nickname.

François's eyes were soft. "You look beautiful," he said.

Inside she glowed. Her eyes met his for a brief interlude before she waved away their compliments with a lace-gloved hand. "Did you see it?" she demanded.

"Did we see what?" François asked.

She went to her desk and retrieved a pink vellum envelope covered in elaborate calligraphy. "Gentlemen, this is what an offer for ten thousand livres looks like." The king's aunt, Madame Adélaïde, had offered to buy her painting. "It was very difficult to turn down their offer to buy this painting, but I heeded your Machiavellian advice, Alexandré." She smiled. "And you will not believe what has happened."

"Well?" Alexandré prompted.

Returning the first envelope to the drawer, she pulled out a second one. "The Mesdames have commanded me to present myself at Versailles on Tuesday." Instead of accepting their offer, she had written a letter to the princesses begging for the opportunity to paint their illustrious persons in a suitable fashion.

First François, then Alexandré swept her up in a crushing embrace.

"I demand a commission," Alexandré said.

"Gentlemen," she laughed. "Don't wreck my invitation. I need it to get into the palace."

One week later.

Adélaïde could not believe she was in Versailles, the palace of the king. Her body still rattled from the twenty-mile coach ride. She dragged the skirts of her court dress through a long corridor behind a liveried servant who carried her sketchpad in a large fabric bag. Struggling to keep up, she admonished herself to stop looking around. But it was the home of the royal family, the source of all the stories she had heard as a child.

At last, they went through two antechambers, then a huge, marble-lined octagonal drawing room filled with musical instruments, finally arriving at Madame Adélaïde's library. The room was lined with wooden bookcases whose decorative carved edges matched the rose swags painted on the wood paneled walls. Red leather-bound books lined the bookshelves. Doric columns rose to support twenty-foot-high ceilings painted with clouds. Louis XIV chairs, a desk, and multiple tables piled with books cluttered the room. It was rumored that Madame Adélaïde had spent more to decorate her chambers than the king had spent on his, but the opulent furnishings, tapestries, and carpets did nothing to disguise the smell of damp in the air nor dispel the chill permeating the rooms. Despite her brisk walk through the palace, cold struck Adélaïde through her heavy gown.

Then she was bowing her head, tucking her right foot behind her left, holding her back straight as she spread her skirt wide. She held her breath to keep her chest from heaving from the long walk, then bent her knees to within eight inches of the floor, executing a flawless curtsey before Madame Adélaïde and Madame Victoire.

The king's aunts sat on rose velvet chairs facing a fireplace where two large logs blazed up the chimney. Madame Adélaïde, tall, thin, and severe looking at fifty-three, put down her knitting and appraised Adélaïde. The woman's younger sister, Madame Victoire, rounder of face and double chinned, looked on Adélaïde with more warmth.

From her place in front of the hearth, Adélaïde waited for a gesture by Madame Victoire, then sat as directed on a tufted footstool between the two women. When she sat, Adélaïde saw the fleur-de-lis embroidered with gold thread on the velvet of the princesses' chairs, saw the lions' paws carved into their scrolled feet. It was not a dream. She really was in Versailles.

A log in the fireplace behind her snapped, startling her. She tucked the fabric of her skirts closer and hoped her dress would not catch fire.

Madame Adélaïde spoke. "We very much liked your work at the Salon."

"Thank you, Your Royal Highness. I am most honored."

"We are looking for someone to paint our portraits."

"We do not want any feminine nonsense."

The words bounced between the sisters like a ball at a tennis match.

"I assure Your Royal Highnesses that I will portray your persons with dignity and respect and in the utmost good taste." Adélaïde forced herself to maintain a straight face. She now knew why the former king had called his elder sister Rags. Beneath the scruffy woolen shawls they wore to overcome the chill, the two princesses wore nightgowns over their panniers.

"We want our royal heritage to be clear in these paintings." Madame Victoire helped herself to a chocolate candy from a box on the table to her right.

Adélaïde promised that her paintings would transform them to glory, power, and place. "I will use backgrounds and symbolic props to indicate your royal heritage. I will show you with the instruments of France, a bust or painting of your father, and documents certifying your heritage." Her enthusiasm built, and she ignored the heat of the fire at her back. "I believe your paintings will be the first history paintings of royal women in France."

Madame Victoire looked intrigued. "And painted by a woman," she said.

Adélaïde's hand tingled. She pulled her sketchbook out. "May I?" she asked, then executed two quick sketches, showing first one sister, then the other standing among the symbols of France. She fleshed out each woman's face, her sepia pencil flying, as she spoke to them and observed their expressions. When she turned the sketchbook toward the sisters, she saw the fleeting look of approval that crossed Madame Adélaïde's face.

"You shall do for our purposes," the princess said.

They ordered several paintings from Adélaïde, untroubled by the exorbitant prices she suggested. Madame Victoire waved the numbers away with an imperious hand. "The queen pays more for her portraits."

Adélaïde assumed Madame Victoire meant the prices charged by Élisabeth Lebrun. Well, she was not a shopkeeper's daughter for nothing. Her face retained its pleasant smile. "I have reduced my prices for your Royal Highnesses, but on the condition that I be named First Painter of the Mesdames."

The two sisters were flattered. "As you wish," Madame Victoire agreed.

Victory swelled in Adélaïde's heart. Having accomplished what she had come for, she arranged a schedule of sittings, then waited for Madame Adélaïde to dismiss her. Curtseying, she backed out of the room. Once in the music room, she twisted her arm behind her back and pulled the scorching fabric away from her skin.

Half an hour later, alone in her hired coach, she leaned forward on the seat and fanned herself as the conveyance rumbled its way back to Paris. The heat at her back dissipated, and she relaxed against the seat. A wide smile split her face. With her mind's eye, she pictured her work hanging on the walls of Madame Adélaïde's library. She could not wait to return to Paris and write to tell her father that her paintings would now grace the grandest palace in Europe. And even about the small painting of hers making its way across the Atlantic, sold to the United States' Minister to France, Thomas Jefferson.

A mote crossed her rosy daydream. As a young princess, Madame Adélaïde had trained in science and calculus and had refused to give up her studies and her freedom unless she married a monarch. Adélaïde had thought to meet a kindred spirit in her namesake. Instead, she had encountered the desiccated lives of two maiden princesses relegated to knitting in the back rooms, aging along with their rotting palace.

Something François said years ago came back to her. What had Vien advised his students? In Art, there were beauties to follow, defects to avoid. Now that she had become the recipient of royal patronage, she understood the true meaning of these words. If she wanted to retain her place as First Painter to the Mesdames, she would have to be more successful at this than any other artist who painted them. But of all the challenges she had faced, this surely would be the easiest.

CHAPTER 27

FEBRUARY 1788

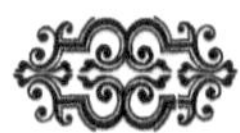

T he studio was too quiet.

Adélaïde put down her quill and looked around the room. It was Monday, a month after her father's death and her first day back in the studio. Concentrating on the minutiae of record-keeping this morning to dull the ache of her father's passing, it had taken a while to realize something was amiss.

Marie was at a canvas, brushing paint into a background. Isabelle stood at another, transferring an outline. Marguerite was not there, but she had gotten married on the first day of the year and left the studio. Her absence in their morning household routine had felt odd, but that was not what was wrong. The rest of the girls had gathered around a wooden Madonna wrapped in a red scarf, sketching the fabric folds that fell at the statue's feet.

No one spoke.

On Monday the girls regaled each other with their Saturday afternoon escapades and giggled over the love letters they had received on Sunday. Monday mornings were a time of chatter, excitement, and singing.

Singing.

Her eyes swung to the canvas at the far end of the room, a portrait for a client waiting final touches. The chair in front of the easel was empty.

"Where's Justine?" Adélaïde asked, rising from her seat. The sudden death of her father had made her feel edgy, as though something bad could happen at any moment.

When no one answered, she turned to Justine's closest friend, Jeanne Bernard. "Well?"

"I'm sure she'll send around a note," Jeanne said. "She left on Friday at noon saying she had an errand to run for her family."

"Wasn't she here on Saturday?" Adélaïde asked.

"No," Isabelle said.

"But didn't she say she might not be here on Saturday?" another student asked.

"I don't remember that," Isabelle said.

"Maybe she's not feeling well," Marie suggested. "Last week, most of us had a cold."

Adélaïde returned to her writing and the girls to their sketching, but inside, unease stirred. Justine would not leave her studio without telling her. The sounds of pencil shading and the scratch of Adélaïde's pen as she tallied up the month's results grew loud in a room silenced by Justine's missing voice.

On Tuesday morning, lessons began without her.

"She's never missed a day in four years," Adélaïde said.

"I'm sure she'll show up," Isabelle said. "It's her turn to teach the class this afternoon. She would never be late for that." But one o'clock came. The younger afternoon students waited for their lesson to begin, sketchpads in hand. No Justine.

"I'll take the class," Marie said.

At two o'clock, the bell jingled and the door to the studio opened. A woman entered. Not Justine.

"May I help you?" Adélaïde asked as the woman pulled her umbrella closed. A sheet of rainwater fell from its pointed tip onto the wood floor.

"I have an appointment for a sitting." The woman removed her coat. Adélaïde saw the woman indeed was dressed in her best finery.

"Madame, I apologize, but I don't seem to have you on my schedule."

"Oh, no, I'm here for Marie-Justine de Beaumont."

Marie stopped teaching in mid-sentence. Adélaïde's students froze, as though they had joined the wooden Madonna in eternal stillness. Her own heart missed a beat.

Isabelle came and pulled her aside. "Madame, something's

dreadfully wrong," she whispered. "Justine would never miss a sitting. She needs the money."

"I know," Adélaïde said, her heart thumping madly now. She rescheduled the disgruntled woman's sitting and sent her on her way. Then she hurried up the stairs and pulled out her record box. After finding what she was looking for, she donned a heavy jacket over her work dress, put on a hat, and returned to the studio. "Justine lives on Rue St. Honoré, not far from here," Adélaïde told her students. "I'm going over there to find out if she's taken ill."

The black slate numbers above the doorframe matched the numbers on the paper in Adélaïde's hand, but the address was a restaurant in a row of restaurants and shops, closed until the evening. No one appeared in the windows, and no one answered the locked door. Pacing back and forth on the rain-slicked street, Adélaïde wondered what to do. Could Justine have written down the wrong house number? She returned to her studio, more troubled than before.

At six when afternoon classes were over, Isabelle straightened the studio while Adélaïde and Marie pulled on their cloaks and returned to the restaurant.

The balding man who answered the door wearing a white apron over his black work clothes did not recall a Marie-Justine de Beaumont. "Perhaps you mean Marie Beaumonde?" he asked. "Pretty girl, dark hair?"

"That sounds like her," Adélaïde said.

"She hasn't worked here for some time."

"Worked here?" Marie's eyes widened.

"Do you know where she went? Do you know where we might find her?" Adélaïde asked.

The man went into the kitchen to consult the chef. He came back with the name of a tavern on the way to Faubourg Saint-Marcel.

When Adélaïde and Marie stepped out of the restaurant, darkness had fallen. They maneuvered their way through the sedan chairs and foot traffic back to the studio. Then Adélaïde went to get François. The tavern was on the south side of the river, and women of their class did not visit taverns alone.

As she and François hurried across the river, snow flurries melted before hitting the ground. After the earlier rain, the cobblestones turned slick and icy. They visited three establishments before they had any luck.

"Ran off a couple of days ago," the proprietor said. "Just before the Sabbath, leaving me with a lot of disappointed customers." He slammed a tankard down on the bar top. "She was my best singer. What am I to do now?"

"None of this makes any sense," Adélaïde said to François.

"Do you know where she lives?" François asked.

The man pointed at the ceiling. "Left everything in her room. I won't be keeping it for her for long, I can tell you that."

"May we see her room?" Adélaïde asked.

"Not much to see but follow me."

Adélaïde wanted to rush the man's lumbering form up the stairs and was glad when he stood aside after unlocking the door. François, who held a lit candelabrum, entered first. Justine was not there.

A narrow bed, its yellow coverlet smoothed with precision, a dresser with a bottle of lemon verbena its sole ornament, a familiar guitar leaning against a ladder-back chair. Three dresses hung on hooks by the door.

"This is her room," Adélaïde said. "These are her clothes." She shivered in the frigid air. "But her cloak's missing."

Just then a wind gust tugged at the candle flames. The window was open. Adélaïde went and pulled it closed. Tiny droplets of moisture, melted snowflakes, covered the windowsill, and glimmered in the candlelight.

Looking for clues, François pulled opened the dresser drawers. In the top middle drawer, he found a stack of letters wrapped in blue ribbon, an unfinished one on top. He read it, then handed it to her and held the candelabra out.

Justine's handwriting.

Friday, 8 February. Dearest Maman, just a few lines to dash off before my morning class. Please don't fret. I have found a way to afford your medicine. By the time you get this letter, the money will be on its way. I've obtained a commission at the Louvre. I'm off to class now but can't wait to write you all about it.

A feeling of horror spread through Adélaïde. "She's been missing for five days."

Back downstairs, François asked the tavern keeper if he remembered anything else. Had Marie been courting someone? "No," the man said. "She's a good girl, keeps to herself. Out at another job all day, then back at night to sing."

How could she not have known this about her student?

A barmaid approached, her green eyes dark with concern, freckles standing out on her pale face. "Someone delivered a letter to Marie on Thursday evening," she said. "She read it but left it at the bar because she was singing. She forgot to take it upstairs when she finished for the night. I saved it for her, but she hasn't been back to get it." The girl went behind the counter, pushed aside the row of wine bottles on the shelf beneath, and retrieved the note.

The envelope bore the imprint of the Royal Academy's address at the Louvre.

"This man asks Justine to meet him on Friday afternoon to assist him with a painting, but I don't recognize his name. Do you know him, François?"

François took the letter. "I have never heard that name. We must find out who he is."

Back out on the street, the snow had stopped. François hailed a fiacre and told the driver to hurry. The carriage careened through raucous night streets, filled with drunken revelers despite the weather, the driver shouting for everyone to get out of the way.

"Whatever possessed her to go off to a stranger's apartment for a painting job?" she asked.

"Maybe she eloped," François said.

Her gut told her otherwise.

The apartment number led to a locked gallery. François glanced at the note. "This wing was closed last year when the roof collapsed after a heavy rain. I do not know of any Academy member who lives this way."

By the time they roused the Academy guard and returned to the locked gallery, La Samaritaine's clock struck two. Outside, the storm clouds had scattered, revealing a full moon that threw bright patches of light across the floor tiles at every window. Their footsteps echoed in the empty halls as they walked for what seemed like miles after the guard unlocked the gallery door. The keys at his belt jingled with each step and he wheezed as they hurried along. His lamp made a feeble arc of light that jerked across the numbers painted in brass plates on each paneled door. The smell of mold billowed out at them when they skirted a scaffold placed beneath a boarded-up ceiling.

"Here it is," the guard stopped to catch his breath, then tried various keys. None fit. He banged on the door and yelled, "Open up!" When no one responded, he turned to go. "No one's here. We'll come back in the morning and have the builder let us in."

Adélaïde shook the door handle and pushed on the door with her gloved hands. "No, we have to get inside now. This is the last place she went. We have to find her, even if we have to break down the door." She shoved at the door.

The guard and François gave each other a knowing look, then hunched down and threw their shoulders against the wood. After a few tries the wood splintered and gave way. The guard kicked the broken boards aside.

Adélaïde gathered up her skirts and followed the men into a large chamber, bare of furnishings except for an easel and a chair in the middle of the room. When she saw that the place was empty, she breathed a sigh of relief. A faint sickly-sweet odor met the back of her throat.

Then a strip of silvery light from one of the side windows struck the far corner of the room. There, in the shadows, a roll of dark ochre cloth lay against the frescoed wall. Justine's cloak.

"No. No, no, *no*." Adélaïde cried. She pushed past the men and ran to Justine, who lay wrapped in her cloak, still as stone, her face marble in the moonlight.

Adélaïde felt as though she had separated into two pieces. Part of her was above the scene, far away, telling herself she was in a nightmare. The guard was shouting at François, but she could not hear him, even though he waved his hands in the air and his breath spewed from his mouth in gusts of fog. Then he was flinging open windows and running from the room, leaving François to guard the door. The other part of her was still inside her shaking body, trying to forget the smell of death, the gut wrenching, gagging awfulness of it, the blood, pooled in icy black patches along the hard floor, Justine's bare skin, cold like butter from an icehouse, unresponsive to Adélaïde's beseeching hands. Her emptied stomach quivered again, and she turned away, hugging herself, her eyes squeezed shut, praying to wake up.

When the Comte d'Angiviller arrived, he regarded Justine with the dispassion of a man used to guards rousing him in the middle of the night to decide what to do with a dead body. His voice calm, he ordered the guards to retrieve officers from the Châtelet.

He has seen many young men just as mangled on a battlefield, Adélaïde thought, but it was Justine lying in a lonely room with snow falling through the collapsed ceiling.

Arriving minutes after the comte, Director Pierre was another matter. When he saw the stab wounds, his eyes bulged, and he ran out into the hall. The sounds of his retching made her stomach lurch again, but there was nothing left inside her gut to lose.

A clink of metal broke the silence. D'Angiviller dropped gold coins into the hand of the lieutenant who stood next to two officers holding a stretcher, handkerchiefs tied beneath their averted eyes. The white trim on the officers' navy uniforms flashed in the torchlight as they knelt and wrapped Justine's body in a blanket. Their boots a parade of shadow and light, the king's officers lifted her onto the stretcher and stood up.

The smell of death curled through the room again. Adélaïde pressed her scarf over her nose and mouth. Even then, she wanted to tell the men to be careful, that it was Justine they held between them, but her mind screamed, *Get up, Justine. Get off that stretcher. You must come back. We can't survive without you singing to us every day.*

The officers brought their silent burden to the door. A tangle of brown hair spilled over the side of the stretcher and Adélaïde thought she smelled lemon verbena. Her knees buckled. She had not realized François was holding her up until he staggered against her back.

How could she tell the girls that Justine had been murdered? She wished this day had never happened, the week had never happened, that she could unwind all the events that had led to this moment. Her studio would never be the same.

"Madame Guiard, may I have a word with you?"

"I—my student . . . I must stay with her, Monsieur le Comte."

His eyes bored into hers. "No, madame, you are to remain behind." He turned and spoke sharply to Director Pierre and the Louvre guards. More money changed hands before the guards left. Pierre bowed himself out without a word.

With the torches gone, gray light filled the gallery. Clouds had returned with the dawn.

When the guards' footsteps faded in the hall, d'Angiviller turned on her. "God almighty, woman, can you not keep track of your students? How did this happen? What was she doing here?"

She wanted to fall over from the force of the comte's anger. François grabbed her elbows, steadying her.

"I–I believe she was working, monsieur," she said. *How could Justine have been safer singing in a tavern than in my studio painting?* "We have to find the monster who did this."

"No, madame, we do not. If anyone asks, you are to say that Mademoiselle de Beaumont left town. What happened to this girl will not be mentioned again. From the moment that you step out of this room, you are never to speak of it. Do you understand, Madame Guiard?" He set his stubble-lined jaw.

She burned with the effort to keep her mouth shut.

When she did not answer, d'Angiviller turned to François. "You understand, do you not, Monsieur Vincent? Such a scandal could endanger our entire program. I will not tolerate it. If this gets out, there will be ramifications."

Beside her, François said, "We understand, Monsieur le Comte."

The comte's wooden heels sounded a measured retreat down the hall.

Adélaïde went and picked Justine's cloak up, saw the dried cranberry stains in the dawn's ash-gray light. She folded the garment gently, inside out, thinking, *I will have to give this to her mother.* A roaring started in her ears. She forced herself to think through it. "François, I need you to call me a carriage."

"What? Where are you going?"

"To Versailles."

"Adélaïde, you cannot go now. We must get back to your students."

She shook her head. "I can't go back there right now."

He put his hand on her shoulder. "You heard the comte. We need to figure out what to say to them."

She shrugged his hand away. "You had no right to speak for me, François."

"I was not trying to speak for you."

She blew out a breath. "If you weren't trying to speak for me, you would have said nothing."

"I was not sure you could speak. It seemed he demanded an answer. I was just trying to do what was best in the situation."

"What was best for me? Or what was best for you?"

"You heard the comte, Adélaïde. The situation is . . . complicated. We need to consider the repercussions."

She shook her head. "It's not complicated at all. Justine did not deserve this. What the comte said sickens me. I'm not going to let them pretend this never happened." She stopped and stared at him. "And you, François, I can't believe you'd even consider it."

He sighed. "All right, then, but let us at least go back to your studio until you compose yourself. You are distraught—"

"Don't talk to me about what I am. Just get me that coach." Hugging the cloak to her chest, she pushed past him into the hall.

CHAPTER 28

VERSAILLES AND PARIS, WINTER AND SPRING 1788

The princesses stopped their backgammon game and stared at Adélaïde.

"Did we schedule a sitting today?" Madame Victoire asked.

The two sisters sat at a game table beside the fireplace in Madame Victoire's blue-lined library. Heavy silk drapes embroidered with blue and gold fleur-de-lis pushed back the dreary winter afternoon. Inside, candelabra brightened the room. The scent of beeswax fought with wood smoke from the fireplace. Adélaïde resisted the urge to cough.

"No. Your Highnesses, forgive me." Averting her eyes, Adélaïde curtsied again. After all these months, it still shocked her to see the princesses in their undergarments. She held out a painting she had done of Justine. "I need to tell you a story, the story of a working girl trying to support her family with her talent, the story of an innocent lamb succumbing to danger in a world that offers such girls no protection at all."

François had been right to get her to change out of her bloodied clothes and to think before she acted.

"I do not know where else to turn, your Highnesses. We need your help."

Madame Adélaïde set her snuffbox on the green felt tabletop and took the portrait from her. "Such beauty interrupted." Her tobacco-stained fingers smoothed the image of Justine's face.

Adélaïde wanted to tell the princess not to touch the portrait but clenched her teeth.

"So much talent lost." Madame Victoire put the long stem of her porcelain pipe to her lips and puffed.

"The light has gone from our studio," Adélaïde said. Her mind replayed the scene in her studio that morning, when she and François had returned, and Marie Capet had demanded to know where Justine was. To watch the grief that fell upon her students, tender, naïve, hopeful, waiting for their own work to support them. She could not stand it. When the wailing started, it felt worse to Adélaïde than losing her brothers, her sister, her parents, her marriage, everything. This had happened to a student of hers, someone for whom she was responsible. She had never felt such rage, such helplessness. Now, she trembled with the effort to keep those feelings off her face. "I don't know what to tell her mother. Her family depended on her."

"This study here." The older princess tapped the portrait. "Perhaps you could paint our dear departed sister in this pose."

Madame Victoire puffed out a vapor of smoke. "We will send you to our nephew, the Comte de Provence. He is always looking for a worthy project." She straightened her pile of black chips on the table and picked up a shaker. When Adélaïde made no move to leave, she said, "That will be all."

Trying not to think, Adélaïde bowed herself out of the room. The footman closed the double doors behind her. Through the narrowing crack, dice snapped inside the shaker cup.

"What a lovely gift." Madame Victoire's muffled voice. "I shall hang this portrait beside the fireplace."

"Clearly, I should have the painting," her sister said. "It matches the colors of my apartments."

"But it will show better in contrast here, my dear."

Three weeks later, on a bright spring day, Adélaïde received a summons to appear at the Palais du Luxembourg at midday. Having used the intervening time to study the Comte de Provence's interests, she was prepared. She brought a roll of sketches, a small box of pastels, and her largest sketchbook.

The footman showed her into a capacious hall with a line of perhaps a hundred servants holding silver cloched dishes snaking their way through the room. The caramel smell of roast beef, sweet bitter parsnips, and sharp lemon with fish tantalized her nose, made her ravenous. At the far end of the room, at the head of a table capable of seating forty dinner guests, sat an enormous man, dining alone. Wondering what to do, she gripped her summons and tried to catch the attention of the silent throng of black-garbed waiters. One of them shrugged his shoulders and gestured toward the table with his platter of strawberries.

'The prince saw her approach, lifted his thick wrist, and waved his serviette toward the chair on his left. She eyed the folding stools placed at the foot of the table and hesitated. "We are not pointing at anyone else," he told her.

Across the table, a servant poured wine into a silver chalice and stared down at her with frosty eyes as she perched on the seat beside the king's brother. A set of waiters removed the soup tureens and servers moved forward in the line. Ten came before the Comte de Provence, five on each side, and removed the covers from their dishes, presenting the starters. The meats arrived in similar fashion. The prince forked food into his mouth at a steady rate. His cheeks reddened from the effort of eating and his forehead glistened from the heat of the candelabra squeezed among the gleaming silver bowls.

When the table service was changed for salad plates, and the prince dabbed his mouth with a fresh serviette, Adélaïde seized her opportunity.

"Your Highness, I propose to paint the act of your donation to the Knights of St. Lazarus." The prince had recently donated funds to the order to build a hospital. "I will use the themes from antiquity where kings presented the church with building models."

The prince motioned for a servant to clear the dishes so he could see her drawings.

"You will be the center of the painting." She took her chalk and drew a shadowy sketch of the prince on a fauteuil, holding a tiny wooden building in his hands. She slimmed his face and made his body heroic. "I will include all the Knights of St. Lazarus in the painting and many royal onlookers."

The prince peered at her sketch while she drew the figures of his aunts. When she drew the prince's cousin, the Duc d'Orléans, standing next to him, he said. "No, no, we do not want such persons in our painting."

She stopped drawing, caught the twinkle in his light blue eyes and the affront of the wine steward standing behind him. Taking out a small piece of rubber, she erased the face of the duke and inserted the haughty face of his servant, adding the towel draped over his arm, the wine bottle in his hand.

The prince laughed, a lusty rolling sound. His chins quivered above rows of lace. "Let us have only the knights at the front of the painting," he said. "The aunts may be up there," he pointed to the gallery.

She thought for a moment. "I will draw them sitting in a royal box. I will visit the subjects in the painting to sketch them. I will hire my best students to work on the painting. These students can compete with any Academy student at the Louvre. In funding such a project, your Highness will save many desperate girls from destitution." Across from the royal box, she drew young women in a gallery, saluting the prince with roses. "I, myself, will paint the faces and persons of the key figures and add precious metals and gold to the painting. I will paint your person clothed in emerald-green velvet, lined with ermine, studded with golden lilies. The knights' armor will be painted with silver."

The prince ate his salads and puddings.

Adélaïde crosshatched color into the clothing with quick strokes. "Your Highness, there will be no other painting like *Les Chevaliers de St. Lazare*."

Before the waiters could place the fruit platters in front of the prince, she named a bold price.

He set down his fork, wiped his mouth, and ordered the disapproving servant to bring her a chalice. "Done." He toasted her, his blue eyes liquid from wine.

Adélaïde left the palace, tipsy and starving but elated.

The night after the Comte de Provence approved her commission, Adélaïde brought a sketch of her concept to François's studio. He was working on his commission from d'Angiviller while Alexandré worked out a cabinet design at their father's old drafting table.

"I'm planning a painting seventeen planks wide," she said.

François examined the drawing in the candlelight. "This is an ambitious project. It should keep you occupied for a while."

"Two to three years, I think. I need a wood for the ages, one that will not warp or crack."

"What about mahogany?" Alexandré came to look at the sketch. "It's about the hardest wood you can find."

"Doesn't mahogany grow only in the Americas?"

"You can buy it on the docks in Bordeaux, straight off the ship. I saw it on my way home from Italy," Alexandré said.

"But how would I manage that?"

"I could take you," François suggested.

A picture of France appeared to her, one known to her only through woodcuts and hand-painted plates in books, complete with maps of hand-drawn rivers and mountains. "Could we go to Limoges?"

François's hazel eyes blazed. His half-smile appeared. "I do not see why not."

"I've always wanted to go on a boat," Adélaïde said. She had never thought of travelling until that moment, but now she wanted to go on a boat with the fervor of a child.

Alexandré said, "We could also visit—"

"You're not coming," they said in unison.

Two weeks later, Adélaïde and François sailed down the Seine as Monsieur and Madame "Dubois." They marveled at the rise and fall of water as draft horses dragged the barge through the Briare Canal locks, took in the beauty of the duke's palace in Nevers. They traveled by an overnight coach to Limoges, toured the porcelain works, boarded a wine-laden barge bound for Bordeaux. The watercraft pushed through the limpid waters of the Dordogne. From their improvised wine cask seats on deck, Adélaïde and François drew the gabled houses along the river, caught the lines of cream and gray on the sun-splashed castles dotting the hilltops above them with their pastels.

When they arrived in Bordeaux, they learned that no ship was expected from the Caribbean for a week, so François hired a yacht, and they followed the estuary out to the ocean. By day, they breathed in fishy air, licked salt off their lips, observed the curve of the earth from the pebbled beach. At night, they watched flashes from torchlights guiding ships into the mouth of the estuary. The moon rose. Waves crashed against the rocks. Swells and undertows frothed and sighed while François and Adélaïde held hands, and the stars shone down on the endless black of the Atlantic.

At day's end, in whatever cabin or inn they found themselves, their bodies formed an ancient rhythm that made Adélaïde forget the pain of her father's death, the horror of Justine's. In the mornings, François rose before her, lithe, lean, narrow hipped—a man of perfect lines her hands ached to capture on paper. But where could she display such art? He became her clay—formed, shaped, sculpted into being each day, and her hands were satisfied.

When the crane lifted the huge log off the bare-masted ship tied to the pier, Adélaïde almost wished the innkeeper had not roused them to say a ship from the West Indies had been spotted offshore. Their yacht raced the ship up through the estuary so she could bid on the wood herself.

"I could have stayed at the beach forever," François said when the dockworkers rolled the timber away.

But a letter found her in Bordeaux.

The king's aunts had persuaded the king to grant her space in the Bibliotèque du Roi.

Five years after being admitted to the Academy, she had received an entitlement of lodgings. And four years after she herself had fought for it, she had won the blessing of the king. It was as though a millstone had been removed from her back.

Excited, she threw her clothes and art supplies into her portmanteau.

"Let's go back to Paris," she said. "It's time to get to work."

CHAPTER 29

VERSAILLES AND PARIS, SUMMER 1788

Justine's great tragedy should not have led to Adélaïde's greatest triumph, but it did.

Watching her excited students pack, Adélaïde paced her studio, her emotions a jumble. The sharp tap of hammers nailing boxes shut punctuated effervescent laughter, male and female. Outside, Alexandré directed François's students as they loaded a waiting cart. Wooden boxes scraped the parquet, and boot falls blended with the swish of skirts.

"Be careful," Adélaïde said. "You'll scratch the floor."

At the empty bay window, the girls paused to watch François's students pile boxes in the street. "By the day's end, we'll have all the space and light we need," said Jeanne Bernard. She had taken Justine's place as an advanced student.

"But you'll have no art supplies if you keep throwing them around," Adélaïde said. "Pack the pastels this way."

Isabelle rolled her eyes. "Madame, we know how to stack crayons without breaking them."

"And don't pack the newspapers. I haven't read them yet."

"We won't, madame. You've told us not to at least ten times. And not to pack the lemonade or biscuits." Marie laughed, her exuberance overpowering her reserve.

When Adélaïde protested the way they rolled the canvasses, the girls pushed her out the door. "You're interfering with our work." They giggled.

Outside, Alexandré heaved crates onto the cart.

Adélaïde rushed up and grabbed a pastel box from him. "Don't drop the boxes into the cart, Alexandré."

"Yes, madame," he saluted her.

"Let me show you how." She stood on tiptoe to load the pastels herself, and a student with a pile of crates bumped into her.

"That's it," Alexandré said. "Go back inside. You're in our way."

"They already threw me out."

"Take a walk, then."

When she hesitated, he made a shooing motion. She could almost hear Justine saying, "Why so troubled?" She walked toward the Seine. The sunlight fell on her uncovered face, and Parisian air, dark and gritty with notes of river water and undertones of perfume and sewage, filled her nose. *Eau de Paris,* she thought and let out a shaky laugh. At least she and her girls would no longer have to breathe dray dust.

At a fruit stall along the river, she bought a plum. Biting into the soft purple fruit, Adélaïde watched a boatman descend the stone steps at the river's edge and climb into a small rowboat. From the adjacent stall, newsboys shouted the headlines.

"'Necker Scrambles for Government Funding. Time Running Out!'" cried one who looked to be about seven years old.

"'Duc d'Orléans Exiled!'" piped another.

"Hang Necker," spat the ferryman picking through winter apples in a wooden barrel. "And hang d'Orléans," he muttered under his breath. "I'll not pay another livre in taxes."

"It's time the gentry and the church paid their share," the fruit seller agreed. "We're taxed too much as it is."

"Next they'll tax us when we take a piss in the river."

Adélaïde cleared her throat.

"Oh, pardon me, your highness." The ferryman clicked his boots together and tipped his three-cornered hat at her.

"What will happen to the Palais Royale?" she asked the fruit seller as the ferryman walked off with his sack of apples.

"The duke's shops, theaters, and restaurants will do just fine," the man replied. "Especially because he doesn't pay taxes. But for Necker to do his job, the duke had to go."

"But why?" she asked.

"The duke has been one of the loudest protesters against Necker raising taxes on royalty and the clergy. The king can't have his cousin undermining him."

She tossed her plum pit into the water, thinking she would have to pay closer attention to the actions of the government now that she was dependent on the royal family.

Hot from her walk in the sun, she returned to her studio in time to see the heavy-laden cart head off on its short journey along Rue St. Honoré. She watched the cart until it became lost in traffic, then followed its familiar route in her mind. The King's Library was around the corner from the site of À La Toilette. As a child, she had gone with her brothers during public hours. She could almost hear her brothers calling her to play hide-and-seek in its drafty halls, examine one of its giant globes, or decipher one of its charts tucked away in its many drawers.

A part of this beloved space would now be her workplace. Alexandré had designed a grand studio for her, complete with a kitchen, workroom, and dormitory to house student apprentices and young working artists. When she asked him why he had never received his architecture degree, he shrugged and said, "Too dull. François is the one in the family who studies hard, not I."

Having so many young women under one roof brought new responsibilities. When Adélaïde advertised for a housekeeper and chaperone, another part of her childhood returned to her. One of the first applicants was her former maid, Claudette.

They met at the King's Library, where, downstairs, the students had already started to work on *Les Chevaliers*. The ceiling shook as workmen demolished walls on the floor above them with sledge-hammers.

"You've grown thin," Claudette exclaimed. At forty-one, her sharp features had softened into adulthood, but her dark eyes snapped and mocked as before.

"And you haven't lost your tongue—or your freckles," Adélaïde said. They laughed. "I almost didn't interview you when I saw you didn't provide a reference."

"You would think that at my age, no one would bother me

anymore, but at my last position, I refused my employer's advances. His wife turned me out."

Adélaïde shuddered. "I assure you, no one will bother you here." Before the silence grew awkward, she changed the subject. "I recall that you married that bookseller of yours and retired from the life of a working girl."

"In fact, your mother had no more need of my services," Claudette corrected. "I had to find another job."

"But—" Somehow, she recalled it differently. "That was a lifetime ago—almost twenty-five years. What has happened to you since?"

Claudette shrugged. "All things come to an end. He was in his sixties and in failing health. Unlike your parents, he was never a good shopkeeper. We struggled to make a living, feed our daughter, and pay the rent."

"You have a daughter?"

Claudette shook her head. "When my husband died, we sold the inventory, but it was insufficient to cover his debts. Our daughter helped when she could, but when she became pregnant, that ended."

"You're a grandmother?" Adélaïde asked, amazed.

"For all of one day, and then I was no longer even a mother." Claudette's voice turned bleak. "Annie was nineteen." She looked away. "That was four years ago. No shop, no children, no grandchildren, and no place to live. I took up work as a housekeeper."

Adélaïde tried to imagine Claudette's life and loss. "I'm so sorry, Claudette." To avoid another silence, she offered Claudette a tour of the studio. They watched her students climb the scaffolding with life-size pieces of tissue paper and tack them into place on a wooden canvas attached to the wall.

"This is the largest canvas I have ever seen," Claudette looked back at the double doors. "How did you get it into this room?"

"The carpenters constructed it right here." Adélaïde described how the carpenters had sawed planks an inch thick, twice as thick as a normal canvas, then glued and braced the boards together. "When they polished the surface, the red-grained wood glowed. The woodworkers claimed it was a sin to cover the wood with glue and linen but cover it we did." It had taken her students weeks to apply fifteen layers of gesso, wait for each layer to dry, then sand the surface to perfect smoothness again.

"It looks like ivory."

Adélaïde nodded. "The gloss will cause light to shine from within the painting."

"You said the wood was red? I've never seen mahogany before."

Adélaïde pointed to a gleaming red wood desk. "My desk is made from leftover remnants of the log."

Claudette ran her hands over the glass-smooth surface. "A desk for a queen," she said. "What are the girls doing on the scaffold?"

"They're transferring images onto a grid to ensure that the proportions are correct. The diagonal lines you see determine the vanishing point. That helps maintain proper perspective. More than one hundred people will appear in this painting."

Claudette stared at her. "Is this the same girl who sat in her bedroom sketching still life after still life? The one who bored us to death with innumerable drawings of her brothers?"

"The very one." Adélaïde dipped her head. "In fact, I will paint my whole family in the gallery of onlookers at the top of the painting, waving to someone outside the painting. In the bottom right corner, you'll see my arm saluting them." She flexed her fingers. The call from her hands was strong. "I can't wait to get up on the scaffold and do my part."

They went upstairs to view the housekeeper's quarters, stepping around men stacking remnants of rotted wood.

"Where is your room?" Claudette asked.

"I'll have a bed in my office downstairs," Adélaïde said. "but I also have rooms on Rue Neuve des Petit-Champs not far away."

"Why?" Claudette asked.

"I must come and go from Versailles to work on the studies for the painting and will be in and out at all hours."

Her father had ordered the executor of his estate to sell his cottage and use the proceeds to secure a long-term lease in the Roches' mansion for the remainder of her life. *"Daughter,"* he had written in a letter she had received after his death, *"I can no longer help you, but you will never lack a place to live."*

When Claudette seemed about to ask another question, she added, "This way I won't disturb anyone." Claudette did not need to know the rest.

Her former maid raised her eyebrow and gave her a knowing look.

∼

The cart had been gone for some time before Adélaïde re-entered her studio. Her students stood gossiping as they drank the lemonade and ate the cookies. Their voices echoed against the ceiling in the empty room.

Marie poured her a glass.

Sweet tartness slipped down Adélaïde's throat, melting away the heat of summer.

"Here's your newspaper." Isabelle plucked it out of the last box in the room.

Adélaïde took the paper to the bay window.

"We should get to our new home while the light is still out," Jeanne said. "Are you coming, madame?"

"What are you reading, madame?" Marie asked when Adélaïde did not reply.

"About the Duc d'Orléans leaving the country. Can Necker really force royalty and the church to pay taxes, do you think? We certainly can't afford any more taxes." She thought of the angry workmen out on the river. "How will Necker solve this?"

"Today is not the day to worry about the world's troubles, madame," Jeanne said.

Truly Justine's replacement, Adélaïde thought.

"Read the article on the back page instead," Marie said. "The back page is always more interesting than the front."

The girls trooped out the door.

Marie stepped back inside. "You'll be along soon?"

Adélaïde nodded.

"Watch the time," Isabelle called through the door. "Madame Claudette expects you before dark."

In the sudden silence, Adélaïde turned to the scandal section. 'Where is Jacques Louis David?' the headline asked. Full of innuendo, the writer implied that the artist had not been seen since the death of his student in Rome.

I wonder how he likes being the subject of scurrilous stories circulating in the papers, she wondered, thinking of the pamphlets about her that

David had passed out to his students. Her stomach churned, but then she forced the thoughts away and tossed the paper into the stove. She had other things to worry about.

She looked around the bare studio. She had managed well enough on d'Angiviller's stipend. Covering construction costs for the new studio while she waited for the Academy to reimburse her and paying wages for the new painting until the prince paid her would be a challenge. What if he did not pay?

"That's impossible," she said aloud as she climbed the stairs. "Everyone knows the king pays his family's debts when they don't. Besides, it's already done."

Isabelle's corner in the bedroom had disappeared, the crates filled with clothing and carted away. The screen that had marked Marie's side of the room had been folded and shuttled off to a new life in the King's Library. Only the landlord's furnishings remained.

Yellow bars of sunlight fell across the muslin bed linens.

An image hit her mind's eye: the Sunday Justine had come to the studio to work on a project with Marie and Isabelle, the Sunday Adélaïde had learned of her father's death. Adélaïde had sat on the bed, clutching Claude Labille's last letter, staring at nothing. When the students heard her cry out, they had crept into the room.

"How will I live without Papa's letters?" Adélaïde had asked. "He has written me every week for fourteen years." His letters had been full of droll country events, wry advice, and encouragement. In return, she entertained him with the events of her days in the city, told him of her successes, and confessed her failures. Always, his letters had lifted her up. "My entire family is gone." She gulped in a breath, but grief took up all the space in her chest.

Marie and Isabelle had crawled onto the bed and cradled Adélaïde between them. Justine had knelt on the floor beside her, placed her cool hands on Adélaïde's fevered temples, and said, "We are your family now."

Now, the light on the bed shifted.

"Justine, we're leaving," Adélaïde breathed into the quiet. Her hands flew to her mouth. Suddenly, she could not remember the press of Justine's cool fingers against her skin. She sank down onto the floor where Justine had once knelt. The tears she had held back for months to be strong for her students, to do what she must, spilled down her face and jagged gusts of sorrow exploded from her chest.

Twilight had gathered shadows into the room when she felt a presence beside her. François. She inhaled his familiar scent of sandalwood, bergamot, and citronella, and was glad for his presence.

"Adélaïde, whatever is wrong?"

"Why does it all have to be so hard, François?" she asked.

He sat down next to her on the floor and pulled her into his arms.

"I just don't know if I'm doing the right thing with this move."

"We all go into a murky future we cannot see," he said. "But I know it will be all right." He smoothed her hair with his hand.

"How can you be so sure?"

"As long as we have each other," he said. "It will be."

The floor was a hard place to be, and then it was not.

Lightened of her grief, Adélaïde locked the studio door for the last time while François waited, staring into the bay window, its sheer curtains drawn against the empty room inside. When she turned, his eyes, dark green in the shadows of the torches, looked into hers. He held out his arm. "Let me escort you to your new studio, madame."

"Thank you, kind sir." She took his arm.

They followed the path the cart had taken earlier in the day. "Your secret is out, you know," he said.

"What secret?"

"Rumor has it that d'Angiviller visited Director Pierre today. People could hear him yelling out in the Academy halls."

"I've had nothing to do with d'Angiviller for months."

"D'Angiviller wanted to know who had approved your commission from the Comte de Provence."

"Not that it's any of his business, but the prince himself approved the commission."

"But for thirty thousand livres, Adélaïde?"

She liked the sound of the number. "Yes, what of it?"

He stopped and stared at her. People flowed around them. "You do know that is the highest price paid to an artist to paint a painting ever, do you not?"

A slight smile teased her lips. "What I know is that my students will not have to live above taverns, sing for money, or fall prey to dangerous men ever again."

"D'Angiviller fears that all artists will want commissions like that."

"I'm sure they will."

"That took some . . . backbone, Adélaïde."

"I'm a woman, François. I don't have any . . . backbone, remember?"

PART V
REVOLT

CHAPTER 30

VERSAILLES, JANUARY 1789

Two more miles. Adélaïde pushed the curtain back across the coach window and thrust her gloved hand inside her fur muff. At eleven o'clock in the morning, the sun had yet to make an appearance. Outside, ice clung like glass bristles to the barren branches that arched over the Versailles Road. Beyond the birch trees, snow covered fields sloped up to hills shaded to slate under dark gray clouds.

Even bundled in blankets, her booted feet on a warmer, each indrawn breath was a torturous path of arctic cold to her lungs. She knew it was worse for the coachman and his son out on the box seat, and she would not have put the three of them at risk but for the promise by the Mesdames' aide that a long overdue payment awaited her at the palace.

Once she had moved her studio to the King's Library, she had spent the summer traveling back and forth to Versailles, painting the Mesdames and hunting down each of the knights of the order of St. Lazarus to sketch their faces. She spent hours viewing the work of her fellow Academician, Anne-Marie Vallayer-Coster. She studied the way that a kitchen knife floated in space, the depth and breadth of music instruments that thrust off the canvas as though they were sculpture instead of flat art, then experimented with her own techniques to make the central figures of her painting appear three-dimensional. She would fulfill her promise to the Comte de

Provence that there would be no painting like *Les Chevaliers de Saint-Lazare.*

Her experienced students spent their days on the scaffolds, building up layers of background paint, while younger students worked on studies for the painting and learned how to portray drapery, silk, and velvet in oil or gouache. Claudette managed the growing household of female apprentices as though she were operating a boarding school for privileged young men.

"And why not?" she said. "Here in the King's Library, we have access to information from across the world."

In the semi-dark confines of the coach, Adélaïde mentally tabulated her ledger, deciding what bills she would pay, what funds she would set aside for food. Until autumn, the only clouds on Adélaïde's horizon had been invoices sent month after month to the Mesdames, rarely paid, and progress billings for *Les Chevaliers de Saint-Lazare,* never paid. More and more of her earnings from bourgeois portraits paid for her students' work on *Les Chevaliers.* Then the worst winter anyone could remember arrived. Bad weather destroyed grain crops across France. Mills stopped working and food supplies did not make it to the cities. In Paris, the price of bread soared. Sustaining a household of twenty became her daily preoccupation.

Suddenly, the coachman shouted and hauled on the brakes. Adélaïde felt a bump, as though they had hit something in the road. The coach swayed, spun. Something cracked. The coach came to a stop, almost on its side. Adélaïde flew out of her seat, then slammed into the opposite seat, her face hitting the coach wall. The foot warmer tumbled out of its wooden frame. Heat bit through her dress. With a cry, she kicked away from the metal box, then tried to pull herself up. Untangling her skirts, she rose to her knees, dazed. Pain radiated through her upper body.

The coachman and his son yelled for help, then tried to extricate the horses from their traces. Burning wool alerted her to coals from the warmer boring through the carpet. Stamping out the embers, she pushed at the door. She had to get out.

She made her way around the coach, trying not to slip on the ice, then recoiled. They had run over the naked body of a child, perhaps seven or eight years of age, twisted in a fetal position, hands and feet blue, face white as the birch trees above them, except for a nose blackened with frostbite between sunken cheeks.

The little girl was frozen to the road.

She tried to look anywhere but at the mangled body, but it did not seem possible.

A farmer, his scarecrow frame wrapped in rags to ward off the cold, tromped down the hill. He bent and examined the dead child. "Every day they come through the woods on their way to the palace," he said. "We have nothing to offer them."

Adélaïde removed her checked wool scarf and covered the child. Ice-cold air snapped at her exposed throat.

"Why are her clothes off?" she asked. A muddy blue dress and a white bonnet blackened with mud lay crumpled next to the child.

"Who knows?" The farmer made the sign of the cross. "Perhaps the cold makes them mad."

Horses whinnied in the distance. Soon, a posting coach pulled to a stop behind them. The post boys dismounted from their horses and discussed with her coachman how to move the damaged coach. A wheel had broken in the accident. With the help of the horses, the men dragged the conveyance out of the snowbank. On the other side of the coach, in the piled snow, they discovered two more bodies, a woman and a teenaged boy.

The woman's face resembled a skull, but no frostbite marked her extremities. The boy, on the other hand, bore signs of frostbite and lay curled against his mother's body, his shirt beneath him.

The farmer crossed himself again. "We must get the village mayor," he said.

The posting coach door opened. A man in heavy furs put his head out. "We don't have time for that. I have to get to the palace."

"But we have to remove the child from the road," the farmer said. "Other travelers will come along."

"I'll get my shovel," her coachman muttered.

Her breath coming in jerks, Adélaïde moved to the side of the road. She turned away and covered her ears to stop the sounds of metal striking ice and rock, the grunts of the men as they worked.

When the coachman told her it would be some hours before he could get the wheel repaired, she climbed into the posting coach, not caring that she was getting into a closed vehicle with a stranger.

The coach had no curtains over its plain glass windows, but it also had no heater. She could not stop shivering.

They had been on the road for perhaps a quarter of an hour when the coach slowed. The man peered out the window and swore at the line of beggars on the road. Adélaïde ignored his invective until he berated her for making him late.

"I was called to the palace myself, sir."

The two of them sat in silence the remainder of the way, the man drumming his gloved fingers on the seat beside him. It was one in the afternoon before they made it past the lines of people and through Versailles's gold-plated gates. For an hour, Adélaïde knelt before a low grate in an antechamber, warming her hands enough to paint, her eyes squeezed shut against the image of the dead family in her head.

"It is dull at the palace today," Madame Victoire said when Adélaïde arrived at the princesses' apartments.

The receiving room had changed in her absence. The princesses' chairs had been moved and placed before a giant glazed contraption painted light green with pink and white roses, its pipe ending just below the coffered ceiling. A stove. For once, the room was hot.

"Come, entertain us." Madame Adélaïde motioned to the ottoman beside her. "What's the news from Paris?"

Collapsing onto the cushioned footstool, Adélaïde could think of nothing to say. A footman delivered her painting supplies.

The older woman picked up her knitting. "Well?"

At the sound of clicking needles, Adélaïde's stomach roiled. She swallowed and said, "Everyone speaks of the weather."

"The weather bores us." Madame Victoire opened a fashion book with the next season's colors. "You have experience with fashion. What color spring dresses should I order?"

Adélaïde glanced at the color plates and read the first description her eyes fell on. "I—I believe that robin's under-breast will be the most popular color this year."

"Gray again? After this winter, you would think they would choose a brighter color for spring. Humph."

"But it is a very light gray," Madame Adélaïde told her sister.

The princesses ate bonbons next to their new ceramic stove while Adélaïde added red tones to Madame Victoire's likeness, reflecting the rouge tint in the woman's flour-dusted wig. Compared to the drafty fireplace, empty now and hidden behind an embroidered screen, the stove worked so well that the chocolates softened. Madame Adélaïde made a moue of distaste, dabbed her fingers on a serviette, and called for a fresh box of candy.

Madame Victoire picked up the discarded box and rifled through the treats. "Oh, they are all ruined," she exclaimed. She picked up her knitting basket and pulled out a sock in progress. "I hear there are people begging outside the gates. Is this true?"

Cautiously, Adélaïde nodded.

"What do they want from us?" Madame Adélaïde asked. "Pâté?"

"I wish they would just go away," Madame Victoire said. "The queen should not insist on giving them kitchen scraps."

Adélaïde could not complete the highlights on Madame Victoire's nose. The image of the dead child's face with its missing nose blocked her view. Her eyes watered, and she bit her lip to focus on the pain. Putting the brush down, she blended red and white paint with slow strokes of the palette knife, as though deriving the perfect shade of rose were the most important act in the world.

At three o'clock, a footman brought a message from her coachman. The coach was repaired, and he wanted to make it back to Paris while the roads were passable. Relieved, Adélaïde folded away her easel and handed the wet portrait to the footman to store until her return.

The coach edged its way through the beggars at the palace gates. A mile down the road, as the sky turned the color of washed indigo, they passed the last stragglers heading to Versailles. The coachman stopped so his son could light the lamps, then urged the horses into a steady trot. The night deepened, the skies cleared, and moonlight glittered like diamond chips atop the snow.

Adélaïde stared out the window, a bank draft gripped in her gloved hand.

Back in Paris, up in the dormitory, Adélaïde cocooned herself in a blanket on the bed closest to the hall. A bowl of steaming onion soup topped with broiled cheese warmed her hands. Her students sat on their narrow cots watching her.

"I thought I wanted a hot bath more than food, but perhaps not." She dug her spoon into the soup. Hot liquid sloshed over the rim of the bowl, burning her hand. "Where's the bread?" she asked.

"There is no bread." Claudette's voice shook. "I went to the market at dawn this morning, but only one baker had obtained flour. The line of people waiting wrapped around the whole market. We stood in the cold for hours, smelling the bread baking. Many in line had not eaten for more than a day. When the bakery finally opened and the baker announced his price, no one could afford it. The women who had been waiting all night tore down the market stall outside his shop and threw vegetables at him. Others threw cobblestones through his window. The police came and the bakery closed without selling a single loaf. I searched all day but could not find another bakery that was open."

Adélaïde sighed. "Perhaps grain will arrive tomorrow."

"How?" Claudette asked. "Will the farm carts run over bodies to get here?"

"The roads are passable now." Adélaïde set the soup down on the bedside table, her appetite gone. "We have money," she said. "We'll go out tomorrow and buy salted meat and vegetables if there is no bread."

"How can we? People are rioting everywhere. They have destroyed the custom houses leading to the city. If the government does not let wine, meat, or vegetables in because people have not paid the taxes on them, how will we eat?" Fear darkened Claudette's eyes.

"The king has called a meeting of the Estates General to deal with the crisis. It's to happen in May."

"That is months away."

"Still, I'm sure he'll solve the situation."

Claudette stared at her. "A king who cannot find bread for his people while he's wearing flour on his head is not fit to be king." Her brittle voice struck like breaking glass.

The dormitory fell silent, as though everyone paused to check for bleeding feet. In her heart, Adélaïde agreed with Claudette, but to voice it was treason. Her career and her future were bound to the royal family. She could not have it said that such thoughts were expressed in the King's Library. She made her voice sharp. "Hush, Claudette. People will think—"

"I do not care what people think, and I will not be silent. If people have no bread in the countryside, and we cannot find it in Paris, what will happen to us all?"

Adélaïde tried to send a message to Claudette with her eyes. "I know you had a harrowing experience this morning, but there's no need to alarm the students."

Claudette crossed her arms. "We should be alarmed. If you are not, then you are a fool."

The students gasped. Adélaïde stood and stopped Claudette with a raised palm. "That's enough, Claudette. I'm sure you would like to retire after your ordeal. You are dismissed."

Claudette snapped her mouth shut, turned, and stalked out.

Adélaïde turned her attention to the silent onlookers in the dormitory. They looked anywhere but at her. "Girls, it's time for bed." No one moved. Snuffing out the candelabra, Adélaïde left the room with the last lit candle. A faint strip of light flickered beneath Claudette's door. She raised her hand to knock, then lowered it and went down to her office at the back of the studio. Closing the door behind her, she pushed aside the screen that hid the daybed and sank down on it with a heavy sigh. She felt horrid for correcting Claudette, but what else could she do? The divide fracturing the country had made its way even into her studio.

She lay down in her street clothes and pulled her cloak over herself, still cold to the bone. She stared into the darkness as though she could see what it hid. Often, life appeared to go along in its usual fashion until something drastic happened that changed everything. Adélaïde knew this was not true. Events that appeared insignificant led up to a dramatic moment, but often one could not perceive this until it was too late. Last summer, the finance minister had tried to impose taxes on the clergy and royalty. When they refused to accept them, Necker raised taxes on the common people, who refused to pay them. The common people rioted, winter came, the grain harvest failed, people starved. The separation between the three estates grew, with clergy and royalty banded together against the common people.

The specters of the doomed family danced before her burning eyes. In their ghostly luminescence, she saw that the world she had known had a giant crack running through it.

CHAPTER 31

SPRING AND SUMMER 1789

The vicious weather that gripped France by the throat held on through spring. Across the kingdom, people plowed through snow to hold elections for men to represent their districts at the meeting of the Estates General. In the coffee houses and cafés of Paris, hungry people warmed themselves on heated rhetoric and filled their bellies with bitter brew.

One blustery evening in March, François escorted Adélaïde between the Roches' mansion and the King's Library. They paused beside a row of townhouses as a group of men dressed in dockworkers' clothing dragged a table out of a coffee house and placed it in their path.

One of the men climbed onto the table. "Why should I pay taxes to support a lazy aristocrat?" he shouted. Torchlight threw wild shadows on his face. "If the government can't help us, we should abolish it."

"We need a constitution," one of his companions said.

Across the way, a cheese seller stepped out of his open doorway and called to the group surrounding the table, "Ordinary citizens must have rights."

"Liberty! Equality! Brotherhood!" the man on the table yelled back, waving his coffee cup in the air. The group in the street hollered and stamped their feet.

A window above François opened. "Sisterhood!" a woman cried.

The people in the street jeered and clapped.

The woman tossed a chamber pot toward the crowd. A stream of yellow liquid sloshed down. François yelped and jumped out of the way.

The horde in the street howled with laughter.

They pushed their way through the milling crowd and made it to the King's Library.

"Perhaps you could stop painting at night," François said as he examined his soiled cloak.

"I can't. I have to get this painting done."

Her students greeted them, then descended the scaffolding, revealing the huge canvas of *Les Chevaliers.* Its center was a gleaming patch of gesso surrounded by half-painted drapes and completed gallery figures.

"You are working late," François said when Marie hurried past him carrying paintbrushes to the dry sink.

"Madame pushes us, monsieur," Marie smiled. "But tonight, we are going to a talk outside the coffee house around the corner."

"Be careful," Adélaïde cautioned.

"I'm going with them." Claudette came down the stairs, a pile of cloaks and coats over her arm.

"An umbrella is probably a good idea," François said.

"Don't forget that you have work, and the king provides you with a place to live," Adélaïde called out as the girls left. Shaking her head, she gathered up discarded paint pots and placed them in the cupboard. "No matter how hard I try to stop it, even my students speak of nothing but politics all day long. It's as though we're being attacked with words from all sides."

"Better that than flying slop." He gave one of his lopsided smiles.

She laughed, but a breathless catch came at the end of it.

"Why are you working everyone so hard?" François asked as she mixed paint onto a palette.

"We've fallen behind. Everyone is distracted by the elections. The Comte de Provence took months to approve the composition at the center of the painting." She pointed to the expanse in the middle of the canvas. "We're going to have to add a lot of architectural detail and shadow beneath the gallery line to blend things together."

After François left, Adélaïde assembled her own palette and chose her brushes. She climbed the scaffold and continued to work on the figures in the gallery at the left top of the painting. While waiting for the prince to make his final choices, she had almost completed her family grouping. She had painted her mother happy and youthful, her sons crowded at the railing around her. Félicité was a winsome teen, and Adélaïde's father appeared as he had when he used to toss her high in the schoolroom, when his own hair still showed under his wig. With raised arms, they hailed her own upraised arm at the right bottom of the painting.

"I don't think you'd recognize the world right now, Papa," she whispered to his image as she painted into being the long hair that had always stuck up from his left eyebrow. "Food is too expensive for anyone to buy, but someone pays for presses to run day and night printing pamphlets exposing the kingdom's faults." She imagined her father running for office as she added a hint of dark sideburns under his wig. "I don't know what will happen."

In the quiet, a familiar dread seized her, a feeling that had haunted her since her trip to Versailles in the snow, that would not let her sleep, that brought her to the studio night after night to paint while the girls slept.

"I wish the royal family had more noble acts like this to commemorate, but that is not what I see."

Her father's eyes stared at her, fierce, urgent. "You must show them how they should be," he seemed to say.

"I have everything I need, Papa, almost everything I've fought for."

Wind moaned around the side of the building and rattled the Palladian windows. "How can it be that some women starve to death out on the road while others grow rich pandering to the vanity of the royal family?" She sank against the scaffolding, feeling weak. "The whole system is rotten." Her hand flew to her mouth. She peered out into the darkened room, at the easels supporting paintings, the sketches she knew lined the walls. "But where would we be if I weren't doing this?"

After a while, she picked up the brush and painted the crinkle at the corner of her father's eye. His expression turned stern, knowing. "Who are you debating, Adélaïde?" it asked. "Me, or yourself?"

~

In May, when the Estates General met, Parisians gathered in parks and on parade grounds to hear the awful news that came along the Versailles Road. According to custom, the king met with the clergy behind closed doors, then met with royalty with the door ajar. But he refused to acknowledge the representatives of the people when they filed past him.

"You would think he would show the least amount of respect," François muttered to Adélaïde as they stood under a chestnut tree just spreading its many-fingered leaves.

"You would," she said, but she knew better. When she had last seen the princesses, the two sisters were angry that they had not been permitted to hang their spring furnishings, due to "all this trouble with the elections," as Madame Victoire called it.

In June, when it came time to vote on a way forward, military guards locked the representatives of the people out of the assembly room. Fearing for their lives, the representatives barricaded themselves in the tennis court. Calling themselves the National Assembly, they vowed not to leave until they had established a new constitution. When this news reached the public gardens of the city, Parisians threw their caps and bonnets in the air.

"If the king cannot do it, the people can," they cried.

Committees and societies supporting the new government sprang up like the tulips and daffodils opening in the squares. Paris assembled an army of thirty thousand men ready to march on Versailles should the king ignore the will of the people. In response, the king hired foreign mercenaries to guard the Tuileries Palace, the Treasury, and the bridges crossing the Seine. People attacked these soldiers with stones and wicker garden chairs.

Fearful for their safety, the aging Roches removed the sign outside their shop that read "The King's Official Lock Maker" and made plans to leave the city. Adélaïde took to the alleyways behind the houses to get to the library, and Alexandré offered his protection to the women of her studio.

On a warm July weekend, a rumor swept through Paris that the king planned to attack the city. Citizens rushed to the armories to arm themselves. Despite the rumor, Adélaïde went to work as usual on Monday, but on Tuesday, when she stepped out into the street, people ran past her, heading toward the river. She went back through the courtyard. The Roches' footman rushed out of the building.

"What's going on?" she asked.

"They say that anyone who has a gun can get food. I'm going out to find one." He threw off his wig, put a rose fashioned out of green grosgrain ribbon in a buttonhole of his liveried jacket, and hurried out of the courtyard. What was he doing? The people of France wore white cockades. What did this mean?

She followed the footman back out to the street, but he had disappeared into the mass of people. She paced while the bells of the nearby basilica chimed the half hours, worrying about her students and scanning the crowd for Alexandré until her eyes ached. Had something happened to him? More and more people sporting green cockades passed before her searching eyes. An hour after Alexandré was due, the street teemed with people so close together that they appeared as a moving mass of arms, legs, and heads. Men, women, and children were indistinguishable but for bobbing hats, bonnets, and caps. She thought of the fifteen girls and Claudette alone in the studio, then thought of Justine. She could not let anything happen to another student. She looked out over the crowd again. No one was fighting. No one was rioting. It was only three blocks to the library. She waded in.

She had made a mistake. It was like being carried underwater in a wave of the ocean, one with sharp elbows and implacable chests. Wherever the crowd went, she had to go or be trampled. She stepped on feet, was stepped on in turn. At times she could not feel the ground. No one spoke, but harsh breathing came from all around her. Her hat ribbon cut into her neck. She could not get her hand up to pull it away. She looked up to the sky, tried to orient herself, to gulp in air, but all she saw were hats and faces chiseled with fear. She began to wonder what would happen to her.

It seemed like an eternity before the crowd lessened and she could move. She stumbled to the edge of the road, collapsed against a shop wall and gulped air into her lungs. She saw she was some-where out on Rue St. Antoine. How had the crowd carried her two miles? Worse yet, how would she get back?

An arm grabbed hers in a harsh grip. She cried out.

"Are you mad, woman?" François hissed.

"Where did you come from?" she gasped.

"Luckily, I am taller than you. I saw you step into the crowd. I have been trying to catch up with you since. It is a good thing you wore that hideous hat."

"Hideous hat?" She gave a little laugh and reached up to untie the double-knotted bow under her chin. She had thought the hat would strangle her in the mob. "I'll have you know this hat has sat on the Queen of Spain's head in a portrait." She pulled out the hatpins that had secured the contraption to her head during the mêlée. The scarlet brim had lost its shape, the ostrich plume had snapped, and the red feathers were gone. "Ruined." It had cost her a small fortune. "What was I thinking, wearing this today?"

François's own tricorn was gone, his cravat untied, and his jacket ripped. "You owe that ugly thing your life. What were you thinking, going out alone?"

"I waited and waited for Alexandré. Why didn't he come?"

"He did not think you would be fool enough to venture out. Somehow, I knew better. I told him to go on to the studio and that I would come for you."

They heard a crack, and then something whizzed overhead and hit the brick building. Stone shards rained down on them.

"Gunfire." François pulled her into an alleyway. Cannons joined the gunfire. Soon a mob's synchronized roars shook the walls of the building surrounding them. A horse and rider thundered past the alley, followed by men running with bayonets. A man cried out in panic, then the horse screamed. François grabbed her hand, dragged her through the alley, then commanded her to run.

"And that is when we think the mob murdered the governor of the Bastille," Adélaïde said.

It was the evening after the burning of the Bastille. Adélaïde, François, Joseph Suvée, and Simon-Charles Miger had gathered for dinner and an artists' meeting at a restaurant in the Palais Royale. While she had never met him before, Simon, the son of a successful tanner, who had worked his way from tutor to secretary to engraver and Academician, had grown up in her old neighborhood. He wore an unadorned black jacket over brown pantaloons. His dark hair was cut short in the new republican style.

"There isn't much left of the Bastille," Joseph said.

Crowds had torn the ancient castle down stone by stone, then set fire to the rubble. Outside, blowing ashes floated down onto the streets like snow flurries. Inside the restaurant, they could hear celebrating out in the street.

"Alexandré saw the governor's head on a pike with his own eyes," François said.

"I heard they forced the governor's daughter-in-law to drink his blood," Joseph added.

Adélaïde shuddered. "This violence must stop."

"Don't lose heart now, Diana." Joseph sneered. "You can't be the goddess of the hunt if you don't appreciate violence." It was the first time he had spoken to her since their falling out over the loss of his female students.

"I'm not," she said. "But how does killing solve anything?"

"But good has come from it," François said. "Prisoners who have lived in darkness and deprivation for years are free."

"Do the ends always justify the means?" she asked. "A more perfect society must be built on reason and rationalism, not violence and emotion."

"Madame Guiard, ever the idealist." Joseph dipped his wine glass toward her.

"Only the future will judge," Simon said.

The meal ended as more artists from the Academy arrived, sat at the tables, and ordered drinks. Looking around the room, Adélaïde realized that the men had transformed their appearance. Like Simon, everyone wore black or brown, and no one wore a wig. No one wanted to look like royalty.

Joseph, François, and Simon stood and addressed the group.

"The National Assembly must gain control of the country," Joseph said. "We artists must create alliances to support this new government."

"They are drafting a constitution based on *The Rights of Man* and have asked us to present ideas," François said.

"The constitution must consider the rights of women too," Adélaïde said from her seat. She was the only woman in the room.

"Perhaps it will." Joseph glanced down at her. "The Assembly promises to tear down the old institutions and build up new ones based on reason and fairness. The Assembly has reached out to the academies and requested recommendations on how the academies should be reorganized."

"Religion should not be a barrier to marriage or profession," François said. "From the time I entered Vien's studio, people questioned my right to be in the Academy. Like the Bastille, these ancient walls must be torn down." François was never one to complain, but the fire that appeared in his eyes reflected his fervor.

"One art form cannot be held in higher esteem than another," Simon said. "Engravers should be treated the same as sculptors or painters."

"And artists must receive their quarterly stipends," Joseph quipped. "The Academy is months behind in paying us."

The men drank to that, then pushed aside their glasses and planned the principal tenets of a new academy. They bickered over voting rights and meeting rules, ending favoritism, and receiving equal treatment in the various artistic fields.

"These concepts should be the central part of our proposal," someone said.

"Let's call it the Central Academy," another artist said, and they voted on the name.

Adélaïde wanted to leave, but with the mob out in the streets, could not. The longer the evening went, the more adrift she felt. She had no possibility of voting, worried about even having opportunities for herself and her students, and had not been paid by the government at all. What was she even doing here? These were not her concerns, and she could not afford to offend the royal family. Without them, she had no real place at all.

The bi-annual Salon opened in August.

Jacques Louis David, back in society after his mysterious illness, submitted three paintings. Given their subject matter and the mood of the people, the king forbade their display. When David's students rioted and his journalist friend, Jean Paul Marat, organized a protest, the king was forced to relent. *The Lictors Bring to Brutus the Bodies of his Sons* went on display at the front of the exhibit. Élisabeth

Vigée Lebrun exhibited a painting of herself and her toddler in togas, a republican Madonna and child. The critics praised Madame Lebrun's work as much as Marat's crowds praised David's awkward, dark painting.

Adélaïde entered her paintings of the Mesdames and their sister, Madame Louise-Élisabeth, who had died in Spain several years before. She had reflected the essence of Spain through a crimson and black palette. Southern sunlight threw blinding patches of light across Madame Louise Élisabeth's black taffeta dress and flooded the tile floor and stone walls of the balcony she stood on in light and shadow. *The Mercure* called Adélaïde's bold new colors acrid. She was used to her work being compared to Madame Lebrun's, but the criticism of her technique and use of color stung. The Encyclopedists were no less kind.

"How could I have gotten it so wrong?" Adélaïde asked François as they walked along the Seine after opening night. It was midnight. Students celebrating the Feast of St. Louis bumped into them, drunk and rowdy.

"It was that ugly red hat," he said, a gleam in his eye.

She pushed him away.

He laughed and took her arm. "It happens to us all."

"But what will the princesses think?" She could not lose her place as first painter.

"Remember, you wanted criticism."

Given the country's dire situation, Adélaïde supposed it was petty for her to worry about criticism, or for people to argue over the placement of a painting, but neither she nor François could have imagined the far-reaching impact of the king's prohibition against David's work.

CHAPTER 32

OCTOBER 1789

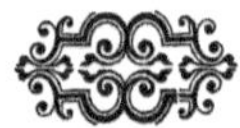

"Bread is thirty *sous* today." Claudette blew through the open doorway to Adélaïde's office.

"What?" Adélaïde rose from her seat. A week ago, the price for a loaf of bread had gone up to ten *sous*, half a laborer's daily wage. How would they eat?

"We have to go to market. We have run out of almost everything we scavenged from the neighborhood cellars."

Those of their neighbors who had country houses had fled to them to avoid the unrest. Shops on the streets around them had also closed. Riots or no, Adélaïde realized Claudette was right. Sighing, she retrieved her cash box. "I'll join you." Even though their relationship had cooled, she and Claudette had resolved to work together to ensure the efficient running of the studio.

"I have nowhere else to go," Claudette had said when Adélaïde asked if Claudette would be happier somewhere else.

"It looks like rain," Claudette said, looking out the window.

They donned cloaks and stepped out into the early morning light. Autumn leaves skittered across their path as they headed toward Les Halles. They had not gone more than two blocks when Adélaïde heard a rumbling noise coming from the direction of the market. She put her hand on Claudette's arm. "Is that thunder?"

"It sounds more like a demonstration." Claudette removed Adélaïde's hand from her arm and stepped away.

The commotion crystallized into the furious boom of drums coming in their direction. A shouted roar shook the building beside them. The terror Adélaïde had felt the day of the Bastille bloomed inside her.

They turned to go back to the King's Library.

A group of women, dressed as though they were out for a stroll in the Tuileries Palace gardens, emerged from a side street, forcing them to stop. One of them looked familiar.

"Madame David?" Adélaïde asked. She had not seen Charlotte David since that day she had gone to confront Jacques Louis David in his studio, but she never forgot a face. "It's not safe to go this way. There's a mob coming."

Market women clustered around Madame David's group, their stained aprons announcing their occupations.

"We've joined these women," Madame David said breathlessly.

"Where are you all going?" Claudette asked.

"To Versailles." A woman thrust herself between Adélaïde and Charlotte. She stank of fish and brandished a gutting knife. Grabbing Adélaïde with a filthy hand, she said, "Come with us."

Adélaïde extricated herself, trying to keep her eyes off the offal still on the narrow knife.

The market women marched on, but Madame David and her friends remained behind. "Why don't you come with us?" she asked.

"To Versailles?" Claudette asked. "Walk twenty miles?" She looked at the sky. "It will rain any minute."

A fevered look appeared in Madame David's blue eyes. "Righteousness will carry us."

"You should not be following these women," Adélaïde said. "You could jeopardize your husband's career."

"My husband doesn't tell me what to do. Besides, what has the king ever done for him? Prevented him from showing his greatest works and stopped the exhibit of his students' art?"

"But you–your family . . . Why are you protesting?" Claudette asked.

Charlotte David's father, the king's builder, had amassed enormous wealth working for the king.

"What has that to do with today?" Charlotte asked. "Royal patronage is a massive fraud on the people. We're going to Versailles to set things right." She gave an excited laugh and linked arms with her bourgeois compatriots. They counted, then stepped off in formation.

At the end of the block, one of the women shouted, "Kill the Austrian bitch!"

Shocked, Adélaïde stared after them. "How can they say that?"

"Many people do not like the queen and hate where she came from."

"I know, but . . ."

More women passed by. In their eyes, Adélaïde saw the look she had seen in Madame David's eyes—a fire, a lust, a madness she had never seen before.

Lightning fractured the sky, followed by a crack of thunder. Rain pelted the paving stones in large gray drops. Gripping their cloaks over their heads, Adélaïde and Claudette dashed back to the King's Library.

Inside her studio, Adélaïde barred the doors and ordered everyone upstairs. "We're going to be in the middle of this." The tightness in her chest made the words difficult to get out. Situated between the river and the markets, the King's Library was an island in the flow of the marchers. Claudette closed and locked the shutters.

"Claudette, are the pails full?"

Claudette nodded. Ever since they had learned that a mob had thrown a flaming brick into Madame Vigée Lebrun's salon, they had placed pails of water throughout the studio.

Soon drums and shouting beat out the sound of the storm.

"What do we do, madame?" Isabelle asked when they were all in the dormitory. Below them, the street flooded with women heading for the Versailles Road.

"We have to get through it, like the Bastille," Adélaïde said.

"Were you able to get anything to eat?" Jeanne asked.

At the reminder, Adélaïde's stomach growled. "No, I'm afraid. When things settle down, we'll try again."

"And when will that be, madame?" Claudette gave her a hard stare, went to her room, and shut the door.

Adélaïde pressed her lips together.

Heedless of the driving rain, Marie opened a dormer window, leaned out, and called down to the women, "What will you do when you get to Versailles?"

A market woman looked up, her hair tangled and wild around a face wet with rain. "Get the king!" she crowed. Her smile revealed several missing teeth.

"Marie, get back inside," Isabelle implored.

"Hey, there's a man out there dressed as a woman," Marie said, leaning up tiptoe. They rushed to see.

"Where?" Adélaïde asked.

Marie pointed at a tall person in a gown and black riding boots. A dark beard edged the jaw jutting beneath the edge of a frilly bonnet.

"Look, he has a gun," Adélaïde said.

They stared out at the crowd of fishwives, housewives, bored young women and the sea of knives, brooms, and hoes.

The tocsin at the Hôtel de Ville sounded. Several students clapped their hands over their ears. The single treble note of the giant bell went on and on, reverberating through Adélaïde's body, sending chills down her arms until she could not stand it.

"Marie, come inside and shut the window," she ordered. The alarm bell, designed to be heard for miles, was no less loud with the window closed.

"Madame, what will happen to the royal family?" Marie asked when the tocsin ceased.

Adélaïde thought of the mayor of the Bastille and shook her head.

"But he's the king . . ." Isabelle said.

Adélaïde understood her confusion and distress. The king represented France. He was France. Through his aunts and his brother, he had become her personal protector, and by extension, theirs. Now this group of crazed women—and men dressed as women but brandishing bayonets—held the fate of the kingdom in their fevered hands.

They could do nothing but wait.

They waited through the night as the noise of the crowds faded along the Versailles Road, then waited through the stillness that follows a devastating storm, when people wait for water to recede before venturing out to assess the damage.

The next afternoon, the sound of horseshoes striking cobble-stones met their ears, and then the blessed smell of coffee drifted through the louvered windows. Adélaïde opened the dormitory shutters, squinting against the light that flooded the room. The coffee seller on the street corner had set out his red umbrella.

"It appears safe to go out," she said. "Let's see what we can do about food."

"Please, Lord," Marie raised her hands in prayer. They had had nothing to eat since the night before last.

Adélaïde went to her office and returned with twenty livres, which she handed to Claudette. "Take Marie and Isabelle with you. See if you can find a newspaper as well. I will stay with the students." From the portico, Adélaïde watched the women walk up the street. If twenty livres did not buy them food, she did not know what she would do.

A few hours later, the women returned. François accompanied them, carrying a wooden box filled with food.

"Look who we found out on the street," Marie said.

Adélaïde and François greeted each other with their eyes as he set the box of food down on the table in the workroom. His clothes were sweat-stained, his face grim. "Are you all right?" she asked.

He nodded and wiped perspiration from his sunburned face. "It may be clear here, but it took three hours to get past the Tuileries Palace."

"This is what twenty livres buys today," Claudette dropped a single denier into Adélaïde's hand, her eyes daring Adélaïde to object.

François whistled.

"We couldn't find bread, soup, or cheese," Isabelle said.

Adélaïde pulled a baked chicken, two quiche pies, a bottle of wine, and a jug of ale out of the box. The odor of bad poultry hit her nose. "I hope we don't get sick."

"How will we get on if a day's meal costs as much as a whole week's worth?" Claudette asked. "You have seventeen mouths to feed."

François ripped off a chicken wing and popped it into his mouth.

"Eighteen," Claudette corrected.

As if I can't count, Adélaïde thought, but spending twenty livres was the least of her worries. All she could think of was the eleven thousand livres the royal family owed her.

Le Journal lay at the bottom of the box. She plucked the newspaper out and scanned it. The headlines screamed at her. 'Market Women Force King from Versailles.' 'Queen Found Hiding.' 'Royal Family Escorted to Tuileries Palace.'

"François, what does this mean?" She searched his somber face. "Which royal family members are in the Tuileries Palace?"

"I heard it was the king, queen, and their children," he replied.

"What about the Mesdames?"

"I didn't hear any news of the king's aunts."

She turned the page of the paper, then groaned. "The princesses left for Bellevue a week ago, but when the authorities searched for them, they were not there. It says here that the aunts eluded capture. Where could they be?"

"Perhaps they fled the country." François took a glass out of the cupboard and poured himself a drink.

A feeling she did not recognize bubbled in her chest. "How can they leave the country without settling their debts?" She lowered her voice. "They owe me three thousand livres."

He looked shocked. "When do these people think of anyone but themselves?"

A terrible thought struck her. "Have you heard anything about the Comte de Provence?"

"Not a word."

Adélaïde searched the newspaper until she found what she was looking for. "He's under house arrest," she wailed.

Footsteps sounded on the stairs as the students came down from the dormitory. "What's happened?" Jeanne asked as they assembled in the doorway.

"The royal family is imprisoned at the Tuileries Palace," Claudette said. "The Mesdames may have fled the country, and the Comte de Provence cannot leave his palace."

A collective gasp went through the room. As one, the students turned to face the far wall where *Les Chevaliers de St. Lazare* awaited its final touches. After three years of labor, the girls had only to put highlights on the clothing of the figures in the gallery along the top of the painting.

Adélaïde pushed past her students and went into the studio. A halo of light shown on the figure of the Comte de Provence, who occupied a throne-like chair at the bottom right of the painting. In the middle of the painting, a knight knelt before the prince. The king's brother was the epitome of dignity and grace as he bestowed the hospital charter. Through her painting, Adélaïde had demonstrated the beauty and nobility of generosity. She had taken her father's advice.

Everyone began talking at once.

"What are we going to do?" Isabelle asked.

"What will happen to us?" Claudette demanded.

"Will we have to leave the library?" Marie asked.

"Let us stop speculating." François made himself heard above the din. "I happen to know food awaits us in the workroom."

Adélaïde listened to the clank of plates, the ting of silverware, but made no move to enter the workroom.

"Madame, aren't you going to eat?" Marie came back into the studio, a full plate in her hands.

"No," Adélaïde said. "I'm not hungry. You go ahead."

Lowering her voice, Marie asked, "What will you do about the painting?"

Darkness hovered at the edge of Adélaïde's eyesight. She thought she would faint. "I–I don't know. I can't think right now."

"You should eat." François joined her in the studio.

"I can't eat right now." She wanted to cry, to scream, to howl, but needed to do it alone. She had not been to her apartment in the Roches' almost empty mansion for weeks, but the thought of imprisoning herself in her windowless office was intolerable. "I have to get out of here."

"Where are you going?"

"To my apartment."

"I'll go with you." François went into the backroom and came back with a large slice of quiche filled with leeks and spinach. He ate the egg pie as they walked the short distance to the Roches', excusing himself for eating as they walked along. "I am starving. There has been no food by the Louvre for the last two days. All the stalls are closed. We can be thankful, at least, that it appears to be a bloodless coup."

She made a choking sound.

He stopped and searched her face. "Adélaïde, what's wrong?"

"They–they're . . . I never imagined this would happen."

"I know how you feel."

"No, I don't think you do," Adélaïde said. "I've tried to collect my fees from the royal family for months. If the king does not come out of this, financially, I will be destroyed. I've spent eight thousand livres in labor and materials for *Les Chevaliers*. He hasn't paid one denier."

"Dear God, Adélaïde."

A great weariness overcame her. "I have no idea what to do."

They walked on in silence. When they neared the outer door to the Roches', François said, "You need to know something else. On my way to your studio, I ran into Monsieur Lebrun. He was rushing about, frantic to hire a coach to get his wife and child out of the country tonight."

Her stomach clenched. "What happened?"

"Revolutionaries broke into their house. They had just repaired the damage from the firebomb. Apparently, one of the revolutionaries was a neighbor of theirs. He told her that she needed to leave town for her safety."

"Why would revolutionaries want to harm an artist?"

"This man said they are coming for any friend of the queen. Adélaïde, you should think about planning an escape. Just in case."

The air was stale in her room when Adélaïde let herself into her attic apartment. When her father's bank had arranged for the lease, she had chosen her old rooms back. They might have been tiny, but they had the best light in the building.

She opened the window and looked out. The skyline presented its familiar forms to her: the narrow triangular rooftops of the row houses, the squares and rectangles of churches and palaces towering over them, the chimneystacks belching smudge into a salmon sky.

Night tumbled slowly into the room. A great darkness fell over the city. Globes of pulsating light wavered below her, people carrying lanterns through the streets, but as far as she could see, the lamps strung across the intersections remained unlit.

D'Angiviller was right, she thought. *I am a fool. I'm a painter, but I thought I could be a sculptor, chipping away at the Academy and the art system to reveal perfection within.*

She had caught glimpses of the weakness in the stone but ignored them. Then the stone fractured and revealed its hollow core, leaving a void as big as the buildings dissolving into the night sky.

How would she ever recover?

CHAPTER 33

OCTOBER 1789

Autumn air woke Adélaïde, her mind chasing the remnants of a dream. The tendril that remained was the sight of one of her students exiting the Royal College, a book in her hand. Justine perhaps? Adélaïde could not tell, but knew she herself wore the robes of a professor . . . Was the dream a vision of what the Revolution would bring?

An hour later, she let herself into the studio. Setting a cloth sack on the worktable, she surveyed the room. Her students turned to watch her, looking like gardenia bouquets in their billowing white skirts. She kept her face impassive for a long moment, then said, "What are you sitting around for? We have a painting to finish. And breakfast to eat." She opened the bag, and the smell of roasted chestnuts wafted out.

Laughing with relief, the girls swarmed the worktable. Soon, joyful banter bounced between the young women on the scaffold and the girls mixing paints and passing supplies up to them.

Adélaïde went into her office and sorted the correspondence on her desk, looking for an invitation from the Marquise de Condorcet. Claudette came and sat in the wooden chair across from her desk. "You've already spent a fortune on this painting," she said. "How can you keep this up? How will you pay for it all?"

"I'll find a way."

"You know the royal family isn't going to pay you."

"I don't know that. They just can't pay me right now."

"You do know it."

Adélaïde stopped moving papers around on her desk. Why did Claudette always have to question her? "I want to be paid, yes, but it's more than that. I've wanted to be an artist my entire life. I've given up a lot for this dream. My paintings and my students are my family. And my legacy."

Claudette fiddled with her sleeves, seemed about to say something, then pressed her lips together. "I do know you," she said at last. "From the time you were a girl, once you started drawing, nothing could stop you."

"*Les Chevaliers* shows how royalty can serve us through deeds that put the needs of the downtrodden and indigent above their own. I want people to see this message."

Claudette rolled her eyes.

Marie appeared in the doorway. Glad for the interruption, Adélaïde motioned her in.

Claudette stood. "Well, madame, you keep on painting, and I will keep trying to figure out how we will eat. A bag of nuts won't last for long."

Marie stared after Claudette, then sat in the seat she had vacated. "How will you get paid, madame?"

"I have no idea," Adélaïde said.

The pink envelope appeared beneath a stack of bills. She extracted the pale pink pages inside and checked the date. "Oh, no. The Marquise de Condorcet's salon is this afternoon. Would you please send François a note to escort me?"

"You've decided to go?" Marie leaned forward and lowered her voice. "But don't they want to weaken the monarchy?"

Adélaïde closed her eyes, her stomach queasy. "Their group advocates for the education and advancement of women. I should be there." She looked at the clock. "I have four hours to write a speech."

"Shall I cancel our committee meeting tonight?" Marie asked.

"We can't stop now. With the new government, we have a chance to be heard." In the end, Adélaïde had decided to organize her own committee of women artists.

Alone in her office, Adélaïde took out a piece of paper, sharpened her quill, and began to write.

∼

After the tumult of the past two days, the afternoon was calm. François and Adélaïde crossed the bridge, the river sluggish and brown beneath them.

"I've decided to finish *Les Chevaliers*," she told him.

"Why?" He looked troubled. "What have you to gain?"

"I may never receive another commission like this. I don't want anyone to say that it was too ambitious, that I couldn't honor my word."

"Still, you are taking a big risk."

"I need to get paid when this is all over." She pulled at the bow in her bonnet strings. "How can I tell the girls I have to stop paying them? How will they feed or clothe themselves?"

He had no answer. For a while, they walked along in silence.

"François, with your committee work, do you know who could help me now?"

"Most people either support the monarchy or want to overthrow it."

"There must be a middle ground. I can't afford to offend the king. I don't want to be forced to flee the country like Madame Lebrun, but how do I support the royal family and push for change at the same time?"

"If this is what you want, are you certain you should be going to the de Condorcets?" he asked.

Everyone doubted her today. "Who else is working to change the rules for women? We can't continue this way, where a few of us are promoted and then learn it was done to quiet our voices. Behind our backs, the Academy leaders laugh while they press their thumbs on the scale to keep us from succeeding. It may be a game to them, but our lives are on the line." The water sucked at the pilings under the bridge, and a small taxi boat lurched forward. Her stomach felt like the passengers in the boat, who cried out. "My biggest fear is being forced to move out of the library."

"Well," he grinned. "If you lose your lodgings, you may have to decamp to the Louvre with the rest of us. Imagine an army of women invading the comte's domain, throwing themselves at his mercy? He would have to accept you then."

She snorted. "We could disrobe and sing and dance before him, but he would be unmoved. Whichever side d'Angiviller is on now, he's never been on mine."

"Some men are brutes," he agreed. "Humanity has a long way to go, but things are improving. It has taken almost two thousand years for men to follow the work of the Romans, but we are on the right path now." He told her of his visit with Thomas Paine, the author of the *Rights of Man*. "His work is everything I've longed for since I left Switzerland. Monsieur Paine wanted me to paint his portrait, but I had to turn him down."

"Why?"

"My vision is too blurred," he said. "I cannot."

She stopped and stared up at him. François, not capable of painting a portrait? She thought back over the past few months, the evenings when he had complained that his eyes were too tired for him to paint, the struggle of mixing colors as he had intended, the details in a painting he was not happy with. "François, this has been going on too long. You must see a doctor."

"With my committee work, I have had no time."

She searched his face. "Promise me you will make time."

He changed the subject as they turned in the direction of the Hôtel de Monnaie. "You are right not to set yourself against royalty. They will never pay you if they resolve their difficulties and learn that you went against them. I suggest you contact the Feuillants. They want constitutional changes but wish to preserve the monarchy." They arrived at the stone steps leading up to the Hôtel de Monnaie. "I wish I had better answers to give you."

She squeezed his hand. "You have always been a wise counselor to me."

He looked out over the river. A bleak look chiseled his face. "You know I would be more."

She willed the pain away, her eyes following the foot traffic along the river. "What you are is always enough to me."

When Adélaïde stepped through the double doors of the de Condorcet's drawing room, she understood François's elation at finding the world he had searched for all his life.

Thirty or so people congregated around chairs and curved sofas placed to facilitate conversation. Several of the guests were women. Adélaïde should not have been surprised. Many salon leaders, females themselves, did not welcome women, but ideas were the entrée to the Marquise de Condorcet's salon.

Dressed in a fashionable but practical dark blue dress over narrow panniers, Sophie de Condorcet flowed like water between her guests, greeting them in Italian, French, or English. When she arrived at Adélaïde's side, Adélaïde perceived that the young woman's huge, droopy eyes and winsome smile disguised a sharp intellect and forceful personality.

Adélaïde began to curtsey, but Sophie de Condorcet offered a handshake instead. "In this place we are equals, Madame Guiard."

The marquis appeared and bowed over Adélaïde's hand. After Sophie de Condorcet's comment about equals, Adélaïde appraised the man in silence, uncertain how to greet him. Tall, thin, austere of face and form, almost twice the age of his young wife, his high forehead and cool gaze suggested remoteness and unapproachability. She knew, however, that he espoused such radical concepts as the equality of all mankind, man, woman, black, red, or white. A philosopher and mathematician, he taught mathematics and probability at the Academy but spent most of his time writing about rationalism and the progression of mankind. She thanked the marquis for inviting her, then told him how his writings had impressed her.

He inclined his head. "We had heard that you were interested in women's issues and education, and we thought that you might like to lend your support to our cause."

"I'm working to get the Royal Academy to change its admission rules for women and to improve training and opportunities for female artists," she told them.

"Our work pertains to the education of women as a whole," he said.

"And their political and legal rights," his wife added.

"Mankind must have both male and female to function as a species," the marquis said. "The single difference between the sexes is the preferential rights granted to men."

"Women must have equal rights, but to exercise them, they must have equal education," Sophie said. "We're attacking both prongs."

"Not equal rights," her husband corrected. "The same rights."

Adélaïde regarded the couple with amazement. She and

Claudette had once gossiped about the de Condorcets over breakfast.

"I hear that he gives his wife free rein to pursue her own ideas and interests," Claudette had said.

"As though she were a horse, he lets her go where she will."

"That is the nature of marriage," Claudette had said.

"Men hold the leading reins, the purse strings, the whip, and any other rope you can think of," Adélaïde had agreed.

She realized how wrong she had been about this husband and wife.

"We're searching for women who have succeeded despite the current restrictions," Sophie said. "The Comtesse d'Angiviller assured us that you are such a woman."

Adélaïde marveled how this one woman had influenced the direction of her life.

When she remained silent, Sophie de Condorcet asked, "Were we wrong?"

"No. No. I've believed this my entire life." Embarrassment at how breathless and girlish she sounded rouged her cheeks. She fought to return her voice to its usual cadence. "How can I help?"

"We are friends then." Sophie took Adélaïde's arm and tucked it into hers. "Come meet women and men who agree with us. We meet each week to discuss the ways we can improve the lot of women." She pulled Adélaïde toward a group of women arguing animatedly on a rounded settee overlooking the river. A woman in a bright red dress gesticulated while another waved her green-gloved hands in response. Leather writing books, paper, quills, and inkwells littered the low table in front of the settee.

"Dear ladies," Sophie de Condorcet interrupted them. "May I introduce Madame Guiard, artist, member of the Royal Academy of Art and Sculpture, teacher. She is here to speak of her experiences."

The women rose to greet her. The green leather gloves belonged to the oldest woman in the group, a thin person wrapped to the throat as though enduring the harshest winter even inside a stuffy apartment in early September, her hair powdered and tinted lavender to match her purple dress. Her dark brown eyes shone with excitement. A poet and essayist, she had taught the Duc d'Orléans's children and told Adélaïde that the challenge was to teach girls

Latin and Greek, get them into the royal colleges, and then into the universities.

While Adélaïde had studied Latin and Greek under her brothers' male tutors, she had never heard of a female tutor for young boys. "That is far beyond my humble task to fight for women to study art at the Louvre," she said.

Sophie de Condorcet then introduced Olympe de Gouges, a feminist, abolitionist, playwright, and political pamphleteer. Madame de Gouges, whom Adélaïde took to be close to her own age, wore a simple dress with a shawl draped about her neck, her hair pulled back in a bun styled after a Greek statue. Adélaïde felt like a giant standing next to her.

"I'm writing a tract regarding the rights of women," Olympe said, her voice gravel deep for one so small.

"I'm familiar with *The Rights of Man*," Adélaïde said.

"That treatise ignores the existence of women." Olympe waved a dismissive hand. "Women must have the right to financial independence."

"Well, they do, as long as you can find an honest man." The woman with the green gloves laughed.

"Why wait for that?" Olympe asked. "Women must have the right to inherit, the right to divorce, even the right to have relationships outside of marriage."

Adélaïde's face heated again. Did Olympe know about her? She looked at the group around the couch, then relaxed when the woman with green gloves said, "Exactly right, Olympe."

"I admire your purpose, but these Church practices are ancient." Even if wrong.

"The Church is a cruel, inhumane institution that must be abolished," Sophie said.

"The idea seems extreme . . ." She could almost hear her mother's screech. The memories of her Church trial, the leering men, the terrible questions, rose in a flash. Why had this never occurred to her before?

"Every original idea, when proposed, seems extreme," Olympe said. "But its righteousness and resulting actions defend the idea."

The young woman in the carmine dress was a traveling actress Adélaïde had seen at the Comédie Française. "Women must participate in all aspects of the Revolution," she said.

"Even violent ones," agreed her young companion. In this girl, Adélaïde recognized the granddaughter of the chocolatier who had sold her parents the chocolate drinks they offered their guests.

How small the world of the Revolution, she thought.

"We work to feed and clothe our children." The last woman did not wait for an introduction. "We pay our taxes. But what do we get?" Her deep-set brown eyes blazed. "No power. We still have to beg men to protect us. We must have the right to bear arms."

"While I do not believe violence should be the answer to anything"—Adélaïde shook the woman's hand—"I look forward to debating the issue with you." An unexplained joy shivered through her.

"We cannot wait to hear your perspective, Madame Guiard," Olympe said.

Sophie de Condorcet waved Adélaïde forward, then perched on the arm of the sofa.

For a moment, Adélaïde was reluctant to tell a group of strangers of her darkest days, but then she realized that these women were not strangers to her experience.

"The ideology of liberty and equality has shone a light on the fact that not only do women not enjoy liberty or equality, they also do not have the basic right to provide for themselves." A spring opened in the earth and her words poured out. "I am a woman artist and an employer of women. The rules were written to keep us from succeeding. Many of you know this already."

The men stopped their huddled conversations and moved behind the women on the sofa. Adélaïde stopped speaking. "I'm sorry," she said. "Was I too loud?"

The marquis waved an imperious hand. "Continue," he ordered.

Thirty minutes later, she finished, saying, "Women should not be called immoral when they try to earn a living. The right to live is the most moral imperative on earth. Ladies and gentlemen, this view must change."

No one spoke. For a terrible moment, she thought, *Was I that awful?* Sweat gathered on her forehead. Her face grew hot. Then loud clapping delineated the silence.

"We have found our orator," the marquis exclaimed.

"No other woman in our group has made it into a Royal Academy," Olympe de Gouges said.

"Or has an education in Greek and Latin," the woman with the green gloves said. "You should write our pamphlet on the need for women's education."

"I'm an artist, not a writer."

"I will help you," Olympe offered.

"With a speech like that, Madame Guiard, I cannot believe that you have written nothing," the marquis told her.

She dipped her chin. "I have drafted a few petitions."

Adélaïde floated down the steps of the Hôtel de Monnaie and onto the bridge.

Coming to the de Condorcets, she had worried about the king, about what others would say, about her place in the world. Instead, she had found people who believed as she did, who listened to her ideas without laughing, who wanted her help to build a new way to live. She felt loosed.

Halfway across the bridge, she stopped and looked back. To the left of the Hôtel de Monnaie, the Latin Quarter with its universities and teeming students, to the right, the ancient neighborhood of St. Germain-des-Pres. Up and down the quays, men loaded cargo onto squat boats while children played on flat barges, and women hung laundry across the bows. On the far shore, the Louvre Palace faded into the tapestry that formed Paris. For once, the palace with its Royal Academies and arbitrary rules seemed trifling and inconsequential, but she knew they were part of the strictures that kept people burdened and suffering. Tonight, she would begin to tear that fabric apart.

When Adélaïde and her students left for her meeting at the Louvre a few hours later, Olympe met them at the bottom of the library steps.

"I'm inviting myself to this Society of Artists meeting of yours," she said. "I want to observe women in action. Perhaps I will join your group."

Adélaïde linked arms with her. "Then we'll call it the Society of Artists and Friends of Artists."

By the time she stepped up to the podium at eight o'clock, one hundred thirty women— artists, wives of artists, and daughters of artists—were gathered in the Apollo Gallery. Their faces glowed with the light of a thousand candles lining the platform floor, but even more, Adélaïde thought, with the inner light of anticipation. Above the candles, the air grew hot.

"Imagine, my friends, a world where you can change the laws that hold you back, bind you in poverty, keep you powerless. A world where young girls can study alongside young men, where women can rise to positions as leaders and teachers."

Could they do it? The women cheered and waved their fans. In the crowd, she saw the same hope, the same desire she felt deep inside.

She raised her fist. "Tonight, my friends, we are here to create that world. Let's get to work."

At midnight, Adélaïde, Olympe, and her students returned to the King's Library. She threw her redingote on the worktable and collapsed onto a chair. Olympe sat down across from her.

"I can't believe we raised sixteen thousand livres," Marie, the society's new secretary, exclaimed. She retrieved writing materials from Adélaïde's office and handed them to Olympe while Isabelle lit the chandelier above the worktable. Then Marie and Isabelle followed the rest of the students up to bed.

"With this fortune, we cannot fail to get women into the Academy," Adélaïde said to Olympe as silence settled over the King's Library.

"You are an inspired speaker." Olympe pulled a small knife out of her reticule. "The women listened to your every word."

"For once, they heard something that gave them hope," Adélaïde said.

Her brow furrowed, Olympe sharpened a quill with the knife.

"But you're the writer, Olympe, and I'm glad you're here to draft this letter. What we say to the National Assembly when we send them this money is paramount to get them to act on our behalf."

Olympe arched her brow. "But why should they regard this letter?"

"Support will be the new influence, not titles, not family connections," Adélaïde said. "Surely you heard that this morning. And sixteen thousand livres is a lot of support."

Olympe set her knife down. "Do you really believe that your new society can accomplish its goals through money alone? That you can buy change?"

"Of course not. The National Assembly must see that we have earned our place too, that we wield power through the funds we've amassed with our own efforts. We just need the right words to get the assemblymen to understand our needs."

"How is that any different than the old way?" Olympe had yet to put a word on the paper before her. "Did the National Assembly approach you?"

She shook her head.

"Do they know who you are?"

They stared at each other.

"Somehow, I don't feel like you're helping me," Adélaïde finally said.

"It's not that," Olympe said. "I question whether money alone will be enough. You need a position on one of the committees already working with the new government. Or the backing of a political club. I myself belong to the Girondist club."

"I've tried to avoid politics and make it about the issues."

"Is there a difference?"

"When you want to get paid, yes."

Olympe's eyes flashed under her dark brows, but the sound of her scratching quill filled the silence, and Adélaïde let out her breath.

The dark of night was lifting when Adélaïde proofread the final letter. "Thank you for writing this."

Olympe stretched and yawned. "Personally, I believe you're in, all the way, or you're out."

"I hope you're wrong," Adélaïde said.

CHAPTER 34

1790

"Raise the curtains," Adélaïde urged her students in a loud whisper. The excitement on her girls' faces ignited her own. Marie and Isabelle stood on ladders at opposite ends of her studio. Between them, red fabric hanging from a rod divided the room in half, *Les Chevaliers de St. Lazare* on one side, a select group of friends and artists from the Central Academy on the other. The girls pulled on the cords, and the drapes swooshed aside with a clank of brass rings.

Afternoon sunlight struck the painting. In the light, the figures appeared to dance and wave. There was a moment of silence, then someone shouted, "Bravo, madame!" The men clapped and whistled.

Joseph Suvée came up to the painting, then stood back, staring at the Comte de Provence seated on a fauteuil, his outstretched hand offering the deed of a hospital to a knight kneeling before him. In the middle of the painting, two knights exclaimed over a tiny building model that radiated in flecks of silver. A third knight eyed the viewer with sparkling eyes, his arm inviting the viewer into the painting.

"The figures shift to include us in the painting," Joseph marveled.

Ducis walked the length of the painting, turned, and walked it in the other direction. "The figures in the gallery," he said. "When you turn, they turn. They wave at us, the audience. How do they do that?"

"The painting shimmers with light and energy," another artist exclaimed. "But how?"

"Is it the metallic effects and gold leaf highlights?" Simon Miger examined the clothing on the central figures and the dignitaries behind them.

Everyone walked the painting to get the full effect.

"You were right to finish this painting." François handed her a glass of champagne.

Joseph raised his glass to her. "The greatest female artists have been in your studio all along. And it is because you taught them."

She carried her glass to where he stood and said in a low voice, "I never meant for you to lose your students, Joseph. I've been fighting for them ever since. You must believe me." She searched his face. "Friends again?"

He tipped his glass.

"Good," she said. A little tension eased from her spine. She raised her voice. "These girls came to me with talent." Her students stood beside the painting, pointing out the parts they had worked on to an Academy professor. "Together, we were able to accomplish something no one has done before."

"Madame, your work is a crowning achievement in a century of art," Simon admired.

"How *did* you make the illusion work, Adélaïde?" Joseph asked.

"If I'm permitted to hold a class at the Louvre, gentlemen, I'll be happy to teach you my technique."

The men laughed.

"I wish Vien could see this," François said. "Now that he's director, he needs to know what you and your school of students have accomplished."

"I have a meeting with him tomorrow," Adélaïde said. "Depending on how things go, I may offer him a viewing."

"Everyone should see this painting," Joseph said. "Too bad they can't."

The room fell silent.

Adélaïde looked away. It hurt that the debut of this work, the most ambitious of her life, went off with so little splash. It was a small party, made so by the times and the now controversial subject matter. No one wanted to see a painting of the royal family these days, and the subject of her painting remained under house arrest.

Ducis's jolly voice broke the sudden quiet. "Madame, I must say, this isn't your usual style."

"What do you mean?"

"Your usual habit is to paint our faults with unrelenting cruelty. But here you've made the king's brother look downright heroic. Not like a man who eats for sport all day long."

She chuckled. "Be kind to the man. What else is a prince to do, locked up in his palace with nowhere to go?"

"Such a prison," Joseph said. "If ever I were arrested, I'd like to be locked up in a palace, surrounded by food, granted my every wish by a thousand servants."

"Palace or no, I would not want to be imprisoned," Simon said.

"Nor I." Ducis shuddered. "Poor fellow. But, really, Adélaïde, did you have to give the man a halo?"

"I didn't." She pointed to the roll of paper in the prince's hand. "The light is traveling to the prince from the charter, not the other way around. It's the act of giving the deed that transforms the man."

He tilted his head and considered. "I have to say you've been more successful than d'Angiviller at elevating the royals. He was complaining about that last night."

"What do you mean?"

"I was witness to the most dreadful dinner party."

"Do tell," she took his arm and drew him away from the painting.

"The d'Angivillers have finally finished their remodeling. They invited some forty people to celebrate last night. The most interesting guest of the evening was Joseph Vien, who got into an argument with the comte."

"An argument about what?" François turned at the sound of Vien's name.

"Vien wanted to know when Academy members would be paid. D'Angiviller told Vien to take it up with the national treasury. Vien said there was no need. He understood that the comte had received funding for the Academy months ago, and he wanted to know where it was. With everyone looking on, d'Angiviller had to say he would look into it."

"Well, he should." Joseph joined them. "We're owed three quarters now."

"And then Vien brought up the protests. Apparently, Jacques Louis David's students marched on the Louvre parade grounds yesterday, demanding an end to grace and favor positions."

"Talent should be the only consideration," Adélaïde said.

"D'Angiviller told Vien that the students could protest all they wanted, but he would never grant their request. Vien responded that the protesters had a point, that some change was necessary."

"Vien's support should be good for our cause," Simon said.

"Don't be too certain," Ducis said. "D'Angiviller told Vien he hadn't hired him to be weak. He had hired him to bring dignity and glory back to France, not to support rabble-rousers. Vien grew quite red in the face, got up from the table, and left. Even the musicians did not know what music to play after that."

"If I had been invited to dine at the d'Angivillers', I would have eaten my dinner and kept my mouth shut," Joseph said. "Their dinner parties are famous."

"Rightly so." Ducis patted his round belly. "My landlords invite me to every party. My job is to drop Shakespearean quotes to support the comte's positions at appropriate intervals. After the guests left, d'Angiviller said he'd spent his whole life protecting the kingdom of France. He asked how could everything have gone so wrong. 'O, where is loyalty?' I replied. He grew angry and reminded me that I too ate his food and drank his wine. He told his wife that all he'd ever tried to do was turn men's hearts to serious matters. How else could he bestow dignity on a young king with no dignity at all?" Ducis laughed at their shocked expression. "He really did say that. To which I replied, 'The king is but a man,' Richard II, thank you. The comtesse said perhaps it hadn't gone wrong at all, that the whole country was fighting for France, even the poor."

"How will Vien respond?" Simon asked.

"I'm about to find out," Adélaïde said. "I have a meeting with him in the morning. Now that the painting is done, it's time for me to focus my efforts on the Society of Artists' push to get more women admitted to the Academy."

Joseph laughed. "You may have better luck collecting what you're owed on this painting."

～

"It's good to see you, sir." Adélaïde had had little to do with Joseph Vien since she had painted his portrait years earlier. "Permit me to congratulate you on your appointment as Academy Director."

From his seat behind the desk, Vien inclined his head, his expression as remote and tight-lipped as she remembered.

"May I sit down, sir?" He had not risen at her entrance.

"No need. This will be quick, madame. We do not permit outside groups to speak before the Academy, and we have never heard of this society of yours."

"We are well known to you, sir. Our group includes wives and daughters of Academy members."

He shook his head. "They have no standing here."

"But, sir, you invited me to come." Perspiration slid down her back.

He held up a stack of letters. "It seemed the best way to stop your ceaseless requests."

Disappointment hit her. "If you won't let our Society of Artists address the Academy, then permit me to speak as an Academy member."

"You, too, have no standing to speak."

"But I am an Academy member."

"As you did not take the Proces Verbaux, you have no right to speak."

"The Proces Verbaux? The vow I stood ready to take? That I waited years to take? That the Academy wouldn't let me take because I am a woman?"

"I do not make the rules, madame."

She slapped her hand on his desk. "Then let me take the oath now."

He reared back in his chair. "I have no authority to render the oath, and I cannot change the rules, so do not waste your breath uttering a vow you have no right to make."

"How convenient. Did the Academy plan this all along?"

"I am sorry, madame." He looked anything but sorry.

She thought of the women depending on her. Desperation took over. "Would you treat your wife—a fellow Academy member—this way, sir?"

His eyes glacial, he rose from his seat. "It is time for you to leave, madame. We have no further business to discuss." He opened the door and stood back.

Her wooden heels clicked as she passed him. "You can't hide behind unjust rules forever, Monsieur Directeur."

The door banged shut.

Later that day, François, Joseph, and Simon met her at a coffee house. She bought four cups of coffee at the counter, brought them to the table, and slammed them down.

"Careful, Adélaïde." Joseph moved his chair back. "I'm grateful you're paying today, but I want to drink the fruit of these Arabic beans, not wear it."

She told them what had happened that morning. "Knowing they are doing this on purpose makes me so angry." Olympe had been right when she advised Adélaïde to work from the inside. "We women stand ready to do our part, but we aren't making any headway. To be successful, we need to be on the committees already working with the government. Ones that have broad support. Your Central Academy is such an organization." She stared into their eyes.

"Oh no." François looked alarmed.

"Gentlemen, make me a member of your Central Academy. It's the only way. I'm begging you."

Joseph groaned. "I knew this coffee would come with a price."

"Of course we will help you," Simon said. "I'll add your petition to the engravers' proposals at the next Academy meeting. The meeting is months away, but that gives us time to prepare."

"Is that the only way? I would prefer to present our petitions myself."

"Even if you join our committee, the Academy will not permit you to speak," François reminded. "Without the Proces Verbaux—"

She threw up her hands. "Do not say that phrase to me, François."

"Calm down." Joseph looked around the room. "Simon Miger is a good orator. You can trust him."

But could she?

CHAPTER 35

1790

In the months leading up to the Academy meeting, Adélaïde drafted her pamphlet for women's education and followed François's advice, turning to the National Assemblymen who called themselves the Feuillants.

Lobbying them the way she had lobbied Academy members a decade before, she painted their portraits and discussed her issues. In this way, she witnessed the heart of the Revolution, recording the faces of its leaders with her brush while she listened to their ideas and added her own.

"The new order is rising before our eyes," she told François and Alexandré. "If Jacques Louis David can be the Revolution's cartoonist, I shall be its portraitist. These men listen to me. Some even take notes." To know that her paintings documented history and that she herself could shape the new order in some small measure filled her with excitement, and equal amounts of pride and humility.

Alexandré de Lameth, a seasoned soldier who had fought in the American Revolution, insisted on freedom of the press and fought to ensure that the right to declare war rested with the National Assembly and not the king. He worked on the *Declaration of the Rights of Man and of the Citizen*, but did not support the rights of Black men.

"What about the rights of women?" she asked.

Charles, his brother, who had also fought in the American Revolution, founded the Society of the Friends of the Blacks. He repaid the government his military education and renounced his noble titles. "But who will be the friend of women?" she pressed.

Adrien du Port de Prélaville, Freemason, attorney, and mesmerist, was famous for his speeches. He supported trial by jury for criminals and organized a new judicial system. When Adélaïde heard him speak on the assembly floor, his control over the crowd thrilled her as much as it frightened her. When she asked him how he got the audience to do his bidding, he told her, "Find the magnetic energy field of the audience. Move it. Use it. When you capture the people's energy, you can get them to do anything. Go out in the streets and watch it happen."

Antoine Barnave believed in free speech and the protection of private property, but despised the king and the clergy, and insisted that church property be confiscated. He disagreed with Adrien du Port de Prélaville, saying that a crowd's energy and power was dangerous and should be checked by a monarch who had popular support. Adélaïde thought he might be right but observed that individuals acting alone could also be dangerous. Soon after she finished his portrait, he proved her point, shooting a man who disagreed with him in a duel.

"Are we going to settle our differences with attempted murder?" Adélaïde asked François. "Do you still believe the ends justify the means?"

He did not answer.

The Duc D'Anguillon, young, impetuous, dilettante lover of music and theatre, threw his lot in with the Third Estate in the way that the young reject the ways of the old. Chubby, indolent, but desiring glory, he joined the Republican Army as a general.

"He has no idea what he's doing," Adélaïde told Olympe.

"Most of them don't," Olympe said. "But that's what makes it exciting."

The Vicomte de Beauharnais, a member of nobility born in the Americas, had fought in the American Revolution. He became President of the National Constituent Assembly. She spoke to him about liberty and equality for women.

Jean-Baptiste-Charles Chabroud, judge and statesman, was thin and solemn with large dark eyes. He was the writer of the new criminal code and did not believe that a death sentence could be executed humanely. Impressed, Adélaïde debated with him how changes could be made to the law for the compassionate, equitable treatment of women.

François LaBorde de Méréville, descended from a long line of bankers, managed the finances of the new government but questioned whether the Revolution would take France in the right direction.

She spoke to him about the plight of poor women, then asked, "Do you think I will ever get paid?"

Prince Louis-Victor de Broglie, an army marshal who had fought in the American Revolution, had such zeal for the ideals of the Revolution that he would not tolerate anyone who suggested that the Revolution would fail. She painted his portrait and did not argue with him.

Louis-Philippe, Duc d'Orléans, exiled by his cousin the king, had renounced his title and returned to France upon his cousin's imprisonment. Calling himself Philippe Égalité, he used his vast fortune to finance the Revolution. His features were so like his cousin's, the Comte de Provence, that Adélaïde thought she was painting *Les Chevaliers* all over again.

Chevalier de Beaumetz, member of the Second Estate representing Arras, supported a constitutional monarchy and called for the end of torture during judicial proceedings. She agreed wholeheartedly. He called for all sides to work together to find positive solutions to stem the violent turn of the Revolution. Adélaïde wished him success.

Last to sit for her was the Bishop of Autun, who listened to her ideas about the education of women and agreed that something must be done.

She reflected the light falling on their faces, added dots of white to their irises. While they debated, she layered life and luminosity into their images, revealing the person through his glance, the curve of his lips, and the stance of his body. Gone were pre-revolutionary trappings of backgrounds with symbols of status and wealth, just a stark background and a face brimming with life and remembered conversation.

By day, she visited the Tuileries Palace and watched the Feuillants debate in the National Assembly, struggled through the packed streets to the club where they met in the evenings, and sketched while they drafted new laws. Then she walked home in the darkness, escorted by Alexandré when François was caught up in committee meetings of his own, and finished the men's likenesses by candlelight. Her shoulders ached, her fingers cramped, and her eyes burned from the late nights, but she knew she could not stop. She never missed a weekly salon at the de Condorcets and continued to speak and write on working women's issues.

Back in her studio, her students mixed her paints and prepared her canvases, the older students taught the younger ones, and her new friends read and edited her pamphlets and speeches.

"It's working," she told the women of the Society of Artists and Friends of Artists. "Some of the National Assemblymen have agreed to incorporate our ideas into their floor debates, but we must press forward on all fronts."

To her, the early days of the Revolution and the changes it brought were the back and forth of a minuet played in a music hall along the Champs Élysées. She whirled between its movements with light steps like everyone else. But as time wore on, drums and cymbals replaced the flute trills and violin notes. Clamor and discord grew.

"Kill the king!" the Montagnards cried from their tabletops along the sidewalk.

"Preserve the king's life at all costs," the Royalists insisted from inside the coffee houses.

The factions fought it out in the streets, fists punching, boots kicking, and rocks flying. One night, as she and Alexandré pushed through the teeming streets, a freshly painted canvas between them, a man standing on a table turned and pointed at her. "Hey, isn't that the woman who painted the king?" The man's shirt was torn, and torch flames made his sweat-stained face look as if it were melting. He grabbed a cobblestone from a pile stacked on the table and threw it at her.

Before they could react, objects from the crowd flew at them in the darkness. Alexandré tried to use the painting as a shield, but a rock struck him in the temple. He staggered and blood poured down his face. Adélaïde grabbed his elbow and hurried him to the studio, the painting abandoned in the crowd.

There, her students rushed to help.

"Oh, your face," Isabelle exclaimed.

"I'll get the medical supplies." Marie ran to the back room.

Alexandré flopped down on a chair beside the worktable with a groan. "Is it that bad?" He touched the wound.

"Let me look." Adélaïde batted his hand away.

"Here, madame." Marie appeared with a brown bottle and a stack of torn fabric.

Alexandré yelped when Adélaïde placed a vinegar-soaked towel on the wound.

"Sit still," she ordered. "You may need stitches."

"Not from you I don't." He scrambled to his feet. "Have you ever touched a needle in your life? Everyone knows you weren't the girl sewing samplers when you were a child."

"I'm sure I can figure it out."

"No thank you." He grabbed a fresh towel and pressed it to his head, then regarded the bloodied cloth. "Really, Adélaïde, is all this worth it?"

"I'm sorry about your pretty face, Alexandré, but if I can't speak for myself, my art must. And you just cost me hours of work. I'll have to repaint that canvas from memory."

Alexandré flung his hands out. "Girls, I protected your teacher from harm, got wounded for it, and all she cares about is her painting. Where's the gratitude for my heroism?"

"Luckily for you, I've got one painting to go after this. Maximilien Robespierre has finally agreed to sit for me."

"Who cares about Robespierre?"

"Crowds flock to him every night, Alexandré. We ourselves went to hear him speak last night. Afterward, I asked him why he hadn't responded to my letters, and he told me that jealous gods had prevented him from having the Graces paint him. He supports the rights of workmen, slaves, and Jews. Imagine if he took up our cause?"

Beneath the towel, Alexandré's lips turned downward. "Isn't Miger speaking for you?"

"Yes, his Academy speech is tomorrow, but I have to know that I've done everything I can for our cause."

At that moment, a knock sounded at the studio door. Simon Miger stepped inside, a sheaf of papers in his hand.

"Speak of the devil," Alexandré muttered.

"Ah, Simon, good evening," Adélaïde greeted him. "Come, we

have a podium for you. Everyone, gather the chairs." She turned to Alexandré. "I'll let you know when I need you to take me to the Jacobin club."

"Watch out, Simon," Alexandré pouted as Simon passed him. "Madame Guiard has us all doing her bidding. Be careful you don't get injured too."

"Alexandré was just leaving." Adélaïde nudged him toward the door. "We need to focus on Simon's speech, not your histrionics, so off you go. Girls, take your seats."

It was three in the morning when Adélaïde blew out the last candle in the studio and crawled onto the daybed at the back of her office.

Marie lingered in the doorway, her lamp outlining her figure. "Monsieur Miger's almost as good a speaker as Robespierre. I wish we could hear him speak tomorrow."

"Well, you can't," Adélaïde said. "It's a closed-door Academy session. Even I am stuck up in the women's balcony. But I feel much better about tomorrow's outcome. With that speech, Simon could persuade a king to give up his kingdom."

CHAPTER 36

NOVEMBER 1790

S imon's speech was a disaster.

Adélaïde should have known something was wrong when Simon, dressed in his usual black linen, stepped into the speakers' box, looked behind him at the Academy officials sitting on a raised platform, then glanced up into the gallery. His gaze passed over her as though he did not see her, the only woman in a press of men, standing at the railing of the balcony, smiling, and waving her fan at him. Confused, Adélaïde sat down in her prized seat, the one she had refused to give up when the speaker's floor filled, and Academy members joined her on the balcony.

Without looking up again, Simon read from his notes. "Monsieur Vien, Secretary Renou, Academy members, we are here today to decide the future direction of the Royal Academy of Painting and Sculpture. The National Assembly has asked many constituents to assist in reforming the institutions of government. Today, I would like to put forth the recommendations the Central Academy group has made for the Royal Academy of Painting and Sculpture and to discuss their rationale."

The man to her right yawned.

A sour taste rose in her throat. This was not the speech Simon had delivered in her studio the night before, a speech that flowed from him in effortless, cadenced rhythm and had her students leaping to their feet. Now, Adélaïde strained to hear his monotone drone of words over the pulse thudding at her temples.

"As we organize our nation around the principles of liberty, equality, and humanity, we must apply the same foundational concepts to our Academy. And as the laws of a nation are granted by the people who agree to be ruled by such laws, so too must the rules of the Academy be granted by the members of the institution themselves."

Behind the speaker's box, Vien picked at a piece of lace peeking from his jacket sleeve, looking bored. The man beside Adélaïde emitted a soft snore.

Put some passion in your speech, Simon, Adélaïde implored.

"We call for the end of closed-door sessions where officers hold meetings in secret and make decisions that impact all of us without our discussion or approval. All Academy members must have the right to direct the governance of the Academy."

"Hear, hear," someone on the speaker's floor said.

Where was the sentence she had helped Simon draft about women having the explicit right to vote?

Behind Simon, the Academy officials whispered among themselves. Secretary Renou sat at a small table to their side, writing the meeting minutes into the Academy's ancient tome.

"Secondly, we recommend that the Academy be open to all. The only entrance requirement must be talent—not age, rank, wealth, or connection."

What about sex? What was going on?

Several men clapped, but Joseph Vien started tapping his foot.

"Further, we must free ourselves from the taint of the corruption, injustice, and favoritism that are the fruits of a patronage system acting in secret. Thus, we call for salon admissions to be decided by a committee of academicians using rules and principles that make the process fair and transparent."

Simon tapped his notes on the lectern as though he were done. The papers aligned with an audible clack. Tepid applause scattered through the room. Surely that wasn't his entire speech?

Simon looked up and saw her on the balcony, her hands raised as if to ask, what happened? His jaw ticked. "And as pertains to our three recommendations, female artists who display the same level of talent and dedication to their art as men must be admitted under the same conditions as men and must enjoy the same rights and privileges of men, from admission of works to the salon, to governance of this august body." The words burst forth in a rush.

The man beside her jerked awake. "Did that man just say females could rule the Academy?"

The Academy officials seated behind Simon looked furious. Joseph Vien's hands snapped into fists, a second scowled his disapproval, the third jumped to his feet.

"What makes you think you can bring such an outrageous proposal before this body, Monsieur Miger?" he asked.

Simon turned to face the officials. "Times change. Governments change. The Academy too must change. Everywhere, women who contribute to society must be awarded their rightful place."

Central Academy members shouted "Hear! Hear!" from the speaker's floor, but to Adélaïde's ears, their cries were ineffectual accent notes, not the crescendo of approval that was to have followed the rousing speech that Simon did not deliver. How could he have betrayed her like that? She wanted to run out and throw up.

Joseph Vien rose to his feet. "Gentlemen, we seem to have an insurrection happening in our midst. Monsieur Miger, you did not come here to change this institution. Instead, that woman"—he jabbed his finger toward the balcony—"has stirred you up and enticed you to act on her behalf."

Uncomfortable laughter met his remark. The man seated to her left shifted to stare at her.

"Young man, you should guard against the influence of such a woman," Vien sneered.

Simon rocked back on his feet, fists clenched, his face reddening.

Men began to murmur, then argue, on the speaker's floor. On the balcony, the men were silent, but she felt their eyes watching her. Adélaïde held herself rigid, but heat prickled up her spine.

Secretary Renou stood. "Gentlemen," he addressed the crowd. "Two roosters can live together in peace but introduce one hen into their midst and the fighting begins."

Laughter broke out. Perspiration soaked Adélaïde's dress.

"Let the cock wars begin," someone cried.

Behind her a man shouted, "Cluck, cluck."

Male laughter filled the balcony. The men below turned to stare up at her.

"Cock-a-doodle-doo," someone crowed.

Renou turned to Vien. In a loud, pitying voice he said, "Monsieur le Director, we must forgive Monsieur Miger his confusion. Since time immemorial, women have lured men to their destruction. It is an established fact that even judges known for their integrity cannot be impartial when they judge the work of a woman. These men of the Central Academy have been blinded by Madame Guiard, who has spread her shining wares before them."

Adélaïde jumped to her feet. "How dare you, sir?" She pushed her way through the men seated in her row and stormed down the stairs, ready to accost the man. When she made it to the speaker's floor, the room erupted into shouting and flying fists.

Adélaïde did not know how she made it home. She only remembered flashes of people as she pushed through the streets, wielding her umbrella at anyone who got in her way. She wished Vien with his smirking face were before her now, or Renou with his sneering pity. She would have beaten their straight noses to a bloody pulp. If she ever saw Miger again, she would strangle him with her bare hands.

"What happened?" Claudette cried as Adélaïde barged through the studio door.

"Just leave me alone." She went into her office and slammed the door. Her whole body shook with the effort not to lash out.

CHAPTER 37

1790

Aloud knock woke Adélaïde up.

"What is the bestselling pamphleteer on women's education doing hiding in her office?" Olympe shouted through the office door. "Adélaïde, open the door."

Adélaïde raised her head from the desk and looked around, bleary eyed, wondering why she was not lying on her daybed. Then she remembered. Groaning, she buried her face in her hands. "Go away," she said.

"Adélaïde, if you do not come out, we are going to break the door down." Claudette rattled the doorknob. "Someone, get a hammer."

"I'm coming. No need to destroy the place." Adélaïde rubbed the sleep from her eyes, smoothed her hair, and opened the door. Marie, Isabelle, Claudette, and François peered at her from varying heights above Olympe. After the dark of her windowless office, sunlight blazing behind her friends stabbed her eyes. She sprang back, shading her eyes.

"Are you well?" Marie asked.

"I fell asleep." She rubbed the crick in her neck. "What time is it?"

"Nine in the morning," François said. He hovered behind the women, a large tart in one hand, a jug in the other.

She sniffed the air. "Is that apple pie I smell?"

He nodded.

She sniffed again. "And chocolate?"

He grinned and held out the tart. "Come and eat."

They sat down at the worktable. While François served Adélaïde an extra-large portion of pie, Olympe asked her what had happened.

Adélaïde set down her fork and told them. "What was Miger thinking? Why'd he change his speech?"

"He was warned," François said. "He was told just before the meeting that if there were any theatrics, he would be expelled."

"I can't believe the Academy would go that far. Will we always have to live in a world in which we have no say, in which men hold authority over us and act together to keep us out?" She speared an apple slice with her fork. "How can I go out in public again? I may have to retire to the country."

"You're not going anywhere," Olympe said. "Society will change when enough women sacrifice their pride and keep fighting."

"But why do you have to be the one to sacrifice?" Claudette asked.

Marie turned to François. "Monsieur Vincent, can't you do something?"

"It's not his place to protect me." Adélaïde shoved the pie plate away.

"Perhaps it's time to reconsider." François rubbed the back of his neck. "Perhaps Claudette is right. Why do you need to put yourself through this? You know you are a good artist. You do not need these men to tell you that."

"Stop fighting them," Claudette said. "You could lose everything if you continue."

"You can't let them win," Olympe said.

"Oh, I won't." Bravado made Adélaïde's words strong, but the pie settled unhappily in her churning stomach.

"Just how do you plan to do that, Adélaïde?" François folded his arms across his chest.

"I don't know, François, but I should have been the one to speak before the Academy. I knew better."

"Miger could have been Aristotle himself, and they would have acted the same way," he told her.

"Well, I can't let them black my eyes and stomp all over me."

She pictured Vien and Renou jeering at Simon and deflated in her chair. "But I don't know how to fight them anymore."

"If you give up, what will happen to us?" Isabelle got up to clear the dishes, her face averted, but Adélaïde heard the fear in her voice.

"Everyone will give up, that's what." Marie stood to help her friend.

"You can't let that happen," Olympe said. "One hundred and thirty women depend on you to succeed. I saw them at your society meeting. I heard you make promises to them."

"I know you're right, Olympe, but—" Adélaïde pondered the conflict ahead. Her enemies would continue to demoralize and discourage her. Could she prevail before they destroyed her? Or before they destroyed the ones who supported her? She looked at the familiar faces around the table. Love, encouragement, trust, fear, and hope looked back at her. Marie and Isabelle headed into the backroom, their bodies filled out, healthy, no longer emaciated as when they had come to her. Where would they be if she stopped fighting? Where would they go? Where would she go?

She took a deep breath. "The Academy cannot be allowed to treat anyone the way they have treated me."

"How will you do it, madame?" Marie rushed back into the room.

"Perhaps you could speak to the Comtesse d'Angiviller again," François suggested. "I don't think the Central Academy has any more sway in this."

She pictured herself groveling in the d'Angivillers' ornate drawing room a third time. "I won't debase myself before d'Angiviller again." A thought struck and she straightened in her chair. "François, have the Academy members been paid yet?"

"No."

"But didn't d'Angiviller receive the money to pay you?"

"So they say."

Isabelle asked, "Where could the money have gone?"

"No one knows. We have heard nothing from Vien's inquiry."

She recalled Ducis's comment about new dining room furniture and new porcelain dishes from Limoges. Her mind's eye saw the elaborate frescos and marble statues in process at the d'Angivillers' mansion the last time she had visited. "I think I know where the money went."

"What are you planning?" François asked. "That look in your eye makes me nervous."

"It's time to bring d'Angiviller down. Olympe, I may need you to help me write some letters."

"Anything," Olympe said.

Just then Adélaïde remembered what Olympe had said outside her door that morning. "Olympe, what did you mean about my pamphlet?"

Olympe smacked her head and swore. "I forgot. I came bearing glad tidings. Yesterday the printer told me he had begun a second printing of your pamphlet on women's education. The first printing has sold out."

"Is this true?" For the first time since leaving the Louvre, she felt like she could breathe.

"I went to the booksellers to see for myself. Adélaïde, people stood three deep in line waiting to read it. And who should I run into at the bookseller but the Bishop of Autun."

"Talleyrand?"

Olympe nodded. "He had come to purchase a copy. He intends to ask you to speak on the plight of poor women before the National Assembly."

Excitement coursed through her. "Are you teasing me?"

"Of course not. Do you realize what this means, Adélaïde? You will have the opportunity to speak for yourself—for all women—on the biggest stage in the land." Olympe stared at her, her pointed chin raised in challenge.

Adélaïde admired Olympe's cagey wisdom. "You are something, you know that?"

"Still feeling defeated?" her friend asked.

"No, I don't think I am." Energy flowed through her like wind catching the sails of a ship.

"This calls for a celebration." François held up the jug, but they were out of hot chocolate.

"Let's wait to celebrate when—*if*—it happens. Right now, we have something we must do." Adélaïde stood up. "François, how quickly can we assemble a group to visit the comte?"

CHAPTER 38

1790

"Madame, you have become a thorn in my side." The Comte d'Angiviller stood with his desk between them, arms folded across his chest.

"Oh no, please do not think of me that way, sir. One can extract a thorn. I would prefer you to view me as a burr digging in for the duration."

Joseph Suvée stifled his laugh in a cough while François directed his gaze to the paintings on the wall behind the comte. Simon Miger maintained his stoic demeanor.

"Do not tell me you have come to waste my time petitioning for the support of fan painters." The comte's medals quivered against his burgundy coat.

"Lord preserve us from fan painters." Adélaïde snapped her ivory fan open and wielded it with expert effect in the stuffy room. "I'm here to discuss my outstanding invoices. You have not authorized a single payment on the repairs made at the King's Library. This is unacceptable, sir."

The comte's face took on a pink hue. "You must understand, madame, that in this troubled era, things take time."

"Deliberately ignoring my invoices has nothing to do with the times." Adélaïde made her voice cold.

"And we demand to know where our stipends are," Joseph said.

"What does any of this have to do with me?" d'Angiviller asked.

"Everyone knows you make the ultimate decisions for the Academy," Adélaïde said.

The comte shrugged. "Even I find it impossible to get funding right now." He left his desk to open a window. A late morning breeze swirled into the room.

"If that were true, workmen would not be plastering your ballroom ceiling at this moment." Adélaïde snapped her fan shut. "We called upon you at home this morning. Massive funds are being expended in your house right now. Where is that money coming from, I wonder?"

The comte made a movement toward her, and François stepped between them. "We have come here to resolve this amicably, Monsieur le Comte." He looked down on the man from his superior height.

"But if you do not meet our demands, we intend to take you to court," Adélaïde said.

"You will never succeed," the comte said. His face had turned from pink to red.

"I would not be so certain of that," François told him.

Anger, then fear flickered in his eyes. "What is it you want, Madame Guiard?"

"You have denied an entire body of men and women access to their livelihood. Stop blocking our efforts to speak at the Academy. Allow us to present our ideas, then put them to a vote."

The comte sat at his desk and sharpened a quill. "As you have said, madame, I and I alone am responsible for the Academy. All this fomenting of ideas wastes everyone's time. I have already implemented all changes necessary." He dipped the quill into a bottle of ink and began to write as though he had forgotten they were there.

"Sir, can you not see that changes are required?" François asked. "We no longer live in a time when one person can dictate how society will operate."

D'Angiviller squared his jaw. "I have made my position clear, Monsieur Vincent."

Adélaïde said, "Then, sir, I must inform you that we will report you to the National Assembly. We will call for an accounting of the money spent since you became Director of Building Works. The world needs to know how you've built yourself a palace while you forced hundreds of artists to starve."

His face the color of his velvet jacket, he stood again. "Do you threaten me, madame?"

"If you have nothing to hide, you have nothing to fear."

"This is extortion."

The four artists looked at each other. Finally, they had him where they wanted him.

"Consider it terms for peace," she said.

Simon placed a document on d'Angiviller's desk. "Here are our demands. You allow us to present our proposals without interference, changes which, I will remind you, the National Assembly requested."

The comte picked up the paper, rubbing his jaw. "The Academy may consent to hearing your ideas."

"You let me speak on behalf of women artists," Adélaïde said.

"Madame, in one hundred forty-two years, no woman has ever addressed the Academy."

"Then it is a hundred and forty-two years late," Adélaïde retorted.

He pulled at the ruffles circling his throat. Several minutes passed before he relented.

"Our petitions get put to a vote," François said.

"We will do this at our next quarterly meeting," the comte agreed.

"No. Call a special meeting for next week," Adélaïde said. "We are tired of waiting."

When the artists left the Louvre, they stopped at a beignet stand along the river, then sat on a stone wall to eat the pastries. A sharp pebble pressed into Adélaïde's thigh. She flung the rock out into the roiling wake of a passing barge.

"I can't believe it," she said. "The comte has made life difficult for years, but it took just one threat to make him change his mind."

"It was not a small threat," Joseph said.

"The man has done immeasurable harm while enriching himself," Simon said.

"Who knows what he intended," François said. "What is done is done. Let us focus on what we must do next. We need to get

Academy officials talking to the Central Academy members again. And we must line up votes."

"Perhaps we should get Chevalier Roslin involved," Adélaïde said. "He's the most powerful artist in France. He and his wife have always supported me."

"I will secure votes among the engravers," Simon said. Ever since the debacle of his speech, he had been eager to redeem himself.

"And I must find a way to reach the hearts of Academy members with my speech," Adélaïde said.

"Many of them will not listen to ideas they think come from a woman," François warned.

"A 'failed man' cannot possibly have a valid thought in her head." Adélaïde rubbed her hands together. "Gentlemen, I wonder, is Nature full of failures and successes by virtue of one's sex?"

"Of course not," Simon said.

"Adélaïde is teasing you," François told him.

"Look to Greek and Roman history," Joseph advised. "Consider Plato. He said that nothing is more ludicrous than for men and women not to follow the same pursuits with all their strength and mind. When they do not, the state of the whole being is cut in half."

"How is it that we're still debating this thousands of years later?" She tossed her beignet into a flock of pigeons and stalked off.

On the evening Adélaïde addressed the Academy, the centrist movement chose its most venerable members to speak before her. Night air chilled the audience hall but sweat trickled down her back as she waited her turn. A stage occupied the front of the room, complete with a lectern and a table where Secretary Renou recorded their speeches in the minute book.

Jean-Georges Wille, seventy-five years old and blind but full of passion for his fellow artists, called for elevated status for engravers. The audience loved him and cheered, clapped, and stomped. When he finished, Simon Miger assisted him down the shallow stage steps and led him to the seat beside Adélaïde in the first row.

"Well done, Monsieur Wille," she whispered. "Your petition is sure to pass."

He groped for her hand and squeezed it. "Good luck, my dear."

Chevalier Roslin spoke next. "Ladies," he acknowledged the director's wife, Marie-Thérèse Reboul, and her friend, Anne-Marie Vallayer-Coster, who sat in the front row with Adélaïde, "and gentlemen, we now turn to our petitions regarding the entrance and participation of women. Who better to introduce them than a woman? And what a talented person she is. You may have heard her speak in the salons and political clubs of Paris, read her booklet on the education of poor women, or seen her artwork in the Salon. Known in the Academy for her clarity of vision, realistic portrayal of people on canvas, and dedication to her art, she is celebrated throughout Paris for her determination to improve the lives of working women. Ladies and gentlemen, I give you Madame Guiard."

Listening to the applause as she bounded up the steps to the stage, Adélaïde thought, *Who could have imagined this is who I would become?* She faced her audience without notes. "Once there was a little girl who liked to draw. For her fifteenth birthday, a kind person arranged for her to see the famous art collection of Pierre Crozat. From the very moment she saw the works of Mademoiselle Carriera, this girl knew that she wanted to produce work like that."

After their raucous response to Monsieur Wille, the men had quieted, but heads nodded when she mentioned Rosalba Carriera.

"No one told her that it was improper or immodest, or that she could not do it. Her muse called, and, as men and women have done for centuries, she responded. With the support of her father, she commenced the serious study of art." Standing before these men, she yearned to be a part of their body, to make decisions that would move art in new directions. She knew she could do it, had proven it over and again, but they had to let her in, had to stop seeing her as the enemy, and to see her as they saw themselves. She looked out at the faces in the crowd, impassive, polite. What were they thinking?

"She was happy to do what she had been born to do. But as she continued her studies, a curious thing happened. When the boys in her art classes excelled, they won scholarships and prizes. They could attend the king's university, study in Italy, look forward to a brilliant career in the Academy. But if she did well . . . nothing. Nothing at all. Those doors were closed to her." She looked around and saw that some men were listening. "How would you feel if you were told that because your hands were small, you could only paint porcelain, or that you could never paint a serious subject because you were incapable of intelligent thought?"

That got their attention.

"Would you be insulted? Would you be angry? Would you be discouraged?"

Someone shouted, "Yes."

"Despite these setbacks, this young girl joined the Academy of Saint Luke. Then the government closed the guilds. As a female, she was denied admission to this Academy. Unable to earn a living, she faced starvation and homelessness. Gentlemen, I ask you, how does society commit such a moral outrage?"

Several men shook their heads.

"Now, this young woman was determined"—she saw François's faint smile—"and did not wish to starve, so she knocked on every door that she could think of and kept knocking until the Academy admitted her as one of the four females permitted to its distinguished body. She could now support herself, grow as an artist, and propel art in new directions. Still, doors remained closed. The Academy denied her the entitlements of living quarters and studio space." She paused again. "Gentlemen, how would you like to be put out of the Louvre? How would your students feel? How would it impact your business?" She let the questions sink in. "Even if the Academy found you alternate housing, or paid you to find your own studio space, you would protest. You would know that your career would suffer, your business would suffer, your students would suffer." The crowd booed. Were they with her? Had she made her point? Many of them were on the edge of their seats. "The final insult would be for your students to be permanently barred from this esteemed body, forever casting your legacy in doubt."

They waited for her to speak again.

"While I have met with success beyond my wildest imaginings, I cannot stand by and watch while other women face what I have encountered or let another starve while she waits for another exception to be made."

Cheers came from different parts of the room.

"Doors should never be closed to opportunity solely because you are a woman. Past Academy leaders have justified their actions under the spurious and convenient premise that women cannot contribute meaningfully to art. Facts say otherwise. Science and Nature tell us that men and women are two halves that make a whole. Thousands of years ago, Plato observed that as long as we prevent half our members from pursuing their dreams, our society will be hobbled by those unjustified restraints. How can we as a society continue to ignore this evident truth?"

Applause greeted her question. Had she changed their hearts and minds?

"Socrates said that the secret to change is to build something new, not to fight what is old. I do not come here today to battle the old order or to right past wrongs. I come instead to advocate for Plato's whole society. This new order is the hope of our young nation."

Several men stood and clapped. Would they vote with her now?

"Today, I stand before you, knocking at this last door—the door of opportunity, of equality, of justice. I ask you to open that door and invite women in. Consider their work, and those whose quality, originality, and expertise warrant it. Let them in, and in the words of that famous member of the Academy of Art in Florence, Artemisia Gentileschi, 'Illustrious sirs, we will show you what a woman can do.'"

The audience clapped for five minutes. When everyone returned to their seats, Secretary Renou nodded. It was time. She presented her two petitions—one for the Academy to accept women in unlimited numbers, the other to create a position of counselor to permit women to participate in Academy leadership.

Monsieur Wille pushed himself to his feet. Leaning on his cane, he turned to face the room and called out, "Madame Guiard has proven that we must admit women without restricting their numbers. The Academy must admit members based solely on talent, not on the sex of the artist. I support this petition."

François stood next. His voice carried over the tumultuous audience as he said, "I support Madame Guiard's petitions."

Members of the Central Academy movement stood to join him and called out, "Hear! Hear!" Clapping and cheering followed.

Joy swept through her at François's public support. She thanked the chevalier, the director, and the officers of the Academy and the members, then walked off the stage to cheers, whistles and thunderous applause.

When she sat down, Monsieur Wille grasped her forearm with a trembling hand. "Bravo, my dear."

The chevalier addressed the Academy leaders. "As agreed, you have promised us that you would put our petitions to a vote tonight."

From his place on the stage, Secretary Renou initiated the roll call. Men's voices sounded around the room, the sonorous rhythm of yays and nays broken as the vote passed by the three women.

Renou tallied the votes, then announced, "With respect to the petition to allow women to be admitted to the Academy in unlimited numbers: passed. With respect to allowing women positions of counselor: passed."

Exultation swamped her. She brought her hands to her mouth to restrain the whoop that escaped. She half rose out of her seat, before falling back as relief weakened her legs. Beside her, Monsieur Wille grabbed her arm and congratulated her. She heard the chevalier's congratulations through the applause that broke out. François, who had been seated on the other side of the knight, dragged her out of her seat and shook her hand, his eyes burning with pride.

Suddenly, she realized that not all the clamor was cheering. She turned and watched as Jacques Louis David led a group of men to the doors at the back of the hall. Among them she recognized her harshest critics. At the door, he looked back. His tumor throbbed and contorted his face like a magic lantern image. He shouted something but his words sounded like barking. Spittle flew from his lips.

The doors slammed shut. A band of pain circled her head as arguments ricocheted across the room and the shouting rang to a deafening roar. How could this be happening again?

Joseph Vien and the Comte d'Angiviller climbed on the stage and conferred together. Then Vien pounded his walking stick on the platform and bellowed for silence. "Gentlemen, take your seats." He banged his walking stick until quiet returned, then took out a handkerchief and wiped his forehead. Tucking the square back into his jacket, he turned to Renou. "Monsieur Secretary, I order you to strike these votes from the record. Academy members have no right to change the charter. That right belongs to the Academy's officers alone. We will retire to consider the matter."

Renou drew a line through the tallies in the ledger and sprinkled sand on the ink. He waited for the ink to dry, closed the book, then tucked it under his arm and left the stage. Vien followed, beckoning his wife to join him.

Anne-Marie Vallayer-Coster took Madame Vien's arm. As the two women passed Adélaïde, they averted their gaze.

When the comte moved to follow, Adélaïde stepped into his path. "Why did you revoke the vote?"

D'Angiviller looked down his nose at her. "I agreed to put your petitions to a vote. I did not agree to accept that vote." Then he, Joseph Vien, the remaining Academy officers, and those who had voted against her petitions walked out.

Silence fell.

Adélaïde's hands shook. Her lips trembled. She clenched her fists, bit her lips, and looked around the room. Only those in the centrist movement remained. Her supporters.

Beside her, Monsieur Wille asked in a confused voice why the Academy had not voted on his petition. She shook her head, then realized he could not see her. Picking up his cane, she placed it in his hands. "I have no idea."

François approached, his face expressionless. "Shall we go?"

CHAPTER 39

1790

Two weeks later, the Comte d'Angiviller and Joseph Vien called a special Academy assembly to announce their decision regarding Adélaïde's petitions.

Whatever happens this evening, Adélaïde thought as she shifted on aching legs in front of the stage, *the Academy will not be able to hide what they have done.*

Despite the onset of winter, the people of Paris packed the Louvre's Apollo gallery. Adélaïde's students, women from the former Guild of Saint Luke, those who had read of the controversy in the news journals, those who saw a crowd and followed. The Society of Artists and Friends of Artists, dressed in white, thronged the floor around her.

Up on the stage, Vien opened an embossed leather portfolio and prepared to read a statement. Beside him, the comte glared out at the crowd. His angry gaze sought and held Adélaïde's. Chin lifted, she stared back.

"The officers of the Academy have expended considerable debate on the petitions of Madame Guiard, despite the fact that, as a nonvoting member of the Academy, her petitions were improper and invalid. Following our deliberations, we find that no changes to Academy regulations are warranted." Vien looked out at his audience. "Not only do we believe it inappropriate for women to interfere in the business affairs of men, but we also question the morals of the women who mix themselves in administrative work contrary to their nature and who occupy their time disrupting the important mission of art. Given recent events, and to avoid future disturbance to our operations, we hereby bar women from attending our deliberations."

Boos resounded through the gallery as Vien paused to turn his statement over.

"Turning to the other petitions we have before us . . ."

Adélaïde could not hear the rest of Vien's speech over the angry buzz in her ears, only registering when Vien closed the folder and adjourned the meeting.

From the stage, d'Angiviller directed a look of triumph at her. Then he followed Vien down the steps.

Later that evening, Adélaïde met with Joseph and François at a quiet cafe.

"I achieved everything, and they took it away like that." She snapped her fingers. The bottle of brandy on the table wavered, and she wiped her eyes. "I have never felt so naïve." *Or so hopeless.* "I just can't believe their duplicity." A sour feeling of defeat spread through her body.

"Their actions weren't directed at you," Joseph said. "They denied all the Central Academy positions, not just yours."

"Vien did not call you or your students immoral, Joseph." She pushed away her empty glass. "What a hypocrite. I remember when Vien had nothing but accolades for my work."

"I have to agree with Adélaïde." François took her glass and refilled it. "David and the men who walked out with him formed a Society of Fine Arts. They wrote a letter to the National Assembly accusing the Academy of discouraging talent. They claimed that its very existence fostered favoritism and cronyism."

"They might have a point," Adélaïde said bitterly.

"You won't agree when you hear what happened next," François told her. "The National Assembly elected David to a committee to investigate the rules and regulations of the Academy."

"How can he do that?"

"You must have forgotten that David ran for public office on the Jacobin platform and won."

"But what about the Central Academy's work?" Her mind spun. Until that moment, she had thought only of her own losses. Now she wondered what would happen to all of them.

Joseph pursed his mouth. "In David's official capacity, he will be able to influence the Assembly far more than we will."

"When will David present his findings?" she asked. "I want to be there."

"He's due to deliver it soon, but—" François shared an uneasy look with Joseph.

A lump gathered in her throat. "I can't battle the two of you and my enemies as well."

"You may as well tell her," Joseph said. "She'll read it in the journals tomorrow anyway."

"Word has it that David claimed you exert too much influence over the Academy. His group has called you a Joan of Arc," François said.

"I've been elevated from hen to witch?" She threw her hands up into the air. "Are they planning to burn me at the stake?"

"It's no laughing matter, Adélaïde," François said.

"Do you see me laughing?"

"No," he said. "But it gets worse. David's group has demanded that the nation forbid women from studying art."

Perspiration gathered on her temples and the back of her neck. "What does this mean for my position in the Academy?"

"We do not know," François said.

"Could I lose my ability to teach?"

"It's anyone's guess," Joseph said.

Wind howled around the building and the cold of night stole into the restaurant. A crushing pain filled her chest. "I was on the ground before, but now they want to stomp me into the dust."

Waiters moved through the room, lighting lanterns. François and Joseph sipped their brandy in silence. Adélaïde's hands hovered above the lamp in the middle of their table. Inside the glass box, the candle emitted light, but its weak flame could not warm her spread fingers.

The street door opened, and frigid air blew through the restaurant. With it came the shuffle of slippers. Letting out an exclamation of relief, François jumped to his feet. "The cavalry has arrived."

Olympe, Sophie, Isabelle, and Marie bore down on them, shedding their winter coats. A waiter scurried for more chairs while another struggled under a pile of coats and wraps.

"What do you mean, you don't know what to do?" Olympe demanded when Adélaïde told them the latest news. "You come back at them, twice as strong."

"Have you sent your letter to the National Assembly?" Sophie demanded.

Adélaïde shook her head.

"Was your threat to d'Angiviller just a bluff then?" Olympe asked.

"Of course not, but, foolishly, I took him at his word."

"Well, it's time to report him," Olympe said.

Sophie rested her hand on Adélaïde's shoulder. "You have many letters to write." She smiled down at her.

"And we are here to help," Marie said.

"While we're at it," Sophie continued, "let us reach out to the Bishop of Autun. Did he not say he would invite you to speak to the National Assembly? If they permit Monsieur David to present his position, they must also let you present yours."

All business, Olympe handed out quills, Marie passed out stationery, and Isabelle opened bottles of ink.

Strength returned to Adélaïde's spine. She picked up a quill.

CHAPTER 40

MAY 1791

Low clouds obscured the morning.

"Not an auspicious start to the day," Marie worried as she looked out a studio window. "It's beginning to mist."

"Hush," Sophie said. "No matter the weather, it's a glorious day when a woman makes history addressing our new government."

"Are you ready?" Isabelle asked as Adélaïde stood before the cheval glass by the door, rouging color onto her cheeks.

"You have to be." Olympe's face appeared below hers in the mirror. "You've practiced enough."

"As though practicing my speech a thousand times were not enough, you all tormented me in my dreams last night." Adélaïde pulled on her woolen cloak. She stared at herself in the mirror again. If she failed today, female artists could lose their right to the very study of art. The responsibility of it crushed her. A double row of wrinkles etched their way across her forehead. She blew out a breath.

"You'll do fine," Olympe said. "Just remember, don't be over-wrought. Don't be overcome. Speak out for women everywhere with confidence and strength." Olympe pulled the hood of Adélaïde's cloak over her hair and tied the ribbons under her chin as though Adélaïde were a child.

"Remember your students, madame." Marie turned from the window as a parade of girls descended from the dormitory. "We'll be up in the gallery cheering you on. Look for our scarves." They pulled pieces of bright red fabric from behind their backs and waved them at her.

Adélaïde laughed and sniffled at the same time. "Let's go. If I stay another minute, I won't be able to squeeze a word out." She could not fail.

When Adélaïde had visited the ocean, she had observed its currents, swells, and undertows. She had heard waves crash against a sea wall in the dark and watched flashes of light that warned sailors as ships came and went in the harbor. Today, in the Tuileries Palace, on the floor of the National Assembly, a sea of humanity surrounded her, waves of boisterous, black-clad men, a shoreline of note takers, scribes, and journalists who roamed the floor behind her. Swells of women with festive cockades crowded the galleries above. Every Parisienne who could squeeze into the gallery had come to witness this historic moment. Voices bounced against the ceiling and echoed through the chamber.

When she mounted the speaker's platform, women in the gallery cheered and clapped. Several men on the assembly floor added their applause, but others continued their conversations. Three argued over a newspaper article that had been published that morning. Another group continued a loud debate on voting rights through the Bishop of Autun's introduction of her.

It surprised Adélaïde to see how the assemblymen ignored one of the most powerful men in France. Still, an encouraging smile cracked the bishop's narrow face as he limped to a seat on the platform beside her.

"It's all yours, madame," he said.

She looked out over the crowd. There must be at least a thousand people here, she thought, her heart skipping. How would anyone hear her over this teeming mass? *Remember what Ducis taught you*, she told herself, then focused her breath. "Ladies and gentlemen—"

A shout drowned her out. "Why have you put a woman before us?" Four men dressed in long, striped pants and red liberty caps pushed through the crowd. "What can a woman have to tell us?" By their cultured accents, she knew these men were no dockworkers.

"Did knowledge or wisdom ever come from the house of whores?" a man with a hawkish nose and heavy cheekbones bellowed. He pounded his fist on the platform.

She felt the vibration through the soles of her shoes.

"A woman has no place here. This chamber is for serious business, not dramatic spectacle."

Adélaïde stared down at the costumed man in disbelief. He seemed familiar.

The bishop stood and moved to the edge of the platform and addressed the man. "Who better to address the needs and interests of a woman than a woman, sir?"

"Don't worry," one of the protestors assured his comrade. "She won't have the courage to speak. No woman can speak to a crowd this size."

Then Adélaïde recognized the man as one of the Jacobin artists who had walked out with Jacques Louis David the night she spoke before the Academy. She could not believe that David had sent his cronies to destroy her before the nation.

The third man turned and shouted at the crowd, "In our new empire of liberty, a woman's place is to inspire her husband to serve the nation and to raise children to do the same. Women have no business debating in the halls of government. Send this woman home."

The hall quieted as people noticed what was happening.

Hadn't she accomplished enough in her life to be treated with a modicum of respect? Hadn't she endured enough? What did she have to prove to these idiots? Her heart expanded as though it would explode from her chest. She could not get any air. She turned to the bishop to tell him she could not go on.

"Let her speak. Let her speak," chanted the women up in the gallery. Her students crowded at the balustrade, waving their red scarves, shouting in unison.

"Send this clucking hen home to feed her chicks," one of the Jacobins gestured to the gallery.

When she made an instinctive move toward the steps, a victorious look crossed the man's face. Just in time, Olympe's words reverberated through her head. *"Don't be overwrought. Don't be overcome."*

She looked down into the man's raging eyes. Silencing her was what he wanted, and she had almost fallen into his trap. She looked up to the ceiling, looked to her students, then moved to the front of the platform and faced the man down.

"If gentlemen like you are to speak for us, sir, humanity is lost indeed." Her voice was shaky but loud enough to be heard throughout the room. "It is toothless old cocks like you who must be put in a pot and boiled, fit for nothing but broth stew."

Shocked laughter broke out on the assembly floor.

"She has put you in your place, sir," Autun grinned.

Male voices on the chamber floor took up the mantra from the gallery. "Let her speak. Let her speak."

All eyes were on her now. Willing her heart to stop its thrashing, she regarded the raucous crowd, distinguishing individual faces. She recognized the National Assemblymen she had painted, signaling encouragement. Standing beyond the heckling Jacobins, Adrien du Port de Prélaville raised his forearms as though invoking the gods.

Catch the energy, his dark eyes told her.

Taking a steadying breath, she returned to the center of the stage. Projecting her voice as Ducis had taught her at the Comédie Française, she began again. "Gentlemen of the National Assembly, distinguished ladies in the gallery—" Her voice penetrated to the back of the chamber. A cheer went up in the gallery. "As the Bishop has said, I have come to speak to you about the education and work opportunities of women. I will speak to you of destitute widows, desolate mothers, desperate daughters—women who must make the most heinous, unnatural decisions to save themselves or their children, all because these women have no way to provide for themselves."

A roar from the upper gallery stopped her.

"I will speak to you of women who, with no other recourse, must enter the world's oldest profession, whether as an unwilling wife who has no choice but to throw her fate into the hands of a man, or as a courtesan living behind palace walls, or as a streetwalker plying her trade in the darkest of alleys."

Another roar.

"I will speak to you of bright young women, hungry for education and learning, women who long to attend France's government-funded colleges and universities, but who cannot, while young men from all over Europe enjoy that experience for free."

The women roared again.

"And I will share with you the facts about the earnings of women—one tenth the wages earned by men. I will tell you of the poorest servants, women who work long hours for a pittance and a corner of a kitchen to sleep in. Gentlemen, this desperation, this degradation begins with women's education, which, for most of us, ends when we reach eleven years of age."

Adélaïde saw herself as a lantern on the rocks flashing into an oncoming storm over the ocean. Each sentence she spoke met with a cheer from the crowd that hit her with the force of a buffeting wave. She grabbed that magnetic energy and absorbed it into herself.

"But first, I will tell you the story of a beautiful young woman, the tragic tale of a life lost too soon. You may have heard about Marie-Justine de Beaumont." Adélaïde pictured Justine in her mind's eye, laughing, singing, as she painted. "Justine was an artist with all the promise and dedication to become a great master, to be the Rosalba Carriera of her generation. Her family needed her to succeed—her father had died, her mother was ill, and she had two young sisters to feed. This capable, accomplished artist had the skills and experience necessary to provide for her family. But she could not sell her works and did not have the protection of the Academy or a guild system to help her. Why was this? Because she was a woman. One night, in secret, desperate to earn money to buy medicine and food for her family, she left my studio to paint a portrait. Instead, instead . . ."

She cleared her throat, struggled to see Justine as she had painted her, not as she had last seen her. "Instead, her ravished and broken body was found a week later in an abandoned corridor of the Louvre."

The men in the chamber before her listened from their seats, riveted, while the women in the gallery above her stood spellbound.

"Think of it, gentlemen. An eighteen-year-old girl lies in her grave, brutally murdered because she tried to support her family. Sirs, I submit to you that the most imperative natural right on this earth is the right to live. To live, we must be able to take care of ourselves. Following that, we must be able to take care of the ones we love. Gentlemen, have you ever known what it is to be poor? Please, raise your hands."

Many hands on the chamber floor went up.

"Have you ever known what it is to be hungry?"

Fewer men raised their hands.

"Have you ever known what it is to be starving, homeless, and to have nowhere to go?"

A smattering this time.

"What would happen to you if you were out on the streets without education or training, if you were not allowed a profession and you could not find a situation as a servant? What if prostitution were the one profession open to you? Has any one of you been in that situation?" When there was no response, she said, "I do not see any hands." She raised her hand, then looked up and called out, "Members of the gallery, have any of you been in that situation?"

The men on the floor turned and looked up. Up in the gallery, many hands dripping lace and bows raised.

"Thank you, ladies." Adélaïde lowered her hand. "For many of you men, had you found yourself in this desperate situation, you would have used your education and training, even your right to earn a decent wage, to extract yourself from this situation. In fact, I know that many of you did start out with limited means but were able to lift yourselves up. It cannot be right, it cannot be rational, it cannot be reasonable then that half of our population does not enjoy the basic right to support themselves. When we look at the natural world, we see that this prohibition contravenes the laws of Nature. All animals have the capacity to care for themselves, whether male or female."

She waited for the shouting in the gallery to die down. "Our nation has called upon us to create a new and improved society, and we women have responded to that call, from the market women who have protested the price of bread, to the wealthy women who have nurtured the ideas of freedom and equality in their salons. The successful women of Paris—writers, artists, fashion designers, shop owners—have even funded this revolution through their earnings and personal wealth. But at every turn, women have found their way blocked. Without rights, without control of their own property, without the liberty to work as their talents provide, women have no control over their destiny. Without education, a woman has no hope."

Adélaïde paused, swallowed, wished for a glass of water. Up in the gallery, a wild tempo of waving scarlet urged her on. Her voice strengthened. "I was lucky. Although I found myself in a terrible circumstance, my father had given me an education, and I had friends who took me in and helped me. For many women, however, their recourse is a life working the streets. For some, a brutal life, for others, life as a mistress or courtesan, but in all cases a tragedy for any woman who has the dreams and capability to work but who is denied a place or position on account of her sex."

She searched the expressions of the men before her, willed them to understand. "Would you want this for your daughters, should something happen to you? Would you want this for your wives?" Many men would not meet her eyes.

"Gentlemen, I ask you, as you draft the laws that form our new constitution, please provide for the education and training of women, and then make provision for them in the workforce. When we empower women, we lift society up. With will, purpose, and generosity of spirit, we can allow everyone to enjoy the full benefits of our new nation. Then Marie-Justine de Beaumont can rest in peace, knowing her death is not in vain."

When she finished her speech, she turned to the bishop, her hands over her heart. The roar from the women in the gallery drowned out her expression of gratitude. Women threw their cockades into the air. Red handkerchiefs disappeared in a kaleido-scope of scarves and ribbons. The balcony floor shook with their foot stomping, shouting, and clapping. Through the rain of scarves and rosettes, the men on the Assembly floor sat, silent, sober, thoughtful.

Autun rose from his seat. He limped to the podium, cleared his throat, and wiped at his eyes. "Madame Guiard, you have moved us to tears. I assure you that this governing body will address the situation concerning women's education and make appropriate changes."

Adélaïde made it through the handshakes, embraces, and congratulatory comments, then walked through the courtyard and emerged beneath the portico of the palace. The fog of the morning had burned off, and early afternoon sunlight gilded all in golden light. The garden fountains flung jets of water high into the sky. A rainbow shimmered in their trajectory.

A feeling of happiness and well-being coursed through her. Her face stretched into a wide smile when Olympe and Sophie joined her, behind them, an entourage of students.

"Madame, you were incredible," Marie said.

"How did you make us hear you all the way up in the gallery?" Isabelle wanted to know.

"Weren't you frightened?" Marie asked.

"You were inspired," Olympe said.

"I'm flattered." Adélaïde smiled. She moved toward Rue de Rivoli with a skip in her step.

"Wait for us." Sophie fought to catch up. "You walk too fast."

"Your legs are too short." Adélaïde grinned. "Let's go eat. I could slay and eat a lion right now."

"You just did," Olympe said.

The women moved along the riverside, as joyous and light as a fleet of sailboats skirting the shoreline on a brisk summer day.

CHAPTER 41

JULY 1791

"How can a king abandon his country?" Marie set her pestle down on the worktable and wiped her brow. It was a warm Monday afternoon. She worked at the center of the long table in the back room, grinding colors to make pastel crayons for the week ahead. Bowls containing chalk, clay, and oatmeal whey lined the table, ready to mix with the pigment. Drying pans waited on the shelves behind her.

Claudette sat at the foot of the table, cutting small rectangular strips of paper, and writing the names of colors on them in her elegant script. "We've given this man everything—our loyalty, our fealty, our wealth, the labor of our backs, the lives of our sons," she said.

"In turn, he must lead us, give his life for us." Isabelle picked up a bowl of crushed verdigris and poured it into the chalk mixture. "Not run away."

"We can't be led by a coward," Claudette agreed.

Totaling columns in her ledger at the other end of the table, Adélaïde made no effort to defend the king. Recent events had overshadowed her wait to find out how the National Assembly would respond to her speech. In June, the royal family had fled the Tuileries Palace in the night. A week later, they were apprehended near the Austrian border and returned to Paris in disgrace.

Dressed as a sansculotte, Alexandré had watched soldiers return the king to Paris and reported that the crowds turned their back when the royal coach rolled past. An hour after the king's ignominious return, the National Assembly had suspended his duties. Today word had come from Austria that the Comte de Provence, who had escaped from his palace at the same time the royal family fled, was ensconced in the emperor's palace.

"What will happen now that both the king's brothers are in Austria?" Marie asked.

"There will be war," Claudette predicted.

"It's possible the king meant to raise an army in Austria. His brothers may still try. One can't know for certain," Adélaïde said.

"The people will never tolerate the king going to war against them," Claudette stabbed the point of her scissors into the table for emphasis.

Adélaïde could not imagine a king fighting his own people.

"But who are we? Who is France without a king and a royal family?" Marie asked.

Claudette lifted her chin. "We are a nation."

While Adélaïde did not know what would happen, she did know one thing for certain—all hope for receiving payment for *Les Chevaliers* was lost. The new government would never pay for the portrait of a traitor, the king could do nothing confined to a small room off the National Assembly floor in the Tuileries Palace, and whatever the Comte de Provence was doing in Austria, he was not concerned about paying his debts. There was nothing more to say. Her mind felt like the copper powder under Marie's pestle. She pushed the bills for lapis lazuli, unground cinnabar, and gold flake aside with a sigh. "I should have used Prussian blue and synthetic vermilion instead."

"Never," Marie said.

Claudette pointed to the pastels. "Maybe we should start selling our own pastels to raise money."

Adélaïde did not respond. Her grand plan to help women work as artists had failed. Most of her lucrative afternoon students had left because their parents thought it no longer safe for their daughters to navigate the streets of Paris. Worse, Adélaïde had had to send many of her best students away, unable to continue to support them.

Jeanne came into the back room and handed a sealed envelope to Adélaïde. "Madame, a letter from Monsieur Vincent."

Adélaïde inhaled the scent of François's sandalwood cologne on the envelope, then opened the note and read his scrawled words. All thoughts of war and unpaid bills vanished.

Glorious Diana, you have pursued your quarry with cunning and persistence and gained the prize. Today the National Assembly announced that the Salon will be open to all, male and female, regardless of affiliation.

Her mind repeated the words. This was so much more than she had expected, so much more than she had asked for. Elation swept through her and her heart pounded with excitement. She jumped up and ran into the studio.

"Girls! Girls!" she shouted.

"Madame, what is it?" Marie ran after her.

When she told them, her seven remaining students gaped at her.

"Did you not hear me?" She waved the note. "You can exhibit in the Salon this year. You have two weeks to get your paintings submitted."

Bewilderment turned to joy, laughter, and hugs.

"Madame, you did it," Isabelle cried.

The girls executed an exuberant jig around her that ended when an easel tipped over.

"Enough." Adélaïde extricated herself from their midst. "After you clean up this mess, bring out your best work, and let's have a look."

One morning a week later, Adélaïde stood before the members of the Society of Artists and Friends of Artists in the Louvre's Apollo Gallery.

"Friends," she said. "A new era has arrived. No longer are you left behind, treated as less, not allowed to participate because you are female. While many of you have waited years for this moment, some of you are just starting out in your profession and will never know the struggles and difficulties that have led to this moment. But for all of you, you may now exhibit and sell your work, the same as any man in the Royal Academy."

The women, old, young, and in between, cheered and tossed

red, white, and blue cockades into the air. Watching the ribbon rosettes fly, Adélaïde thought how it had been necessary to tear down an entire system to change things. For so many years, she had tried to work within the system, following the rules, proving she was worthy, but in the end, it had required toppling the regime to make things right.

～

"Everyone is elated, and I am thrilled for them, but the one painting that I would have wanted to show, I cannot," Adélaïde told Olympe as they lunched on Rue St. Honoré that afternoon.

"Times have changed," Olympe shrugged. "But you have righted centuries of wrongdoing."

"I can't help feeling that it doesn't mean a thing." She pushed her plate of sauteed fish away.

"What do you mean?"

"I wanted a leadership role in the Academy. The members approved it, but the directors didn't honor their vote."

"Perhaps that will change now that the National Assembly is investigating d'Angiviller."

"Perhaps," Adélaïde said. "But when I asked for a place in the government, I was given a job teaching tapestry and embroidery at the new Institute for the Deaf." She laughed. "Everyone knows I don't embroider. And what I know about tapestry is about as much as the amount of lapis lazuli as I would leave behind in a mortar bowl." She pinched her fingers together. "But when François sought a position in the new government?"

"He was appointed to the National Museum Commission. I know." Olympe set down her fork. "Your position may be a bone thrown to a dog, Adélaïde, but this—the opening of the Salon to all —you've changed the course of history."

"If the Academy follows through, Olympe. Believe it or not, after all this time, I still have not secured lodgings. If the king . . ." Adélaïde did not want to voice her fear.

"We still have work to do," Olympe said. "But you've won a battle in a great campaign." She folded her serviette into a triangle, smoothed it and bared her teeth in a fierce smile. "And tomorrow, I take up the challenge."

In the morning, Olympe's book, *The Rights of Woman*, would be available at booksellers everywhere. In the evening, Olympe would give a reading in the de Condorcets' grand ballroom.

"I can't wait," Adélaïde said.

The next evening, François arrived early to escort her to the de Condorcets. He brought a sheaf of papers into her office and set them on her desk. "Would you please read these notices to me? Everything is blurry today."

She glanced at the documents. A feeling of alarm swept through her. "You can't read this?"

"No."

She read the letters from the Museum Commission aloud, trying to keep her voice calm over the thudding of her heart. The writing was crisp and clear. What was happening to him? "Have you seen a doctor?"

"Not yet."

"You have to." She returned the letters to him. "The good news is, you'll be busy for quite a while."

He grinned. "Securing the nation's artwork and setting the standards for a national collection could occupy the rest of my life. Imagine searching for all the art of value in France and deciding what to display in d'Angiviller's new museum at the Louvre?"

"You had better make sure that something of mine is in there."

He laughed.

The de Condorcets' ballroom was large enough to hold a thousand dancing partners. Tonight, it was filled with women seated in row upon row of chairs. When they entered the ballroom, Adélaïde's students stopped in surprise.

"How many women are here?"

"Where did they get all these chairs?"

Sophie de Condorcet had rented more than fifteen hundred chairs. Still, so many people had come that men and women stood along the back and sides of the room. Adélaïde pushed through the crowd to the front. There, Olympe sat with Sophie de Condorcet on her left, an empty seat on her right. Further along the row, Adélaïde saw the Comtesse d'Angiviller.

Adélaïde greeted the titled women, then turned to her friend. "I see you followed my advice." She gestured to Olympe's fire orange redingote and black underdress. "You are a signal flame. Everyone will be able to see you up there."

"Thank goodness you're here." Olympe rose from her chair, her eyes large in her heart-shaped face. She gripped Adélaïde's arm. "There is no one I would rather have than you as my focal point tonight." Olympe regarded the preacher's pulpit installed for the occasion. "I hope I don't trip and make a fool of myself."

"You won't," Adélaïde said. "It's only steps." They embraced.

"I cannot conceive of such a crowd."

Olympe trembled against her.

Adélaïde hugged her the harder. "Remember, here, you are among friends. As you once told me, don't be overwrought. Don't be overcome."

The Marquis de Condorcet greeted them and sat down beside his wife. Then Marie and Isabelle arrived.

Embracing Olympe, Marie said, "When you look out over the audience, you'll see orange handkerchiefs, Madame de Gouges." Isabelle showed her handkerchief. The women who attended the de Condorcet's weekly salon took their assigned seats in the front row, all clutching squares of orange fabric.

A gong sounded.

"It's time." Adélaïde squeezed Olympe's arm.

Olympe climbed the pulpit and looked down as she sought Adélaïde's face. Adélaïde waved her own orange scarf. Olympe smiled, then looked out over the crowd. Calm settled over her face.

"Woman, wake up!" Olympe cried. When the timbre of her voice reached the back of the ballroom, a cheer went up. The room brightened with flying orange. "The tocsin of truth rings out. The universe hears it. Take your hands off your ears so you hear it. It tells you that Nature has created us equal, but man has stolen that equality from us." Olympe stood unflinching and fearless, a goddess, as she made her *Rights of Woman* come alive. A fever of emotion swept the room. "The flame of truth has burned away the clouds of folly. Open your eyes. See for yourselves. Man has shrugged off his bonds and set himself free but has turned and trampled upon woman. What advantage have you received from the Revolution? On the contrary, you have been rewarded with scorn and disdain."

Adélaïde pictured the giant alarm bells ringing at Paris's ancient city hall, imagined their deafening sound. Then she thought of her battles with the Academy, the years she had spent fighting, the money she had lost, the speeches she had given. She thought of her unpaid bills, considered her unresolved housing, remembered the day the Academy had recalled her votes. What had she gained? The tocsin of truth reverberated through her.

"No longer must we live with prejudice, superstition, and lies. Throw off the chains of slavery and be free."

The roar of women shook the mansion. Adélaïde cheered and waved her scarf until her voice was hoarse and her arms grew sore.

CHAPTER 42

AUGUST 1791

The next night, a muggy blanket of fog and smoke settled over the city. Adélaïde was alone in her studio painting when the door opened, and Jean-François Ducis stepped inside. Tannery smells from the river and an odor of perspiration followed him in. His hat was missing, and his leonine mane straggled about his face. His beard needed trimming.

"Don't you look beaten down." Adélaïde set down her paintbrush. "What happened to you?"

He plopped down in her mother's chair and dropped his valise on the floor with a thud. Pulling an embroidered handkerchief from his waistcoat pocket, he mopped his face. "'What am I, so withered and wild, that semble not an inhabitant of this earth?'"

It appeared she would not have a night of quiet and reflection, but she had no intention of searching her brain for a literary reference. She shrugged, shook her head.

"*Macbeth*." He folded the soiled linen away. "Your band of Amazons has rendered me homeless. A glass of ale for my parched throat, dear lady, and then I will tell you of the end of our favorite couple, one that would rival any star-crossed pair of Shakespearean lovers, dare I put pen to it."

She went to the backroom and returned with a bottle of brandy. Apricot and cedar mingled in the air as she poured. "My students are out with Claudette at a political meeting. Hurry and tell me before they return."

He tossed back the drink and held out the glass for more.

"That's fifteen-year-old Cognac, Ducis."

He took the bottle from her, sniffed, nodded, and poured himself another glass. "Last night, the comtesse and I were reading aloud from *The Rights of Woman* when d'Angiviller burst into his wife's salon. I don't think he saw me or the footman at his post. Rivulets of sweat left a gooey flour trail at his temples." Ducis wiped his brow as though something sticky ran down his face. "If there ever were a debate against powdered wigs, this scene would settle it."

Adélaïde laughed.

"D'Angiviller grabbed the comtesse by the elbow and demanded she come with him. She went, tripping over her skirts and protesting he was hurting her. Half the household staff came running. Of course, I had to follow." He set the empty glass on her paint stand. "D'Angiviller dragged his wife into his dressing room, then opened the cupboards and started tossing his clothes on the floor. You should have heard the valet." He screeched to demonstrate. "We thought d'Angiviller had lost his mind, but then he picked up a shoe bag and begin to stuff coins and jewelry in it."

"He didn't." Adélaïde drew in a breath.

"Oh, he did. I wasn't close enough to hear what he said next, but I heard the comtesse say, 'What investigation?' and d'Angiviller say something about the Central Academy."

"They finally acted?"

"Finally acted," he snorted. "Well played, Madame Guiard. Apparently, d'Angiviller is to appear before the National Assembly for questioning. His wife wanted to know why, and he said, 'How can you be so naïve, Élisabeth? Funds are missing.'" Ducis laughed like a madman.

Goosebumps rose on Adélaïde's arms. She did not know how the actor did it, but his face had changed, his nose appeared pinched, and his lower cheeks puffed out along the jawline. He looked like d'Angiviller.

"'Where do you think the money for the parties came from, Élisabeth? How do you think we paid for all this work?'" Ducis's voice was high and hard like the comte's.

"I knew it." Adélaïde's fist hammered the air.

"He said they had to leave the house as though they were going out for a walk. The comtesse began to cry and asked how he could have done these things, how he could have done this to her."

Adélaïde pictured the comtesse, a woman who had spent her life helping others, in a closet, comprehending the perfidy of her husband. A sliver of guilt pierced her triumph.

"'You and your liberal ilk, Élisabeth.'" Ducis looked down his nose and continued in d'Angiviller's cold voice. "'The people needed a firm hand to keep them down, not liberality.'"

Adélaïde rocked back in her seat.

Ducis gestured to the walls. "He said, 'Go out in the streets and look where your ideas to help the poor have led. Now idiots and lunatics are in charge.' His wife asked if he cared not at all for the people starving in the streets, and he said he was not talking of the poor but of the leaders in government." Ducis looked at Adélaïde. "Imagine, the valet, the housemaids, the footman, and I, standing outside the open dressing room door. At this point, the comte was stuffing stickpins and rings into his waistcoat pockets. A diamond ring fell at our feet. One of the housemaids snatched it up. When the comte told his wife that radicals would destroy everything he had worked for, she said, 'You had a generation of artists teach your republican ideals to the masses. Where did you think this would lead?' 'I wanted to bring back the glory of France, not bring down the monarchy,' he said. By this time, his pockets bulged. He put on his cloak and told her to get her valuables."

"She didn't go with him, did she?" Adélaïde breathed.

Ducis shook his head. "'I'm not going anywhere,' she said. 'I won't slink away in shame.' 'I command you,' the comte said. 'You cannot force me to do a thing,' she said. 'I am one of the radicals you disdain.' The comte stared at her for a long time. 'I cannot go to prison,' he finally said."

"He as much as admitted his guilt." Adélaïde clapped her hands together.

"The comtesse asked him where he intended to go. At this moment, he seemed to come out of his trance. He turned and saw us standing in the door. A great fear came over his face. 'Our lips are sealed,' I told him. The valet and I backed away so he could come into the bedroom. I tell you, Adélaïde, he had the face of a hunted man." Ducis's shoulders hunched and his eyes shifted back and forth.

"As he should," Adélaïde said.

"Stop interrupting my scene, madame." Ducis picked up the candelabra and rose. In the pool of light, his face changed into something that resembled the Comtesse d'Angiviller's face, catlike, chin pointed. "'If you wish to leave, I will not stand in your way.'" Ducis's voice was feminine, the words crisp and clear, a martyr laying down her life. His face changed and he appeared as the comte. "'Come with me.'" His face grew angry. "'You'll regret this, Élisabeth. You have no idea what's coming.'" Ducis shrank back, straightened his shoulders and said in a cool feminine voice, "'Perhaps I do not, but at least I have the courage to stay and face it.' "'People will die, Élisabeth,'" Ducis said in the comte's voice.

Ducis loomed over Adélaïde. His face morphed into a chimera, rigid, angry, threatening, and she sprang to her feet. Pushing at her arms, he drove her toward the door. Adélaïde tried to get out of his way, fear flashing through her. Was he still acting?

The light from the candelabra was hot in her face. Ducis's hair stood in wiry points and his eyes bored into hers, crazed and terrible, yellow flames dancing in them. He pointed to the door and, in a monstrous female voice, hissed, "'Go then. Get out while you can.'"

PART VI

TERROR

CHAPTER 43

SEPTEMBER 1791

Chaos reigned at the Salon.

"I wish you would not go," François told Adélaïde when he and Alexandré arrived at the library to escort her and her students to the Louvre.

"The streets are more dangerous than ever." Alexandré touched the ragged scar on his forehead.

"Would they really accost a group of young girls in the daylight?" Adélaïde asked. "My students should not have to wait another moment to see their work on display. We already missed opening night because of the fighting in the streets."

"Who knows what the mob will do next?" François asked.

"As long as there's no rioting today, we're going. We'll be as careful as we can." Adélaïde topped her upswept hair with a simple cap and grimaced as she tucked stray hairs inside. In the last year, her forty-second, the tresses had grayed at the edges. "Look at me." She pointed to her dark blue redingote jacket that covered an unadorned gauze dress. "Who's going to accost an old headmistress and her students?"

François snorted. "You're not old."

"You spend your whole adult life putting powder in your hair, then one day you don't have to." She picked up a red, white, and blue rosette and held it against her jacket. "Should I wear a cockade?"

"If you wear that, I may have to beat up one of my new friends." Alexandré had taken to dressing as a sansculotte to go between the Louvre and the King's Library unaccosted.

"Yesterday you could not wear green. Who knows what color is out today?" François added. "You are not making a political statement at the Salon, so do not make one on the street."

"Given the subjects of my paintings, some people may think otherwise," Adélaïde fretted. She had submitted a portrait of a National Assemblymen, then at the last moment, included her painting of Robespierre, reasoning that it was safer to have paintings of representatives from more than one political party on exhibit.

"The Jacobins have encouraged the mobs to visit the Louvre this year. Last night, they walked past our apartments, banged on the windows, and threw rocks," François said.

"We're ready, madame," Marie called from the stairs. "If we leave now, we'll arrive just in time for the doors to open."

The three of them turned and watched her students come down from the dormitory. To Adélaïde, in their simple white gowns, her students resembled Greek caryatids. A flush of excitement bloomed through Marie's cheeks, and Isabelle's eyes lit up with expectation. Jeanne twirled around the room to show her anticipation.

Adélaïde turned back to the two men. "I know the circumstances are far from ideal, François, but no mob is going to steal this victory from us."

The Salon organizers had abandoned any attempt to organize the paintings on display. Most senior academicians, focused on political activity, had submitted little or no work. François himself did not exhibit, saying his eyesight was too poor. As a result, student and outside artists' paintings overwhelmed the walls, many of inferior quality.

Fit for the rag pickers' heap, Adélaïde thought.

No livret had been printed, so their group went room by room looking for her students' work. Graffiti covered many of the placards bearing artist names and work titles.

They came across Adélaïde's painting of the Prince of Bauffremont. The prince had chosen to commemorate his ascension to the Order of the Golden Fleece. He sat at a table dressed in sap green velvet and wrapped in a red cloak. The sash of his new order hung from his neck; the medal of the order pinned to his jacket. A feeling of sumptuous luxury permeated the work, which Adélaïde had painted in the old style, before she had run out of time to paint more than just the essence of a man.

Three sansculottes stood before the painting. As their group passed, one of men spat on the floor. "Anyone who paints royalty should be locked up," the man muttered.

Idiot, Adélaïde thought. *Don't you know a patriot when you see one? That man is a Feuillant.*

"Or run out of town," his companion suggested.

"Or strung up." The third mimed hauling a rope.

Fear surged through Adélaïde. The man's fevered gray eyes made her feel he could do it right then. She hurried the girls out, hoping they would find her students' work soon. Above all, she wanted to leave. She entered the next gallery, François close behind. A man exiting the room charged into her and knocked her off her feet. She fell into François, who steadied her as she caught her breath. Behind her, her students cried out. She regained her footing, but the man did not move, forcing her to back up. Heat radiated off his body. His musk cologne was strong. She straightened her cap and looked up.

In person, Jacques Louis David was taller than she had thought, his shoulders broad, his face craggy and distorted. A group of his students filled the chamber behind him.

"Excuse me, Monsieur. You're blocking our way."

David did not move. His brown eyes burned into hers. He said in a hard voice, "Madame Guiard, you and you alone have destroyed the Salon. The works displayed here should be used as firewood."

His forefinger jabbed her breastbone, and shock spread through her chest. She could not imagine a man touching a woman in this manner but recognized the look in his eyes from the days of her marriage. She fought for calm.

"How can you say that, monsieur? We do see many amateur pieces presented, which is unfortunate, but that is the consequence of the Academy not having time to create entrance requirements."

How could he blame her for that? She cast a glance toward his students. "I am certain that your students' work is of the highest caliber, as is the work of mine."

"She doesn't know he's referring to her work," one of the students behind David said.

François moved to stand between Adélaïde and David. Alexandré stepped in front of her students. David's students pushed their teacher aside. They shifted on the balls of their feet, fists raised, ready to fight. The three men standing in front of her painting had not moved. In her peripheral vision, a dagger blade flashed. One of David's students had a knife. When she saw the blood lust in the young man's eyes, Adélaïde took François's arm and backed up. "Girls," she said. "Let's come back when the company is more hospitable."

David folded his arms across his chest. "If you return, we will be waiting."

They passed the three men in front of her painting, who stared at her, their arms folded across their chests. Adélaïde understood then that David had sought her out to provoke an altercation.

Back at the King's Library, the girls took their usual places, pulled out sketchbooks and pencils, but sat idle, their faces downcast, their excitement extinguished. Adélaïde sat at the worktable, staring into space. With d'Angiviller gone, they had begun to make progress. But now this.

François paced the room, feinting punches at the walls. "You should have let me hit him."

"Hit a man whose father died in a duel? Whose own face was disfigured in a duel? Who knows what he's capable of?" The threat from David was physical, his hatred visceral. She had never felt such fear when dealing with d'Angiviller, Pierre, or Vien. She realized she had vanquished one enemy only to encounter a more virulent one, one lurking under the surface all along, one she did not understand. "What have I done to provoke this man's hatred?"

"You stole his glory."

"What?"

"When you were admitted to the Academy at the same time as

he was. It was ever thus in Vien's studio. David hated anyone who competed against him."

"Why me and not Madame Lebrun?"

"Since she fled to Italy, she is no threat to him."

"Isn't it enough that when I joined the Academy, he and his students drew cartoons of me?" She put a hand over her stomach. She never thought of those cartoons without getting ill. How did one fight such an enemy? "Maybe I should appeal to Maximilian Robespierre to put a stop to this. He's the head of the Jacobin club now."

"Do not waste your time, Adélaïde. They say Robespierre treats David like a rabid dog on a leash and uses him to do his dirty work."

"But when Robespierre sat for me, he seemed so young and earnest. His ideals filled me with hope. How could he have changed so much?"

François sat down at the table beside her. "It makes you wonder what the Revolution is about anymore."

Dressed as a sansculotte, Alexandré returned to the Louvre to search for her students' paintings. He never found them.

CHAPTER 44

SEPTEMBER 1792

Darkness engulfed Paris. Months ago, the lamplighters had left their posts when the government could not pay them. Fearing the mobs, householders shuttered their houses before nightfall, ignoring the law to leave candles burning in their ground floor windows until midnight. Adélaïde crossed the Pont Royal accompanied by Sophie de Condorcet's footman, her lantern doing little to pierce the gloom. Several blocks to the north, a crowd milled, the flames of their torches making the buildings glow. Chanting from the mob carried on the wind. She stopped at the foot of Rue Neuve des Petit-Champs.

"I can go on from here," she said.

"Are you sure, madame?" The footman's lamp illuminated a boyish face, eyes wide with fear.

"Yes." She pointed with her own lantern. "I'm the fourth building on the left. Get back across the river before that crowd arrives. Hurry now."

She kept her head down and made eye contact with no one, praying not to be accosted, not to have to explain her presence on the street at this hour, not to have to defend her political affiliations. Once inside her building, she locked the outer door and dragged herself up the stairs, her lantern and skirts growing heavier with each flight. Exhaustion permeated every part of her body. Up in her apartment, she lit a fire in the stove. The bells of St. Eustache chimed. How could it only be midnight? She sank down in a chair, kicked off her street shoes, removed her cap. Even her scalp was tired of being pulled by the weight of her hair.

The cadence and rhythm of the revolution had changed. Cacophony eclipsed melody. Once the government took the king's powers away, the entire social order changed in an instant. Nobility lost their titles, but on the good side, Jews obtained citizenship, and slaves their freedom. Everyone now had the right to worship as they pleased.

For François, the signing of the constitution had been a day of celebration and thanksgiving. "No more mistreatment, no more religious discrimination. Imagine if my father had lived to become a citizen of this great nation." But the Pope condemned the constitution, and the rest of Europe declared war on France. Cymbals clanged the alarm, drums impelled a mad, impossible beat, and trumpets blared radical voices that obliterated the ones calling for patience and calm.

Tonight Adélaïde had come away from the de Condorcet's weekly salon appalled by what she heard.

The moderate women said, "When do we stop? When should we be satisfied with what we have achieved? Haven't we done enough?"

"Things have changed for men, but not for women," Olympe insisted. "Where is our freedom? Where is our equality? If we cannot inherit, manage our money, or determine our destiny, we are still chattel."

"But haven't we achieved much for women?" Adélaïde asked. "Women now have a right to education and more rights as workers."

"We've achieved nothing," the radical women in the group took up the argument. "And women who do nothing are harming our cause."

"Complacent women are the same as satisfied cows chewing their cud in the field," they said.

"Milked by men until they have nothing left," a woman laughed.

"But some women are happy as they are," another protested.

"Complacency is death," Sophie said.

"The women who don't act, their bones should be scattered in the desert."

"Surely if women knew better, they would act. Without education, women don't have the words to think, let alone the ability to imagine the possibility of their freedom," Adélaïde said.

"Then we must shake those cows out of their complacency," Olympe said.

Sophie agreed. "We have to continue until the old ways are eradicated."

"But at what price?" Adélaïde asked.

"We should force women to dress as men so there is no perceptible difference between them," a newcomer said. "That will get us there."

"No, no," said another. "Even nature has a differentiation of the sexes."

"We must conscript women and compel them to fight," another said.

"Not everyone wishes to bear arms," Adélaïde said.

"Why do you mock our logical ideas?" the newcomer asked.

"I'm not mocking anything," she said.

"Do we acquiesce and join our oppressors?" Olympe asked. "Do we compromise? Do we quit the field?"

"Never," Sophie cried. "Who are we fighting for? Ourselves or every woman, whether they know it or not?"

"Then the blood of women must be shed," Olympe said.

The mob's ceaseless roaring vibrated through Adélaïde day and night, filling her with anxiety, even as her own arguments twirled in her head without end. But tonight's argument among her friends had especially rattled her. She was tired of fighting. She had set out to become a great artist, then a teacher, then an advocate for women. Each day that work became more dangerous.

She had given it her all and achieved much, but not to a level equal to the male artists of the Academy. And that was why she could not stop, she told herself. At any moment her lodgings could be taken from her, and she and her students would be homeless again. Did she not have a responsibility to herself to hold those accountable who had stolen her victory at the Academy, who had taken away the possibility of her having a tenured position like the men? Did it even matter anymore?

~

A sharp knock on the door. She jerked awake, fear like frigid water down her back. Had something happened at the studio? No one ventured up these stairs unless they were seeking her out.

Dear God, had the mob broken in? She sprang to her feet, her heart racing. Where could she hide?

"Adélaïde, let me in," François's voice came through the door.

Her spine went limp. "I'm coming." She smoothed her hair and groped for her shoes. They had disappeared into the dark. She opened the door in her stockinged feet.

François entered, panting as though he had run up all five flights, his gray hair wild, a pamphlet in one hand, the key to the downstairs door in the other.

"I sprinted all the way from the King's Library," he said, gasping for air. "After my meeting with the National Assembly, we were called into the offices of the Museum Commission. I am sorry I was not there to walk you home."

"I can take care of myself." She motioned him to take a seat at the table, opened the cupboard and extracted a bottle and two glasses.

François caught his breath, then sipped the brandy. "Good Cognac." He emptied the glass.

"I know," Adélaïde said. "It's the last bottle from Bordeaux."

"Oh," he said, regarding the bottle.

She opened the casement window and looked up the street. Had the torches moved closer? "I heard a rumor tonight that Austria will attack Paris."

"They say priests and prisoners are conspiring to aid the Austrians."

"Journalists have called for a mob to defend Paris. I think they're assembling at the Opera House right now."

He nodded. "The Museum Commission ordered us to secure the nation's art. I must be at the Louvre by daybreak. No point to sleep tonight."

"Well, let's finish this then." She poured him another glass and joined him at the table. "How did your meeting with the National Assembly go?"

"Very well." Excitement entered his voice. "We presented our draft language for divorce to the National Assembly tonight. We asked for many of the restrictions to be lifted, and added new grounds for cruelty, insanity, desertion, emigration."

"Emigration?" Her tired mind stuck on the word.

"If France goes to war with Austria, anyone who has left the country will be considered a traitor and an enemy. Without this provision, those whose spouses have fled abroad could be charged with treason and lose their property."

"Do you mean that the Comtesse d'Angiviller, whose husband fled to England, could be treated as an enemy of the people?" How could this woman, who had helped so many women, and now opened her purse to feed the poor be made to atone for her husband's misdeeds?

"Yes, but that is not what is important to us." He took her hand. "Adélaïde, the same rules will apply to men and women, rich or poor. Do you understand? At long last you can be free."

"Free?" She fiddled with her glass. "I don't even know what that means, François. Years ago, I gave up on the idea of being free. I've learned to accept my status as it is."

"But why would you accept that?"

"We are taught from childhood that marriage is forever, and has been so forever, a finality whose sole recourse is death."

"That is about to change, Adélaïde."

"But will it?"

A log snapped in the stove.

"Surely you have hoped for something better."

She shook her head and tried to make him understand. "It's like I am a fish with a hook in its mouth. There's a line that follows me everywhere, that constrains my movement at every turn. As long as I stay near the shore, the pain is bearable."

He cupped her face in his hand. "But how would it be to have the hook removed?"

His eyes gleamed in the lantern light as he waited for her response.

I would get as far away from shore as possible and never come back, she thought, but said, "I could never endure another trial. The damage caused in setting me free could be worse than the hook."

"I refuse to believe that." He gripped her hand. "After all these years, we have a real solution to our situation."

"Are you proposing to me?" She smoothed her hair again and curled her stocking covered toes under the table.

"Not yet, but the day is coming."

The mantle clock chimed one.

"I should go." François touched her arm to rouse her.

She had fallen asleep.

"Adélaïde, remember our week in Bordeaux, when we pretended to be husband and wife?"

"How could I forget?"

"That was the best time of my life. I have been waiting for the day when we can be together again, only not as a pretense."

She saw the perfect black circle of his irises, the sweep of his eyelashes, the straining edge of his cheekbones. Without his touch, she felt the intensity of his desire, and knew that he lived on hope, a hope for something she had stopped believing in when she had walked down the aisle toward Nicolas a quarter century ago.

For a moment, she allowed herself to believe as he did, that one day she might be free.

Voices from the street intruded. She went to the window and peered out. She heard feet on cobblestones before her eyes perceived movement—dark forms in darkness. Men marching. Adélaïde thought of the things that François had fought for, the things she had fought for—religious rights, women's rights, the right to be married, the right to be divorced, the right to work. Issues both large and small, issues that required the toppling of institutions and sacred ideas. It seemed miraculous that they were so close to achieving everything, but with war coming, it could all be taken away.

She came inside and took his hand. "Wait until morning." For once, she did not care about mobs, did not care whether Austria attacked their city, did not care what people thought. She wanted to forget the arguments of the women tonight, to escape her fears. Who knew what would happen on the morrow, or even a few hours from now? She wanted to feel safe and warm. She wanted to be with François.

Her bed was too small for two people, two people who were growing older, two people who had not been together for a long time.

Her bed was just the right size for two people, two people who were growing older, two people who had not been together for a long time, high above the troubles that fomented below them.

CHAPTER 45

SEPTEMBER 1792

At four in the morning, François dressed in the dark. Their short night was over. "Are you sure you don't want me to escort you to the library?" he asked as he shrugged into his jacket.

"I don't want to wake Claudette or alarm the girls." She walked him to the door. "Besides, you have a lot to do today." Once they moved the nation's art, François's friends intended to move their own works into the Louvre's cellars. "I just wish I could secure my works."

"I will send Alexandré to the library the moment I see him." He gave her a quick kiss and ducked out the door. On the landing, he turned back. "Do not do anything foolish while I am gone."

"Don't worry about me." She yawned. "I'm just going to sit here until the sun comes up. At dawn, I'll take the alleyways to the library."

Rough iron pinched her fingers when she barred the door. Shaking the sting out, she went to dress, then pulled a wooden chair into the dormer window and sat down to watch the edifice of St. Eustache shoulder its way out of the night sky, hulking over the homes huddling in its shadows.

The wild clangor of bells woke her to broad daylight. The noise came from everywhere—St. Eustache, the closer basilica, the churches beyond the river. Not the calls to Sunday mass, but the tocsins of distress. The calls to aid.

Pain shot down her neck. Ignoring it, she opened the window and stepped out onto the roof. Revolutionaries guarded the intersections in both directions with swords and muskets. Smoke rose from the giant windows of St. Eustache. A wordless panic seized her. The route to her studio was blocked. How could she have fallen asleep and left her students alone?

A man yelled for help. Down the street, a priest ran from the basilica, his woolen habit flaring behind him. A group of men, perhaps ten, chased him with swords and cudgels. The priest had almost reached the Roche mansion when his sandal flew off. He tripped and fell to his knees. An assailant grabbed his cowl and pulled him up. Adélaïde saw a rim of white hair. The men beat the elderly priest with their clubs while he begged for his life.

Two men rushed out of her building, the neighbor from the third floor and the chocolatier from the ground floor, who ordered the men to stop, saying, "This is a man of God."

One of the attackers turned and ran at the would-be savior with his broadsword. In horror, Adélaïde saw the blade slice high in the air, then lop downward into the chocolatier's neck. His head slipped forward. A crimson geyser shot up. The shopkeeper dropped in the road, his head at an awkward, impossible angle.

Her neighbor from the third floor turned back, but it was too late. The mob hacked him down. Then the ringleader, who still held the priest by his clothes, looked up and called out, "Does anyone else want to save this enemy of the people?"

Transfixed, Adélaïde could not cry out, could not breathe.

"You there? You want to save him?" The ringleader had spied her standing on the ledge. The attackers looked up, then rushed into her building. She heard the outer door crash open, and men shouting in the vestibule. She rushed back inside, a scream caught in her throat. There was no one to hear, no one to help. Most of her neighbors had left the city. Revolutionaries advanced up the stone steps, shouting and banging on the doors at each landing.

Alexandré's iron bar looked insubstantial against the door. Could the men rip it out of the wall? She searched for something to block the door. The sideboard. She pushed at it, but it did not move. The attic stairs creaked, and a man's heavy breathing sounded outside her own door. Her heart raced, then slowed down as though the moment stretched. Gritting her teeth, she shoved with all her strength. The sideboard screeched across the floor, china tumbling inside.

The man rattled the knob, commanded her to open the door, kicked at it when she did not. She held the marble bust of her father above her head, ready to use it as a weapon if the man made it into the room. Her arms trembled and her breath came in short high gasps. The door shook, but the bar held. After an interminable time, the third step below her landing creaked, then the fourth step groaned. Adélaïde collapsed on the floor, crying with relief.

The hours of hell are the hours of helpless waiting. The coppery smell of blood rose high enough to reach her attic refuge, but she was too frightened to close the window. Around noon, the church bells stopped pealing and the screams of the dying faded. In the eerie silence came the sounds of shattering glass, explosions, and gunfire. Smoke from the churches billowed across the rooftops, and ashes gathered along the floor.

Curled in a ball on her bed, she thought of her students, her friends, François, and prayed. The pillow and cover over her head did nothing to stifle the roar of the mob below.

The rampage ended on Thursday. After three days, the water in her kettle had run out, she had emptied her last jug of ale, and the last round of cheese was not even a memory. A fortune in scented candles could not block the stench of death that made its way through the old building. Adélaïde was tired, thirsty, hungry, and weak. She lit her last candle and wrote a letter to the king, telling him that she knew he was occupied solving the Nation's crisis, but that a single word from him to grant her space in the Louvre would do her a great service and would protect the students in her care. She readied for bed in darkness, her lips dry, her throat burning. Would the king respond to her plea this time?

On Friday morning, carts filled with debris rumbled along the street below. Adélaïde exited her apartment, then paused on the landing when she heard soft footsteps on the stairs below. She wanted to collapse with relief as Alexandré, Marie, and Isabelle appeared on the landing below.

"We came as soon as we could." Alexandré, dressed as a sansculotte, waited for her to pass him on the stairs.

"Are you all right, madame?" Marie asked.

"I'm not lying dead in the street, so I must be all right." She straightened her coat. "How are things at the studio?"

"Claudette sent everyone home when the tocsins sounded," Isabelle said.

"How could they go?" Adélaïde asked, thinking of those whose parents lived outside of Paris.

"She accompanied them," Marie said.

"We stayed behind," Isabelle said. "Someone had to protect the artwork."

"Besides, where would we have gone?" Marie asked. "You are our family. We were lucky Alexandré showed up right after Claudette left. He was with us the whole time."

"You were supposed to be there," Alexandré accused. "François expected me to protect all of you."

"I know," Adélaïde's voice was agonized. She had had many hours to berate herself for falling asleep. "I'm so glad you were together. Where's François?"

"You haven't seen him?" Alexandré asked. "He was to come here when he finished at the Louvre in case you could not make it to the library."

She thought of her neighbors hacked to death, thought of François lying somewhere injured or worse. Cold dread spread through her chest. "We have to find him." Her voice rose.

"Let's try the Louvre," Alexandré said.

When they exited the outer door, Isabelle told Adélaïde not to look, but her gaze fell on the trio of dead in the street. A woman stripped the clothes off the body of the man from the third floor while a man rifled through the blood-caked pockets of the chocolatier. Adélaïde's stomach heaved.

They picked their way through the fragments of statues, marble heads, plaster feet, and terra-cotta arms that the mob had blown off the city's church doors and rooflines. The stone eyes of the broken statues cried up to her as she gathered her skirts and stepped over them. She wanted to bend down and piece their shattered faces together.

"Adélaïde, come on," Alexandré said.

"Is the Revolution going to destroy everything?" she whispered.

"Going to?" he asked.

At Rue de Rivoli, revolutionary guards brandishing muskets prevented them from going any farther. Beyond the guards, hundreds of soldiers massed on the Louvre parade grounds.

Adélaïde's heart dropped. There was no way they were going to make it through this blockade.

"Unless François finds a way through the sewers, he's not getting out of there for a while. Should I dress as a rat and go find him, madame?" Alexandré's voice was nonchalant, but his smile did not reach his eyes.

"The palace is not damaged. Surely your brother is safe inside," Isabelle said.

Looking beyond the soldiers, Adélaïde saw that Isabelle was right. She let out a breath. "We have to believe he's safe."

They stood for a moment, trying to decide what to do. Finally, Adélaïde said, "We need to check on Olympe. She lives just beyond the Tuileries Palace."

They turned and cut through the palace gardens. Already, autumn had turned the foliage brown. In a clearing among the trees, a narrow metal and wood contraption, painted black, loomed above them.

"What's this?" Adélaïde stopped to examine the machine's sharp edges, its narrow two-foot-wide frame and perhaps fifteen-foot height. The thing crouched on a raised platform at head height, with eight steps leading up to it. At the top, an angled blade with a shallow notch in it.

"A guillotine," Alexandré said. "Designed to remove people's heads without causing them pain."

"It looks like a narrow metal window," Marie said.

"One that looks out to a new dimension of evil," Isabelle agreed.

The chocolatier's head flashed in Adélaïde's mind. "There is nothing humane about any of this," she said. The blade glinted in the sun. "We have to find François."

They came upon the long-decommissioned church of the Feuillants, home to the Feuillant political club. Beneath its tympanum portico, the doors gaped open. Adélaïde had spent hundreds of hours in this building, painting members of the National Assembly.

The last time she had visited, she had sat on a chair in the nave, sketching Antoine Barnave as he argued with another club member over the monarchy.

"We can get news here," she said.

They stepped inside.

Broken furniture lay strewn about. Bloodstains etched the walls and pillars in jumping spikes. Blood pooled on the floor and turned the parquet to black. More blood, this time in the outline of human forms, covered the bottom part of a huge, unfinished painting in the apse. Gouges in the wooden canvas told their own horrifying tale. Feeling exploded through Adélaïde. Her mind wanted to escape what she saw and leave her behind. Had her friends been murdered? In the middle of the gore, a lone figure clutched a reddened rag, a wooden bucket at her feet.

They must have made some noise, for the woman startled and turned toward them. It took a moment for Adélaïde to place the disheveled young woman as the defiant Madame David whom she had last seen marching on the Versailles Road.

Adélaïde's voice was hard. "What happened here? Where are the Feuillants?"

Charlotte David glanced at the painting. "They're not here. The . . . Jacobins made them leave some time ago."

"Whose blood is this then?" Alexandré demanded.

"A mob attacked the palace. Some of the Swiss guards protecting the king ran in here. The mob followed them." Her voice trailed off.

Adélaïde's gaze went to the torn canvas. Had the unfortunate foreigners thought they were entering the sanctuary of a church?

"But what are you doing here, Madame David?" Marie asked.

The young woman gestured at the painting. "This is my husband's studio."

"He turned the Feuillants' club into an artist studio?" Adélaïde asked.

Shame clouded Madame David's face. "He needed more space for this painting."

"Where are the Feuillants?" Adélaïde asked.

"I don't know." The woman shifted on her feet. "An order has been issued for their arrest."

Those who had protected the king, those who had helped her. It was unbelievable, impossible, terrible. "But you . . . What are *you* doing here?" she repeated Marie's question.

Madame David drew in a ragged breath. "My husband wanted me to see the damage done to his painting when the mob used the soldiers' bayonets against them. He rejoiced. He was happy to sacrifice his art to the Revolution. He said the monarchy could no longer hide. Then he. . . he smelled the blood as though . . . as though . . . he loved it. He said he helped to plan all this." Her voice faded away. "He went out. He wants to bring his friends to see." She stared into space. "I'm trying to clean up, but I cannot do it." A tear trailed to her jawline. "My husband has lost his mind."

Adélaïde abandoned any thought of reaching Olympe or finding François for the time being. She crossed the space and gathered the woman's resistant body into her arms. "Let's get you out of here."

They escorted Madame David to her home in the Marais. The new townhouse with its yellow stucco and white-framed windows was calm and untouched, a world away from the violence a neighborhood over. The woman invited them in, and Adélaïde devoured her first real meal in days—potato quiche, a serving of roast chicken that Charlotte herself brought from the kitchen, and two bottles of wine. They saw no servants.

Alexandré paced the dining room while the women listened to Charlotte's story. "My husband has always had his excesses, the things he does that I don't understand. Every day he presses for the death of the king. I supported the Revolution, but this . . ." She looked around the room, decorated with simple yet elegant furnishings made up in last season's gold chintz. "The royal family has made my father wealthy beyond measure." Her voice broke. "I don't know what to do. I cannot stay. I cannot go. Last week my husband told Robespierre he would gladly sacrifice his children to the Revolution." She dragged her hands through her hair. "How could he say that?"

Adélaïde recognized the desperation she saw on Charlotte's face and remembered believing that no one could help her. "You must leave your husband."

Alexandré's eyes bulged. From the door, he signaled to Adélaïde to stop talking.

She looked away. "Take your children and go to the country. I know a group of women who can help you. They can provide money and transport when it's safe to leave the city."

Charlotte stared at the roses woven in silk covering the wall in front of her. A clock chimed in another room. At last, she nodded. "I can go to my parents' estate," she said, her voice subdued.

"We need to go," Alexandré said. "Now."

Charlotte's eyes widened, as though she too realized the danger. "You cannot be here when he gets home."

They went to the door. "Will you be all right?" Adélaïde asked. "Should you come with us?" She made the offer but wondered how any of them could help anyone else now.

"I can't. The children are up in the nursery."

"Aren't you afraid of the mobs?" Isabelle asked.

Charlotte laughed, a short, harsh sound. "My husband and his friends rule the mobs," she said. "I am quite safe." She followed them to the door.

"Please let us know if you need anything," Adélaïde said.

"You've been very kind." Charlotte's hand touched Adélaïde's, a fleeting pressure Adélaïde thought she imagined. Her eyes flicked between Alexandré, the girls, and Adélaïde, then she whispered, "No one must know that I told you this, but my husband has vowed revenge for himself against anyone who's ever crossed him. He sits on the Committee of Public Instruction now. He can do what he wants, and no one can stop him. He has spies everywhere. His students are watching you."

Out on the street, Alexandré said, "Are you out of your mind, Adélaïde? Why would you offer to help that woman? Haven't she and her husband done enough to you already?"

"I don't expect you to understand, Alexandré, but right now, we don't have time to argue. We have to find François, and we need to find out what the Committee of Public Instruction does."

Alexandré's rare anger dissipated as they encountered more dark stains along the way back. At a bookseller's shop, he ordered them not to move until he came out. Minutes later, he breezed through the door. "Madame, your wish is my command." He handed a pamphlet to Adélaïde with a deep bow. He then grandly escorted them to the King's Library.

"How can he still joke?" Isabelle asked.

"I'm sure his brother dropped him—" she started to say but lost the direction of her thoughts when she saw the white sign posted on the double doors to her studio. The hand-painted sign read Closed Until Further Notice. "Who put this here?" she demanded.

"Madame Claudette," Marie said.

"How dare—" Adélaïde stopped.

Inside the studio, the walls were bare save for *Les Chevaliers,* which glowed in the late afternoon sun. Her stomach dropped. "Where's my artwork?"

"After Claudette left, we moved all the art we could down into the basement. Come, see for yourself how busy we were," Marie said.

In a dark and windowless room that smelled as though it had been used to age meat in centuries past, the girls had lined her works along the walls.

"You did all this for me?" Remorse flooded her.

"Alexandré turned it into an adventure." Marie giggled.

Back up in her office, Adélaïde opened the pamphlet and learned with dismay about the Committee of Public Instruction's mission.

An hour later, Marie and Isabelle, dressed as shop girls, carried notes to Adélaïde's closest friends.

We must meet, Adélaïde had written. *Come to my apartment as soon as the sun sets.*

CHAPTER 46

SEPTEMBER 1792

Blue seeped from the sky as Adélaïde and Alexandré walked to her apartment. Revolutionary guards still patrolled the crossroads, but the rubble had been cleared away. To her relief, the bodies were gone.

"How long will François be trapped at the Louvre, do you think?" she asked.

"He'll find a way out," Alexandré said.

The odor of sewage assaulted them when they reached the fourth landing. Alexandré rushed past her, saying, "I told you so."

François waited on the attic stairs, filthier than any person she had ever seen.

"I knew you'd find a way out," Alexandré said.

"You do not want to touch me." François eluded his brother's embrace but looked pleased. "Once we had moved all the artwork, we found ourselves trapped behind the revolutionaries. But Joseph and I had discovered an old tunnel when we put our artwork in the cellars, so he went one way, and I went the other." François told them how he had encountered men planning their escape from France in the sewers and others plotting government assaults. "It took me two days to find my way to the tunnel under this street and forever to find an open grate. I had to swim through a cesspool to reach the ladder."

Alexandré doused his brother with water down in the courtyard, while Adélaïde went to the third floor to hunt for clean clothes in her dead neighbor's apartment. She pulled a shirt and pair of pantaloons out of the man's wardrobe, wondering how stealing the man's clothes from his home was any different than taking them from his person out in the street. What had they all become?

"Do you have any food?" François asked when they were all back in her apartment.

"None whatsoever." She told him of the deaths outside her building and what had transpired since.

He swore and pounded the table with his fist. "I should never have left you. Can you forgive me?"

"I too made a terrible mistake. But we're together now, that's all that matters."

"No, it isn't," Alexandré said, staring into her empty cupboard. "If we don't get out of here, we're going to starve."

Nightfall was complete before Olympe huffed her way up the steps, swearing at Adélaïde for living on such an uncivilized floor.

Marie and Isabelle arrived next, bearing a note from Sophie de Condorcet, who sent the couple's apologies. Jean Ducis arrived last. "The Comtesse d'Angiviller would not answer my knock," he said. "They tell me she has not left her apartments since her husband absconded." Ducis had moved into his dressing room at the Comédie Française.

They sat in the close atmosphere of her apartment, the windows shuttered. Candlelight flickered across faces ravaged by the terror of the past week. Olympe fanned herself. Sweat trickled down Adélaïde's back. Her chest tightened. She could not spend another night in this place. "We have to get out of here," she said. "We're living in the middle of a battlefield."

"Should we leave the country?" Marie asked.

"If we do, we would be charged with treason," Isabelle said.

Adélaïde thought of the guillotine. A sour taste invaded her throat.

"My production of *Othello* opens next month. I cannot leave," Ducis said. "People are still attending the theatre," he said when they stared at him. "They don't come to see blood and gore these days, though, so I've changed the ending."

"We're weeks away from achieving our goals," Olympe said. "If you leave now, Adélaïde, how will you oversee your petitions?"

"I'm not leaving the country, and I won't stop fighting, but we do have to leave Paris."

"I met a man in the tunnels who was desperate to escape," François said. "He has a house out in Pontault-en-Brie, not far from here. I have twelve thousand livres, but he is asking more than twice that amount."

"I'll match your figure," Adélaïde said. It was almost everything she had left.

"We can help," Marie said.

"How?" Adélaïde asked.

Isabelle's eyes shone with pleasure. "You paid us out of your own funds, madame. How could we spend that money?"

Once again, her students humbled her.

"Then it's agreed?" François asked.

Marie covered her mouth with her hand. "I can't believe it's come to this."

They stared at each other in the darkness.

Olympe stood. "I will not run away, so leave me out of your plans."

"Most of the Feuillants are running for their lives," Alexandré said. "They fought to save the monarchy but now are fighting for their own survival."

"The fight over what to do with the king has brought a crisis on all sides," François agreed. "I heard that Lambeth, DuPont, and the Duc d'Anguillon are planning their escape."

Fear prickled through her. These men had advanced her cause in the National Assembly. "It seems that anyone who has had a part in forming our new government has fallen from favor."

"The Feuillants are traitors," Olympe said. "They oppose war with Austria, but we need war to wipe the slate clean and establish our country as a nation. If some men fall from power for the needed change to occur, so be it."

"I joined this revolution to support the rights of women to work and to support artists, not to go to war or to murder my countrymen," Adélaïde said. "How can one justify what happened this week?" Thinking of the deaths she had witnessed made her ill.

"The mobs have committed atrocities, but the Revolution must continue until we achieve our goals," Olympe said. "We must wait it out."

"I don't believe we can. Even now this house is being watched." Adélaïde told the group of Madame David's warning. "When I learned what the General Committee of Instruction does, I realized that David has the power to carry out his plans for his enemies. This committee is responsible for schools and universities, libraries and museums. It controls the education of children and adults, even moral education. It will manage all examinations, prizes, and schol-arships, and control the hiring, firing and wages of teachers and professors. The committee's first project is to go throughout France and destroy any information it finds to be unpatriotic."

François whistled. "David is on this committee?"

"You report to him," Adélaïde said.

"Everything makes sense now," François said.

"I will not leave Paris until my work is finished." Olympe gestured with her forearms out, palms down.

They saw the resolve on her face.

"Aren't you afraid?" Isabelle asked.

"I will not bow to fear. If I were to leave Paris now, everyone would say that woman is weak and fearful. It would make a mockery of *The Rights of Woman*."

"But how will you be safe?" Marie asked.

"The Girondists will protect me."

"You cannot rely on any one political party to protect you. David's political club controls the mobs," François warned.

"I refuse to be swayed by the Jacobins. With the right mix of leaders, the violence will stop."

"While I subscribe to your ideals," Adélaïde said, "our enemy has become one of the most powerful politicians in the land. A man who offers up his children as a sacrifice will stop at no depravity."

"He would think it his obligation to the nation," François said. "Remember his painting, *The Lictors*."

Olympe raised her eyebrows. "Right will prevail."

Their meeting ended, Adélaïde stood at the top of the stairwell and watched Olympe wind her way down to each landing with

Ducis behind her. These days she no longer knew whether right would prevail. She worried for her friend and wished she could have been more persuasive.

"How can we make arrangements to leave if we're being watched?" Adélaïde asked when the outer door closed.

"I will do it," Alexandré said. "No one's watching my movements."

François sketched a map of the tunnels for his brother. Then Alexandré, Marie, and Isabelle left for the King's Library. François and Adélaïde stayed behind, securing her apartment. Wrapping the bust of Adélaïde's father in a bundle of her clothes, she forced herself to think of the task at hand, and not the abandonment of the place that was supposed to be hers for life.

François carried her small leather chest as they headed down the stairs.

"Are we running away?" Adélaïde asked. Her voice echoed in the stairwell.

"What choice do we have?"

The two days it took Alexandré to find the man in the sewers felt like two weeks. In his absence, François and Joseph Suvée, who had made his way out of the sewers, sealed Adélaïde's works shut in the basement. While the men worked, Adélaïde, Marie, and Isabelle went to market. Claudette still had not returned.

"Where can she be?" Adélaïde worried.

"It's only Sunday," Marie said. "She'll be back."

On Monday, Alexandré bounded into the studio. "Ladies, your carriage awaits. The house is empty. We can move in today." Down in the alleyway, a donkey brayed. They rushed down the library steps, to be met by the sight of a farm cart drawn by two donkeys.

Isabelle and Marie laughed.

"Alexandré, can't you be serious for once?" Adélaïde asked.

"The donkeys came with the house," he said. "And this is how we're going to get out of town without spies reporting us." He handed each of the women a bundle of clothing with something heavy inside. Wooden shoes.

Les Chevaliers could not be moved down to the basement, but since the unrest had begun, Alexandré had devised a way to protect the painting, working long hours in secret while Adélaïde and her students attended exhibits and political meetings. Now, he, Joseph, and François threw off their cravats and rolled up their sleeves. They cleared a large space in the middle of her studio and pried up the floorboards, exposing coiled ropes and grooves under the slats. They heaved on the ropes and Adélaïde watched with amazement as the parquet floor lifted upward in one piece. With the section upright, the men rotated the false floor. On the other side was a false wall, complete with chair rail and thin wooden panel insets painted to match the insets on the other walls. They eased the moving wall along the grooves, working until the new wall rested inches before *Les Chevaliers*, then nailed ceiling molding and baseboards into place.

Alexandré touched up the nail holes with paint and returned the scuffed floorboards to their place over the grooved track. Finished, he knocked on the wall in a few places to prove it did not sound hollow. "I defy anyone to find your painting, madame," he bowed. "It's protected from everything except fire."

"Ingenious, Alexandré. I forgive you every annoying antic from childhood on."

He mimed profound relief. Everyone laughed. Then Adélaïde returned the chairs and easels to their original positions, and the men went down to the alley to load the cart.

At that moment, Claudette appeared in the studio. Her narrowed gaze scanned the empty room. "Where's the artwork?" she asked.

"Someplace safe," Adélaïde said. "I was just leaving you a letter. We're heading for the country. Will you join us?"

"I have seen enough of the countryside to last a lifetime, thank you."

"Where will you go?"

"I will stay right here. Someone needs to protect this place."

"How can you be safe?"

"I have friends."

"Then let me leave you some money and show you where we stored some food for you." Adélaïde was not going to waste time arguing with someone else who wanted to stay behind. They had just minutes to leave. She handed Claudette the last coins from her cash box and showed her where they had stored wine, cheese, and vegetables. "We won't be far, and we'll check on you every time we come to town."

~

Outside, the October air had turned cold as the sun slid along its westward journey. Adélaïde slipped on the tattered woolen cloak Alexandré had given her earlier and joined Marie and Isabelle on the cart bench.

"You all look a sorry sight. I hope you make it in this derelict conveyance." Joseph Suvée thumped the cart with his fist and stepped back.

Alexandré, dressed as a farmhand, shook the rope attached to the donkeys' halters. "Don't insult our carriage," he said. "It's worthier than a king's conveyance."

Adélaïde, Marie, and Isabelle huddled together in the crisp air. Their wooden sabots ground leftover hay and discarded lettuce leaves into the wooden planks that covered their supplies and clothing.

François, in long pants and heavy boots, a straw hat pulled over his face, regarded the sun. "Hurry now," he said, taking up the rear. "We have to get on the road to join the rest of the farmers leaving the market."

The cart lurched forward, moving up the alley toward the Versailles Road. As they neared the Châtelet prison, a horrible stench clutched at them. Adélaïde gagged and covered her nose and mouth with the rough cloak. Marie moaned and covered her face. Corpses rotted in the open air. Hills of bloated bellies, arms, and legs were swarmed by buzzing flies.

A figure stalked the dead, sketchbook in hand. He crouched, his face inches away from the frozen faces of death, staring intently. They watched him straighten, tuck a pencil behind his ear, then move aside a stiffened body to get a better view of the face of his subject. The body slid off the pile and thudded to the ground with a puff of dust. The man squatted and resumed sketching.

Beyond the Châtelet, Alexandré slowed the cart. They turned to look back.

Engrossed in his art, Jacques Louis David never looked up.

CHAPTER 47

PONTAULT-EN-BRIE, WINTER
1792-1793

"Did moving here bring us any safety?" Adélaïde asked as she and François walked out of the clerk of court's office.

François waited until they negotiated the stone stairs and stepped into the street. "What next? The color of our clothes?" he asked.

"If we run out of money for bribes, one of these days we won't come back from the mayor's inquest. He just made that law up." It was their fifth fine since moving to Pontault-en-Brie.

"He wants to hold us accountable for every aristocratic act that ever occurred in this village." François scanned the street. Empty. "Let's go home." It was past noon; they had spent hours inside the city offices and were hungry but knew better than to enter one of the small taverns along the street. A sense of impending doom weighed on them.

Yesterday François had refused a command of the Committee of General Instruction to enter Academy members' ateliers and order the destruction of any painting that did not reflect Revolutionary values.

"I have no idea what those values are anymore," he had said when he made it back from Paris. He slumped at the farmhouse kitchen table, emotions warring across his face.

Adélaïde put down her dishtowel and poured him a glass of ale.

"I won't participate in it." He dragged his hands through his hair and rubbed his eyes as though waking from a dream. "This never happened under the old system."

How could it be that the old system was starting to look good?

Now, they walked through the small village on their way to the farmhouse. Bare tree limbs groaned with each gust of wind.

Adélaïde shivered and pulled her woolen scarf tighter about her head, hurrying to match François's long stride. "François, what's going to happen to you? What will David do now that you've openly defied him?"

"I may be arrested."

She took his arm, tried to press him against her side, but his body was rigid. Taut with fear or cold, she could not tell.

The next day, they appeared before a second village judge, signing powers of attorney to allow Isabelle and Marie to manage their affairs should either of them be arrested. They returned home to wait. Wait for what, she did not know. For her petitions to be answered? For miracles to solve their problems?

Even the king could not solve his problems. Now plain Citoyen Louis Capet, the king awaited trial in the Tuileries Palace while Girondists and Jacobins fought over his life. One of the loudest voices calling for the king's execution was Paris Commune Deputy Jacques Louis David.

Until the situation with the king was resolved, their lives were on hold.

Cannon balls screamed overhead. Pounding drums shook the square. Their furious report thundered against the palaces edging the square. Adélaïde felt the vibrations in her heart.

A guillotine loomed against the sky. Through its frame, she observed hundreds of soldiers in formation, and beyond them, a sullen crowd. A shadow darkened her view, the slanted blade rising on its guide rope. Morning sun struck metal and blinded her for a split second. In the sudden silence, a clank of metal, then a *shush-thunk*. Blood sprayed the soldiers nearest the scaffold.

The executioner reached into the basket before him and held up the king's head for the crowd to see. Then came the cry. "The King is dead! Long live the Republic!" The soldiers resumed their mighty drumming.

Hanging by its hair in the executioner's hand, the king's head turned and sought Adélaïde in the crowd. His eyes burned into hers. His bloody lips parted. She heard him say her name.

She woke, her heart knocking in her chest. Disoriented, she sat up in the darkness. A lightning flash illuminated the familiar shapes in the farmhouse bedroom. She flopped back against the pillows as thunder rolled over the house, her cold sweat seeping into the bedsheets. Another nightmare.

It had taken a week for the news of the king's death to reach their refuge in Pontault-en-Brie. No one could get into or out of the city. Soldiers blocked every intersection with guns and bayonets. Elsewhere, revolutionaries armed with pikes roamed the streets, accosting people at will.

"God have mercy," Isabelle cried.

For days they wandered the farmhouse like ghosts. Outside, snow fell but did not reach the ground. They could not eat; they could not sleep. How did the earth continue to spin when the world had been knocked out of its natural order? They had all fought for change, but none of them could imagine a world where a people murdered their king. The highest authority in the land, whose authority came from God, was dead. Who could control France now?

A packet arrived from Claudette, inside it a letter to Adélaïde from the Royal Academy. Standing under the portico of the farmhouse, Adélaïde braced herself for bad news. Was this her notice to vacate the King's Library, to surrender it to the new Republic? When she read the note, heat, then cold went through her. She released a shaky laugh. "I don't believe it."

"What does it say?" François demanded.

She looked up at the sky. It was still blue. "After eight years of fighting, I have lodgings at the Louvre. I am to present myself next Monday to pick up a key and order any necessary repairs."

"Why now?" François asked. "With everything the leadership has said and done, I find it hard to believe the Academy would relent."

"Perhaps the king's death?" Marie offered.

Adélaïde could not speak for guilt.

Now, lying between clammy sheets, waiting for day to extract her from her dark thoughts, she recalled the letter she had written to the king in the summer. "A single word to grant an artist studio space to follow her talent would do her a great service."

Had the king given that word? Had it been one of his last acts?

When morning arrived, François, Alexandré, and Adélaïde left for Paris. A sole footman greeted them at the de Condorcets' mansion. Adélaïde recognized him as the young man who had escorted her across the river months ago. Upstairs, no servants scurried through the corridors; no visitors convened in the hall outside the drawing room. Adélaïde had never seen the salon devoid of people.

Sophie and her husband sat on the settee that faced the river. They did not turn when the footman announced Adélaïde's presence. "Go on in, madame. They may not hear you because of the drums and the artillery. They attended the execution."

Sophie started when Adélaïde appeared. "What are you doing here?"

"I came to see how you are doing."

The Marquis stared out over the roiling Seine.

"Don't you know how dangerous it is to be seen here?" Sophie asked. "We expect an arrest warrant at any moment."

"Oh, Sophie." Adélaïde sat next to her friend and embraced her. She touched the Marquis's arm.

His hand twitched. "The world is against us now," he said in a faint voice.

"My husband did everything to save the king's life," Sophie cried. "Now, who will save my husband?"

Adélaïde could smell their fear.

Their visit to the Louvre was brief. Young men patrolled the halls of the Royal Academy, dressed in long white coats with golden epaulets and blue trousers, the same design David had fashioned for the revolutionary army. When she saw the dark-haired young man who had threatened them with a knife at the Salon, Adélaïde took François's hand, and they hurried into the director's office.

Joseph Vien wrote out the number to her new quarters on a slip of paper. His penmanship wavered under his shaky hand. An unfinished sketch lay on his desk. Adélaïde marveled at how it took the director seconds to give her what the Academy had fought years to keep from her. She had planned to tell Vien that she would still fight for her counsellorship but refrained. Today he was an unworthy opponent, frail, elderly, unrecognizable as the teacher who had struck fear into his students, the man who had held her future in his resistant hands.

The student with the dark hair entered Vien's office. "Get me a drink of water, old man," he said. "And hurry up with your drawing. David wants you to prove whether you are a capable artist or not."

They left Alexandré to inspect her new quarters and sketch designs for the workmen, while they went to check on Claudette at the King's Library. Mustering an optimism she did not feel, she instructed Claudette to have her paintings moved out of the library basement as soon as work was complete in her new studio.

Claudette's eyebrows went ceiling-ward. "And when will that be, madame?"

"Soon, I hope."

In the afternoon, they headed back to Pontault-en-Brie in a hired carriage.

"How could that young man treat Vien like that?" she asked. "I may not like the man, but I'm not sure we should have left him alone with those students."

François nodded. "It's getting to be the same at the Museum Commission."

The coach turned onto the main road outside Paris. She grabbed the leather strap to keep from tumbling off the seat. "Am I insane to consider moving back to Paris? Or just wild with hope that things will return to normal?"

Alexandré handed her the news journal he had been reading and pointed to the headlines. Spain, Sardinia, Sicily, and Naples had joined Austria's coalition against France. And Robespierre had introduced a new program to instill virtue in the people through terror.

"Wild with hope," he told her. "The mad ones are in charge."

CHAPTER 48

PARIS, 1793

Divorced. Restored to her maiden name. Adélaïde stepped out of the new Family Court on the Île de la Cité beneath a morning sky studded with clouds that caught the sun and took on the hue of pearls. Above her, the lead markings of stained-glass windows in the towers looked like metal lace. She wished for her pastels, thinking, *Does everything appear beautiful when you are free?*

She stood up tall and breathed in, all the way to the bottom of her lungs, then set out for the Louvre. Leaving a note for François in the Academy offices, she visited her new studio where two white-clad workmen spread plaster on the walls. The schlock of wet sand and the scrape of trowels across stone blended with the peace and promise of a new space. Her gaze roved the room, seeing where she would hang large paintings, where her students would paint. She walked through the living quarters, imagining the rooms populated with furniture, the walls decorated with chinoiserie. Beyond the Palladian windows in the dining room, opened to let out the sharp scent of new paint, a cherry tree grew in a huge planter in the courtyard, its barren branches loaded with green nubs.

Footfalls came from the studio. François entered the dining room, stopped and stared at her. "You look . . . beautiful," he said. "Your eyes have a sparkle I have not seen in a long time."

"Isn't it wonderful?" She spread her arms wide to indicate the day, her new lodgings, the tree. "I don't care what people will say. I will put an easel right here in the dining room."

He gave her a quizzical smile.

She took his hand and guided him to the window. "I've never lived on a ground floor or had a tree outside my window. And it's all mine."

He pulled at the back of his neck.

"Just imagine the studio finished, light falling through the windows, the statues, the live models." She moved to the door. "Come, I want to show you where I was thinking to set aside a space for Academy professors to critique my students' art."

He made no move to follow her. "What happened this morning, Adélaïde? How did it go at Family Court?"

"No more Madame Guiard," she said. "You are speaking to Citizen Labille." It sounded both alien and familiar. She wondered who this Citizen Labille would be.

His eyes shone. "It's official?" When she nodded, he straightened as though a great weight had lifted from his shoulders. "We can begin to make plans then."

"Plans?" She grinned and looked around the empty room. "I have enough plans to last for the next few years."

He stepped back. "What do you mean, Adélaïde?"

A sinking feeling settled in her stomach. "François, I . . . It's too soon." He looked like he wanted to argue, so she reached up and took his face in her hands. "Please, don't say anything right now. Let me enjoy this moment."

They looked at each other for a long time, then he gathered her into his arms with a soft growl. His heart thudded against her cheek while she willed him to be patient.

The bells of La Samaritaine intruded. She pulled away. "I have to visit Olympe."

He released her. "Do you want me to walk with you?"

She shook her head. "The streets are quiet this morning. I know you have appointments today."

Out in the corridor, the dark-haired young artist who had threatened Vien roused from his lounging position against the wall, opened a small book, and made a notation as they passed.

At her knock, Olympe called out, "The door's open."

Adélaïde entered the small apartment, passed a desk that overflowed with half-written manuscripts and found Olympe lying on a red velvet settee, one arm flung over her eyes. She sat up and made room for Adélaïde beside her.

"You shouldn't leave your door unlocked, Olympe," Adélaïde sank down into the worn cushion. "Someone followed me all the way to Rue St. Honoré."

Olympe appeared not to hear her. She regarded Adélaïde with red-rimmed eyes. Hanks of hair had fallen out of her bun. "I've made a terrible mistake. I've led people in the wrong direction, and I–I have to warn them."

"What are you talking about, Olympe?"

Olympe got up and paced the Turkish carpet's already threadbare path edging the room. "The king did not deserve what happened to him. Despite that, he went to the guillotine full of conviction and bravery." She shuddered. "He should not have lost his life for a kingship he never wanted."

"A few weeks ago, you championed any avenue the Revolution took," Adélaïde reminded her.

"That was before his execution. A system that holds a king accountable under the law is one thing, but a system that removes a king to make room for a tyrant will never be free. We are watching the rise of tyrants, Adélaïde."

Adélaïde thought of Robespierre's power grab and David's rage. "Perhaps the best way to stop them is to get out of their way."

"By the time a tyrant seizes power, it's already too late. The Jacobins will destroy everything we've fought for."

"People will realize what's happening and journalists will call for the mobs to act."

Olympe stopped pacing and stared at the wall with wide eyes as though she saw a terrible vision of the future. "There won't be any journalists left. The Jacobins' only goal is to gain power and rule through terror. The Revolution has taken a wrong turn. We can't wait. We have to stop it now."

"Stop the Revolution?" Adélaïde's question ended on a half laugh. "The Revolution is a roiling river sweeping us along. Olympe, you can't turn back the water."

"Then we must change its course."

"Please come to Pontault-en-Brie with me and ride this out." Adélaïde took Olympe's arm and shook it, tried to bring her friend back from wherever her mind had gone. "Look at all you've accomplished. Women have the right to inherit, and today I'm a free woman because of you."

"It's not enough." She turned to Adélaïde. "You're divorced, then?"

Adélaïde released a breath, relieved to have her friend's focus on something less dangerous. "I'm sure François is going to propose to me. Years ago, I wanted to marry him more than anything. Now, I'm dreading the question." She knotted her hands together. "I've spent my whole life fighting for the right to work, to be treated as an equal. Now, I have the right to control my life. If I were to marry him, I would give that up again. I want to know what freedom tastes like. Am I selfish?"

"Marriage." Olympe's face twisted. "You just freed yourself from those bonds. Why put them back on?"

"You don't think François and I would be different?"

"Marriage is the graveyard of trust, hope, and love."

"Why do you hate marriage so much, Olympe?"

A darkness crossed her friend's face. She averted her gaze. "When I was seventeen, my parents forced me to marry a seventy-year-old neighbor to align our property holdings. He raped me every day of our marriage. If I did not say I enjoyed it, he beat me until I did. I ran home once, but my father delivered me back to that torturer. I rejoiced the day that man died, and once I had my widow's portion, I left and never looked back." She turned to face Adélaïde. "I've seen nothing to change my mind since."

Adélaïde's gaze roamed the red-painted walls, the mirror over the fireplace, the books stacked along the floor. She could not think of a thing to say. "I'm sorry, Olympe."

Olympe waved her hands in the air. "Well, I'm glad you're divorced, but I did not ask you here to talk of marriage." She handed Adélaïde a small manuscript from her desk. "I have a plan."

Olympe roamed again while Adélaïde read the essay. "Olympe, no printer will publish this now. He'd be charged with treason."

"Therein lies my problem." Olympe stopped moving and cast a challenging look at Adélaïde. "But if I create a set of hand-drawn posters, I don't need a printer." She waited. "I do, however, require assistance." Her gaze sharpened.

Adélaïde imagined the two of them being caught hanging posters on street corners in the dead of night. How could Olympe ask this of her? She cleared her throat. "Putting them up could get us arrested or worse."

"I'm asking for your artistic skills, not for you to post them." Olympe watched the emotions play across Adélaïde's face. She moved into the middle of the room and pressed her hand over her heart as though she were an actress in one of her own plays. "I will never reveal your part, I swear."

"How can you promise that, Olympe?"

"This is war, Adélaïde. Right now, we must do what it takes to save the people from disaster." Olympe's look turned calculating. "If things continue this way, what will happen to you, to what you've achieved? Are you willing to lose the liberty you've just won?"

Adélaïde thought of the new studio she could not use, thought of how she had to hide in the country, thought of the young man who had followed her out of the Louvre and had shouted after her, "We don't want you here." What would she do to defend her freedom, her place in the Louvre?

"It's like letter writing, only drawing." Olympe's gaze impaled her.

Adélaïde thought of all the hours Olympe had spent helping her with her fight against the Comte d'Angiviller. How could she not help her friend pen a few posters? But these posters were far more dangerous than her letter-writing campaigns. She thought of the joy she had experienced in her new studio this morning, felt again the fear of David's student threatening her. Would they ever let her live in peace at the Louvre?

"Is anyone ever truly free, Olympe?"

"Isn't that what we're fighting for?"

Now that she had fought for this, had gained it, how could she permit another person to take away that feeling, that hallowed place from her? She straightened and smoothed her hair with a hand that trembled. "I'll help you." She swallowed back her fear. "Maybe, just maybe, we can stop this madness."

～

When Adélaïde left Olympe's apartment that evening, François materialized from the shadows at the bottom of the stairwell. "I thought you were one of David's spies," she gasped. "What are you doing here?"

"What do you mean, what am I doing here? What are *you* doing here? I came looking for you hours ago, but you were not here. I returned to the Louvre, but you were not there either. At the Library, they told me you and Olympe had left ten minutes before. What was I to think?"

"I'm sorry, François. I lost track of time."

"No one loses track of time right now, Adélaïde. What were you and Olympe doing?"

"You tell me." She folded her arms. "Seems like you've been following my movements closely enough."

"What are you talking about?" He stared at her. "I came to escort you home." A door opened on a landing above them. "Let's not argue in the middle of the hallway." He guided her out and whistled for a fiacre.

Adélaïde sat with her back away from the filthy seat, her arms crossed, her ink-stained hands clenched against her sides. The warning messages she and Olympe had painted on the posters tumbled through her head. Her insides quivered.

Outside the coach, the white stucco shapes of Paris, outlined in blackened beams, changed to the skeletal trees of the countryside, bits of springtime green unfurling on their upheld arms. The wind picked up and the light fled before the oncoming clouds.

"Another night of storms," she said.

Sitting across from her, François assessed her mood. "Shall we celebrate tonight?"

"Celebrate?" Her voice sounded loud in the rented vehicle.

"Your divorce. I thought we could throw a small party at the farmhouse."

She went limp against the seat. "I don't feel like it."

All she could think about was a piece of paper behind the desk in her office at the King's Library. One of the posters had shot between the desk and the wall. She and Olympe had started to move the desk to retrieve it, but Claudette had entered Adélaïde's office unexpectedly. They had had to leave the poster behind.

How could she have been so careless?

CHAPTER 49

PONTAULT-EN-BRIE, 1793

Adélaïde squinted at her hands in the candlelight. The lye soap was working but how it stung. She picked up the blackened rag and scrubbed at her hands again. Beyond the farmhouse, thunder rumbled in the distance.

A knock sounded at her bedroom door. Her hand jerked and knocked over the candlestick. She grabbed the candle before it rolled off the washstand. Hot wax seared her knuckles. She hissed in a breath and plunged her hand into the water.

"Adélaïde, let me in," François said in a low voice.

"One moment." She dried her hands, stuffed the towel into the wardrobe, and opened the door.

François entered, a candelabrum in his hand. Setting it on the washstand, he eyed the gray water in the washbowl. His hands sought her roughened fingers. He examined them for a long moment before saying, "You are keeping secrets from me." His voice was soft.

She pulled her hands away. "Sometimes it's better that way."

"How can it be better to hide things from each other?"

She pressed her lips together. Lightning flashed outside.

He sat on the edge of her bed. "From the beginning, we participated in the Revolution together. Now, we spend all our time apart, even though we live in the same house."

She sat down next to him. "We're not on the same committees, François. Our goals are different."

"No matter the Revolution, our goals should be the same. Who knows when, or how, the Revolution will end?" Lightning lit up the room. "We should get married while we can."

Not now, please not now. "Are you proposing to me, fair sir?" She let a half smile tilt upward.

"Well, yes." A matching half smile quirked his lips. In the semi-darkness, his love and longing gleamed with a brilliance impossible to suppress.

"François, I just got divorced." She tried to keep her voice light.

"I love you, Adélaïde. I have always loved you. I would do anything for you. But for you to be my wife . . . I have lived for this all these years. No matter how impossible it seemed."

"You've always told me that the most important thing was for us to be together."

He shook his head. "Right now, I need more."

Her shoulders drooped. "I like us as we are. Why do we need to change?"

"Adélaïde, there is no we as we are." He made a restless movement. "I am tired of hiding from rumors, hiding our love, hiding us."

She edged away. "Those who matter know."

He took her hand. The back of it had started to blister, and she gritted her teeth against the pain. "The future may be a disaster," he said. "But I want to spend it with you. I want to protect you. I have stood by for months—years—as men have said terrible things about you and had no right to defend you."

"I don't need your defense, or your protection. I need your support, and you have supported me beyond imagining. We don't need marriage for that."

"I do not understand what you mean, Adélaïde."

"Our relationship has always been about love. Why do we need a piece of paper to prove that?"

"What kind of love is not willing to commit?"

"François, you know I love you."

He stared at her. "Do you, Adélaïde? Do you really?"

Her body recoiled. For a moment, she could not catch her breath. "François, how can you ask me that? Of course I love you."

"Saying it is not enough."

"But I can't offer you more right now." Her stomach trembled with upset. "My war is not over. The fight for women is too important for me to stop now, even for marriage. Especially for marriage. Once the Revolution's over, we can speak of marriage."

He searched her face as though he had never seen her before. "You are so focused on your battles that you have lost sight of the things happening around you. You did not bother to ask what the doctors had to say today. Do you not care that I am going blind?"

In the lamplight, new lines etched his face. She had not even noticed that he wore a thicker pair of glasses. Remorse sliced through her. "Oh, François, I forgot about your appointment. What did they say?"

"They do not have a cause, but for now, I must curtail my painting." He dragged his hand through his hair. "How can you be an artist and not paint?" His voice rasped.

She took his hand while she searched for something to say. "Can you still teach?"

"As long as I can see well enough to be of any use."

"I can't believe this is happening to you." It was every artist's fear. "Thank goodness you have your museum position."

"I may not have it for long. At the commission meeting today, they questioned my loyalty."

"Why?"

"Because I refused to search the artists' studios."

"What will you do?"

"I am more determined than ever not to do it," he said at last.

"Even if they arrest you?"

"Even so."

She thought about what he had said about keeping secrets. "François, I too have done something for which I could be arrested."

He took her arm. "Adélaïde, I will not permit you to put yourself in danger."

And there it was. The clank of shackles. It was as though a vice had squeezed her head. "You have no right to permit me to do anything or to forbid me from doing anything."

"You know I did not mean it that way."

"Yes, you did," she said. "The issues of women are important. I must see them through. You have no right to stop me."

His voice subdued, he asked, "When will all this fighting be enough for you, Adélaïde? When will you let it go and just live?"

She turned her head away. Bleakness stole over her. "This is my life, François. Why is it acceptable for you to risk your life, but not for me to do the same? Aren't the things I'm fighting for just as important? If we married, you would have the right to determine what's important for me. I would give up all my rights to determine the course of my life."

He rose to his feet. His chest heaved. "I am nothing like your husband was."

"I can't take that chance right now."

He retrieved his candelabrum from the dresser and walked to the door. When he turned, she saw a look on his face she had never seen before. Something broken. "Did you ever love me, Adélaïde? Or did you just use me to get what you wanted?"

The door shut behind him with a faint click. Raindrops on the rooftop obliterated the sound of his retreating steps. At the window, Adélaïde stared out into the darkness, gripping her blistered hand. Water sluiced down the glass and pooled on the pebbled driveway.

Since the king's death, people had tiptoed around the edges of their lives. They had hoped to avoid notice while the world convulsed, terrified that whatever new form it would take would turn and rend them to pieces. Instead, they were tearing each other apart. François's love had always been the one constant in her life. Where would she be without it? Part of her wanted to run after him and beg his pardon. But the other part insisted that he had been wrong to push her.

Lightning tore the darkness apart and thunder shook the house. Then glittering white stones hurtled from the sky, pounding the roof like angry missiles.

CHAPTER 50

PONTAULT-EN-BRIE, AUGUST 1793

Mist wrapped the poplar trees along the drive, and translucent points of moisture settled on Adélaïde's hair. "Do you think it will rain today? Will we need an extra tarp?" From the porch, she directed her questions to the group surrounding the farm cart. Another biennial Salon had arrived. With the collapse of the art market, no one had much hope for the outcome, but Isabelle and Marie had completed entrance pieces and now loaded their finished canvasses into the cart.

When François did not respond, Alexandré spoke. "We probably do."

"I believe you are right, brother." François turned and walked to the barn for another oilcloth. Adélaïde watched the distance stretch between them, like the gaping hole of silence that had grown since the day of their argument.

A horse galloped along the main road. Soon a rider emerged from the fog, his horse lathered in sweat, sides heaving. It was Laurent Dabos, François's student. Perspiration darkened his clothes, and he was breathing almost as hard as his horse. He dismounted and said something Adélaïde could not understand. Mopping his brow, he repeated it.

"The Academy abolished?" François had returned from the barn, a yellow cloth folded over his arm. "How is that possible?"

Adélaïde had a strange feeling of having been here before,

standing on the steps of Saint Symphorien when the Academy of St. Luke was shuttered. A haze descended over her vision, and she could think of nothing.

Laurent Dabos's voice came from far away. "Jacques Louis David did it."

Rain began to fall. François and Alexandré flung the tarp over the cart, then ran up the porch steps to join the rest of them under the porch awning.

"David rules the arts world now," Laurent continued. "Earlier this week, the Committee of General Instruction closed down theaters they considered unpatriotic. They arrested twenty actors. David said he could do no less with artists."

"How can an institution be closed at the whim of one man?" François asked.

Adélaïde found her voice. "Which actors?"

"I don't know them all, but we do know that Jean Ducis was taken."

Adélaïde thought of the last time she had seen Ducis, following Olympe down the stairs, arguing he should be the first to the door.

"What do you mean, he would do the same for artists?" Isabelle asked.

"David has joined Robespierre on the Committee of Public Security. He plans to use the Law of 22 Prairial to purify the arts."

"The Law of the Great Terror," Adélaïde breathed. Olympe had written Adélaïde about the law, writing of Robespierre's demand for a law he could use to go after his enemies and of the weak men in the National Assembly who had given it to him. Adélaïde would not forget Olympe's last words: *Things are grim in Paris,* Olympe had written. *Stay away.*

Adélaïde had wanted to write back and tell Olympe that things were bad in the country as well, that the mayor harassed them, that she and François were not speaking, that she had no idea how to mend the rift between them.

Laurent nodded. "David has ordered his students—he calls them his generals—to search the artists' studios at the Louvre. He wants any artist who conspires against the Revolution, or who does not support the Revolution, to be rooted out. I have come to warn you that his students are ransacking the studios at the Carousel right now."

"What are they looking for?" Adélaïde asked, glad that her own atelier was empty.

"Incriminating evidence the Revolutionary Tribunal can use."

"What's a tribunal?" Marie asked.

"It's a new trial court," Adélaïde explained, then turned to Laurent. "I understand that if you are called before this Tribunal, you don't have the right to counsel, and neither you nor the Tribunal can call witnesses. They can only find you guilty or innocent. Is this true?" She thought of the politicians she had painted. Many who had not fled the country were now sitting in prison under the system they had helped to create.

"Yes," Laurent said, "and if you are found guilty, it's the guillotine." He made a chopping motion with his hand, then dropped his voice as though even miles from Paris, Parisians could still hear him and report his words to the authorities. "Everyone is a spy now."

"But we support the Revolution," François said. "There is nothing to find."

"Joseph Suvée was arrested this morning," Laurent said. "I watched them bind his wrists with rope and take him away in a cart."

Adélaïde wanted to fall down and weep. "Joseph has done nothing," she cried. "He was among the first to call for change."

"I heard there were some sketches in his studio that David's students found aristocratic," Laurent said.

François swore and kicked a porch column. "David's using this law to settle old scores."

"What about the Salon?" Isabelle pointed to the cart. "We're on our way to drop our pieces at the Louvre."

"To participate in the Salon, artists must bring their art before a committee who will inspect it to determine whether its contents support the Revolution."

Fear spread down Adélaïde's spine like ice.

"What should we do?" Marie asked.

"If they could arrest Ducis and Suvée, we can't take the risk." Adélaïde saw her students' stricken faces, the anticipated disappointment on Laurent's. To forbid her students from participating in the Salon after their years of effort felt like thrusting a knife into them herself, but most of their paintings were of politicians.

"What do we do about your studio, sir?" Laurent asked. "They will search it soon. They may have done so already."

"Yes, what happens to your lodgings?" Alexandré asked. "I quite liked your apartment, François." He sounded forlorn.

François sat down on the porch swing, which hit the farmhouse wall. "My whole life has been built around the Academy." He pinched the bridge of his nose and took a deep breath.

Adélaïde wanted to join him on the swing but had no idea how to comfort or cheer him. Instead, she glared at Alexandré.

"Sir? What do we do about your studio?" Laurent asked again.

François did not move. "There is nothing there. We removed the art months ago."

"Even though your paintings are gone, that doesn't mean David's students won't find something else," Alexandré worried. "We need to make certain there's nothing in your studio that could be construed as aristocratic or against the Revolution."

Adélaïde's mind raced through her own studio, thinking of what searchers might find. *Les Chevaliers* was safe behind its false wall, but could they find the paintings hidden in the basement? She went through the list. They were all paintings of National Assemblymen, men who had led the Revolution, but men who were in trouble now. What would happen if they were found? What about the letter from Robespierre in her desk? Surely that would be in her favor. Then she thought of Olympe's poster, lying in wait behind her desk all these months. Sweat gathered at the back of her knees and slid down her arms. If that poster were found, she would be arrested. What if the authorities linked her to Olympe? She had to get to that poster before someone else did and destroy it. But how could she get to her studio, past the phalanx of spies that followed her everywhere each time she went to Paris?

Another horse approached. The rain had lightened enough to see that the rider flying up the drive on a black horse was a revolutionary.

"What now?" Marie asked.

"It's Sophie de Condorcet's footman," Isabelle exclaimed.

The footman dismounted and executed an awkward bow before them, his sopping Phrygian cap with its bedraggled red, white, and blue cockade held to his chest. His cropped blond hair was plastered to his head, and he looked nothing like the young footman who had walked her across the Pont Royal in the dark.

"Come out of the rain," Adélaïde said.

Isabelle ran into the house and returned with a towel.

Wiping his face, he told them that the Marquis had been charged with treason for defending the king. "He's gone into hiding. His wife sent me to tell you not to visit their house under any circumstance."

Adélaïde's spine curved forward. Her body felt weak. "Disaster upon disaster," she said.

The footman nodded. "Yes, madame," he said. "Olympe de Gouges has been arrested. The police searched her apartment, then took her to the Châtelet prison. The authorities are hunting for her accomplices."

Prickling heat flashed beneath Adélaïde's skin. For a moment, she could not breathe.

"I have a note for you." The footman pulled a damp envelope from his coat pocket and handed it to her.

The handwriting was Claudette's. Adélaïde tore the envelope open. "David's students have been here," she read. "Come now. I will not be able to hold them off for long."

CHAPTER 51

PARIS, AUGUST 1793

When Adélaïde, Isabelle, and Marie arrived at the King's Library that afternoon, they found the courtyard outside her studio filled with young women fanning themselves in the summer heat, students Adélaïde had not seen since the troubles began, and students Claudette had sent away during the massacres.

"What are you doing here?" Adélaïde asked Jeanne.

"We were ordered to come," her former student said. "But since we arrived, they have made us stay outside."

Claudette met her at the entrance. "I tried to keep them out."

Adélaïde stepped inside the studio, then stopped in disbelief.

Young men in white coats and long blue pants swarmed her studio, throwing open drawers, dumping their contents out, smashing the empty drawers against the floor. Others opened cupboards and threw her students' canvasses on the floor. David's students. One of them grabbed an easel and snapped it over his knee. Wood splintered. Another student laughed, picked up the jagged stick and rammed it through a painting. She wanted to storm at them, to scream, *Stop!* but could not move, could not say a word.

The young man who had spied on her at the Louvre strode across the room and grabbed her by her arms. His fingers dug into her biceps. "Where is it?" he shouted, his breath hot on her face.

Did he mean the poster? *Les Chevaliers?* Something else? Against the crashing furniture and sketches raining down on their heads,

377

against her heart that seemed to have stopped working, she could not form a response. Then a student opened the workroom cupboard and tossed the boxes of handmade pastels into a heap. A moan escaped her when he ground them beneath his boot.

"Hey, look at this," he shouted to his comrades, and reached into the cupboard and pulled out the jar of gold leaf. "Is this real gold?" He held it up to the light, then threw it against the false wall. Golden powder and glass shards showered the air. The young men cheered.

Behind her, Claudette said, "Stop this at once. What you seek is not here. Check the basement. She said they were in the basement."

Releasing Adélaïde, the man rushed out into the courtyard, followed by David's other students.

Adélaïde ran into her office and shut the door. If this was what they did when there was nothing to find, she did not want to imagine what they would do if they found the poster behind her desk. She crouched at the back of her desk and thrust her hand behind it. Rough plaster scraped her knuckles, but her hands encountered only dust. She strained as far as she could reach, but it was no use. She could not reach the poster. She lay down on the hardwood floor, and looked under the desk, unable to believe her eyes. Where could it have gone?

She heard the swish of skirts and looked up. Claudette loomed over her.

"What are you doing here?" Adélaïde gasped.

"I did knock," Claudette said.

Adélaïde scrambled to her feet. They stared at each other.

"Were you perhaps looking for this?" Claudette withdrew a scrap of paper from her pocket and held it out. A small triangle of black paper with an orange border, charred at the edges, dropped into Adélaïde's palm.

Her mind scattered. "You burned it?"

Claudette thrust her face in front of Adélaïde's. "Did you think I would let you put us all at risk?" she hissed.

A girl's sharp cry sounded behind Claudette. *Jeanne.*

David's students were back, their coats filthy from the foray into the basement. The ringleader dragged Jeanne into the middle of the studio. "We found the hidden room," he said. "But the big painting wasn't there. Tell me where it is." He shook her.

"I don't know," Jeanne cried. "I truly don't."

Adélaïde pushed her way past Claudette and pulled Jeanne away from the man. "Let her go. She has nothing to do with this."

"Then you." The man turned and jerked Claudette toward him. Claudette landed on her knees. The man grabbed her hair and pulled her head back, exposing her neck. "Tell me where it is." His knife flashed at Claudette's throat.

Several girls screamed.

"I do not know." Claudette's voice shook. Her eyes sought Adélaïde's. Normally sharp, lids narrowed and mocking, now they were dark and wide. Unfocused like the day the two of them had met. The day of the noise in the street, the overturned carriage, the housemen and Adélaïde's father pulling a broken body from beneath it and lifting a woman and child through the vehicle door that faced the sky. Her father leading the injured woman and a ragged, white-faced urchin into their shop, and saying, "We must help them."

Experimentally, David's young student drew his knife across Claudette's neck. A thin line of red appeared. Claudette whimpered and the man's lips lifted in a caricature of a smile.

His look of pleasure and deadly intent made Adélaïde's heart stop.

"There! It's right there." She pointed to the false wall.

The next few minutes were pandemonium, David's students trying to destroy the wall and failing, Adélaïde ordering her students to flee. When David's students left to find sledgehammers and crowbars, Adélaïde ran through the studio's backrooms and up to the dormitory, searching for Claudette to help her. She could not find her. With a sense of unreality, Adélaïde returned to the studio. The time it took David's students to pry open and tear apart the wall, for them to call Jacques Louis David over from the Jacobin Club, for him to follow his students through the courtyard and down the cellar stairs, was a time where blood stalled in her veins. She was underwater, unable to breathe, falling to the bottom of the ocean.

And then, a stirring of air and the feel of a malevolent presence passing by as David's black cape brushed against her. He moved into her studio as a force, kicking aside broken chairs and tumbled easels with his red riding boots. He stopped before *Les Chevaliers de Saint-Lazare.*

"Shall we destroy the painting, Monsieur?" David's students stood in a semi-circle before the painting. One of them hefted a sledgehammer.

To this point, Adélaïde had avoided looking at her painting. She lifted her eyes from the overturned furniture, the crushed pastels, the precious gold flake that glittered over the mess. Hidden from view for almost a year, the painting blazed before them. The glory of its colors and movement dazzled in the afternoon sun. Sunrays lit the figures in flashes of ruby, sapphire, emerald, topaz, and gold. Jewels dazzled. Beneath their colorful clothing, the people in the painting turned, their gazes sought Adélaïde's, their open mouths cried out to her. She saw her father's desperate wave.

"No!" she said.

David turned at her voice. Jealousy, awe, fury, and hatred pursued each other across his face. The sword scar sliced downward through his jaw, white against the pulsating purple tumor and reddened face. He opened his mouth but hesitated.

In that moment, she knew, and he knew, and everyone else in the room knew, that she was the better painter.

"No," she said, more calmly. "You won't destroy it."

She moved a chair out of her path, righted an easel, pulled a canvas out of the dust. "Look what your students have done, Monsieur David." She thrust the canvas at him, then put it on an easel. "My students have done nothing to you. They have done nothing to your students." She retrieved a crumpled drawing from the rubble on the floor and waved it at him. "Many of my students are children. Just children." An emotion she had never felt fomented in her chest. "Get out." She grabbed a broken easel leg and advanced on the young men.

"Hey," one of them cried as she hit his leg.

"I said get out." She pushed him toward the door.

She batted at their legs, shoving and thrusting until they turned and went to the door.

"We're going. Stop hitting us," one of them said.

Her students moved aside as she drove the men through the doors.

Adélaïde stood in the shadows of the portico, her chest heaving, the broken wood a bayonet by her side. She squeezed her eyes shut and wished she could wake from this nightmare. When she opened them, her students were staring at her.

"I can't believe you did that," Marie said.

"You aren't supposed to be here," she said in a shaking voice.

"We didn't leave," Jeanne told her.

"You were a virago," Isabelle admired.

"I was terrified." Adélaïde went back inside and moved through the ruined studio. A moan escaped her. Dust motes floated in the last rays of light and a coating of plaster covered the floor. She stepped over chunks of the false wall, her shoes crunching ceramic potshards hidden in the plaster dust. The jagged edges of china cut through the soles of her shoes. Behind her, the girls made their own way through the room, picking up drawings, smoothing them out, placing ruined canvasses back on the easels that could stand.

"Oh, no," Marie said, when she saw the broken easel leg thrust through her painting. "Look what they did."

"I know," Isabelle held up her own damaged work. "Look at this."

Adélaïde made it to the one unbroken chair and collapsed. A memory returned. "Did I really push David out of the room?"

"You did," Jeanne said.

Adélaïde imagined being arrested and led away, her wrists bound with rope like Joseph Suvée. She imagined entering the Châtelet, that awful place where so many years ago men had smirked at her and told her what they would do to her, imagined her students dragged there with her, imagined the men's groping hands. She covered her face with her hands. "Oh, what have I done?"

CHAPTER 52

AUGUST 1793

T he order came within an hour, delivered by three revolutionary soldiers. Two wore the same attire as David's students but were armed. The third, an officer dressed in red, carried a sword at his side. Curious Parisians spilled into the studio behind them, elderly men and women, young artists, men dressed in sansculotte.

"Citizen Guiard?" the officer asked, his voice hard and deep, theatrical for the benefit of the onlookers.

Adélaïde wanted to say that was not her name, but when she opened her mouth, no sound came out. She felt Marie and Isabelle's trembling against her back as though it were her own, heard the catch in Isabelle's breath. Then she thought of Olympe's arrest and stepped forward.

She took her time breaking the seal and unrolling the document. Would she have to go with these men? Would she have time to say goodbye? "Madame Guiard, you are hereby ordered to . . ."

For a moment, her heart stopped. Darkness clouded the edges of the room. Her legs gave way.

Sometime after the soldiers had ushered the crowd out of the studio, François and Alexandré arrived to find the girls cleaning up, and Adélaïde sitting in the lone chair, the order resting on her knees.

Alexandré surveyed the gaping false wall, his laugh lines erased. "Who betrayed you?"

She shook her head.

François picked up a broken chair, tested it, then sat next to Adélaïde.

"Your apartments?" she asked.

"Empty. They even took the bed."

"Your paintings?"

"Safe in the tunnels."

"Well, that's something." She handed him the order.

He squinted at it and gave it back. "I cannot read it."

Isabelle came to stand beside them. "It says that for Madame Guiard to prove her loyalty to the Revolution, she must bring *Les Chevaliers* and its studies to be burned at the Place du Carousel tomorrow evening at five o'clock."

Marie joined them. "She must also bring her paintings of members of the National Assembly to be destroyed."

"Devoured," Adélaïde murmured. "It says for my paintings to be devoured by fire."

"She has to deface any royal person in the paintings before arrival," Isabelle added.

"How can they do this to me?" She could not steady her voice. "I have done nothing wrong. I have fought for what is just and fair, nothing else. Isn't that the spirit of the Revolution?"

"Fairness and justice no longer matter." Alexandré pushed at a piece of his false wall with his boot.

The studio was silent but for the swish of a broom across the floor and the clack of broken pottery as Marie gathered it up. When long shadows of evening fell across the room, Isabelle lit the candelabra lining the walls. *Les Chevaliers* took on its nighttime perfection. Plum, garnet, and maple yellow glowed among the indigo and obsidian, etched in silver and gold. The dot that was the diamond in her mother's wedding ring flashed along the gallery rail and her painted figure turned toward them.

François gazed up at the painting. "It takes your breath away," he said.

Adélaïde sprang to her feet. "Can you imagine? David couldn't bring himself to destroy it. He couldn't even order his students to do it. So he's forcing me to. Well, I won't."

"You have no choice," Marie said. "You'll be arrested if you don't."

"I must be able to appeal to someone. Vien. A judge."

"David signed the order using his position on the Committee of Public Safety. There is no higher authority in the land," Isabelle reminded her.

"And anyone who is found guilty at the Tribunal will be sent to the guillotine," François said. In the past few hours, worry had etched deep lines in his forehead.

"I don't care."

"Adélaïde, you must think with a clear head right now. First the Jacobins went after the politicians. Now they are arresting artists, actors, writers, even their families. On my way here, I learned that they arrested Élisabeth Vigée Lebrun's husband and brother and that they fired Olympe de Gouges' son from his post."

"It's a good thing we aren't married then."

Isabelle froze, the broom in her hand, while Marie stared at her over the stack of crockery in her arms. François swore and turned away.

The words hung in the air, beyond her reach to take them back. How was she supposed to make sense of what was happening? "The world has gone mad." She went to *Les Chevaliers* and tugged at its frame. "We need to get this out of here."

"It's too late," François said.

She had fallen into a never-ending well and had nothing to grab in the darkness. A terrible pain twisted inside her chest. She could not swallow it away and could not breathe past it. She beat at her breastbone with her fist.

Her friends looked at her, helpless.

When she could speak past the grief choking her, she said, "I won't do it."

"Adélaïde, they do not want your death, just the destruction of your works." François's hazel eyes implored her.

"How can you say that to me?" She saw herself painting study after study, creating figures at first lifeless, then breathing and moving, remembered the calluses on her finger pads, the pain in her eyes after late nights, the times she slept on the floor beside the painting. "If I don't have my work, what do I have? They may as well kill me." She imagined her work incinerated, saw ashes like dark powder fall from the sky, slip through her sifting fingers, nothing to scrabble for but charcoal smudges. She turned from the painting. "We have to save it. Please, help me take this painting and hide it where no one can find it."

A smell of lavender, then Claudette stood before them. "This painting is going nowhere. It's aristocratic. It must be destroyed." Her face was white above a strip of cloth covering the knife wound on her neck.

"Madame Claudette," Marie cried. "You're still bleeding."

Claudette put her hand to her throat where red seeped through the bandage. "For once, think of someone other than yourself, Adélaïde. You may wish to martyr yourself, but I have no desire to die on your behalf."

Adélaïde felt like a fish caught in a river trap. She looked at her friends, knowing that she had to think about what would happen to the girls if she went to prison, or to Alexandré who had built the false wall, or to François who had supported her all these years. Claudette had almost lost her life. But what would happen to her if she lost herself?

Weighed in the balance against her friends' lives, what was there to weigh?

"If it is any consolation, I—" François began.

She cut him off. "There is no consolation."

The bowels of the Châtelet prison were much more terrifying from the inside than imagining them from the outside. The guard pocketed his bribe and led her down the stone steps, worn in the middle from centuries of prisoners walking to their doom. Moaning emanated from the stairwell, as though the ghosts of those who had gone before warned her to flee. Water from the river seeped through the walls in dark stains and sloshed beneath their feet. A strong scent of excreta coiled about her. She prayed that her wooden street shoes would be tall enough to keep her feet out of the muck. Telling herself to be brave, trying not to breathe, Adélaïde lifted her skirts and followed the guard's wavering lantern. By the time they reached a tunnel deep in the earth, their breath fogged the air.

Olympe sat writing at a table in her cell. She looked up when the guard unlocked the door, her face pale, her eyes dark and hollow. A lone candle formed a weak pool of light about her and cast faint shadows on the moss-covered walls. She put down her pen, then maneuvered to avoid brushing against the walls or scattering a stack of papers on the pallet beside her. Adélaïde stooped to avoid the low ceiling. Their embrace was brief, but long enough for Adélaïde to feel Olympe's ribs and the ridge of her backbone through her dress, the delicate embrace of a sparrow. Olympe's body shook with cold. Adélaïde removed her shawl and wrapped it around her friend.

Olympe pulled the garment tight with a nod of thanks. "Did you bring paper? I will need lots of paper, quills, and ink." She possessed a restless energy that frightened Adélaïde.

"I'm sorry. I didn't think of it."

"Then why are you here?"

"I'm a selfish idiot, coming to trouble you."

Olympe moved the papers to the table, and they sat on the squalid cot. Damp from the mattress rose through Adélaïde's dress as she told Olympe what had happened. "Olympe, why'd you do it? You didn't have to show the police your papers."

"Did hiding your works save them?"

"No, but that's different. You led them right to yours." She clasped Olympe's hand, which burned with a strange fever divorced from her shivering body. "Tell me you didn't do that because of the poster we left behind?"

"Of course not. I told you I would leave you out of it and I did. The Committee came looking for evidence."

"But they didn't find any. You could have saved yourself."

"I meant those words when I wrote them. I will not retract them now."

"I guess there's no retracting art. I meant to protect my works until the situation improved, but now I must burn them."

Olympe raised her shoulders. "You could always refuse. You could come and keep me company in here, but I will be very busy." Her eyes turned glassy. "I'm not allowed to hire counsel to defend me. The judge has already said that my words have convicted me.

Now, my words must justify me. I have very little time left to tell people the truth."

"Don't say that."

"I'm already dead. It's just the hour and the moment I don't know." She pulled the shawl tighter and laughed. "Remember when I worried that I would trip on the pulpit at the de Condorcets? Well, now I must think about walking the steps to the guillotine. How will it look if I falter?"

"Who cares if you fall?"

"I must not look weak." Olympe's legs were shaking against the straw mattress. "They wanted me to deny my convictions. They wanted me to prove that woman was weak." She clenched her fist. "I will prove that woman is strong, and like man, can die for her convictions." But then her fist flew to her mouth, and her eyes went wide.

Adélaïde tried to choke back her own fear. "I don't think I can do what you're doing."

"Isn't it better to die trying to make the world a better place, than to live a lie and give in to evil?"

"So, like Arria, you stab yourself? But I find myself the Paetus in this story, unable to fall on my sword. Besides, if you were alive, you could still fight them."

"There's no hope for me. I've already been convicted. But while I wait, I must get the truth out."

"What was the point?" Adélaïde said. "I wanted to be an artist. I wanted my work to be recognized for its worth. I wanted to have my paintings hang in palaces. These goals seem so paltry, but I gave my whole life for them." She could not think about the darkness that awaited them.

"You made it to the Academy, Adélaïde. I would have loved to have achieved Woman of Letters."

"But you, Olympe, gave women their liberty."

"And yet, here we are." They listened to the steady plop of water on the floor. Olympe's laugh ended in a wet, hacking cough. "Rather than be forced to admit women to the Academy, they closed it down."

"I understand now what Robespierre meant when he said that jealous gods had prevented me from painting him. He was referring to David."

Olympe nodded. "They are fallen gods clutching at their lost power."

"And destroying everything while they hang on? What did I do all this for?"

Olympe's fierce face swam in Adélaïde's vision. "You did it to prove you could. You did it to prove what was right. They will have to live with the wrong they've committed."

"But will they? Will they even care?"

"Long after we are gone, our deeds will testify to the truth. My words will live on."

"But my legacy will go up in smoke at five o'clock tomorrow. How can I be justified when nothing is left?"

"No one can take away what you did, Adélaïde." Olympe pondered the arched ceiling. "Why not make your paintings go out in a blaze of glory? Put on a show they won't forget. Make them know the cost."

"But how?"

A drop of water splashed the papers on the table. Olympe moved them to her lap. The prisoner in the next cell called out in his sleep, a gnawing sound of agony and fear. The candle guttered and Olympe gripped her hand. "I can't work in the dark. Do you have money for a candle?"

Adélaïde nodded.

"Get me a candle, then have the guard see you out. There will be no one to fight on if we're both stuck in here. You need to go before I lose my courage and beg you to stay."

Adélaïde looked about the dungeon room. Fear tore at her insides. "Olympe, I can't leave you here."

"You have no choice." Olympe stood and called the guard herself.

Adélaïde bought four candles. "I don't know if I can get back," she said.

"You shouldn't try."

While the guard waited, the two women embraced a final time. Against Adélaïde's chest, Olympe's heart galloped like a wild horse freed from its reins and plunging through the forest.

Adélaïde emerged from the prison, dragging fresh air into her lungs, Olympe's unfinished manuscript hugged against her chest.

CHAPTER 53

AUGUST 1793

Back in the dormitory, Adélaïde stared out into the night as the sky turned from darkness to indigo. Restless in their sleep, the girls threw off their sheets in the hot room. Their sighs formed a troubled caress, their breaths hitched as they faced their own terrors in the night. Beside them, Adélaïde could not get warm. The wild jig that had propelled her quest to change the world had ended in deafening silence. She realized she had blinded herself by what she wanted to see. She thought of the letter from Robespierre locked in her office downstairs. The letter's intricate scrolls appeared as fiery words in her mind's eye. She had come face to face with Evil, sat with him, talked with him, painted his portrait. And Evil had written to thank her for making him beautiful.

What part had she played in this madness?

When she next opened her eyes, morning light flooded the room. Marie sat on the edge of the bed across from her, her face paper white. "Isabelle is downstairs preparing breakfast, madame."

Adélaïde sat up but made no move to stand. "I'm no match for these people, Marie."

Nodding, Marie moved beside her and put an arm around her.

"Did you always know I would fail?"

Marie did not answer.

"Gather what students you can. We'll need their help." Adélaïde went to the mirror and scraped her hair into order. Her face was pale from a second night without sleep.

Today, the sounds of Adélaïde's studio were muffled footsteps, rustling skirts, sliding drawers. Only Jeanne returned to help. François and Alexandré dragged the worktable from the backroom. Claudette and Jeanne gathered Adélaïde's studies for *Les Chevaliers* while Marie and Isabelle brought canvases up from the basement. The pile on the worktable grew.

"Now what?" Jeanne asked

Adélaïde pointed to the paint.

The students blended red, green, and blue and the colors of fire, earth, and sky turned to black. Isabelle loaded the paint onto palettes.

In the defused morning light, the figures in *Les Chevaliers* appeared drained of color. Their painted eyes accused her of betrayal.

"How can I get this painting out of here intact?" she asked.

"You should just cut it up," Claudette said.

"Oh no, Madame Claudette," Marie breathed.

"If a draftsman cannot figure out how to get this painting out in one piece, no one can," Alexandré said.

François rubbed at the stubble on his chin. "We could hire workmen to take it out through the main doors and load it on to carts."

"To do that, we'd have to remove the doors and windows above the entrance," Alexandré said.

"That was our original plan to get the painting to the palace," Adélaïde said. She pictured her painting riding to glory on the carts. An idea formed.

When she told them, Claudette said, "Leave me out of your plans. I experienced enough terror when they ransacked the studio."

"Me too," Jeanne said.

François turned to leave. "We don't have a lot of time. I will go hire help."

"What should we do?" Marie asked.

Adélaïde directed Marie to get a ladder and cover the royal faces in the gallery with X's. Creeping up a ladder in her voluminous skirt, Marie stopped at the highest safe rung. Isabelle handed her a round brush and palette, but Marie made no move to begin. Her shoulders shook and the brush fell to the floor.

"I can't do this," she cried. She started down the ladder, but her foot caught in the fabric of her skirt. Isabelle steadied the ladder while Adélaïde grabbed the palette before they were all covered in black paint.

Yesterday she had vowed not to destroy her painting, but today she realized she would have to show the way. She chose a broader brush and approached the Comte de Provence seated on his velvet throne.

He leaned forward. His eyes ordered her to stop.

"I'm sorry." Her mouth was dry, and the words came out in a hoarse whisper. *Was this what it felt like to murder a friend?* She executed a line of black across his face, starting at his wigged hairline, painting through his right brow, his right eye, his nose, the white of his teeth between his parted lips, the left side of his chin. *You may have been selfish. You may have only cared about your next meal.* She lifted the brush, then started at his left hairline, painted through his left eye, across his nose, through his jowly jawline. *But you gave me hope.* Her nose was dripping, and she sniffed and wiped her face with her sleeve. She moved on to the knight kneeling before the king's brother and placed an X through his profile. *And you, my friend. The hours spent capturing you whole, the hours of the universe.* The center of the X crossed through his wigged curls above his ear. The right line of the diagonal covered his nose and jaw. She did the same to the two men at the center of the painting. The figures stopped moving. Pain welled in her chest. *I'm sorry, I'm sorry, I'm sorry.* She stepped back and bumped into Isabelle and Jeanne. Thrusting the palette into Jeanne's hand, she said in a ragged voice, "That's how you do it."

For the next hour, Marie, Isabelle, and Jeanne painted perfect X's across the painting. Then they turned to the studies and the portraits of the National Assemblymen. Toward afternoon, years of Adélaïde's work lay on the worktable or propped against it, ruined. A hundred wet black X's glinted in the sunlight falling on *Les Chevaliers.* Only the faces of her family remained.

Throughout the day, Adélaïde headed to the back room, picked up the dented metal pail resting outside the open door, and retched into it. Outside on the stone step, she caught her breath and looked up at the sky. Across the courtyard, between the rooftop windows, bedsheets flapped in the wind.

How could anyone do laundry on such a day? Didn't they know that life had ended?

Sunset drove its yellow and orange hues forward as their entourage set out from the King's Library. *Les Chevaliers* balanced on braces across two joined carts. Marie and Isabelle had bought up all the white flowers along their road. They garlanded the outsides of the carts with gardenias and covered the smaller paintings piled in the carts under masses of ivory roses and white lilies until the carts resembled a bier.

The donkeys from Pontault-en-Brie pulled the cart train, their harnesses decorated with white carnations. A sign above *Les Chevaliers* read "Vive la Revolution." Adélaïde had wanted to write "Death to Art" and "Death to Reason" beneath those words.

"Are you trying to get us killed?" Alexandré had asked.

Flanked by Marie and Isabelle, Adélaïde walked before the donkeys, dressed as the Roman goddess Libertas. She wore a white dress and a laurel wreath, and carried a giant chain wrapped around her body like a snake. Marie and Isabelle had also donned white dresses and laurel wreathes. François had hired six carpenters to build the braces. It had taken all of them to lift the heavy wooden painting onto the carts. Now, aided by the payment of Adélaïde's last coins, the carpenters, dressed as revolutionaries, carried torches and walked beside the carts. François and Alexandré took up the rear.

With the unrest of the last few months, the streets of Paris usually emptied at sundown, but this afternoon hundreds of people milled along Rue de Rivoli.

"Make way!" Adélaïde shouted as they maneuvered their way to the Carousel parade grounds. "Make way for Liberty in chains!" People laughed and jeered but began to follow them.

Darkness was falling as they entered the Place du Carousel. A crowd thronged the square grounds, their outlines illuminated by the glow of a giant fire. The donkeys caught the scent of smoke and stopped. Adélaïde tried to pull one of the beasts forward, but he would not budge. Their procession came to a jumbled halt.

François shouted a warning, and Adélaïde turned back. The crowds following them had moved to the side of the road. In that opening, a man advanced toward them, yelling and wielding a club.

Alexandré tried to block the man, but the club connected with his skull. He dropped to the ground. Isabelle cried out.

As François turned to help his brother, a group of men attacked him.

Yelling their names, Adélaïde tried to get to them, but a mob swarmed the carts. She felt herself pushed into the first cart. Flowers fell to the pavement, and the scent of crushed roses assailed her. Splinters dug into her hands. Her knees slammed into the cobblestones. The chain around her neck began to choke her. By the time she untangled herself and got to her feet, the girls were gone.

Beyond the second cart, François's attackers dragged him away. Adélaïde's eyes locked with his for an agonized moment before the crowd swallowed him up. She watched as a group of men lifted Alexandré's limp body and carried him away. Blood poured from the side of his face.

A bugle sounded. Soldiers pressed the crowd back and formed a path to the fire. The revolutionary officer who had handed her the decree yesterday strode through the cleared space, his body gilded with firelight.

"Citizen Guiard?" he shouted above the noise of the crowd and the snap of flames.

Her heart tore a terrified path through her chest. Her lips trembled too hard to form words. She nodded.

"You have the requested items?"

She gestured to the carts.

Soldiers unhitched the donkeys and set them free, then pulled the carts into the square. Members of the sansculottes came out of the crowd to help. Together they dragged the carts toward the fire. The people followed, carrying anything they could find to feed the fire.

In their midst, the fire snapped and roared.

An official examined the artworks and compared them against a list in a narrow ledger. At a nod from the man, the crowd rushed forward.

Men and women danced about her and stomped to the sound of fiddles and drums. Sweat pored off their faces and madness blazed in their eyes. Adélaïde scrambled onto the tongue of the cart and looked out over the crowd, scanning for a familiar face, looking for anyone to help.

No one.

A woman shouted something and lifted a wine bottle to throw at her.

A man dressed in a red cap and polished red boots emerged from the crowd. If the sight of the officer had terrified her, this was so much worse: Jacques Louis David, disguised as a sansculottes.

She recognized his students in the crowd.

David climbed onto the cart and shouted at the crowd, making them laugh. He tossed her artwork down for them to throw into the fire. Two of his students climbed onto the cart.

Then Adélaïde saw the painting David held in his hands, a painting that should never have been on the cart. The madness of the crowd became her madness. She felt herself screaming, felt herself scrabbling onto the cart and grabbing at the first young man she could reach. Felt herself pulling the painting out of his hands.

"Have you no shame?" she cried at them.

"Have *you* no shame?" David shouted back.

The first student held on to the painting while the second student kicked at her. The three of them stumbled into *Les Chevaliers*. The painting tipped in its braces. A heavy soled boot landed on her ankle and an elbow hit her in the ribs. She ignored the pain and fought back.

More men mounted the cart. Hands tore at her, any part of her. The mass of men enveloped her. She was driftwood on the ocean of their strength. A fist hit the side of her head. Stars exploded.

She roused to another bugle call, to the officer shouting for everyone to stand back or face arrest. Soldiers pulled her off the cart and held her in an immovable vice, where she struggled to breathe, her face pressed against one of the men's woolen coats.

"If you value your life, you will stop fighting," the man growled. "Otherwise, I can smother you right now."

～

Through the human trap formed by the soldier's locked arms, Adélaïde watched the soldiers push back the crowds and lift *Les Chevaliers* off the carts. Grunting under its weight, they carried *Les Chevaliers* using its scaffolding. The weight and size of the painting made it impossible for them to toss it onto the pyre, and they could not lift it to straddle the fire. While the soldiers debated how to destroy the painting, two sansculottes mounted the carts and tossed the remaining artwork into the fire. Wooden frames, thin rectangular logs, raged without a sound and sank down into the fire. Sketches on Bleue Hollande curled and shrank until scraps floated on flaming edges into the wind, disappearing in a dot of ember. The fire in the square grew higher, the heat more intense.

Men arrived with axes.

Les Chevaliers loomed in front of the pyre. The figures in the painting, their clothes rimmed in gold, shone in outlined form and gleamed yellow in pockets. Axes struck their bodies. The X'd out faces called to her in fear and pain, but she could not answer.

The men had not anticipated the hardness of the wood. After a few minutes, the heat of the flames drove them back. They decided to bring the fire to the painting and lined up firewood and tinder scraps along the length of the painting, then doused the tinder with oil and lit it with a torch.

Flames crawled along the bottom of *Les Chevaliers*. Adélaïde had wanted a wood for the ages, and now this beautiful wood of hers refused to burn. For a long time, the painting stood untouched in the night air, flames licking at it, dancing around it, but as La Samaritaine chimed its quarter hours, fire asserted its certain victory. First, the scaffolding burned. Then the glue between the plank joints melted. At last, flames moved up the wood, and ate into the gesso layers, higher and higher, until a fiery sign in the dark burned before them. The mob chanted and drank while her work burned. When the flames wavered, they brought more fuel to throw on the fire and roared with approval when a tree branch or a confiscated piece of furniture joined the inferno.

The spirits of *Les Chevaliers* lifted off into the wind, desperate to escape. The last to leave were her parents, whose unmarred faces blazed before her in the upper corner of the painting. They hovered over the fire, then joined the dark clouds of smoke rolling toward the Seine.

La Samaritaine chimed one. The soldiers had long since released her. They stood nearby, talking among themselves, occasionally stamping out embers that got too close. Many onlookers drifted away. Adélaïde's eyes burned, and her chest ached. She pressed her hands together, trying to suppress the sting of blisters on her palms. She could not remember what she had done to burn herself.

Across the square, Adélaïde saw Marie and Isabelle coming toward her, their laurel wreathes drooping, their white dresses in tatters. An immense pressure lifted from her chest. Claudette and Jeanne followed, but François and Alexandré were not with them. Where she should feel François, where the connection in her heart should be, she felt a gaping hole.

"I'm sorry we were afraid," Jeanne told her.

Adélaïde shook her head. "François?" She wanted to scream, but his name was a hoarse croak. "Alexandré?"

No one had seen them.

At two in the morning, coals glowed crimson in the center of the square. All else was gone. They ended their vigil.

Claudette's lantern did little to pierce the smoky darkness as they stumbled home. The girls led Adélaïde along like Belisarius, her eyes blinded from staring at the flames, her heart keening for François. How could she have been so stupid as to have left things unresolved between them? His broken face played over and over in her mind. What if she never saw him again? What would it have hurt for her to have told him she would marry him when things were over? Had he gone to his death without her love?

The women crept into her studio and barred the door, Adélaïde as brittle as teetering glass. Dirt streaked her face. Soot coated her hair. Her clothes smelled of sweat and smoke. She eased onto the unbroken chair. Isabelle brought her a pitcher of water. She drank from it, then poured water over her face.

They spent the night salvaging any remaining student work, cleaning the studio, and stripping the beds in the dormitory. Dawn bloomed over Paris, its pink clouds smudged with smoke layering the skyline. Adélaïde swept the floor a last time, her blistered hands protesting beneath their bandages. Overcome with anxiety and fear for François and Alexandré, she moved the broom across the parquet as though her life depended on it.

When the bells of La Samaritaine tolled their seven laments, she sent runners through Paris advising her students to retrieve their belongings. At nine o'clock, a group of young women stood in the empty chamber, clutching their artwork.

Adélaïde closed her studio.

She surrendered herself to the embrace of her students, but their arms could not melt the chill that had invaded her and turned her limbs to lead. Her arms stayed frozen and heavy by her sides. The room was quiet after the sound of their footsteps receded from the courtyard.

Then Claudette stood before her.

Adélaïde looked at the wound on Claudette's neck and gave her oldest friend a watery smile. "I can't believe you were hurt."

"It was a small sacrifice." Claudette lifted her chin.

"No, it wasn't. I'm sorry it ended this way. I will write you a reference."

A strange light flickered in Claudette's eyes. "That won't be necessary. I'm not going anywhere."

Adélaïde did not understand.

"The Republic has asked me to stay on."

"The Republic? The government?" Adélaïde's wandering focus returned. "What are you saying, Claudette?"

Triumph crossed Claudette's face. "I have pleased the Committee of Instruction with my service. They have appointed me as the library's new caretaker."

"I . . . What?"

"You think I liked being a servant all these years? You had every privilege and opportunity given to you while I had to stand by and watch." She took Adélaïde's arm in a punishing grip. "Your father educated me to a point, but you never made me part of your family and you never included me in your group when I came here. When you looked at me, you saw a housekeeper, nothing else. Now, it's my turn."

They stared at each other.

"Claudette." Her mind reeled.

Claudette set her jaw. "Citizen Guiard, you must vacate this space within the hour."

~

"Madame, we must go," Marie said, her arms gentle.

What more there was to feel of pain, Adélaïde could not imagine. Her very being had ripped apart. "We can't leave until I know what happened to François and Alexandré."

"We may never know, but we have to leave," Isabelle said. She and Marie guided Adélaïde to the waiting coach. The bells of St. Eustache clanged eleven times as the coachman urged the horse into traffic.

They made it to Pontault-en-Brie without incident. The farmhouse nestled beneath the poplar trees as it had for centuries, as though the world had not shifted, as though all that she loved had not disappeared from the earth. Adélaïde stood on the farmhouse steps, bereft, unable to go in. Isabelle took her bandaged hand, but Adélaïde felt nothing. The emotions that had tingled through her fingers and impelled her art had dissipated as though they never were.

"You're as cold as ice," Isabelle exclaimed. "Let's draw you a bath."

Marie and Isabelle heated water and carried the heavy pails up to Adélaïde's room.

"Are you sure you don't want our help?" Marie asked.

"Leave me," Adélaïde said, her voice still hoarse from the smoke.

She sank into the hard metal tub and watched from somewhere outside herself as the bathwater turned gray, then black. When the water grew cold, she rose and dried herself. Climbing onto her bed, she tumbled into a dreamless sleep.

Noon passed before she came downstairs the next day on legs of gossamer, hugging the banister railing.

"Madame, come eat," Isabelle said from the kitchen.

"No," she said. How could she eat if François could not?

She joined Isabelle and Marie in the great room. A ticking clock measured the minutes as they sat waiting. When would they know? What could they do?

The clock had chimed three times when Marie cocked her head. "Someone's coming."

From the window, they watched a cart turn into the lane. Their two donkeys, wilted flowers still braided into their harnesses, plodded along in the shade of the poplar trees.

They rushed outside.

François drove the cart, a plaster across his nose, his eye a ring of black. Alexandré sat beside him, his arm in a sling and a bloodied bandage wrapped around his head.

"Where have you been?" Adélaïde grabbed the reins from François.

"When I tried to fight off the men who attacked Alexandré, we were arrested and detained for the night. For disturbing the peace." François gave his lopsided smile. "They released us yesterday morning."

Relief made her speechless.

"I don't think they knew who we were when they let us go," François said.

"They did," Adélaïde cried, finding her voice. "It was Claudette. They planned it that way."

"But where have you been?" Marie demanded. "That was yesterday."

"As we were making our way to your studio, we encountered David's students, who were out looking for François," Alexandré said. "They made him go to the Louvre, to the offices of the Museum Commission."

"Where they terminated me from my post for insufficient patriotism."

Adélaïde thought she would faint again. "What does this mean?"

"Oh, don't worry. They just ordered me to vacate my studio."

"Which they had already cleaned out for us," Alexandré joked. "But we had some other things to do, and we had to track down these two mangy beasts." He regarded the donkeys with affection.

"This calls for a celebration," Isabelle exclaimed. "I'll go make dinner." She turned for the house.

"We *are* starving," François said. "And if you ladies would step aside, we could get down from this cart."

Adélaïde and Marie moved away from the cart. A hunger pang pierced Adélaïde's stomach and everyone laughed.

"We heard that," François said.

"We could all eat," Adélaïde agreed. "Marie, let's go help Isabelle."

François jumped off the cart, then turned to help Alexandré down.

The men stayed behind as she and Marie followed Isabelle toward the house.

"Aren't you coming in?" Adélaïde turned back.

François's eyes glittered in the afternoon light. "You go on. We will be in in a bit." He and Alexandré worked to lift the wooden seat board off the frame of the cart.

She did not move and watched as they placed a blanket on the ground, Alexandré's movements awkward with his one arm. They grunted as they lifted a heavy object out of the bed of the cart. "Watch your arm," François admonished his younger brother.

From its narrow, rectangular shape, Adélaïde knew it was a large painting. "What on earth?" She returned to the cart.

They maneuvered the wooden panel and set it on the blanket, then leaned it against the cart.

She gasped. In the confusion and distress of the last few days, she had forgotten all about her self-portrait with Marie Capet and Marguerite de Rosemond hanging in the Louvre.

"I tried to tell you I had hidden it in the tunnels, but you would not listen," François said.

Alexandré turned toward her and executed an elaborate bow. "And I, I told the men guarding the art when we came out that this painting was too aristocratic and that we had to destroy it. They even helped load it into the cart."

"I can't believe it," she gasped.

François slipped his hand into hers and looked into her eyes. "I saved it for you."

She gazed back. The windows to his soul were open to her again. "At the cost of your position?"

"No matter."

Sorrow, anger, and gratitude coalesced in her throat.

Isabelle and Marie came out of the house carrying two bottles of wine and several glasses. The group stood in the drive, laughing, crying, and toasting each other.

"After all this time, will you tell us what you were painting in your portrait?" Alexandré asked.

Adélaïde looked at the painting, saw her own face looking back at her, assured and confident, Marie and Marguerite eager and innocent as they stared at the painting hidden from view inside the portrait. She thought of the painting David had thrown into the fire and took François's hand and lifted it up. Staring at their entwined fingers, masculine, feminine, wrinkled now, she observed the veins that moved under the surface of their skin in ways that young veins did not.

"I was painting our studio in the Louvre—the one we imagined —with young men and women painting, studying, learning together. Learning from us." She stopped speaking and pressed their joined hands against her chest.

Marie, Isabelle, and Alexandré examined the painting.

"For a moment, a very brief moment," Adélaïde continued, "we women of Paris looked out on the world and glimpsed what might have been, what we could do, what we could achieve." She paused and drew in a breath. "For a time, that gift was right before us." She struggled to keep bitterness out of her voice. "But it has been snatched away."

Isabelle refilled their glasses, and they lingered before Adélaïde's painting. Sunlight slipped through the trees and evening descended, the air redolent with fading flowers and summer grass.

Using their joined hands, François pulled Adélaïde into his warmth. "For a time," he murmured. "But not for the last time."

AFTERWORD

One day while wandering through the Louvre's Rococo gallery, I encountered a painting I had never seen before. The words of my college art history professor echoed in my head: "No woman has ever contributed meaningfully to the arts." Yet here was a woman in a painting by a woman staring out at me. Her eyes blazed a message that said, "Tell the world about us."

I had to know more.

So began my research into the lives of the female artists of Paris who tried to change the world during the Age of Reason. Unbelievably, the words of my college professor were also spoken by the Comte d'Angiviller, with specific reference to the women of this story and the centuries of women artists who had come before them.

The story of Adélaïde, who accomplished so much for women, but whose greatest work is not among us, especially appealed to me.

In *Adélaïde: Painter of the Revolution*, Adélaïde makes the decision to complete *Les Chevaliers*. While some accounts indicate that the piece was left unfinished, others do not, and I like to think that nothing would have stopped Adélaïde from finishing this work, even if just to honor her word and her work ethic.

After the revolution, Adélaïde continued her case against the government, trying to get reimbursed for her costs on *Les Chevaliers*. Ultimately, she received 2,000 livres.

Following the abolishment of the Royal Academy of Painting and Sculpture, its successor, the Institut des Beaux Arts, did not allow women. Ironically, François-André Vincent was one of its founding members. Under France's new rules of exhibition, Adélaïde could no longer refer to herself as an Academician or a Painter of the Mesdames; she was merely the student of Messieurs Vincent. After her marriage to François, she exhibited as Madame Vincent, a "student of her husband."

Élisabeth Vigée Lebrun, whose Madonna-like *Self-portrait with Her Daughter, Julie,* inspired my quest, spent twelve years in exile before she was allowed to return to France.

Although Élisabeth-Josephe de la Borde, the Comtesse d'Angiviller, supported female artists, there is no evidence that she met Adélaïde at À La Toilette when Adélaïde was a young girl. She did, however, commission portraits from Adélaïde, and Adélaïde painted her image on a locket held by the infant in *Portrait of the Comtesse de Flahaut and Her Son.* The comtesse spent her life in seclusion following her husband's flight from the country.

In my research, I came across François-André Vincent's sketch, *The Drawing Lesson.* I could hardly believe it when I recognized the couple in the drawing: François and Adélaïde seated as close together as only two teenagers can get while seated apart. It was clear their rich and varied relationship had lasted a lifetime.

Adélaïde and François married in 1800 and Adélaïde died in 1803 at the age of fifty-four.

After Adélaïde's death, Marie-Gabrielle Capet painted the scene of Adélaïde in her studio all those years ago, when she painted Joseph Vien in her quest to make it into the Royal Academy. In the painting, Marie Capet presents herself as a much older woman. She looks out at the viewer, grief-stricken, as her painting reflects back on a time of possibility for women. In this painting, Marie demonstrates her mastery of the historical painting genre at a time when women were relegated once again to the background.

In 1795, Adélaïde painted a portrait of François wearing spectacles. He suffered from deteriorating eyesight that ultimately impacted his ability to paint. In my book, François mixed lead into paint, one of the ways in which artists damaged their eyesight. In fact, many painters suffered from ill health as a result of the lead and mercury they used in their paints in the 18th century. Marie Capet would care for François for the rest of his life.

Marie-Victoire d'Avril, referred to as Isabelle d'Avril in the book, was the beneficiary of Marie Capet's estate.

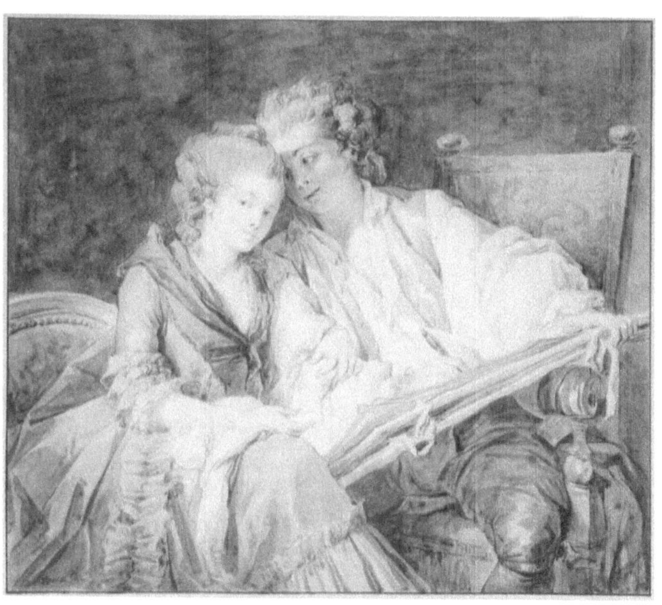

François André Vincent, *The Drawing Lesson*, ca. 1777,
brush and brown wash over graphite on cream laid paper,
laid down, with a framing line in brown ink, 32.5 x 37.7 cm
Image courtesy of the National Gallery of Art, Washington.

ACKNOWLEDGMENTS

I am profoundly grateful to those who helped me bring this book into being, who read version after version of the manuscript, who said this story must be told.

To my sister, Quinda Fukuzawa, who read the first pages—and kept on reading; to my friend Diann Newhouse, who read the first version before it was really anything; and to Mary J. Fry, my friend who believed in my book, always. I don't have enough words to express how much your encouragement, the hours you spent listening to me agonize over sentences, and your advice meant to me.

To Sarah Turitto, who approached each Thursday night read and critique session with boundless enthusiasm, and who provided great ideas when I felt stuck.

I owe a huge debt of gratitude to my writing coaches: Marni Freedman, whose guidance and advice helped me "see" how to tell a story, and Carlos de los Rios, who never let up on his high expectations. A giant shout-out to Jeniffer Thompson, who brought the pieces of me and what I write about into a logical whole.

To the team at Acorn Publishing—Holly Kammier, my publisher; Leslie Ferguson, my book producer; Marci Clark, my editor; Kat Ross, my proofreader—thank you for turning my novel into a living work.

ACKNOWLEDGMENTS

To my daughter, Aimelie, who was born with a pencil in her hand, drawing already, your innate creative talent and artistic drive were my windows into Adélaïde's soul.

Thank you, dear reader, for reading this book.

ABOUT THE AUTHOR

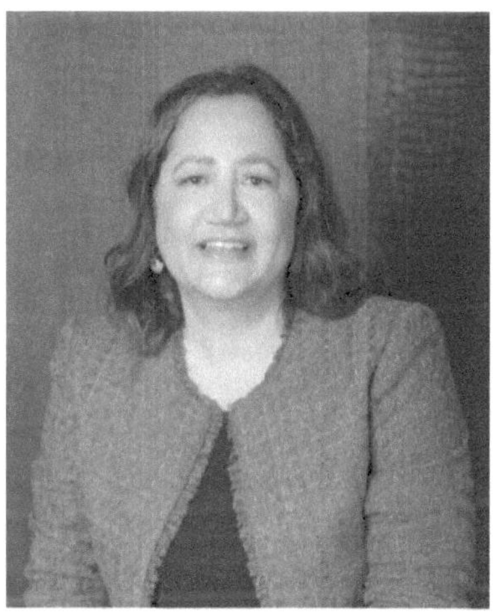

Photo Credit: Julia Badei Studios

Janell Strube makes a mean barbecue sauce. She's also a world traveler, a baker, and a bicyclist. But when she writes, her identity as an adoptee often steers her attention to topics of alienation, erased history, and displacement.

In 2024, a personal essay of hers was published in the anthology *Adoption and Suicidality*. Her work has also appeared in *Shaking the Tree: brazen. short. memoir* and *A Year in Ink*. Her short memoir, "Taking my Blonde Daughter to a Black Lives Matter Rally," was selected for the 2020 San Diego Memoir Showcase, an annual live storytelling event.

While much of her writing is personal, she enjoys the freedom that comes with crafting fiction. Her desire to learn about forgotten female artists who shaped the French revolutionary period motivated her to write *Adélaïde: Painter of the Revolution*.

When not crunching numbers as a tax executive for a hotel chain, she can be found hanging out with Shiloh the Wheaten and plotting her second book.

Visit Janell at janellstrube.com, and follow her on Facebook at Janell Strube and on Instagram @janellstrube.